Invisible Scars

By

Peter Sykes

Published by New Generation Publishing in 2017

Copyright © Peter Sykes 2017

First Edition

The author asserts the moral right under the Copyright, Designs and Patents Act 1988 to be identified as the author of this work.

All Rights reserved. No part of this publication may be reproduced, stored in a retrieval system or transmitted, in any form or by any means without the prior consent of the author, nor be otherwise circulated in any form of binding or cover other than that which it is published and without a similar condition being imposed on the subsequent purchaser.

www.newgeneration-publishing.com

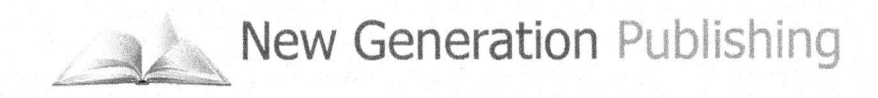

New Generation Publishing

Peter Sykes served as a consultant surgeon for 25 years, later becoming the medical director of an NHS Trust. In 1998 he led the group that became the 'UK Medical Management Team of the Year'. During the final three years of his career, he was involved at a national level in the control of quality of hospital services.

He is now retired, and when not writing, spends his time gardening, golfing, enjoying the company of his grandchildren and occasionally grumbling that *'things ain't what they used to be'*.

****

Peter's first novel **'The First Cut'** was published in 2011. It described Paul Lambert's medical misadventures as he was thrown, bewildered and unprepared, onto a busy surgical ward as a newly qualified doctor.

This was followed in 2013 by **'Behind the Screens'** which tells real-life tales at a time when care and compassion ruled supreme in British hospitals. Some of the stories are humorous, some sad, others poignant, but all are very 'human'. The novel also follows Paul's chequered love life and unveils some of the 'high jinks' that doctors get up to when off-duty.

'First Do No Harm' published in 2015, is set against the political disputes that beset the National Health Service between 1974 and 1976. Again the narrative is interspersed with numerous fascinating tales of the patients treated by Paul and his medical and nursing colleagues.

This book is dedicated to healthcare workers everywhere. May care and compassion be their constant companions

---

All author royalties from the sale of this book will be shared equally between East Cheshire Hospice, Macclesfield and St Ann's Hospice, Stockport.

I wish to thank The Miscarriage Association for their advice, the ladies of the Davenport Golf Club who have searched for errors of spelling and punctuation in the final manuscript and my wife Jane for her patience and for the numerous cups of tea that have sustained me whilst writing.

Above all, I wish to thank the many patients it has been my privilege to serve for giving me the inspiration to write this book.

This book is a novel; it is not literally true. Some characters owe a little to patients and staff I have known, but none of them are real. Likewise, events described are fictitious.

Chapter One: November 1970

Utterly dejected, Paul collapsed into the dilapidated armchair in the corner of the room, his head in his hands, tears in his eyes, his confidence shattered. He was distraught; his mood one of total wretchedness and despair. He felt sick, his mouth was dry, his hands trembled. It was four in the morning and it was the events of those four hours, events for which he had been wholly responsible, that were the cause of his distress. What had happened had been a disaster.

He had been the leader of the team, the one everyone respected, the one to whom they turned for guidance who was supposed to be in control and able to cope with difficult situations; but the night's events had shown him to have been a complete failure. He felt ashamed. He had let himself down, had let the team down and still lying on the operating table in the adjacent theatre, drained of his life giving blood, was the man who had paid the ultimate price for his incompetence. The previous evening William Wilson had been fit and well. He had enjoyed a game of bowls followed by a drink and a chat with his pals in the pub. Now the nurses were washing the blood from his lifeless body in preparation for its short journey to the hospital morgue. Later, they would clean the operating table, scrub the floor and sterilise the surgical instruments in preparation for the next day's list. By morning the theatre would again be spotless, all signs of the disaster that had unfolded in the night erased. If only they could wash away the pain and the guilt that Paul felt as easily.

During his surgical training, he had grown accustomed to the occasional disappointment. There had been lows in his life before, times when his patients had developed complications from treatments he had initiated, such things were inevitable for anyone who chose medicine as a career, but he had never experienced anything remotely like this. He wished the ground would open up and swallow him.

He glanced round the room, his eyes vaguely noting the jumble of discarded caps, masks, vests and pants left behind by the rest of the team as one by one they had drifted wearily to their beds leaving him alone with his misery. Loyally, they had muttered words of sympathy, insisting that he should not blame himself; but their words brought no comfort. He did blame himself; who else was there to blame? His eye settled on the laundry skip in the corner. A loose fold of a gown, heavily stained with blood, hung at an odd angle over the metal ring that formed its lip. A dark stain was forming where blood was dripping onto the floor.

It brought to Paul's mind an image that had haunted him as a child. Whilst on a family holiday, he had seen hundreds of dead pheasants, their bloodied heads hanging limply, at grotesque angles over the side of a trailer, leaving a trail of blood on the rutted earth as they passed. The sight of their ruffled feathers and shattered bodies had sickened him. Walking alongside were half a dozen men, laughing and joking as they drank beer, their guns over the shoulders. Only a few hours before, he had fed the pheasants by hand as they roamed freely through their campsite. They had strutted proudly, bright eyed, their heads held high, showing off the brilliant colours of their beautiful plumage, iridescent reds, brilliant greens and blues. He had suffered nightmares for weeks afterwards.

Paul looked again at the crumpled blood stained gown. Poor Mr Wilson had died as needlessly as those birds and in his heart he knew that he was responsible.

There was a quiet knock at the door and the theatre sister entered, a mug of tea in her hand. She looked at Paul's limp figure.

"It's been a long night, Mr Lambert," she said, a sympathetic smile on her face. "Have a drink before you leave."

"Thanks," mumbled Paul, head bowed, not trusting himself to look her in the eye.

"Look, you mustn't blame yourself. We must accept that from time to time these things happen; not all operations are successful. If all your patients made a full recovery, you wouldn't be human; you'd be a miracle worker. Besides, when a major blood vessel bursts there is a high mortality, you know that as well as I do. Had Mr Wilson not had surgery he would have died. You tried to save him, you did your best, no-one could ask for more."

"And my best wasn't good enough, was it, Sister?" Paul replied.

Sister laid a hand on his shoulder. "Not this time maybe," she said softly, "but I've no doubt that others you operate on in the future will survive. Now drink your tea and go to bed."

Alone again, Paul took off his theatre greens, pulled on his shirt and pants and looked in the mirror. He stared in disgust at the pale, unshaven, weary face that looked back at him.

"Bloody failure," he said to himself, cursing the ambition and misplaced ego that had reduced him to this state. "What the hell are you doing trying to become a surgeon? You haven't the skill to be a success, nor the strength, the resilience to deal with the pain of failure."

Then, turning away from the mirror, he collected his white coat and braced himself for the task that would compound his misery. He had to meet Mrs Wilson and tell her that her husband had not survived his surgery.

Chapter Two: Five months earlier

"So Paul, you're going to be a consultant surgeon for the next few days," Kate said across the breakfast table. She sounded impressed. "Where did you say Mr Potts was going?"

Mr Potts was one of the consultant surgeons on the surgical unit. The other was Sir William, the older and better tempered of the two.

"He's off to London to learn some new skills," Paul replied. "He's planning to start treating diseases of arteries. At the moment the only operations performed on blood vessels are for varicose veins."

"I didn't know there was much call for that sort of work."

"Oh, there are plenty of patients with such problems. Sometimes arteries get blocked which can lead to limbs becoming gangrenous. Sometimes the wall gets so weak that the blood vessel bursts like a bicycle tyre popping. That results in catastrophic bleeding."

"That sounds horrendous!"

"For the poor patient it certainly is, but actually I'm delighted. It will be a new experience for me. I'll be able to watch him at work, another string to my bow."

Paul was training to be a surgeon at The City General Hospital and Kate, his young wife, was a nurse on one of the wards. Since their wedding a couple of years before, they had lived in a flat in the grounds of the hospital and had quickly settled into a comfortable routine. As frequently happens in doctor/nurse relationships, their conversation often reverted to medical matters.

"Will it worry you, acting as a consultant whilst your boss is away?" Kate wanted to know as she rose from the table.

"If I were a proper consultant with ultimate responsibility, it might. But as it is, I'm not going to lose any sleep over it. If there's a problem, I'll simply ask Sir William for help."

"He's such a sweetie that I'm sure he'll be only too pleased to help," Kate agreed.

"Mind you Kate, if I'm to be a consultant, I shall expect to be treated with the utmost respect by the staff," Paul continued, a twinkle in his eye, "especially by the nursing staff. You know, addressed as 'Sir' and offered tea and chocolate biscuits whenever I visit a ward - that sort of thing."

"Yes, of course. I'll see that you're treated with due reverence," Kate replied, grinning broadly as she started to clear the dishes. She executed a neat curtsey. "Your every wish will be my command, Sir."

"I'll keep you to that when I get home tonight!"

"I'm sorry Paul, I don't think a lowly nurse is allowed to consort with a prestigious consultant," Kate replied, as she reached for her nurse's cape and gave Paul a quick kiss. She avoided the grab he made for her waist with practised ease and hurried for the door. She needed to be on the ward by 7.45 for the morning hand over, that daily ritual when the night staff hand over responsibility of their patients to the dayshift.

"Oh and can Sir please wash and dry the dishes before he goes to work and be sure to leave the kitchen sink tidy. Yesterday Sir left lumps of porridge in the plug hole!"

After the door closed, Paul sat for a few moments smiling to himself, thinking about Kate. He delighted in her company and blessed the day they had met. She calmed him when he was angry, cheered him when he was low and teased him if he became pompous. He loved her and thought she was just perfect. He didn't feel that he was in any way special himself and found it difficult to understand why she had chosen him above all others. Paul was not tall, well built or handsome, and he was very conscious of his own deficiencies. He regarded himself as being a rather dull individual, someone who lacked confidence and was socially somewhat inept. She could have had her pick of all the men in the world, yet Paul knew that Kate truly loved him. He had indeed been extremely fortunate and had found great joy within his newly married state.

Suddenly Paul woke from his reverie. He glanced at the clock and groaned. He tried to visit the ward each morning before starting his official duties in casualty or in the operating theatre. It made for a long day but he liked to assure himself that his patients were making good progress. He also wanted his consultant to recognise that he was *'on top of his job'*. Realising he was running late, he threw the dirty dishes, including the porridge pan, into the sink, smiling to himself as he did so. Then he grabbed his white coat and ran across to the hospital. He was scheduled to assist Sir William, the hospital's most senior and respected consultant, in the outpatient clinic and he didn't want to be late.

****

As lunchtime approached at the end of a long clinic, Sir William was reading a letter he had received from one of the local General Practitioners. He felt weary and wondered if his age was finally beginning to catch up with him. Dealing with 35 patients in a morning, with just the registrar to assist him, was exhausting. He saw most of the new patients himself, that was what the GPs expected, but occasionally he passed one to his assistant to see on his behalf. He tossed the single sheet of paper onto the desk.

"Here you are, Lambert," he said with a sigh. "Making the diagnosis in this case shouldn't be too difficult." Then he laughed. "Mind you, you'll probably need all your diplomatic skills if you're to handle things successfully!"

Paul picked up the letter. It was quite brief.

'Dear Sir William
    Re James Cullen   Aged 34
    Thank you for seeing Mr Cullen. I am afraid that the vasectomy operation he had a few years ago on your unit seems to have failed. I would be very grateful if you would see him and advise. With thanks and good wishes,
    James Hattersley MB Ch B'

At this time, vasectomy operations were becoming increasingly popular and, by and large, were proving to be a reliable and safe form of contraception. However, very occasionally, the procedure had been unsuccessful and some men, having subsequently fathered children, had demanded and received financial compensation. This was not because the operation had failed, since that could happen even in the hands of the best surgeons in the land. The payments had been made because the patient had not been warned in advance that there was a possibility of failure. Concerned that this might have happened in Mr Cullen's case, Paul checked the notes, and was pleased to find that the *'consent for operation'* form specifically mentioned this possibility and had been signed by Mr Cullen before the operation was performed.

When Paul went into the small consulting room to see the patient, he found him sitting hand in hand with his wife. They seemed to be a pleasant couple. Mr Cullen was a quietly spoken accountant; his wife was the secretary for a local firm of solicitors. A cautionary bell rang in Paul's ear; she probably had ready access to expert legal advice! If the vasectomy operation had indeed failed, they might be seeking damages. He had read recently of a case in which compensation of over £100,000 had been paid to a couple whose unwanted pregnancy had resulted in the birth of a little girl. They had claimed for everything from nappies, cots and prams for her as a baby, to money for clothes, parties and cinema tickets as a child, then for school fees, holidays and even cosmetics when she became a teenager arguing that she should be treated in the same manner as her older sister. Paul realised he would have to be careful!

Knowing that he needed to ask Mr Cullen some awkward personal and potentially embarrassing questions, he asked if he would prefer his wife to wait outside during the consultation.

"No, I'm perfectly happy for Anne to be present. She's as keen as I am to get this matter sorted out."

Without prompting, Mr Cullen opened the conversation. "I'm afraid my vasectomy operation has failed, Doctor. I'm not blaming anyone; I was warned that it was possible. But I would like to have the operation completed."

At his side, his wife nodded vigorously in agreement. Mr Cullen explained that they had been married for eight years and had two healthy children. Three years previously, having decided their family was complete, he had undergone the sterilisation procedure.

"And you say the vasectomy has failed?"

"Yes, my wife became pregnant and had a miscarriage."

"A miscarriage or an abortion?" Paul asked.

"Definitely a miscarriage, neither of us would ever consider an abortion. It happened a couple of months ago. We were on holiday near Inverness in Scotland at the time. Anne was rushed to hospital. She was bleeding heavily and had to have an emergency operation."

There was a pause as Paul considered how to phrase his next question. "Are you absolutely certain that it's the vasectomy that has failed?"

Mr Cullen looked puzzled, as if no other possibility had entered his mind. "Yes, of course. What else could have happened?"

Paul wondered if his patient was really as naïve as his reply suggested!

"Well," he said, speaking as gently as he could, conscious that Mr Cullen's wife was present, "a vasectomy operation can fail, although such an event is rather unusual. It probably doesn't happen more than once in every couple of thousand operations. However, you must realise that if a woman becomes pregnant, it doesn't automatically follow that her husband is responsible."

"Oh, there's absolutely no question of anyone else being involved."

Paul glanced at Mrs Cullen. He judged that she was probably little more than twenty six or twenty seven. He assumed that she must have been married as a teenager. She wore a smart suit, tailored to her slim figure, over a starched white blouse. A small cross hung from a fine gold chain round her neck. With her skirt cut just above the knee and polished black high heeled shoes, she certainly couldn't be described as 'mumsy' despite having two children. She was a good looking woman who clearly took a great deal of care over her appearance. No doubt some of the young solicitors with whom she worked would find her attractive. But was she flighty? Was she the sort to play away from home? It was impossible to tell of course, but Paul thought it unlikely. She was not afraid to meet his gaze and she appeared to be as shocked as her husband at the suggestion that she might have been unfaithful.

"There's absolutely no question about it," she said. "We're a happily married couple. We're devoted to each other; we love each other to bits."

One of Sir William's favourite expressions came into Paul's head. *'Common things occur commonly'*. If he had heard him say it once, he had heard him say it a dozen times; and a wife cheating on her husband was undoubtedly a more frequent event than a vasectomy operation failing!

"Look," he said, "before we jump to any conclusions, we ought to confirm that the operation has actually failed. The way to do that is to run a sperm check."

"That truly won't be necessary," Mr Cullen replied, placing his arm around his wife's shoulders. "I trust my wife implicitly. I just want to get on and have the operation repeated."

It was an interesting reply. Was Mr Cullen really prepared to have further surgery, rather than risk having to face what might prove to be an unpalatable truth?

"Nonetheless, I do need to arrange the test," Paul said. "From a medical point of view, it would be wrong to arrange another operation without making sure that the first one has failed. It needn't take more than a few days."

"Alright Doctor, if it has to be, it has to be. But I can assure you that it will confirm that the operation has failed."

Paul glanced again at Mrs Cullen, trying to judge if she was as confident of the result of the proposed sperm test as her husband. He had met this situation twice before and in both cases the sperm count had been zero, proving that the vasectomy operation had been successful. It meant that the two men were incapable of fathering children and therefore had to look elsewhere for the cause of their wives' pregnancy. On each occasion, even though the wife had not been present, it had been difficult for Paul to explain the situation and heartbreaking for the man receiving the news. But Mrs Cullen didn't look in the least concerned that the test might prove she had been unfaithful. It left Paul in little doubt that when he met the couple again, he would have to acknowledge the operation had indeed failed and would then arrange for the vasectomy to be repeated.

He completed the request form for the sperm test, told Mr Cullen to go to the laboratory to pick up a specimen jar and to produce a sample at his leisure. This induced a fit of giggling in Mrs Cullen that confirmed Paul's belief that there was no question of her having been unfaithful.

Chapter Three

A few weeks later, somewhat to his surprise, Paul found himself sitting in the front seat of Sir William's car on a Saturday morning. They were on their way to see a patient at the local gypsy camp site. Officially, Paul wasn't on duty but it promised to be a good opportunity to see an interesting case and to observe the hospital's senior surgeon at work. Kate had grumbled when Sir William had phoned to invite Paul to join him. She had just completed an exhausting week's work which including a number of evening shifts; twice she hadn't managed to get home before nine pm. She was tired and eager to spend time with Paul, resting and relaxing.

"It's the weekend," she stated firmly, drying the breakfast dishes for Paul as he did the washing up, "a time for us to be together. The consultants have no right to expect you to work at the weekend."

"Sir William didn't insist that I go, but..."

"Well then," said Kate.

"But I'm glad that he did," Paul replied. "If I'd said 'no', he might have asked someone else. You have to keep in with the consultants, you know that surely, Kate?"

"I suppose so," Kate conceded.

"Anyway, it's kind of him to give me a chance to widen my experience. It would have seemed churlish if I'd refused. Besides, we haven't any special plans for today, have we?"

"No, we've nothing special arranged but you did say you'd help me with the weekly shop," Kate replied looking peeved, "but when I've tidied up here, I'll go and do it on my own."

Paul decided not to reply. He didn't like to disagree or argue with Kate; least said, soonest mended, he thought.

As Paul walked the short distance to Sir William's house, he reflected on the decision he had just made. Was it fair on Kate to put his career before his commitment to her? Had he been afraid to explain to the consultant that it was the weekend, that his wife worked full time and needed some help at home? Would Sir William really have taken umbrage if he had declined to accompany him? Surely not. His boss was a genuine old fashioned gentleman who rarely if ever took offence. Perhaps he was just being selfish; perhaps his love of surgery made the prospect of seeing an interesting case more important to him than spending a morning shopping with his wife. Of course, he wished he didn't have to face such choices but the truth was that to succeed in surgery meant making sacrifices in one's personal life. No-one succeeded if they did not put surgery first. Kate had known that when they got married.

Sir William was not only the hospital's most senior surgeon; he was also the most admired. He had a distinguished appearance with his straight back, silver hair, bushy eyebrows and genial benevolent face. Always the perfect gentleman with his exemplary dress and courteous manners, he was approaching the end of an illustrious career. He was respected by the staff for his wisdom and experience and by his patients for his perfect bedside manner. He lived on the edge of the hospital complex in a small cottage that had once served as the lodge to a large estate, the home of a wealthy industrialist. After the mansion had fallen into disrepair and been demolished, the hospital was built on the extensive parkland where sheep, deer and cattle had previously roamed.

Paul was accustomed to seeing Sir William strolling around the hospital in his immaculate three piece suit, usually with a rose, grown in the garden in which he spent most of his spare time, in his lapel. Now though, he was wearing a comfortable loose fitting sports jacket with leather patches on the elbows and a pair of old corduroy trousers. On his feet were chunky thick soled brogues that were so caked in dirt, they looked as if they doubled as gardening shoes.

He had rather anticipated that his boss would drive a Rolls Royce, Bentley or Daimler, a car suited to his status, but the vehicle in which Paul now found himself was a dilapidated old Morris Oxford. It had rusting body work, worn tyres and an exhaust system which back fired at regular intervals, belching out clouds of black fumes as it trundled along the road towards the city centre at twenty miles an hour. Sleeping on the back seat, was an obese golden Labrador with greying whiskers that was oblivious to the crashing of gears and kangaroo hops caused by Sir William's erratic driving. How Sir William could operate on patients so skilfully yet drive so badly was a mystery that Paul never solved.

There was an overpowering smell in the car that made Paul concerned that his breakfast might reappear. Whether this was due to the stained malodorous tartan rug on which Rufus was lying (that apparently being the dog's name) or whether the odour was due to its habit of farting periodically was not clear. Paul was much relieved and his nausea abated when Sir William had the consideration to wind down his window. Having previously decided not to open his window lest Sir William be offended, Paul quickly did the same.

"Seeing patients in their own homes is both fascinating and instructive, Lambert," Sir William commented as they jerked to a halt at a red light. "When we meet them in the hospital they have been robbed of their individuality; sanitised by the nurses and rendered anonymous in their pyjamas. You learn so much more about folk if you observe them in their own environment. Mind you, there are some hazards to be avoided when doing home visits. You soon learn to be careful; on one occasion I got chewing gum on the seat of my pants having been unwise enough to sit down. And before now, I've come home having picked up some unwelcome visitors on my person; once I got fleas from the family mongrel. Mind you," the consultant added chuckling, "it's quite possible that Rufus has redressed the balance and left his visiting card here and there over the years! Another time I got nits from one of the children," his face creased into a smile, "but that was when I had more hair than I have now. And another bit of advice for you; always politely refuse any refreshment you might be offered. I once ended up glued to the toilet seat for three days after eating a chicken sandwich."

He laughed at these recollections and Paul wondered if the real reason that he had been invited to tag along was that his bachelor boss became lonely at weekends and liked to have some company, as well as an easy audience for his stories. Guiltily, he realised that he really ought to be helping Kate with the shopping; he would find a way to make it up to her when he got home.

As they drove, Paul was surprised to see how little traffic there was. On the rare occasions he took his car into the city centre, he was invariable held up in traffic jams. Then he realised the road ahead was empty because Sir William was driving so slowly and so far away from the kerb that it was quite impossible for anyone to overtake. Further, Sir William seemed deaf to the sound of irate horns from the drivers behind. It was something of a relief to Paul when they eventually reached the now derelict area where the gypsies had set up their camp. In years gone by, it had been the manufacturing heart of this once great northern city; but over time it had been reduced to a neglected wasteland.

"I think you'll find this visit particularly interesting," Sir William remarked as the car ground to a halt outside a heavy wooden gate, the top bar of which was heavily wound with barbed wire. "Have you been in a gypsy caravan before?"

Paul confessed that he hadn't.

"The gypsies are a tight knit community; generally, they don't welcome strangers but Kieran O'Connor, he's one of our local GP's, has their confidence. He's as Irish as they are! Fortunately he's arranged to accompany us, otherwise we wouldn't be allowed onto their site."

The gypsy encampment, enclosed by a forbidding high barbed wire fence, was bordered on one side by a disused garbage filled canal and by an abandoned railway shunting yard sprouting weeds, brambles and rusting metal on the other. The site was overshadowed by two huge brick mills, their walls blackened by the smoke which once rose from the chimneys which served as giant tombstones of a previous prosperous age. The mills now deserted and decaying, had been rendered obsolete by the lower wages paid in the Far East.

Dr O'Connor was waiting for them at the entrance. Almost as wide as he was tall, his clothes were as unkempt and neglected as the surrounding environment. He was wearing a moth-eaten, ankle length, woollen overcoat and a battered trilby hat which struggled to contain the wiry grey hair which sprouted riotously from under the rim. His square face was pock marked by the ravages of severe teenage acne which was only partly obscured by his shaggy grey beard. He could easily have passed for a gypsy himself but for the old leather Gladstone bag he held in his hand. He greeted Sir William with a smile on his face, a twinkle in his eye and an outstretched arm.

"Why hello, Bill, sure 'tis a great pleasure to see you again," he said, taking the consultant's hand and shaking it enthusiastically. "And who might this fine looking young gentleman be that you've brought with you today?"

"This is Paul Lambert, my registrar."

"And a top of the morning to you Sir," Dr O'Connor said, gripping Paul's hand and shaking it with equal vigour. "My dear old friend is showing you the ropes, is he? Well, I hope the old rogue is treating you well. If not, you just let me know and I'll tell you a few tales of the mischief he and I got up to when we were students together. That will take the wind out of his sails." He laughed. "I don't suppose young doctors can get away with the sort of things that we did when we were young, can they Bill?" he added, digging his old friend in the ribs.

Sir William smiled. "Steady on now, Kieran, I have a reputation to maintain these days, as well you know. Don't you go telling tales in front of my staff."

"Sure you have, Bill. Sure you have, but don't you be aworrying," the GP replied with a broad wink at Paul. "I'll not let you down. We old chums have to stick together, don't we? Well come along then, we can't stand here gossiping all day; I've a fascinating case for you to see."

A tall burly looking man of about Paul's age strode to meet them. He wore little more than a string vest, faded jeans and open toed sandals. He was swarthy and heavily tattooed; his dark matted hair tied into a pony tail at the back. A misshapen nose and scarred forehead suggested he was familiar with the rougher side of life. Two large lean Alsatians snapped at his heels. The dogs snarled and bared their teeth at the visitors who hesitated.

"They'll not harm you whilst you're with me," the gypsy said, his voice gruff, his face severe, "but you'd best leave that old lab of yours in the car. These two haven't been fed for a day or two." There was no humour in the coarse laugh that accompanied these remarks. "They make better guard dogs if we keep 'em hungry."

"Hello again Mick," Dr O'Connor said, his voice warm and friendly. If he was apprehensive that the two hungry dogs might take a chunk out of his calf, he certainly didn't show it.

"Let me introduce you to Sir William Warrender. He is, without doubt, one of the finest surgeons in the land; and this is Doctor Lambert his assistant." He turned towards his medical colleagues. "Mick and I both hail from County Sligo in God's own land."

Mick looked at Paul suspiciously. "You said nothing about hangers on, Doc. We don't welcome visitors here."

"To be sure, Dr Paul will be no trouble at all. I know him personally; known him for years, I have. He's an excellent young doctor, always been top of his class, he has," the GP replied, lying fluently. "He'll be as quiet as a church mouse and besides, he'll be helping to look after your mammy if she has to go into hospital, so it'll be good for her to meet him now."

Mick led the way across the site, Paul very conscious of the two Alsatians circling his ankles looking ready and eager to break their fast. Groups of children in ragged clothes all looking dirty and undernourished stopped their games and watched with wary eyes as they passed. If Paul had expected a traditionally painted, wooden, horse drawn gypsy van, he was to be disappointed. Mick's van was a huge metal affair covered with brightly polished chrome strips. A large and apparently new Mercedes saloon stood alongside. Inside, the caravan proved to be remarkably spacious and well equipped. It had a fridge and television. A huge maroon sofa with matching cushions lay to one side and brightly coloured curtains adorned the windows. Numerous Toby jugs and equine brass fittings were displayed on the many shelves. Mick's mother sat, propped up on pillows, in a large double bed that occupied the end of the van furthest from the door. Although the surroundings did not look typically Romany, she certainly did. Wearing a multicoloured patchwork shawl round her shoulders and large rings in her ears, she had dark eyes, long black hair which hung loosely to her shoulders, and the same dusky complexion as her son. Assessing her through medical eyes, Paul noticed that she looked drawn and appeared to be in considerable discomfort. Her skin was dry and wrinkled. She was undoubtedly dehydrated and the whites of her eyes had a yellow discolouration. He was in no doubt that she was suffering from jaundice.

"Hello again Queenie," Dr O'Connor said cheerfully, his voice booming in the confines of the van. "Still in pain, I see. But, don't you worry; I've brought an expert to sort you out. The best in the city, he is. Better than the best the whole of London can offer."

He introduced her to Sir William and Paul adding, "For once, I'm afraid that Queenie's potions and gypsy charms have let her down."

As usual, Sir William took his time eliciting Queenie's medical history in great detail. As he did so, Paul took the opportunity to observe his surroundings. Everything was modern and looked new. He was in no doubt that this luxurious caravan with its rich furnishings and fittings must have cost a great deal of money. It stood in stark contrast to the camp site outside where the children played in ragged clothes on bare earth, in an enclosure separated by barbed wire from the decaying industrial landscape which surrounded it.

Queenie's troubles had started a couple of months before. Hers was a story of indigestion, a slight lack of appetite but a considerable loss of weight. In the last few weeks, she had become jaundiced. Her pain, initially mild and intermittent had become severe and constant. When Sir William examined her, he found a hard swelling in the upper abdomen. His assessment complete, he stood back and addressed his patient.

"I know from Dr O'Connor that you're not keen to come into hospital Queenie, but I think that you're going to need a spot of surgery if we're to sort this problem out for you."

Queenie looked doubtful. "I've no time for hospitals, Doctor," she said, "never been in one in my life. Seems to me, people come out looking worse than when they went in – and some don't come out at all!"

"It really will be for the best," Sir William said gently. "I think you've put up with that pain of yours quite long enough."

"Would it be for long, d'you reckon, Doctor?"

"As long as it takes to make you better," Sir William replied, unwilling to commit himself at this early stage, "probably not less than a fortnight."

"Is it the big C, Doctor? You must tell me if it is. Better knowing than wondering, I always say. If I'm to meet my maker," she crossed herself hurriedly, "there's things I've got to see to."

"You don't need to be seeing to anything at all, Mam," Mick interjected. "Young Rose and I can take care of things, we can sort things out, you know that."

"I know no such thing," Queenie said sharply. "I'll be the one who'll sort things out, thank you."

It wasn't lost on Paul, or indeed on Sir William, that although gypsies were supposed to be a close knit community, there were tensions under the surface between mother and son.

Queenie turned back to Sir William. "Well, is it cancer that I've got?"

Sir William was not afraid to meet her gaze. "That's certainly a possibility," he acknowledged, "but we shan't know 'til we've run a few tests – and it's only fair to warn you that it will probably mean an operation."

Queenie's eyes turned to her son, looking for guidance.

"It's for the best, Mammy," he said, "and I'll be there to make damn sure they treat you right," he added grimly with a sideways glance at Paul who felt somewhat threatened by the remark.

"Okay, that's settled then," Sir William concluded. "Mick, bring your mother in first thing on Monday morning."

"Sure, I will," Mick replied, ushering the three doctors to the door, "and now I'll see you safely back to your car."

As they drove back to the hospital, Sir William turned to Paul. "Well what did you make of that?" he asked.

"It was fascinating Sir," Paul replied. "Not what I was expecting at all. They're obviously not short of a bob or two, not that you would have known from the state of the camp site. I'm sure that was a brand new Mercedes alongside the caravan."

"Yes, that's true," Sir William agreed, "though goodness knows where the money comes from. Looking at the kids you wouldn't have thought they had two pennies to rub together. But that's really not what I meant. What do you think the diagnosis is?"

"It must be a tumour in the pancreas, Sir, blocking the flow of bile to the gut, though I suppose it's just possible that the jaundice might be due to gall stones."

"Agreed," the consultant replied, "and I'm sure it will come to an operation. I don't think her general health is too good though. When she's admitted, I'd like you to go over her thoroughly, particularly to check that her heart and lungs will stand up to a major operation. We may need to build her up a bit before we take her to theatre."

Paul thanked Sir William as he was dropped off at the hospital gates. He walked the short distance to the flat hoping that Kate would forgive him for neglecting her on a Saturday morning. He hated to disappoint her. She meant the world to him and had done since the day they first met when he was a newly qualified doctor serving his probationary period as a resident 'houseman'. She had been student nurse Kate Meredith at the time, the daughter of a pharmacist in the Lake District. Paul was attracted to her from the very first moment he saw her. As the product of a boys' grammar school and coming from a family of three brothers, he had always been ill at ease in the company of the fairer sex. For weeks, despite his twenty three years, he had lacked the confidence to ask her for a date, fearful of being rebuffed.

Although they worked together on the same ward, Paul only felt able to speak with her about their patients and even then he became tongue-tied when discussing Mrs Jones' bowels or Mr Kelly's wound discharge! But whenever they conversed, a subtle change came over him; there was something about her, a chemistry, which made him blush and set his pulse racing. Even discussing a urine sample or the contents of a vomit bowel with her made him feel anxious and self-conscious! He got butterflies in his stomach and felt his heart thumping in his chest. But in her company he also felt more alive than ever before.

In quiet moments he would reflect and wonder what it was that so attracted him; what was it that made her different to other girls? In many ways she was quite unremarkable, the sort of girl you could pass in the street and not really notice. She was of average height, slim with a neat figure and mousy brown hair that was held neatly under her nurse's cap. She had a fresh complexion and blue eyes but could not be described as a classic beauty. It was not a face that would grace the cinema screen or the front page of a fashion magazine but nevertheless one that Paul found highly attractive.

He wondered whether it was simply that she had been kind to him and helped him through his first few weeks when he had arrived on the ward. As a newly qualified doctor, he had been naive and unfamiliar with routine. But he was certain there was more to it than that. He admired the way she handled herself on the ward. She moved easily through the sick patients dispensing a smile here and a kind word there. Whereas Paul had felt anxious in those early days, eager to please, yet afraid of making errors, Kate always seemed to be at ease with herself, content with her lot, enjoying her work, caring for patients without any fuss or bother and certainly not drawing attention to herself in any way. It had taken several weeks for Paul to pluck up the courage to ask her for a date but he had loved her from that day to this.

Now happily married, they enjoyed sharing the domestic duties; shopping washing and cleaning. Kate had shown him how to iron shirts and cook tasty meals. However, the time they enjoyed most was when the day was done, when any friends or visitors had left and the front door was securely locked and bolted. Then they had their home to themselves and they tumbled into bed. Heavy petting apart, they had remained celibate until the day of their wedding, well until the final few weeks anyway, and since then had been on a joyous journey of discovery, finding fulfilment in each other's arms, giving and receiving in equal measure.

Feeling guilty and wondering what sort of reception awaited him, he took the front door key from his trouser pocket. He would take Kate for a walk in the country in the afternoon or perhaps to the cinema in the evening.

"Hello, I'm home," he called. But there was no reply. The house was empty and on the kitchen table he found a scribbled note.

'Out for lunch with Sally. Back later! Ham and salad in fridge.
    Kate xx.'

Chapter Four

The following Monday morning, bright and early, Sister Rutherford was at her desk, her nurses sitting in an informal semicircle around her. Her first job each day, as senior nursing sister on the female ward, was to receive the report from the staff who had cared for the patients through the night. She needed to know of any problems that had developed and hear how they had been managed. Fifteen minutes later, satisfied that she was up to date, she shooed the night nurses from the ward, allowing them to get to their beds for a well-earned sleep. They would need to be fresh when they returned to duty that evening.

Then she turned her attention to allocating tasks to the day staff. On most wards, the custom was for the junior nurses to be delegated the less skilled, more onerous jobs, such as washing bedpans or emptying spittoons before serving the breakfasts. Typically it was the staff nurses who carried out tasks that required more experience; recording pulse, blood pressure and temperature measurements, completing observation charts or dispensing drugs to the patients. This left the nursing sister free to greet any new admissions before spending the day attending to administrative tasks in her office, all the while observing and monitoring her staff as they undertook their various duties.

Gladys Rutherford, though, was not a typical sister; she would cheerfully turn her hand to any of these jobs, a characteristic which made her popular with her staff. She was quite prepared to perform menial tasks herself. Frequently she would assist a student nurse to deal with soiled bed linen or undertake bed baths on patients who were bed bound. The truth was that she enjoyed 'hands on' nursing. She liked to chat to her patients as she worked, getting to know them really well, a tradition that regrettably was rapidly becoming viewed as old fashioned. On this occasion, she helped to serve the breakfasts, asking Kate to attend to a patient who was being discharged and to welcome the two new patients who were expected.

****

When a patient was ready to go home, their husband or wife arrived with a suitcase, the screens were drawn around their bed and five minutes later the patient emerged having changed from night attire into their day-to-day clothes. Kate was often surprised how the simple act of getting dressed could alter someone's appearance. There had been occasions when she had failed to recognise one of her patients as they walked down the corridor to leave the hospital, despite having seen them on the ward every day for a week or more.

Having helped the elderly lady who was on her way home to get dressed, Kate gave her the letter addressed to her GP which detailed the treatment she had received on the ward. She also made sure the patient understood how frequently she should take the painkillers which the medical staff had prescribed for her. She then helped the old lady to walk round the ward as she said her 'goodbyes' and offered good wishes to the envious patients she was leaving behind. Several times she heard people say they would keep in touch although she knew that, as with friends and acquaintances made on holiday, such promises were rarely fulfilled. As soon as the patient had departed, Kate stripped her bed, thoroughly washed its rubber mattress then remade it with clean sheets, blankets and pillows in readiness for its next occupant.

The first patient the porter brought to the ward was called Rose O'Hannagan. She had been waiting nervously on a wooden chair in the corridor for half an hour or so.

"Hello," Kate said. "I'm Staff Nurse Meredith. Welcome to the ward. I'm sorry that we've kept you waiting but we're ready for you now and we'll try to make you feel at home."

Kate then escorted Mrs O'Hannagan to the bed she had just prepared. New patients and their partners found these first moments on the ward awkward and so Kate always did her best to put them at their ease. Men particularly looked uncomfortable when accompanying their wives to a bed in the middle of a female ward, more so than when the situation was reversed. Similarly it was the men who became embarrassed if they were the patient, particularly if their wife made a fuss, or worse, gave them a tearful public embrace before leaving.

Kate pulled the screens round the bed and asked Mrs O'Hannagan to change into her night dress while she went to fetch the equipment she needed to make the base line clinical observations. On her return a few minutes later, she flicked open the case notes she had brought from the office. Normally they already contained the patient's personal particulars, such as their date of birth, religion and next of kin. Also included would be details of their medical problem recorded by the consultant when the patient was seen in the clinic. In this case however, the only information available was the patient's name, address and that the fact that she was a widow.

"I'll show you round the ward and introduce you to a couple of our other patients in a minute," Kate began, "but first of all I need to ask you a few routine questions. I see your Christian name is Rose; are you happy if we call you Rose or would you prefer Mrs O'Hannagan?"

" 'Tis a long time since anyone called me Rose and no-one's ever thought me posh enough to be calling me Missus. I've always been known as Queenie," the new patient said with a smile on her face, "though I'm sure I've never known why. It would sound right queer to be called something else. You just call me Queenie."

"Then you must be the lady that Sir William went to see at the weekend. My husband told me all about your lovely caravan."

For a moment Queenie looked puzzled and then the penny dropped. "You can't be married to Sir William What's-His-Name; you must be the wife of that young doctor, the one the specialist brought with him. He was a handsome young man to be sure, though he didn't have much to say for himself. I don't think I heard a squeak from him all the time he was there. Strong silent type is he?"

Kate thought for a moment, "Yes, I suppose he is," she said laughing before busying herself acquiring the information she required.

"Now, your date of birth, Queenie?"

"You know, I'm truly not sure, dearie. I have my birthday in October, on the 18th but whether I'm 52, 53 or 54 I don't rightly know. You see I don't have a birth certificate. There may have been one once upon a time, but if there was, it was lost long ago."

"And I see that you've been widowed."

"Yes, my Pat had an accident. It happened long ago."

"I'm sorry to hear that," Kate murmured.

"There's no need for you to be sorry, I manage very well without him," Queenie responded, surprisingly cheerfully. "If you've found yourself a good man Nurse, you hang on to him. But if he's nothing but trouble like my Pat, it's no bad thing if he's daft enough to get himself killed in a fight."

"So who should I put down as your next of kin?"

Queenie thought for a moment before answering. "I suppose you'd better put down Mick. He's my eldest."

"Do you have other children?"

"Yes, there's my daughter Young Rose and then there's my youngest, Brendan, though we don't see much of him; I'm afraid we had a bit of a 'falling out'."

Kate completed the admissions process by performing some routine observations. She found that Queenie's blood pressure was raised and there was bile and sugar in her urine. Given that she was jaundiced, the bile was to be expected but the presence of sugar suggested she might be diabetic. Kate also noticed how breathless she became when she walked down the ward to be shown the day room and toilet facilities. Sir William had obviously been right when suggesting that Queenie's general health needed to be improved before she would be fit enough to face an anaesthetic.

"Are you normally short of breath when you walk?" Kate asked.

"I was consumptive as a child, Nurse. I've had a bad chest ever since."

"In that case the doctors will want to do some tests on your heart and lungs. One of them will be along in a little while to examine you. Who knows, maybe you'll be lucky enough to meet the handsome young man who came to visit you at home," Kate added with a smile.

"Tell you what, Nurse, if I was thirty years younger, steal him from you, I would. I knew how to make a young man's heart flutter when I was a girl! The lads always came knocking on my door when they were looking for a good time."

"Hands off, he's mine," Kate replied laughing. She had taken to this colourful character who was sure to liven up the ward for a week or two whilst she was with them. And that would be no bad thing; some of their gloomy patients certainly needed cheering up!

Then the smile on Queenie's face melted away. "Before you go Nurse, would you be knowing what they think I've got?" she asked. "I'm sure that old doctor who came to see me thinks it's something nasty. He had such a long face on him when he visited. And when he said I had to come in, he didn't put me on a waiting list; he gave me the date there and then. That must be a bad sign. I'm sure it must be cancer."

"I'm afraid I don't know what Sir William thinks is the matter with you," Kate explained gently. "You see, because you've been admitted so quickly, there isn't any medical information in your notes. But he's ever so nice and always explains to his patients what's going on; and even if it is something serious, there are excellent treatments these days."

Queenie glanced at Kate's name badge then looked her straight in the eye. "Kate," she said, "I want you to give me your word that you'll always be honest with me – and I mean completely honest – no fibs, no half truths, no little lies to make me feel better. Will you do that for me? Will you make me that promise?"

Kate looked at Queenie's earnest expression then paused, unsure how she should respond.

Queenie noticed her hesitation. "I wouldn't be asking you if I didn't mean it, would I? If the worst comes to the worst there are things I need to sort out before I go; you might call it unfinished business."

Kate could see that she was serious.

"Are you sure that's what you want?"

"Yes, I am."

"Then if that's what you really want, yes I promise."

Kate walked back to the office with a frown on her face. She wondered if she had done the right thing and whether she could cope if later she had to tell Queenie that her condition was incurable, that she was going to die. It was a commitment she had never previously been asked to give. Yet equally, Queenie's request seemed reasonable. Kate knew that if she were going to die she would want to know. There would be all sorts of loose ends in her life that she would wish to tidy up. She went to seek reassurance from Sister Rutherford.

"Are you certain that Mrs O'Hannagan was clear in her own mind, that she didn't have any doubts, that it wasn't a spur of the moment request?" Sister wanted to know.

"Yes, quite sure," Kate replied. "I felt she had made up her mind in advance."

"Well in that case there isn't a problem," Sister commented, "but of course, if and when the time comes, you must keep your promise.

****

When Kate came off duty at five o'clock she went straight to the shops to buy sausages, potatoes and peas for their evening meal. Returning to the flat, she left the shopping on the kitchen table, then went through to the living room to listen to the six o'clock news on the radio; she would cook their supper when Paul got home. Then she started to read a novel. She sighed. She loved Paul dearly, regarded herself fortunate to be his wife, yet sometimes wished he wasn't quite so committed to his patients. This was the third time in a week that he had been late home from work. She recognised, of course, that the long hours he worked resulted from his sense of responsibility which, ironically, had been one of the things that had attracted her to him in the first place!

For a moment, she laid her book to one side and glanced at the photograph which had pride of place on the wall above the fireplace. There was Paul wearing his smartest suit, his graduation robes and mortarboard. She smiled to herself. She recalled the very first occasion she had noticed him. He had been on a ward round, part of a group of medical students. She had been a first year nurse at the time. Paul had been asked by a senior and rather pompous consultant to examine a patient's heart and she had watched as, very self-consciously, he had applied his stethoscope to the man's chest. He had then been told to describe the heart murmur he had heard. The correct term had been an *'ejection'* murmur, but after a degree of hesitation the word that came out of Paul's mouth was an *'ejaculatory'* murmur. The other medical students thought this was hilarious and all the nurses fell about in fits of giggles. Paul had turned the colour of a beetroot. He had been teased about it unmercifully for weeks afterwards especially as the consultant had immediately asked *'whatever were you thinking about Lambert, or perhaps I should ask, which of these pretty nurses were you thinking about?'* Though everyone else had laughed, Kate had felt an immediate surge of sympathy for him and a motherly desire to hug and console him.

When they had been courting, Kate had readily accepted the long hours he was required to work. As a newly qualified doctor, he had been the medical dogsbody, the one at everybody's beck and call. He had been on duty for over one hundred hours each week. However, when Paul returned to the City General Hospital as a registrar, he only had to sleep in the hospital every fourth night. Kate therefore expected those long days at work and the late nights studying surgical textbooks would be over; that she would see more of him. But it wasn't happening. She never knew when he would come home in an evening or whether he would suddenly feel the need to return to the hospital to check on a patient who was worrying him.

She would talk to him about it. She was worried he would burn himself out and was concerned that, like Frederic in 'The Pirates of Penzance', he might be unable to change and would take his sense of duty with him throughout his life. A frown crossed her face; he would need to spend more time at home when they started their family – and that was something else they needed to talk about. Time was passing and she desperately wanted to have a baby.

Kate glanced again at the clock, sighed, then returned to her book but had only read a few lines when she heard Paul's key in the front door.

"Hi, I'm home," he called.

At last, Kate thought. She tossed her book to one side, jumped up and turned for the kitchen.

"Good," she said. "I'll get the supper on. It's sausage and mash tonight."

Chapter Five

Leslie Potts was not a man to hide his light under a bushel. The polished brass plate beside the impressive front door announced in bold block capitals that the owner of this substantial property was **Mr Leslie Potts, MB ChB, PhD, FRCS(Eng). Consultant Surgeon.** The man in question was sitting behind the desk in his private consulting suite. Perhaps slightly less than average height and stockily built, he was aged between forty-five and fifty. His black hair was well oiled and swept back, though greying slightly at the temples. With dark challenging eyes and a tight mouth that rarely smiled, he gave the impression of a man who did not tolerate fools gladly - nor indeed did he!

His secretary, a pretty young brunette with a shapely figure and a cheerful disposition, popped her head round the door. Had Paul seen her he would not have been surprised. When appointing doctors to work on his surgical team, Sir William always selected the graduate who obtained the highest marks in medical school examinations, irrespective of their sex or appearance. Mr Potts, on the other hand, always chose the prettiest of the girls!

"I'm sorry to disturb you Mr Potts," she said, "but I have a gent on the phone who wants to know if you could see him today. He says he's a very busy man and that his problem is painful and urgent. Do you have time to squeeze him in?"

"Yes, that's fine. Arrange for him to come as my last patient," the consultant replied.

He had no objection at all. Private practice was lucrative and at least two of the patients he had seen that afternoon required surgery, which would add significantly to his income. Indeed one of the reasons he had decided to acquire extra skills by training to operate on blood vessels was that it held the promise of even more private patients.

"The more the merrier," he added cheerfully, "and by the way Samantha, do please call me Leslie; Mr Potts sounds far too formal."

When the extra patient arrived, Mr Potts recognised him at once. It was the local MP, Harry Grimshaw, whose photograph featured regularly in both regional and national newspapers.

"Thank you so much for seeing me here and not at the City General," Harry said as he shook Mr Potts firmly by the hand. He laughed. "I'm sure you appreciate that had I been seen in the hospital I should undoubtedly have been recognised. Within two minutes the press would be speculating about my health and wondering if there was soon to be a vacancy in the cabinet. But please treat me just as you would any other Health Service patient."

In other words, you don't expect to be sent a bill, thought Mr Potts!

Fifteen minutes later, when Mr Potts had completed his medical examination, Harry was again up to his tricks.

"You say this is only a minor operation and that I won't be incapacitated for more than a week or so," he said. "However I do have to shoehorn it into a very busy schedule. There's never a good time for me to be away from Westminster." He took out his diary and flicked through the pages frowning.

"I had hoped to get back to London later today to attend a function at Transport House," he said, thinking aloud, "but it's already too late for that. Unfortunately this infected toe is so painful that it's interfering with my work so I'd better get it sorted out at the earliest opportunity. Is there any chance that my operation could be done in the next couple of days? Tomorrow would be best if you could fit me in. Of course, in the hospital I wouldn't expect any special favours."

This rankled with Mr Potts. Harry Grimshaw was an MP, indeed a cabinet minister in a Labour Government that was hell bent on eliminating the private practice that provided him with his lucrative income. Yet he was asking to by-pass the waiting list and dictate the date of his operation; he wanted the benefits of private practice on the NHS.

Mr Potts paused before replying, wondering how best to respond. He could decline to co-operate. He could point out that the waiting time for non-urgent surgery was six months, that the ability to choose a convenient time to fit in with work commitments was relevant to many professional people and businessmen, not just to politicians. Did Harry not understand that anyone with a family or with a holiday booked would also wish to choose the time of their surgery? He looked Harry in the eye, still undecided what to say. The politician seemed to read his mind.

"I know I'm asking for a little favour," he said smoothly, "but as you can imagine, I am quite influential. I'm sure that I'll be able to return the favour in the not too distant future."

You scratch my back, I'll scratch yours, thought Mr Potts.

"All right," he said reluctantly. "Take a seat in the waiting room and I'll see what I can do."

As Harry left the room, he reached for the phone. He dialled the hospital then waited for a couple of minutes, drumming his fingers impatiently on the desk, whilst the switchboard located Paul Lambert, his registrar.

Paul was working in the outpatient clinic alongside Sir William when the call came through.

"Mr Lambert, I have Mr Potts on the line for you. I'll put you through." It was Carol, one of the hospital switchboard operators.

Paul heard his boss's familiar voice, "Lambert, I have a patient with me at the moment who needs to come into the hospital."

Paul presumed, correctly as it transpired, that the consultant was speaking from his private consulting rooms.

"He's something of a VIP," Mr Potts continued. "It's Harry Grimshaw. I presume you know who he is?"

Paul thought quickly. "You mean the politician, Sir?"

"Yes, that's right. He's got an in-growing toenail. Put him on tomorrow morning's operating list as the first case. He'll need to be clerked in as usual of course, but just treat him as a routine patient. Oh, and by the way, you'd better tell Sister to organise a side room for him."

"I presume that he'll be a private patient then, Sir."

The consultant laughed sardonically. "You must be joking, Lambert! With the Labour Party determined to abolish all the pay beds in the NHS, he couldn't possibly risk the press finding him in a private bed. They would hound him out of office for being such a hypocrite. No, he'll be an ordinary NHS patient."

Although an 'ordinary NHS patient' with an in-growing toenail would never be treated in a side room, Paul knew better than to comment. He was a junior doctor. His prospects of progression up the surgical career ladder lay entirely in Mr Potts' hands.

"That's fine, Sir," Paul replied, "I'll pass the message on to the houseman."

"Actually, Lambert, it would be better if you admitted him and managed his care yourself. He's rather a forceful character. The houseman might find him a bit overpowering. Besides, he's very influential so it's important that we create a good impression. Who knows, there may come a time when we need his support."

"And when will he be arriving, Sir?"

"In about 30 minutes."

"Do you happen to know which toe it is?" Paul asked. This was important information. The site of surgery needed to be marked on the patient's skin with an indelible pen and detailed in capital letters on the typed list which would guide the theatre staff the next day. Failure to follow these routines could lead to catastrophic errors which were a disaster for the patient, expensive for the medical insurance company and highly damaging to the surgeon's reputation!

"It's one of the big toes," Mr Potts replied, "I can't remember which side. It will be obvious when he arrives. I'll leave the matter in your hands then."

Despite having said *'just treat him as a routine patient'*, it was clear that Mr Potts intended that Harry Grimshaw should have special treatment. Non urgent NHS admissions were normally notified to the ward a week in advance by the administrative staff, not by the consultant immediately prior to their arrival.

Paul phoned Sister Ashbrook who was in the office on the male ward. She was working on the nurses' duty rota, a weekly chore that she detested. She found it impossible to staff the ward appropriately without denying her nurses the time 'off duty' that they requested.

When Paul mentioned that Mr Grimshaw was to be nursed in a side ward, she became angry. All three side wards were already occupied; the patients in them needing privacy for sound medical reasons. One had an infection and required to be isolated to prevent it spreading to other patients. The second was receiving terminal care and only that morning, she had placed an elderly man in the third side room, where he was receiving more intensive nursing care than was possible on the main ward.

"But that's ridiculous," Sister exclaimed, when told that Mr Grimshaw merely had an in-growing toe nail. "How can I possibly justify moving a sick patient out of a side ward for such a trivial condition?"

"Sorry Sister, but I'm afraid that's what I've been instructed to arrange. Perhaps a cabinet minister's toenail is more important than yours or mine! And Sister," Paul added, "would you mind giving me a bleep when he arrives? I've been invited to give him my personal attention. He's to go first on tomorrow's list so I won't have much time to check him in and organise any tests that may be necessary."

"And you say he'll arrive in 30 minutes? That doesn't give me much time to move a patient who actually needs a side ward onto the main ward, does it?" Sister replied pointedly. Then she posed the question that Paul had asked only a few moments earlier.

"I suppose he is a private patient then?"

"No, Sister. He's a politician who wants the perks of private care on the NHS."

There was a pause before Sister replied. "Oh does he now? Well we'll see about that, won't we?"

Paul smiled at the curious inflection in her voice and wondered what she had in mind. She would no doubt ensure his medical care was to the high standard that she insisted upon for all her patients - but he doubted that Harry would receive the choice of menu, the silver service or linen serviette, those little extras that private patients enjoyed. She might even have some special 'treat' in store for him; Paul knew she was quite capable of it!

Chapter Six

Back in the outpatient department, Paul looked at his watch. The interruption had delayed him and he was running behind schedule. He picked up the next set of notes, those of Mr Cullen and immediately recognised the name. He recalled his initial consultation with the couple and his belief that his vasectomy operation had failed and that he was still able to father a child. He opened the folder and flicked through the pages until he found the report of the semen analysis that he had arranged.

'*Sample of semen*', he read, '*four millilitres of cloudy viscous fluid.*

Number of motile spermatozoa: nil.

Number of non motile spermatozoa: nil'.

His heart sank. The message from the laboratory was unmistakable. Mr Cullen's vasectomy operation had not failed. The sperm test confirmed that he was sterile. He was not capable of fathering a child.

Paul always found it difficult, indeed painful to give bad news to patients. A balance had to be struck between imparting hard facts and offering an appropriate degree of sympathy, all the while trying to avoid becoming emotionally involved. On many occasions it had been his misfortune to inform someone they had an incurable disease. He had experienced the anguish of telling a man that his young wife had died unexpectedly after routine surgery, even had the unenviable task of informing a mother that her four year old daughter had lost her life in a road accident. The present situation wasn't as dramatic but the information he now had to impart would undoubtedly cause significant distress. He had to tell Mr Cullen that his wife had been unfaithful. He held the evidence in his hand.

He entered the cubicle hoping that Mr Cullen had left his wife at home. It would be so much easier to break the news to him man to man. However, it was not to be. They were both waiting to see him and as before were sitting hand in hand. They looked at him expectantly. There seemed little point in spending time on pleasantries.

"Good morning," he said before turning to Mr Cullen. "I have the result of your sperm count here. The sample that you produced did not contain any sperm."

There was a long pause which Paul allowed to continue. He felt it would give the couple a chance for the news to sink in.

"What exactly does that mean, Doctor?" It was Mrs Cullen who asked the question. Paul examined her face carefully; she looked puzzled rather than guilty or ashamed. He thought the implications were perfectly clear but knew he had to be polite and professional.

"It means that the vasectomy operation was successful. Your husband is not able to father a child," he said.

"But that must be wrong," she insisted. "He has fathered a child. I became pregnant."

"Could there be another explanation?" Paul asked cautiously.

It was Mr Cullen who answered, his tone forceful. "If you're suggesting that my wife has had an affair Doctor, you can dismiss the idea. My wife and I love each other dearly. I would never cheat on her and I know with absolute certainly, that she would never cheat on me. I trust her implicitly."

It was on the tip off Paul's tongue to make a sarcastic comment about an immaculate conception, but wisely thought better of it! For a moment there was an uneasy silence.

"I know exactly what you're thinking, Doctor," Mr Cullen persisted, "but there must be another explanation. Could the vasectomy operation be failing intermittently; sometimes sperm getting though and sometimes not getting through, perhaps depending upon the strength of the gush?"

"No," Paul explained, "it doesn't work like that. The vasectomy operation blocks the sperm as they leave the testicles so they never reach the storage reservoir. The ejaculation, or 'gush' as you call it, is the fluid leaving the reservoir and coming to the surface. I've never heard of a case of an intermittent failure."

"Well," Mr Cullen said emphatically, "I still want to have the vasectomy operation repeated. I won't run the risk of my wife having another miscarriage. She had a painful and distressing time. Even after she had miscarried, she had to have an anaesthetic and an operation to ensure that her womb was completely empty."

"Look," Paul said, "if we knew that the operation had failed, as they do from time to time, we would willingly arrange a further operation for you. But with this sperm test, we wouldn't be justified in performing more surgery."

"We would be quite willing to pay to have it done."

"It's not a question of paying, Mr Cullen; it's a question of whether it's the right treatment for you. The operation that you've already had, has achieved what was intended. Having the same operation again wouldn't make it any more complete."

It was Mrs Cullen who spoke next. "I'm afraid that we're not satisfied, Doctor Lambert. If you're not prepared to repeat the operation here, then we'll go elsewhere."

"You're perfectly entitled to get a second opinion," Paul said "but I'm afraid you can expect the same answer if you do go elsewhere."

"Well that's what we're going to do," she said doggedly.

Yes, Paul thought and attempt to persuade another surgeon to perform an unnecessary operation on your husband, when you know perfectly well that you've been unfaithful.

They had reached an impasse and a long silence ensued. Paul needed guidance on how to proceed. One of the advantages of being a trainee was that you could seek advice from your consultant and Paul decided this was an appropriate moment to speak to Sir William. He was in no doubt that the opinion he had given was correct, but throughout both consultations he had been impressed by Mr Cullen's belief in his wife. Perhaps he so desperately wanted to believe in his wife that he was prepared to put his head in the sand and have an unnecessary operation to save his marriage. Or maybe he thought that Paul was inexperienced and there was another explanation of which Paul was ignorant. Paul found it rather unsettling.

"Look," he said after a long pause. "If you'll excuse me for a moment, I'll have a word with my consultant and see what he has to say."

Sir William listened carefully to the story, as he always did. He was not one to be hurried when considering the most appropriate management of a patient. Paul explained that the sperm count done immediately after the surgery, as well as the one done a couple of weeks ago proved the operation had been a success. Not a single sperm had been present in either sample.

"I've never heard of an intermittent blockage," Sir William said, "but I suppose it is theoretically possible. In any case it won't do any harm to get the sperm test repeated. It will be a month or so before we see them again, which will give them a chance to consider the more obvious explanation. Also, since you say she had a miscarriage, you'd better get the notes from the hospital in Scotland, to check that it was well documented."

For a moment he paused, then smiled and added, "But you know what I always say, Lambert; *common things occur commonly.*' The odds must be overwhelmingly in favour of the child being fathered by a third party."

Mr and Mrs Cullen agreed to Sir William's plan without hesitation and were still hand in hand as they left the cubicle. Although Paul was impressed by Mr Cullen's belief in his wife he suspected that eventually he would be forced to accept that she had been unfaithful. He would await the further sperm test result with interest.

Chapter Seven

When Paul was informed that Harry Grimshaw had arrived on the ward, he saw the last of the patients in Sir William's clinic then had a cup of tea and a chat with the clinic staff before going to see the 'Very Important Politician'. There was no reason for him to hurry as the nurses usually took 30 minutes or so to admit a new patient. As he entered the office to pick up Harry Grimshaw's notes, Paul was met by Sister Ashbrook, a slim, dark haired woman with sharp features and a sharper tongue. She ran the male ward with a brisk efficiency. She was never one to hide her emotions whether praising the work of her nurses, or, as was more often the case, criticising some perceived fault by a junior doctor. She was now even angrier than she had been when Paul had spoken with her on the phone.

"He's arrived without any records at all," she fumed, "not even a piece of paper with his name and address on it. And what's more, he hasn't allowed us to do any part of the admissions procedure."

"On what grounds, Sister?"

"He says he's busy. He's working with what he chooses to call his 'secretary'."

"Well, he's going to have to allow me to clerk him in," Paul said, picking up the blood pressure machine and some foolscap sheets which would later be incorporated into Mr Grimshaw's notes. "If he doesn't, he won't be on tomorrow's operating list."

Paul knocked politely on the door, entered the side ward and found Harry Grimshaw slouched in an armchair, fully dressed, a cigarette dangling from the corner of his mouth. There were already two cigarette butts in a saucer at his elbow and a generous scattering of ash both in the saucer and on the floor. Paul had assumed that having started life as a miner, he would have a muscular frame, but if indeed that had once been the case, he had subsequently gone to seed. His belly hung generously over the top of his low-slung trousers, no doubt the result of too many formal dinners. He had a double chin; his neck lost in rolls of fat. His eyebrows were thick and bushy and met in an untidy fashion above the bridge of his nose, duplicating the shaggy moustache he wore on his upper lip, except that the latter was nicotine stained. It was however his nose that was his most striking facial feature. Large and red, nasal hair mingling freely with his moustache, its coarse skin was covered in tiny red blood vessels, suggesting a lifetime of alcohol abuse, evidence of long evenings spent in working men's clubs and Westminster bars. It was immediately apparent why Sister Ashbrook had laid heavy emphasis on the word 'secretary'. The girl sitting on the bed opposite Mr Grimshaw could not have been more than 20 years old. A dyed blonde, she wore a low cut blouse that revealed a generous cleavage and a mini skirt that was little more than a pelmet. She lounged on the bed, her knees at Harry's eye level, as he relaxed in the armchair.

Paul started to introduce himself but was immediately interrupted.

"Don't you know who I am?"

Subconsciously Paul's brain snapped into 'personality assessment mode'. He had only been in Mr Grimshaw's presence for a few seconds but already knew that this was a person he would come to dislike. Over the years, he had found that when meeting someone for the first time, he formed a judgement of them very quickly and once made, this opinion rarely changed.

"Yes," he said, "you are Mr Harry Grimshaw; Cabinet Minister with responsibility for Industry and Commerce. Mr Potts rang me to say that you were coming."

Paul began to explain that he needed to undertake a formal assessment in preparation for Mr Grimshaw's surgery but was interrupted for a second time.

"For Heaven's sake, Doctor, can't you see I'm busy? Come back later." The voice was brusque and authoritative; clearly this was a man accustomed to being obeyed promptly and without question.

Neither Mr Grimshaw nor his 'secretary' looked busy. There were no papers, pencils or notepads to suggest feverish activity but it was clear that Paul would not be allowed to perform a clinical examination at this stage. Deflated, he muttered an apology and left the room, irritated that he would need to return to do the job later.

Paul 'pencilled in' Harry Grimshaw's name at the top of the operating list that had already been drafted for the next day, stating he would have surgery for an in-growing toenail on one of his big toes. *'Side not known at this time'*, he wrote, not wishing to be criticised for omitting this important information. He then busied himself with other tasks, returning to Mr Grimshaw's side ward a couple of hours later. By this time, the nurses had assembled a medical case folder but the only information it contained was Harry's name in capital letters on the front cover. Every sheet in the file remained blank. Mr Grimshaw had still not allowed the nurses to undertake the admissions process! Sister Ashbrook informed Paul that although the 'secretary' had left, her place had been taken by the patient's wife.

Once again Paul knocked on the door, this time waiting for an invitation to enter, before turning the handle. The contrast in appearance between Mrs Grimshaw and the 'secretary' could not have been greater. There was however a certain similarity between Harry and his wife. Both were short, fat and rather hairy! She was wearing an old woollen cardigan, a tweed skirt and brogue shoes. As before, Harry insisted that he was not to be disturbed but this time Paul was more persistent.

"Sir, there are a number of jobs that the nurses and I need to perform if you're to be ready for your surgery tomorrow. It's getting late and we need to get on with them. I have to check that you're fit for an anaesthetic. We also need your signature on the *'consent for surgery'* form."

Once again Mr Grimshaw's reply was uncompromising. "Damn it Doctor, you shouldn't interrupt at a time like this. Can't you see that I have my wife visiting? I'm a busy man. Thanks to my important role in government we're not able to spend a lot of time together. Surely if I'm to have a major operation in the morning, I'm entitled to some peace and quiet with my family this evening."

Paul was sorely tempted to retort that surgery on a toenail could scarcely be described as the most major of operations. He contented himself however by remarking that, for his own safety, certain basic checks had to be undertaken before his surgery could be performed. Whether the MP believed Paul or not, it made no difference to his decision. He wasn't going to waste time on nurses' paperwork, nor would he submit to a physical examination; and that was the end of the matter. Reluctantly Paul left the room empty handed and for a second time, cursed this selfish egotistical individual.

He rang the anaesthetist to inform him that there was a 'special' patient on the list in the morning but explained that he hadn't been able to make any assessment of his fitness for surgery.

"Perhaps you could phone me when you've managed to give him the 'once-over' " the anaesthetist suggested, "and let me know if there are any problems. If there are, I'll visit early in the morning and take a look at him myself. Otherwise I'll see him when he arrives in theatre. You'd better place him last on the list, then if there are any concerns about his chest or heart, he can have an x-ray and an ECG before he comes to theatre."

"I'm afraid Mr Potts has specified that he should go first on the list."

"That can't be right," the anaesthetist protested. "It's a 'dirty' case, his toe nail is infected. We don't want the theatre contaminated by the first case of the day. It isn't fair on the patients who are to follow. It puts them at risk of developing a wound infection."

"I know that, and obviously Mr Potts knows it as well. But those are my instructions."

"If that's what the mighty man wants, I guess that's what the mighty man will get," replied the anaesthetist in a resigned tone, "but it flies in the face of good surgical practice."

Harry Grimshaw's intransigence made Paul extremely angry. Junior doctors worked long hours. Their job demanded sacrifices both of them and of their families. Time off duty was precious and this evening he should be at home relaxing, not wasting time hanging around the hospital waiting to examine Mr Grimshaw. He rang Kate to explain the situation to her.

"Kate, I'm sorry but I'm going to be late home. Mr Potts has insisted that I have to admit our local MP. I think it would be easier if I ate in the hospital canteen and came home when I've sorted him out."

"But Paul I've already cooked our evening meal. You promised faithfully that you wouldn't be late tonight. Please don't let me down again."

"OK, I'll come home and we'll eat together. Your cooking beats anything that the hospital can produce but I'm afraid that I shall have to go back later."

When he got home he found Kate in a fractious mood, demanding to know why Paul had to be the one to admit Mr Grimshaw.

"It's not your job to examine new admissions," she said angrily. "The house officer should be doing it."

"I'm sorry Kate. You're quite right, it should be Janet's job but Mr Potts insisted that I do it. I think he wants to create a good impression."

"You should stand up for yourself Paul. You could have told him it was your night off; that we were going out and you weren't available."

"But we're not going out are we? In any case, if your consultant specifically asks you to do something, as a junior doctor you just have to get on and do it. I depend on Mr Potts for a good reference and I won't get one if I'm stroppy." Paul's day had been long and tiring, he still had work to do and he wasn't in the mood for a lecture.

"You've always got an excuse, haven't you?" Kate responded. "You're always coming home late. You don't think about me or the trouble I've gone to preparing a nice meal for us to share."

"It's probably difficult for you to understand Kate. You're a good nurse and you take your duties seriously, but your hours are fixed. At the end of your shift you're chased off the ward by your ward sister; you're free to come home."

"So why don't you come home at the end of your shift, just as I do?"

"It's different for me, Kate. If one of our patients gets a problem, I've got to sort them out and I'm also at the beck and call of Mr Potts."

"Other junior doctors don't find it necessary to work the hours that you do," Kate snapped as she stormed into the kitchen. Paul heard her venting her frustration on the pot and pans. She returned two minutes later, fortunately in a more conciliatory mood, carrying a steak and kidney pie.

"Look Paul, I'm sorry to be upset, I don't mean to be angry but I've cooked a nice meal and I wanted us to eat it together. This pie looked lovely an hour ago. Now the pastry's gone all soggy."

"Yes, it looks like the flabby belly I operated on today. It's even got a hole in the middle like a belly button where the pie funnel was. But I'm sure it will taste good."

"Paul, I'm being serious. In an evening, when you're off duty, we ought to be able to relax together, maybe watch a film at the cinema or go to the pub with friends for a drink. I don't enjoy spending every evening on my own, reading or watching television, wondering when you're going to finish work. And when you do finally get home, you just collapse exhausted on the settee."

The truth was that she had started to think about the future. She accepted that if Paul was to achieve his ambition of becoming a consultant, he needed further experience and had to acquire more technical skills. Thankfully he had no more examinations to take, but did it really have to be like this?

"How long do you think it will be before you can apply for a consultant post Paul?" she asked.

"Perhaps if things go smoothly, three or four years. Why do you ask?"

"I was wondering when we'll be able to spend more time together. Your recent promotion and my appointment as a Staff Nurse means we have a little more money coming in now."

"Things are still a bit tight though Kate."

"True enough, but we no longer have the bank manager breathing down our necks, do we? We could start to put some money away at the end of each month; you know, save towards a deposit on a house, instead of living in rented accommodation."

"You mean that if we bought a house instead of living in a hospital flat, I wouldn't be able to slip back to the wards on a whim!" Paul said smiling as he tucked into the steak and kidney pie.

"Yes, that's exactly what I mean."

Kate certainly wanted to spend more time with Paul but she also longed to start a family. She wasn't unhappy as Paul's wife, yet when she was alone in the flat waiting to hear his key in the front door, there was sadness in her heart. The truth was that she grieved for her mum. She had only been nineteen when her mother had died, but Kate was still mourning her loss. Her death had left a huge hole in her life and it made Kate yearn for a child of her own. She couldn't explain, even to herself, how having her own child could possibly heal the wound left by her mother's death, but somehow she felt that it would.

She had already spoken to Paul about starting a family. They were both young and healthy and she didn't anticipate any difficulty in having a baby. They had agreed it was really a matter of timing. If Paul was to pursue his dream of a career in surgery, he needed to work long days and live in the hospital every fourth night until he made consultant grade. He had suggested to Kate that if they were to have a child too soon, he wouldn't be able to support her as he would have wished. Then he had upset her by hinting that he was quite content with the 'here and now'. As things were, he had said, when the day's work was finally done, they could relax together, just the two of them, in their own home, their love nest.

It was on the tip of Kate's tongue to raise the issue of starting a family again, to tell him that she thought his attitude was selfish but aware that there was still tension between them she held back; she would catch him at the weekend when he was less tired.

Chapter Eight

Later that evening, long after the patients' visitors had left the ward, Paul returned to the MP's side room. He passed one of the night nurses coming in the opposite direction. Mr Grimshaw's notes were tucked under her arm. She was grim faced and upset.

"I'll take the notes," Paul said, "if you've finished with them."

"Yes, I've finished with them and you're welcome to them – and to him," she added. "He's the rudest man I've had to deal with in a very long time. He'll not be getting my vote come the next election! I'd rather vote for the Monster Raving Loony Party. "Good luck. You'll certainly need it!"

As before, Paul knocked, waited for an invitation to enter then once again explained why he needed to examine him.

"Look, can we get this over as quickly as possible? I've numerous important telephone calls to make. Incidentally there isn't a phone in here. You'll have to me one."

Paul didn't regard himself as a stubborn man although he accepted that, as his mother used to say, when the mood took him, he could become somewhat pedantic! Faced with this objectionable man, he felt more than pedantic; he was possessed of a bloody minded determination that Mr Harry Grimshaw was going to be thoroughly examined, whether he liked it or not. He would overcome whatever objections the man raised, even if it took 'til midnight, even if he was an MP and cabinet minister. It was, after all, in his best interests.

Obtaining details of the infected toe nail was straightforward. It had troubled Mr Grimshaw for about a year, the in-growing edge digging into his flesh causing pain when he walked. However Paul ran into trouble and his patient's humour changed, when he enquired after Harry's general health; had he experienced any symptoms to suggest problems with his heart or lungs such as breathlessness or pain in his chest when walking? Was he able to sleep flat in bed at night? Did he get any swelling of his ankles?

"Are these damn silly questions really necessary?" the MP demanded.

"Yes Sir, of course they are. If you're to have an anaesthetic, they're essential. In any case, there's a lot to be said for having a full medical assessment from time to time. Then if any problems come to light, they can be nipped in the bud."

Questions about his waterworks and bowels were barely tolerated but enquiry about his social habits, the number of cigarettes he smoked and the amount of alcohol he consumed, proved a step too far. Mr Grimshaw's patience was exhausted.

"I've had enough of this bloody silly interrogation. It's time for you to leave." he shouted.

"But I need to examine the toe and mark it for the operation tomorrow."

"Potts examined me, surely that's enough. And it's bloody obvious which toe it is! It's twice the size of the other one; it's as red as a ripe tomato and bloody painful! Now get out."

"Did Mr Potts listen to your chest, take your blood pressure or examine your heart?" Paul asked. He knew exactly what the answer would be, but was determined to make the point.

"Of course not," he roared, "I've come for an operation on this bloody toe, not my chest. Now for God's sake, get out and leave me alone."

It was quite clear that Paul was destined to make no further progress so reluctantly he left the room, his clinical assessment incomplete. Mr Grimshaw's heart and lungs had not been examined, nor had his toe. Further, formal written consent for surgery had not been obtained.

The night nurse was in the office when Paul returned to record these events in the medical case notes. She looked worried.

"How did you get on?" she asked.

"About as well as you did, I suspect."

"Paul, I'm worried. I haven't been able to take his blood pressure or fill in the nursing charts and he refused point blank to provide a sample of urine for me to test. I don't know what to write in the nursing notes. He's an important person. Sister's bound to check his records tomorrow. I'm going to be in trouble if they're incomplete."

"In his medical file, I'm simply going to state that he wouldn't co-operate. Then I shall list the formalities that I've had to omit. I can only suggest that you do the same. By the way, is there a socket for the telephone in that side room? Harry wants one for his personal use."

"Yes, there is. The phone is supposed to be available to all the patients but in the circumstances, to avoid further trouble, I'll wheel it down and leave it for him."

"If he were a child that would be regarded as a reward for bad behaviour!" Paul commented as he replaced the records in the notes trolley.

The nurse smiled. "Maybe it would, but I regard it simply as a case of taking the line of least resistance. Anyway, if he were a child, I would spank his bottom good and hard!"

"I'm sure you'd enjoy doing that," Paul commented. "Perhaps he would too but that really would get you into trouble with Sister!"

Since the night staff were just putting the kettle on, Paul joined them for a hot drink, the first of their long night shift.

Later Janet Smith, Mr Potts' forthright young house officer arrived and together with the night nurse they embarked on the routine evening round to check that the drips were running and that the patients had pain relief and sedation available should they be needed during the night. Nothing was more irritating for a doctor than to be woken in the night and have to leave a nice warm bed, to prescribe a sleeping pill for a patient, especially if with forethought the sedation could have been arranged before the doctor retired. They were just completing the round when Matron's dark shadow fell across the ward entrance.

"Matron must have heard that we have a distinguished visitor on the ward," staff nurse whispered. "We're not usually honoured by one of her visits when we're on night duty, especially as late as this. Thank goodness she didn't arrive twenty minutes ago when we had the kettle on!"

She went to meet Matron who asked to be introduced to Mr Grimshaw but within two minutes she was back. Paul asked what sort of a reception Matron had received.

"Mr Grimshaw was very short with her," she said. "He made it abundantly clear after about 90 seconds that the interview was at an end. But at least he was formal and polite, far more so than he was with me!"

Paul looked at his watch and was immediately struck by a guilty pang. Hell fire, it was eleven fifteen. He had stayed on the ward far longer than was necessary. He could have gone home as soon as he had finished with Mr Grimshaw; Janet was quite capable of doing the evening ward round on her own. Why on earth hadn't he done so? Kate would be furious, and rightly so. He turned to leave then, remembering Mr Potts' instructions, reluctantly told the nurse that if Mr Grimshaw needed attention during the night, Paul was to be called, rather than the house officer. Then he walked the short distance to the flat to find that Kate had already gone to bed and was fast asleep. He crept in beside her, fortunately managing not to disturb her, which was just as well; she was on the early shift in the morning.

Unfortunately, at one in the morning, Paul's slumber was interrupted when he was phoned, not as he would have expected by the ward nurse, but by the senior night sister. She sounded apologetic.

"I'm so sorry to trouble you, Mr Lambert, but I've just been called to see Mr Grimshaw in the side ward on Surgical Five. He says he hasn't been able to sleep and has requested some night sedation. He's also complaining quite forcibly that his blood pressure tablets haven't been prescribed and as a result he's missed his evening dose. Apparently he wasn't told to bring his own tablets with him and of course, the nursing staff can't dispense any drugs without a prescription signed by a doctor. Would you mind coming to the ward to do the necessary paperwork?"

Paul was furious. The MP's medication would have been prescribed and he would have been offered sleeping tablets, had he allowed a full examination.

"Sister, yes I do mind; I mind a great deal!" Paul replied coldly. "His medication hasn't been prescribed because he wouldn't let me complete my clinical assessment. Perhaps you would be kind enough to explain to him that in such circumstances, the law does not permit me to prescribe for him. Then you can ask him whether he's now prepared to answer my questions and let me examine him. If he is, then I will prescribe for him, though you might also tell him that I'm not actually in the hospital at the moment." Paul was at his pedantic best!

"If you would hold the line Mr Lambert, I'll go and ask him."

A few moments later, Sister was back on the phone.

"Mr Grimshaw didn't look particularly pleased; in fact I'd say that he's more in need of his blood pressure tablets now than he was before. But he has agreed."

"In that case Sister, I'll be with you in five minutes."

"What was that all about?" a sleepy voice at his side asked.

"It's our local MP behaving intolerably badly, Kate," Paul replied. "I've got to go back to the ward to sort him out. You go to sleep. I'll try not to be too long."

Kate gave him a kiss then turned away and promptly fell back to sleep.

Arriving in the side ward, Paul subjected Mr Grimshaw to a searching interrogation. He obtained and recorded details of all his previous illnesses and questioned him in detail about his drinking and smoking habits. There was a certain bloody mindedness in the thoroughness of Paul's assessment as he gained a satisfying revenge for being disturbed from sleep. It all confirmed that Harry Grimshaw did not lead a healthy lifestyle.

The physical examination that Paul undertook revealed a significant abnormality. Listening to the chest, he found an area where the breath sounds were unusually coarse, suggesting some disease on the left side. Further investigation would be required, initially a chest x-ray to discover the nature of the problem but given that Mr Grimshaw had been a heavy smoker for 50 years, it was likely to be something rather unpleasant.

When examining his abdomen, Sir William's oft-repeated words came to his mind that *'the examination of the abdomen starts in the groin and ends in the rectum.'* Paul was sorely tempted to subject the cabinet minister to the ignominy of a rectal examination but he relented. In truth, it would have been difficult to justify in a man who did not have bowel symptoms and who had simply been admitted with an in-growing toenail! Paul completed the admission procedure by marking the offending toe nail with an indelible marker and obtaining written consent for the operation that was planned for the next day.

By the time Paul had finished, Mr Grimshaw's face registered unconcealed fury. As Sister had hinted, it seemed he was at risk of bursting a blood vessel at any moment. Paul prescribed his usual blood pressure tablets as well as some night sedation but instructed they be withheld until the patient had also allowed the nursing documentation to be completed.

A chest x-ray was obviously required but if Mr Grimshaw was to be first on the morning's list, there wouldn't be time for this to be done pre-operatively. The anaesthetist had asked to be contacted if the examination revealed any problems but Paul felt unable to disturb him at two in the morning. Instead he attached a note conspicuously to the front of the notes, warning about the chest problem then, quietly satisfied with the nights work, returned to his bed.

Chapter Nine

Sir William laid aside the surgical journal he was reading and looked at the clock on the wall of his office. It was exactly ten o'clock. He smiled, eased himself from his chair, stretched to ease the slight ache in his back then set off down the corridor to welcome the new group of medical students who were waiting for him on the ward. Three times a year, at the beginning of each university term, a group of eight students joined the unit for a period of ten weeks tuition. They were taught basic surgical principles on the ward each morning then attended lectures at the medical school in the afternoon.

He approached the tutorial room with mixed feelings. He enjoyed teaching, deriving great satisfaction from watching these bright young people develop their medical skills and knowledge. The sound training he gave them would be his legacy; something tangible that would continue to help patients long after he was gone. Many of his old pupils had become general practitioners in the city, others consultants in their own right. Many he now counted as his friends and all were grateful to him for the solid grounding in medicine that he had given them. His sadness though, was that this would be the last group of students he would instruct; he was due to retire in less than six months. He vowed, as he always did on these occasions, not only to teach them surgery but to impart to them the common sense and good manners he felt should be the hallmark of all who practised in the caring professions.

"Good morning," he said, as he entered the room.

The students stood. "Good morning, Sir," they said in unison. They all appreciated they had been exceedingly fortunate to be allocated to the care of the hospital's most conscientious tutor. Many of their contemporaries had been assigned to units where students were regarded as something of a nuisance, where teaching was not a priority.

Sir William surveyed the group of eight benevolently. One was Indian, another Chinese, the rest were British, two of them girls.

"Now," Sir William said, "I see you are all wearing your name badges, but I trust you will allow me a day or two to get to know you. Perhaps I could begin by asking each of you to spend a moment or two telling me a little bit about yourselves."

Nervously the students obliged. Sir William learned that all the home grown students had come directly from grammar or independent schools. They were a year or two younger than the overseas students.

"Thank you," Sir William said when the students had introduced themselves. "Now, I want to welcome you to Surgical Five and tell you a little bit about life in the hospital; but first a word about the standards that I, and indeed our patients, expect of us. In the lecture halls and on the university campus it doesn't matter how you dress but in the hospital and particularly on my unit, it does matter. I expect you to be smartly turned out. Men will wear collars and ties. White shirts and grey flannel trousers are preferred and jeans are not acceptable." He looked at the two female members of the group and smiled.

"It would be inappropriate for me as a confirmed old bachelor, to tell you young ladies how to dress, but perhaps the words 'neat, tidy and conservative' will be sufficient to guide you."

Then, addressing the whole group, he added, "At all times, you will be courteous both to our patients and to the staff. You will address the patients as 'Mister' or 'Missus' and the staff as Sister Smith, Staff Nurse Jones or Nurse Brown. It goes without saying that at all times your conduct must be above reproach."

He went on to detail their weekly timetable. For approximately one hour each weekday they would have formal tuition, given by him or, if he were absent for any reason, by one of the junior doctors. For the rest of the morning they would practice what they had been taught on patients on the ward. Surprisingly, most patients enjoyed being examined by the students, even if a few were somewhat heavy handed. It helped to pass the long hospital day and gave them a sense of value, feeling that they were playing a part in the education of the next generation of doctors.

"You are training to be doctors," Sir William continued, "to be members of an honourable profession. As such you will be privileged to share a patient's personal problems and know their innermost thoughts and concerns. What they tell you, you will of course hold in confidence.

No attendance records will be kept," Sir William added, perhaps unnecessarily for most students were eager to learn and unlikely to skip teaching sessions. "I shall make no effort to chase up anyone who neglects their studies."

He knew that the rigorous examination at the end of their training would ensure a satisfactory standard before any of the students qualified as doctors.

"Now, I'm sure you are all eager to get started so I shall introduce you to your first patient." He looked round the group. His eye fell on a tall young man sitting on the front row who wore a luxurious beard to hide an unsightly scar on his face. Early in his student days, on one of the darker streets in the city, he had been invited to hand over his wallet to some yobs. Being a rugby player he had declined and raised his fists but the muggers had produced a knife and his face had been slashed. By chance, he had been treated at the City General; indeed Paul had been the one to repair the damage.

"Mr Morris, please will you ask Sister Rutherford if she would be kind enough to bring Mrs Bradshaw to join us?"

He turned to the rest of the group. "Being a doctor is like being a detective. A crime is solved by interrogating suspects and witnesses, by examining the crime scene looking for evidence and, if necessary undertaking some forensic tests. To make a diagnosis, a doctor takes the same three steps. Firstly, we take the patient's medical history, in other words we ask them to describe their symptoms, then we undertake a physical examination and finally we may perform some tests, perhaps blood tests or maybe x-rays. Of the three, listening to the patient is by far the most important. As they tell their story, they are actually telling you where their problem is and what it is. You should be able to make a good working diagnosis in 70% of cases from the history alone. Your clinical examination will solve the problem in perhaps 20% of cases and various investigations will give you the answer in a further 5%."

He paused and waited for the inevitable question.

"And the last 5%, Sir?"

"In the last 5% you will never find out," Sir William responded with a smile. "Most will simply get better on their own though just occasionally you may need the pathologist to solve the mystery for you with a post mortem."

"Now," he continued as Mr Morris escorted a grey haired lady of about sixty into the room, "your very first patient."

She was wearing a well-worn dressing gown over her nightdress and had woollen slippers on her feet. "I want you to meet Mrs Bradshaw, a lady who has been with us for some time."

He invited the patient to sit in a chair facing the young students, thanked her for agreeing to meet them before making sure she was sitting comfortably.

"Now in a moment we're going to take Mrs Bradshaw's history but before we start I wonder if any of you have already made any observations about her? I'm sure you would normally be too polite to voice them in her presence but Mrs Bradshaw has assured me she doesn't mind."

His enquiry was met with silence.

"Well did any of you notice how she walked?"

After a pause, one of the girls volunteered hesitantly. "I think when she came in she walked with a slight limp, Sir."

"Well done, Miss Seddon, she does indeed walk with a limp and I'm sure Mrs Bradshaw won't mind telling us why."

"Aye, I suffered with polio as a bairn," Mrs Bradshaw responded. "Ma bonny wee sister died of it, poor mite. I was luckier. I dinna die, but it left me with this weakness in ma leg."

"Any other observations?" Sir William asked.

"I think Mrs Bradshaw is Scottish," Mr Morris offered, having heard her strong accent.

"Indeed I am, young man. I'm from Glasgow," the patient confirmed with a smile.

"Anything else?" Sir William wanted to know.

There was silence.

"Mr Solanki, would you care to look at Mrs Bradshaw's hands."

The Indian student walked to the front and examined her hands.

"I am thinking she does much work," he volunteered, at which Mrs Bradshaw smiled broadly. "Aye, indeed I do," she confirmed.

"What kind of work do you think?"

Mr Solanki looked at Mrs Bradshaw's hands again, turning each one over in turn. "Physical work," he suggested, "probably much time spent with hands in water."

"Well done Mr Solanki, anything else?"

"I am thinking she is probably smoking many cigarettes."

"Right again, well done. Mrs Bradshaw has some nicotine staining on her fingers and I think we can smell the faint whiff of her last cigarette on her dressing gown. She also has the face of a chronic smoker, doesn't she? Note those many deep facial skin creases. Now, has anyone made any observations of her general demeanour? What about you Miss Croft?"

Miss Croft was tall, blond with an attractive figure not disguised by the utilitarian white coat she wore; another young lady who was likely to catch Mr Potts' roving eye!

"Well", the student began cautiously, "Mrs Bradshaw seems to be quite confident and comfortable sitting talking to us. It's almost as if she was enjoying it. She doesn't seem in the least bit anxious. If it were me, I'd be worried to bits. It's as if she were used to being in hospital."

"Excellent work young lady. That's a very astute observation and one that is spot on. Mrs Bradshaw has indeed been with us for quite a long time.

Now it's time for us to take our first history. Our patient has a pain in her abdomen; it's under her ribs on the right hand side." Sir William looked round and at the back of the group he spotted a slightly built, brown haired student who seemed to be attempting to make himself invisible.

"Mr Booth, I'd like you to come to the front and ask Mrs Bradshaw a few questions. To begin with, we need to discover how severe the pain is."

Reluctantly the student dragged himself to the front. "Is the pain severe?" he asked in a voice that was barely audible.

"Severe doctor? Aye, it's terribly severe! Cuts me like a knife it does and it's with me all the time."

Mr Booth took a step back satisfied that he had elicited the required information and eager to return to his place.

"Well. Mr Booth, how bad is the pain?"

"It's very severe, Sir."

"Well let's just tease that out a bit shall we," Sir William said. He turned back to the patient. "Tell me Mrs Bradshaw, what do you do when you get the pain? Suppose you were at work when the pain came on?"

"Well I just have to keep working don't I? You don't get paid if you don't work, do you? I just take my pain killers and crack on."

"And what pain killers do you normally take?"

"Maybe an aspirin or two but I'm not really a tablet taker. As often as not, I just struggle on."

"I believe you've had a baby or two," Sir William said, "is it as bad as labour pains?"

Mrs Bradshaw laughed. "One or two, Doctor? I've actually had five bairns but no, it's nothing like as bad as labour pains. They're in quite a different league."

"So Mr Booth, how severe is the pain?"

The young student looked annoyed. "But she said it was severe and it obviously isn't!" he protested.

Sir William smiled patiently. "Yes, that is indeed what *Mrs Bradshaw* said." He emphasised the words *Mrs Bradshaw* to indicate that he wished patients to be formally addressed and not referred to as '*she*'. Then he turned to the rest of the group.

"Let that be your first lesson," he said. "You can't always take the things patients say at face value. If you're to fully understand their symptoms, you have to probe a little deeper. You see, some patients are tougher than others; some are stoical and minimise their symptoms, whilst others exaggerate their problems, eager for them to be taken seriously. You probably recognise from your own experience that some people take a few days off work several times a year with what they call 'flu' whist others, with the same infection, simply call it 'a bit of a cold' and carry on working."

And so it went on, Sir William demonstrating to the students how to elicit the precise site of the pain, its character, severity and duration; all the while impressing on them the need to treat their patients gently and courteously.

"Now," he said finally, "I want you to split up into pairs and put into practice what you've learned. I have a list here of patients on the ward who have a variety of different pains. One of you should take the history whilst the other writes it down. I'll review your notes when we meet tomorrow. And remember I will not tolerate any remark critical of a patient or of a member of the staff. Never forget, either now or in the future, that the case notes are a legal document. They may be produced in court and words you have written may be thrown back at you for you to justify."

Finally he gave each of the students a copy of the 'ten commandments'; his guide to the correct way to write medical records. It was well known amongst the students that on occasion, after someone had written an inappropriate observation in the notes, Sir William ordering him to duplicate the commandments, just as a naughty schoolboy might have been required to write lines at school.

"Before you go though," Sir William concluded, "We must thank Mrs Bradshaw for helping us today. I think Miss Croft you observed that she looked at home on the ward. Full marks to you; Mrs Bradshaw is actually the domestic on this ward. You will see a lot of her in the weeks to come. She was kind enough to agree to act as our patient this morning. And Mr Solanki, you were quite right too, she does indeed work extremely hard keeping the ward so beautifully clean and tidy. We'd be lost without her."

Mrs Bradshaw left the room delighted to have helped the consultant whom she and the rest of the staff admired and respected so much, and glowing with the praise he had heaped upon her.

Chapter Ten

Whilst Sir William was introducing the medical students to the art of communication, Mr Potts was operating on Harry Grimshaw. The MP was indeed placed first on the theatre list, despite the fact that his toe nail was severely infected. Only essential staff members were allowed into the theatre to witness the event. Paul heard afterwards that the anaesthetist declined to administer a general anaesthetic, agreeing that there was a problem in the patient's chest. The operation was therefore performed under local anaesthetic.

Normally at the end of the theatre session, Mr Potts went to enjoy his lunch with his colleagues in the consultant's dining room. On this occasion though he went to see Harry Grimshaw and decided that the MP was fit to go home without delay. However to everyone's surprise, Harry asked if it would be possible for him to stay in the hospital until five pm. After all the fuss he had caused, it was assumed he would wish to escape as quickly as possible.

"My political adviser has arranged for a short press conference to be held on the front steps of the hospital as I leave," he explained. "It will be good publicity for the hospital and it will give me an opportunity to record my thanks to you and to your excellent staff. I do hope that will be alright Mr Potts?"

And a chance for you to have a bit of free publicity in an election year, Paul thought.

Mr Potts raised an eyebrow in Sister's direction. Sister Ashbrook forced herself to smile sweetly and despite wishing to give the side ward back to the elderly man who had been ejected from it the evening before, she stated that this wouldn't present a problem. Paul completed the necessary paperwork to facilitate the discharge, wrote a letter to Mr Grimshaw's GP and prescribed some pain killers for him to take home. He then grabbed a bite to eat and busied himself with his afternoon's duties, content in the knowledge that his involvement with this disagreeable patient was at an end.

Unfortunately this optimism was misplaced. At about 4.30 pm, he received a telephone call from Dr Digby, the consultant radiologist.

"Hello Lambert, I'm sorry to trouble you. I know how busy you junior doctors are but I have some x-rays on the screen in front of me of a patient called Harry Grimshaw; x-rays that you requested. I take it this is Harry Grimshaw, the politician?"

"Yes, it is, Sir."

"I thought it must be. On the request card you suggested there might be a problem on the left side of the chest and I'm not surprised. There's a rather ominous shadow at the root of the lung. It doesn't look too good I'm afraid. I'm sure Mr Potts would wish to know about it. Do you happen to know where he is?"

"I think you'll find him in his private consulting room or if, by chance, he's finished there, he'll be on his way home."

"That's fine. I'll try and reach him on the telephone. Mr Grimshaw will need some further investigation as a matter of urgency but you'd better not mention anything to him until I've spoken to Mr Potts."

Within a few minutes, Paul was bleeped again. This time it was Mr Potts.

"Lambert," he said, "I've had Dr Digby on the phone. I gather he's already spoken to you about Harry Grimshaw's x-ray. I'm afraid I'm tied up at the moment and not free to come. Ask him to remain in hospital. Tell him I'll come and speak with him in about an hour. It sounds as if we may have to pop a telescope down and see what's going on."

Paul looked at his watch. It was five minutes before five o'clock. He went straight to the ward, but Mr Grimshaw had already left.

"Sister and Matron are escorting him to the main entrance so he can make his grand departure," he was told.

Paul raced to the front of the hospital to find that the press conference was just beginning. A well-known BBC reporter was standing, microphone in hand, on the wide flight of steps that led down from the hospital's main entrance. He was linked by wire to his cameraman who was standing a few yards to one side. Mr Grimshaw was stationed on the top step, cunningly positioned such that the reporter was forced to stand one step lower down. To his left, a number of members of staff waited in line, each one step below the next; firstly one of the nurses from the ward, then Sister Ashbrook and finally Matron. Down on the pavement a chauffeur stood, tall and erect, wearing a traditional black uniform and peaked hat. He was holding the Bentley door open in readiness for the great man's departure. A spotlight held aloft by the cameraman's assistant illuminated the scene.

One might have expected that a patient who had simply undergone surgery for an in-growing toenail would be able to walk from the hospital in open toed sandals with a small sticking plaster covering the wound but Harry Grimshaw was no ordinary patient! He was using two crutches for support and his lower limb was impressively swathed in bandages reaching to the level of his knee. Paul decided he would chide Sister afterwards about such an unnecessary and extravagant waste of hospital supplies, though he realised that in all probability she had been bullied by the MP. Surreptitiously, Paul slipped down the steps and placed himself in the line between Matron and the chauffeur.

Mr Grimshaw was an impressive orator. He told his audience how privileged he felt to have been able to receive care from the wonderful National Health Service; a service he used whenever he needed medical treatment. He went on to thank the staff for the exceptional care he had received during his stay and for continuing the excellent work that was the hallmark of all NHS hospitals. He then proceeded to argue that with such an excellent service available, there was no possible justification for private medicine. Why, he asked, should some beds be reserved for the rich? Surely they should be available to all.

Paul listened to the speech with astonishment. The hypocrisy astounded him. The MP had bypassed the waiting list, had come into hospital at a time of his choosing, had gone first on the operating list, been nursed in a side ward and had benefitted from the personal attention of his consultant. He had enjoyed all the perks of private medicine without it costing him a penny; and all because he was an influential politician! Paul stopped listening. It was clearly a party political speech designed for a television audience in an election year. He needed to think what he should say to Mr Grimshaw before he left in his chauffeur driven car.

Eventually, smiling bravely, the MP limped down the steps like a wounded war hero, shaking hands and exchanging pleasantries with each member of staff in turn. Finally, he found himself standing directly in front of Paul.

"I'm surprised to see you here, young man. I thought I'd seen the last of you last night." As he spoke, the television smile never left his lips although there was a cold edge to his voice.

"I know that I shouldn't be here Sir, but I have a message for you from Mr Potts. He wants to have another word with you before you go home."

"And what does Potts wish to speak to me about?"

"It's about the chest x-ray that was taken earlier today. It seems there is an abnormality on it."

His face never flickered; the smile for the camera maintained.

"Do you know what sort of abnormality?"

"Not exactly Sir, but apparently there's a shadow on the lung and the radiologist feels that some further investigations are required; perhaps some more detailed x-rays or possibly a look into the lung with a telescope. Mr Potts asked me to catch you before you left. I think he wants you stay in the hospital for a few more days to have the tests arranged."

There was a slight pause as Harry Grimshaw's nimble brain digested this information and considered his options.

"Is there a back entrance to the hospital and if so, how do we reach it?" he asked.

"Yes, there is. The service entrance is round the back. You simply keep turning left, going round the block, until you get there."

"Meet me there in two minutes."

The conversation was at an end.

Still smiling, still looking relaxed, though the implications of a *'shadow on the lung'* in a lifelong smoker must have been known to him, he gave one last cheerful wave to his television audience and hobbled to the car. The chauffeur assisted him into the back seat, relieved him of his crutches and then walked round to the driver's door before easing the car into the rush hour traffic. It had been an impressive display of quick thinking, combined with a faultless acting performance.

There was a striking contrast between Harry Grimshaw's departure from the front of the hospital and his return a few moments later to the service area at the rear. The limousine looked incongruous in the hospital's back yard parked alongside the vans and lorries that were delivering food and medical supplies and removing rubbish. Mr Grimshaw similarly looked out of place amongst the porters, deliverymen and refuse collectors who stared at him in some surprise. The brief journey round the hospital also resulted in a significant change in the politician's demeanour. As Paul escorted him back to the ward through the service corridors normally unseen by hospital patients, a stern face and a stony silence replaced the smile and pleasantries. Paul left him in the side ward that he had so recently vacated. He received no recognition nor any thanks for identifying the MP's significant health problem, simply a stern, "tell Potts that I'm waiting for him and tell him that I don't expect to be kept waiting."

Mr Potts duly saw Harry Grimshaw within the hour. Paul was not party to the discussion that followed but by the time the night staff came on duty, the side ward was once again occupied by the elderly gentleman who needed specialist nursing care. Mr Grimshaw had been transferred to the private wing of the hospital for his further investigations.

A week later Paul saw an announcement in the newspapers to the effect that Mr Harry Grimshaw had resigned from the cabinet on the grounds of ill health. The same papers recorded his obituary precisely three months later; the MP had died *'after a short illness, bravely born'*.

Chapter Eleven

In the course of the next week, Queenie underwent numerous blood tests and x-rays to investigate the cause of her jaundice; it was becoming increasingly obvious she would need surgery. Despite her problems though, she quickly became a firm favourite on the ward. Permanently cheerful, she chatted freely with the other patients and exchanged lively banter with the nurses. She amused them by giving nicknames to the doctors. Sir William became Sir Lance A Lot. Unsurprisingly Mr Potts became 'Mr Grumpy' and Paul was 'Bashful' named after two of Snow White's seven dwarfs. Kate thought Paul's nick name particularly appropriate in view of his quiet and somewhat unassuming character.

She declined to wear night wear and wandered round the ward in her colourful gypsy attire, often helping the nurses by serving drinks or clearing away the dishes after meals. She read the palms of several members of staff though Kate declined to have her fortune told because of her slightly superstitious nature. However when she offered to foretell the fate of her fellow patients, Sister Rutherford asked her to stop. She felt they already had enough worries without being given predictions about their future; surely that was the doctor's responsibility, though they termed it 'prognosis'.

On the Surgical Five Unit the highlight each week was undoubtedly Sir William's consultant ward round. In advance of his arrival, the sheets on the beds were straightened, pillows were fluffed and lockers tidied. The nurses adjusted their frilly caps, attached newly starched collars to their dresses and wore clean cotton aprons. The doctors straightened their ties, donned freshly laundered white coats and ensured that all the information that might be required during the round was available. They had great respect for Sir William and wanted to ensure that things ran smoothly.

As always, Sir William arrived on time. He strode purposefully into the office where the medical team were waiting. Invariably, after the formal exchange of pleasantries about the weather, Sister Rutherford asked if he would care for a drink before the round began and invariably Sir William declined with the comment that their patients were their priority and should be seen first. Then, after thanking them for their attendance, he held the door for Sister Rutherford so that she could lead the team onto her ward. Sir William was followed by Paul and then by the house officer, pushing the notes trolley in time honoured fashion. A gaggle of nurses and medical students brought up the rear.

Sir William was always keen to involve the medical students on these occasions so when they reached Queenie's bed, he asked which of the medical students had taken her history. This proved to be Mr Booth, the most reserved of the group. Accordingly he was invited to come forward and present the story of her illness to him.

"Mrs O'Hannagan has had pain and jaundice for about four weeks," the young man said, timidly. "The GP didn't know what was the matter with her, so he asked you to see her at home ..."

"Mr Booth," Sir William interrupted, "may I ask you how you know the GP was unable to make a diagnosis."

"Well, Sir, he's a GP. He would need the hospital to make the diagnosis for him."

"I'm sure that by that remark you mean he would need access to the hospital's x-ray and laboratory facilities to confirm his diagnosis. As it happens in this case, the GP was able to make a working diagnosis every bit as good as mine from the history he took and from his clinical examination. It would be a mistake to suggest that doctors who work in the community are in any way inferior to those of us who work in hospital. And don't forget GP's have the advantage of seeing patient in their own homes which gives them a great insight into the way they lead their lives. Mind you, consultants occasionally do visits as well. In fact, as you say, I met Mrs O'Hannagan at her home recently.... and a delightful home it was too," he added with a smile to his patient.

"Home visits can be very interesting, you know," Sir William began now addressing the whole group.

Paul groaned inwardly. He fear that Sir William was about to embark on a long winded story, probably one he had heard before – and so it proved!

"On one occasion I met a delightful elderly couple living a genteel existence in their pleasant semidetached home. It was clean, tidy and immaculately furnished. When the consultation was over, I admired the decor; there was an exquisite arrangement of fresh flowers on the table, Dalton figures were displayed on the sideboard and there were some beautiful watercolour paintings on the walls.

Indeed whilst there, I broke one of my guiding principles and partook of camomile tea and freshly baked scones with them. At a later date though, I had the misfortune to visit their attached neighbours. Weeds were growing through the remains of an old car in the front garden, a motor bike was leaking oil in the front room and an Alsatian dog roamed freely around the property. The smell was awful. The kitchen sink was piled high with greasy dishes, the children were dirty and unkempt and their father wandered around wearing little more than a sweat shirt and filthy jeans. I felt really sorry for their neighbours."

Sir William was now in full flow and would happily have continued to reminisce but Paul had a dozen jobs waiting for him when the round was over. He coughed politely.

"Sir," he began, "when Mrs O'Hannagan was admitted, the nurses discovered some sugar in her urine and further tests have confirmed that she is diabetic. We may have to defer her surgery for a few days until we can get that under control."

Sir William grinned at Paul, "Well done Lambert. It's as well that you keep me focussed."

Mr Booth, grateful that he was no longer the focus of attention, quietly took a backward step and rejoined the crowd.

Sir William turned to Queenie. "It seems there's going to be a little delay before your operation but hopefully it won't be too long before we have you back at home. Then you'll be able to put your feet up and have a nice rest."

Queenie thought this was very funny. "You must be joking Doctor. There will be a hundred and one jobs waiting for me when I get home; meals to put on the table, not to mention the washing, ironing, and cleaning."

"You're quite right," the consultant replied, glancing sideways at the ward sister. "Sister Rutherford often tells me that when a man comes into hospital, his wife shops, cooks and feeds herself and still finds time to visit. However if the boot is on the other foot and she's the one in hospital, her friends and neighbours automatically assume that her husband is completely helpless. He gets invited out for meals and his washing is done for him!"

Paul coughed again, a little more pointedly. "So shall I schedule Mrs O'Hannagan's surgery for the beginning of next week, Sir?"

"Yes do that, and you're quite right, we must keep moving."

Slowly but surely they worked their way round the female patients. Throughout Sir William was relaxed, was his usual benevolent self and frequently digressed from clinical matters. Whenever this happened, Paul sought to keep the round moving as surreptitiously as possible. His legs began to ache and his concentration wandered whenever Sir William drifted into some long winded tale about his student days or his life as a trainee surgeon. But more importantly it wasted time, a commodity which was precious to hard working junior doctors.

Finally arriving back at Sister's office, Sir William was again offered a cup of tea and to Paul's relief he declined. He took a quick look at his watch.

"My, my, "he said, "look at the time. Now if we've seen all the patients here we must hurry across to the male ward. It's right that we should see the ladies first but we mustn't keep the men waiting."

Chapter Twelve

When the notes documenting Mrs Cullen's previous treatment in Inverness arrived through the post, Paul studied them with interest. They included a copy of the letter written to her GP summarising the treatment she had received whilst in hospital. It stated she had been admitted as an emergency with vaginal bleeding. She had told the staff that her periods *'were always erratic'* but admitted that *'she might have missed a period or two.'* Her urine test was strongly positive, indicating that she was pregnant. For forty eight hours she had been held on the ward for bed rest in the hope that this might avert the miscarriage that was threatened, but regrettably this policy proved unsuccessful. She had continued to bleed and then started to pass clots and tissue. Subsequently, she had been taken to theatre and her uterus had been emptied. The operation note, written by the consultant who performed the surgery, stated that *'the products of conception'* were removed. There seemed to be no doubt that Mrs Cullen had indeed been pregnant and then miscarried but for final confirmation, Paul looked for the pathology report of the tissue that had been removed from the womb. But there wasn't one. Since Sir William had been the one to suggest they obtain the Scottish notes, Paul discussed the situation with him.

"Has the second semen analysis been reported?" he asked.

"Yes it has; and the result is the same as before; no sperms were seen."

Sir William thought for a moment. "Alright, I haven't met the couple yet, but when they next come to the clinic, we'll see them together. In the meantime Lambert, you telephone the laboratory in Inverness. It will be useful to know whether the tissue removed from the womb was actually sent to the lab. It's just possible it was sent and analysed but for some reason the report never found its way into these notes. My job will be to speak with one of the gynaecologists at St Margaret's. Gynaecology is not my specialty; it will be useful to get the view of an expert."

So it was that a week later, Paul was in the clinic, introducing Sir William to Mr and Mrs Cullen.

"Have you had the result of my sperm test and the report from the hospital in Scotland?" Mr Cullen asked eagerly. His arm was around his wife's waist but Paul observed that for the first time there was a little anxiety in his voice and a hint of concern on his face.

Sir William deflected the question by commenting that he would come to the information from Inverness in due course.

"Mr Lambert has told me about this problem," he began, addressing Mrs Cullen, "but first I would like you to tell me the story yourself."

Paul wondered if Sir William was simply being thorough, taking a history for himself to check that he had all the facts, or whether perhaps, he was quietly making his own judgement of the couple, particularly about Mrs Cullen. Without challenging her directly, he had placed her in the position of having to restate her loyalty to her husband, which she did without hesitation. In the background, Paul listened to the tale with which he was already familiar, all the while carefully observing Mr Cullen. He suspected that a doubt was beginning to develop in his mind; perhaps he was now beginning to think the unthinkable about his attractive young wife.

"I see," said Sir William when Mrs Cullen had finished her story. "Now let me tell you the result of our detective work. The repeat semen analysis confirms the previous one, no sperms were seen."

As he spoke Paul now watched Mrs Cullen. He could detect no trace of concern in her face, no sign of guilt, she just looked puzzled. If she had indeed been unfaithful, she was a remarkably good actress.

Sir William paused. "We also have the notes from the Inverness hospital where you were treated. The consultant there was in no doubt about it. He was certain that you were pregnant and he was certain that you had a miscarriage." Sir William paused again, all the while watching his patient and for the first time there was undoubtedly a flicker of alarm on Mrs Cullen's face. As Sir William allowed the pause to drag on, the hint of concern became a look of panic.

Eventually Sir William continued. "However, perhaps unwisely, they did not confirm the diagnosis by sending any tissue to the laboratory. There was no analysis of the contents of the womb."

"So what does that mean?" Mrs Cullen asked hesitantly, a mouse trapped in a corner, desperately looking for a means of escape. "It means that they never actually proved that you had a miscarriage. It is just possible that they made a mistake."

"Well that's it," Mr Cullen remarked immediately, turning to his wife, relief written all over his face. "That's the explanation. You mustn't have had a miscarriage after all. It must have been something else. Oh, thank you Doctor, thank you so much for sorting it out. We've been desperately worried and this is such a relief. And, even better, I suppose it means I don't have to have another vasectomy operation after all."

They flew into each other's arms and hugged long and hard. Mr Cullen had his back to Paul, but over his shoulder he could plainly see his wife's face. She looked enormously relieved. She caught Paul's eye and for a moment she smiled. Then there was the suggestion of a wink as she mouthed *'thank you'* silently to him.

After they had left, Paul spoke with Sir William. "I know there was no pathology report Sir, but surely a consultant gynaecologist can recognise the products of conception!"

"Yes, I'm sure he can," he replied. "I rang and spoke with him and he was in no doubt whatsoever. In fact, the reason that he didn't send the specimen to the laboratory was because he was certain of the diagnosis."

"And the pregnancy test on the urine was positive as well," Paul said.

"Yes, it was."

"Then surely you don't believe that there's been a mistake. You do accept that she was pregnant."

"Lambert," Sir William said quietly. "It doesn't matter what I believe or what you believe; it's what Mr Cullen believes that matters. I don't know whether he suspects his wife has been unfaithful or not. It's possible that in his heart he knows that she has. But he obviously loves his wife and clearly wants the marriage to continue. Besides, there are two young children to consider. What would have been gained by forcing an unpalatable truth on him and risking a break up of their marriage? Better to leave things as they are; but I do hope Mrs Cullen has learned her lesson."

Afterwards Paul reflected on the whole episode. He was in no doubt that had the situation been left in his hands, had he not sought Sir William's advice, he would have insisted that the vasectomy had not failed and left Mr Cullen to draw the inevitably conclusion. But Sir William had shown great wisdom. He had seen the wider implications and demonstrated there was more to medicine than simply making the correct diagnosis.

Chapter Thirteen

Mr Potts strode into the surgeons' changing room in ebullient mood.

"Good morning, Lambert" he said to his registrar. "Have you come to learn something new?"

"Indeed I have, Sir" Paul replied, equally enthusiastically. "I haven't even seen an aneurysm of the aorta before, let alone watched one being removed. I'm looking forward to it."

"It'll be the very first one that's ever been treated in the city. Provided it goes well we must make sure the press get to hear about it. If we're going to develop a successful vascular service we shall need a bit of publicity. Besides it will be good to let the locals know that they have a brave skilful pioneering surgeon in their midst!" The man's ego knew no bounds!

The aorta is the huge artery, the largest in the body that runs down the back of the abdomen. It carries blood under pressure to the pelvis, buttocks and legs, indeed to the whole of the lower half of the body. It runs alongside an equally large vein that returns the blood to the heart. As wide as your thumb, it sometimes develops a weakness of its wall resulting in a local swelling called an aneurysm, a condition akin to a 'blow-out' on a bicycle tyre. If untreated the swelling gradually gets larger until eventually it bursts. The rapid blood loss that inevitably occurs is usually so catastrophic that it results in sudden death although just occasionally a patient will survive long enough to reach hospital. Ideally the condition is recognised and treated before it bursts when an operation to replace the 'blow out' is usually successful. However if heroic surgery is attempted after the blood vessel has burst, the mortality rate is enormous.

Mr Potts had set aside the entire morning's theatre session for the operation. To prepare himself, he had been to a specialist centre in London to learn how to perform the procedure. He had watched experts operating, then acted as an assistant and finally had performed the operation himself under supervision. This though was to be the first time he would attempt to remove an aneurysm unsupervised. He appeared to be ultra-confident and was clearly relishing the opportunity to shine, his personality so different from that evident at other times. On the wards, he was dour and uncommunicative but in theatre he was talkative and effusive; he came alive. He delighted in the opportunity to display his technical skills to the junior doctors and to the nurses, especially those with a pretty face or a shapely ankle! He eschewed the unisex green cotton shirt and trousers worn by the rest of the theatre staff, having insisted that the hospital provide him with a tailored blue theatre suit emblazoned with his initials. Together with the crepe sweat band around his brow and the head lamp he always wore, a modification of the old miner's head lamp, he was an impressive figure.

As Paul donned the shapeless pyjama top and bottoms, he noticed Mr Potts searching on the shelves for his personal suit - but it wasn't there. He flung open the door into the theatre and shouted for attention, not caring who saw him in his underpants and socks.

"Sister, my theatre gear is missing. If it's not here in two minutes I shall operate in the nude!" He roared with laughter. "That should wake them up," he added, as an aside to Paul.

Ten minutes later, with Mr Potts suitably attired, the patient was anaesthetised and lifted gently onto the operating table. The skin of the abdomen was washed with an antiseptic solution, the surgical drapes were put in place and all was prepared. The specialist instruments that were required had been purchased and Sister had familiarised herself with their names and functions. She had accompanied Mr Potts when he had gone for training. Her husband, aware of the consultant's reputation, had been apprehensive of his wife accompanying her boss on these overnight excursions but she appeared to have survived unscathed!

Mr Potts had selected his first patient well. He was as thin as a rake, which always made surgery easier; indeed he was so skinny that as he lay exposed on the operating table, the swelling in his abdomen could be seen pulsing to the rhythm of his heart. Paul took his place opposite Mr Potts, Janet stood at his left side and the anaesthetist gave the go-ahead.

"Is everyone ready to make a bit of local history?" Mr Potts asked of the world in general, "if so, we'll make a start."

His task was to expose the aorta and place two clamps across it, one above and one below the 'blow out'. This isolated the aneurysm and stopped blood flowing through it. He then had to remove the length that contained the 'blow out' and replace it with an artificial tube made of Teflon. The graft would be three or four inches long and had to be stitched, end to end, to the remaining aorta so that when the clamps were removed, the circulation to the legs would be restored.

It was helpful to the junior doctors that the consultant was in the habit of describing the procedure as he operated.

"A big incision is essential," Mr Potts said, as he incised the skin from ribs to pubis. "It's dangerous to faff around with a little hole."

Within five minutes the abdomen was open, the intestines were laid to one side allowing the aneurysm to be seen. It was the size of a tennis ball and pulsed alarmingly.

"My God, it looks as if it could pop at any moment," Janet commented in some alarm.

"It's because it will rupture if it's left untreated that we're dealing with it now," Mr Potts replied. "Right, now we get to the dangerous bit. We have to create a little space all round the aorta so we can put our clamps across it."

With great expertise he very gently applied clamps across the aorta above and below the 'blow-out', carefully avoiding the large vein that lay in contact with it throughout its length.

"O K Sister. Get ready with that suction machine and have some sutures handy. I'm going to cut this thing open."

Boldly, he sliced right down the front of the aneurysm with his scalpel. Immediately the blood and clots that had been trapped within the swelling when the clamps were applied burst out. The blood was removed with the sucker, the clots Mr Potts lifted out by hand.

Sister then supplied Mr Potts with the artificial tubing which he skilfully inserted to replace the length of aorta that had been removed. The sutures passed through the artificial tube with ease but the cut edges of the aorta were somewhat thickened which created a little difficulty. Finally the clamps were removed restoring the circulation to the lower half of the body. Mr Potts checked that his suture lines weren't leaking and replaced the intestines in the abdomen.

The difficult part of the operation over, Mr Potts visibly relaxed as he started to close the wound, a routine that he must have performed hundreds of times in his career.

"Nearly through now," he observed, as he stitched the abdominal muscles together. "It will soon be time for lunch and then I'm off for a game of golf. I think I've deserved it, don't you. I've being playing quite a lot recently and though I say it myself, I'm quite a useful performer. I've only been a member of the club for a couple of years but already my handicap is down to 14. Actually, the club are quite fussy who they admit. They have a long waiting list but I chanced to operate on the club secretary and he jumped me to the top of the queue." He laughed. "I never imagined that removing a bunch of nice juicy piles could be so rewarding!"

Paul always felt awkward when Mr Potts started talking of his personal life style as he often did in theatre; be it golf, his home, his daughter's pony or the frequent skiing holidays taken with his family in Switzerland. He was either completely unaware or possibly just didn't care, that the theatre nurses, porters and technicians were struggling to make ends meet on a salary that was a fraction of his.

To Sister's annoyance, he then helped himself to a pair of long handled forceps from her tray of instruments, took a step back and gave a demonstration of his golf swing using the forceps as a club. There was a metallic clang as the tip of the forceps hit the large overhead operating light.

"Woops, sorry about that Sister," he said, as he casually tossed the instrument onto the floor because it was no longer sterile.

"Mr Potts, I would rather you didn't do that," Sister said primly. "I have a responsibility to check all the instruments are present and correct at the end of this operation and it doesn't help if you throw them onto the floor. Besides it sets a very bad example to the junior nurses."

But the consultant merely smiled at her. "I'm just showing you how it's done, Sister dear. You may want to take up the game one day but you'll have to find a club that takes lady members. Not all golf clubs do you know. Our committee rather stupidly allowed women to join a couple of years ago but fortunately only if their husbands are already members. That keeps the numbers down, thank God; most fellows are not foolish enough to allow their wives to join!"

Under the theatre lights, buoyed with success and with pretty nurses as his audience, he was in his element.

"I reached the semi-finals of our club knock out competition last year and was runner up on Captain's Day. I shall do even better this year. I plan to win one of the major prizes. I want to see the name **'Leslie Potts'** in big gold letters on the trophy board in the club house. I've always been able to hit a long straight ball but my putting lets me down. Mind you, I've had some lessons recently and my gardener has prepared a large putting green in my garden for me to practise on. No one is going to beat me this year!"

"I'm told that chipping and putting is where the game is won and lost," Paul volunteered. "Isn't there an old saying that you *'drive for show and putt for dough'*?"

"You seem to know a bit about it Lambert. Do you play?"

"I used to play a bit at college Sir, but was never particularly good. And of course, I don't have time for golf these days. It must be twelve months since I got my golf bag out of the cupboard."

"Were you a member of a club?"

"No, I wasn't a member anywhere. I used to play on municipal courses."

"And did you have a handicap?"

"No, at least not an official one. I used to try to get round in about 90 shots."

"90 shots eh? That would mean a handicap of about 18. Not quite up to my standard but not bad though. We must have a game. I'll fix it up."

"I'm not sure about that, Sir," Paul replied backpedalling furiously. "I don't have a lot of free time these days and there are always plenty of household chores to keep me busy. My wife is a nurse as I think you know. She works shifts so we share the domestic duties."

"Rubbish, Lambert. Housework is for women and wimps. Besides, if you work long hours, you're entitled to some relaxation."

"It would be enjoyable of course Sir, but I really don't think that I should. I don't spend enough time at home as it is without going off playing golf."

"Nonsense my boy. Are you a man or a mouse? You're beginning to sound like a henpecked husband. You're not 'on call' next weekend are you? I'll contact you when I've arranged a time."

Paul's heart sank and privately he cursed himself for making his casual comment about golf. He would now have to spend four or more hours in Mr Potts' company biting his tongue whenever his boss polished his overinflated ego, when he could and should be at home with Kate!

The operation had taken the best part of three hours but had gone without a hitch. There were many aspects of Mr Potts' behaviour that Paul disliked; his abrupt manner, the pleasure he took from embarrassing his junior staff should they make an error and his attitude towards the female sex but he couldn't fault his technical ability.

"Well what did you think of my surgery?" Mr Potts asked as he put the last stitch into the muscles.

"Extremely impressive," Paul replied with total honesty.

"I thought so too!" responded the consultant, beaming behind his mask. "Mind you, in due course, when the word gets out, neighbouring hospitals will be sending us all their aneurysms, including those that rupture in the middle of the night. They present a much greater challenge and a horribly high death rate."

With that he looked at the clock on the theatre wall. "Right," he said, "I've done all the hard work. I'll leave you to tidy up here Lambert. Sister, do you think one of your delightfully pretty young nurses could make me a cup of coffee."

With that he stepped back from the table, ripped off his cap and mask, tossed them in the general direction of the laundry basket and marched out of the theatre singing '*When I rule the world*'!

"Indeed extremely impressive," Sister echoed as she passed Paul the sutures with which to close the skin. "But Sir William would have thanked his team for their help, wouldn't he?"

"Yes, he would," Paul agreed, "but you can't deny that he's performed a remarkably skilful piece of surgery."

Paul knew exactly how his boss was feeling. It was an emotion that he too had experienced when he had successfully completed a difficult operation or had brought a patient back from the dead. It gave him a 'high' every bit as powerful as any drug. The feeling was one of exhilaration; an intoxicating mixture of pride and joy. And it was addictive, it made one strive to experience it time and time again. Basking in the admiration and gratitude of patients and their relatives when pain had been relieved, or a tumour removed was undoubtedly gratifying. But there had been times when Paul had experienced painful emotions just as keenly; the profound feeling of inadequacy when a desperately ill patient defied diagnosis or the appalling sense of personal failure when an operation had gone wrong and a life had been lost. Then one could be torn apart by self doubt and recrimination.

Chapter Fourteen

It only took a couple of days to get Queenie's sugar levels under control but regrettably there was then a further delay. A shadow was found on her chest x-ray and for the second time her surgery was postponed. Three more days elapsed before it was decided that the shadow was not significant; it was no more than a scar from the tuberculosis she had suffered as a child.

All the while, her jaundice became more obvious, an ominous development and one evening Queenie asked Kate for a quiet word.

"The doctors think I've got cancer, don't they?"

Kate, very conscious of the promise that she had made to be open and honest, was obliged to agree that this was by far the most likely diagnosis.

"Then why would they be wanting to operate? What's the point if my numbers up anyway?"

"Because they need to be certain. You see, there are lots of different causes of jaundice; gall stones for example or certain infections. They can produce a similar picture. Even if the problem is a cancer, they can do an operation to by-pass the blockage. That would get rid of the jaundice and make you feel a whole lot better."

"Sweet Mother Mary, I wish they'd get on with it. I'm looking more like a Belisha beacon every day! Sure if it goes on much longer, they won't be needing electric lights here at night; they'll just stand me in the middle of the ward and stick a lamp shade on my head!"

Kate smiled. "Operations have risks Queenie, and so do anaesthetics. The doctors want you to be as fit as possible before they take you to theatre. It would be a disaster if your problem was simply due to gall stones but you didn't survive because they'd operated too soon."

Life had not been easy for Queenie; at times it had been exceedingly tough. She had worked hard, often in difficult circumstances, always on the move as the family travelled from place to place. She had born the resentment of conventional folk who distrusted gypsies, regarding them as rogues and petty thieves and she had brought up her family despite losing her husband. She chose to present herself to the world as a tough, cheerful, outgoing character, someone who was more than able to take care of herself. But all was not as it seemed. She was troubled by events that had happened many years before. She had done something she knew to be wrong, something that had caused pain and suffering to someone she loved - and it continued to distress her. Feelings of guilt gnawed away at her, intruding into her quieter moments by day and disturbing her sleep by night. When healthy and busy with her daily routine, she was able to put her worries to the back of her mind but in hospital, with time on her hands, her conscience would not be denied. She had decided that if she was destined to die, she must be free from the demon that had haunted her for so long. She must act to set things right before it was too late. She reached out and took hold of Kate's hand. Looking into Kate's eyes, she spoke quietly and earnestly.

"Kate, if I haven't got a lot of time left, there's something I need to do before I go. Many years ago, when my Pat was alive, there was a terrible rift in our family. Mick and his younger brother, Brendan had a terrible row. We were in the London area at the time, selling pegs, working the local fairs, scratching a living as best we could. Then Brendan got the glad eye for a girl. Head over heels he went and I wasn't surprised, a right pretty thing she was with her blue eyes and long blond hair, though that probably came straight out of a bottle. She was full of airs and graces too, looking down at us with her fancy clothes and stuck up manners. She wasn't our type at all. She came from a posh family, they were well-to-do people. Her dad was a banker or lawyer or some such sort; worked in the city he did and drove a flashy car, but worst of all, they were Protestant."

"Surely that doesn't matter much these days."

"Oh yes it does, especially to folk like us. Many a family's been torn apart by religion. Anyway Brendan insisted he wanted to marry this girl. Mick and Pat were furious and I'm afraid I spoke out against it as well. It was never going to last; as different as chalk and cheese they were. She'd been brought up to be a young lady; she wasn't used to hard work; certainly not the sort to roll up her sleeves and get her hands dirty. She was never going to adapt to the gypsy way of life. She wanted them to live in a house in the town, wanted Brendan to take a job in an office. But he was a free spirit, a wild fox, far too young and restless to be tamed and trapped within four walls like a rabbit in a hutch.

Then the girl fell pregnant and her family insisted they got married before it showed too much, though I'm sure they disapproved just as much as we did. So Brendan walked out on us, bought a suit and a tie and started to work as a clerk in her father's business. It all ended in pain and tears of course as I knew it would. They came from different worlds and they broke up soon after the babe was born; a little boy it was too."

"So you have a grandson. That's nice. Do you see much of him?" Kate asked.

"I haven't seen Brendan or the baby from that day to this, though I think he does keep in touch with our Rose."

There were tears in her eyes as she continued. "Kate, I have to make my peace with Brendan before I go. I need to apologise. Even though I knew the marriage was doomed, I was wrong to criticise. He was my son, he was a grown man, I should have given him a mother's love and support and I didn't. It's a burden I've carried in my heart ever since.... and I'd love to meet my grandson; he must be five or six by now."

She handed Kate an envelope on which an address had been written in a rough hand.

"I want you to post this to him. I need his forgiveness before it's too late - and I'll pray to the Good Lord that he doesn't turn me down. Oh and Kate a word of warning; it would be best if Mick didn't get to hear of this, he wouldn't be best pleased."

****

When Kate rejoined the nursing team that evening, having taken the opportunity during her afternoon off duty to post Queenie's letter, her first task was to prepare the ward for the daily invasion by the visitors. At 7pm the hand bell was rung to allow them access to the ward. It was not a time that the doctors particularly enjoyed; it was difficult to do much work with visitors sitting at the bedside. It was no coincidence that the evening meal in the doctors' residency was served at this time. Paul found it particularly inconvenient. As his working day was coming to an end, he liked to check that all loose ends had been tidied up before he went home and the presence of the visitors delayed him. Whilst working on Surgical Five he had developed a strong sense of possessiveness; this was *his* ward, they were *his* patients. He wanted the best for them and he wanted to give them his personal attention. He resented the intrusion of visitors onto the ward almost as much as he would have resented the presence of strangers in his own home.

Many of the nursing sisters in the hospital also disliked having visitors on their wards, feeling that they interrupted nursing routines and made the ward look untidy. Sister Rutherford however took the opposite view. She saw it as an opportunity to help patients and visitors alike. She cheerfully made herself available to visitors and many took the opportunity to seek information or reassurance about their loved ones. Others sought to satisfy themselves that their nearest and dearest had told the staff everything they considered to be relevant to their illness; *'He tends to put a brave face on his troubles, Nurse.'* *'His pain is actually very severe and he's had it for years'.* *'You do know that he's allergic to penicillin, don't you Sister?'*

Kate found it fascinating to observe the behaviour of visitors. Often conversation flourished for five or ten minutes but then languished. The visitor then sat at the bedside for the next 50 minutes, glancing at the clock periodically, having exhausted things to say but afraid of giving offence by leaving early. For others, visiting seemed to be a duty. A wife might accompany her husband when he was admitted to the hospital at 4pm and then be back visiting at 7pm. There had scarcely been time for her to take the bus home and have a meal before she returned to the hospital. It seemed rather unnecessary to Kate although she supposed it gave the patient moral support. Some received visits from distant friends or relatives who had ignored them for years. Were such visits motivated more by morbid curiosity than by genuine concern for their health? The patients though, generally welcomed visiting time; it helped to break a long day.

At 8 pm, Kate rang the bell again, to indicate it was time for the visitors to leave. As the chairs were tidied away and goodbyes were being said, some cheerfully, some sadly, Kate was approached by a woman whom she thought must be Young Rose, Queenie's daughter. She had the same long black hair, dark eyes, high cheek bones and dusky complexion. At her side was a rough looking character whom Kate rightly assumed was Mick, the older of Queenie's two sons, the one Paul had met at the gypsy encampment.

"May we have a word with you please, Nurse?" Rose began.

Kate led them to the office and offered them a seat.

"What can you tell us about our Mam?" Rose asked.

"I'm pleased to say she seems to be settling in very well," Kate replied.

"We know that. Isn't it a tough life that she's had? She can settle in anywhere, fancy room or farmer's field, bed of feathers or a bed of straw, it's all the same to her. But what we need to know is 'what's the matter with her'?"

"She's got jaundice as you can see, but we don't know what's causing it yet. It could be lots of different things. We're still running tests and it may take an operation before we know for sure".

Then Mick butted in. "Is she going to die?" he demanded. "We want to know if she is."

Immediately alarm bells rang in Kate's head. She didn't know the reason for the question but she had her suspicions. She went on the defensive.

"Gracious what a question. I suppose we're all going to die sometime. Why do you ask?"

There was a pause. "We're just concerned that's all" he replied sheepishly, but Kate recognised the lie.

Then Mick lent forward and spoke again, this time forcibly. "Now look here Nurse. Mam has told us she's sent a letter to our Brendan, though only the Devil knows why she's done that after the way he's treated her. It's possible that he might try to visit. If he does, he's not to be allowed to go anywhere near her. Do you understand? He's not to be given any info on her either. Is that clear?"

Kate was taken aback by Mick's glaring eyes, fierce expression and by the ferocity of the words. "Look," she stammered, backing away slightly, "we can't control who visits. It's up to the patient, up to your mother, who she sees."

Mick's fist crashed onto the desk, sending some loose papers flying on to the floor. "Now you listen to me," he shouted his face only inches from Kate's. She felt a few drops of spittle on her face, "if you know what's good for....."

But Rose restrained him before he could issue his threat. "Holy Mother Mary," she cried, "d'you want half of the world to hear you Mick?"

She turned to Kate. "It's just that her youngest, Brendan is a nasty piece of work. He's no good for our Mam. He's caused her no end of grief over the years. He'll only upset her and make her condition worse. When you find out what's the matter with her, it would be best if you only spoke to Mick or me about her. Truly it would. You can do that for us, can't you Nurse?"

Fortunately, Kate's formal training came to her rescue as she remembered the hospital's official policy.

"When it comes to a question of medical information," she said, "every patient has a right to privacy. We can only divulge confidential details if the patient has given their permission. So if someone asks about your mother's condition, whether that's you or Brendan, it's up to her to decide what to say."

"But Nurse," Rose whined, "in the circumstances, surely you can...."

"No," Kate said, "Your mother will be the one who decides whom she sees and she will decide what they are told. Is that clear?"

Mick was furious and looked about to explode but Young Rose took him by the arm and led him away.

"If the nurses won't keep Brendan away I'll damn well do it myself" Kate heard him mutter as they left, which left her feeling rather disturbed. She remembered that Queenie's husband had died in a fight. The last thing they wanted was violence on the ward.

When the couple had gone, Kate sat for a few moments to let her pounding heart settle. Then she went to see Queenie and related the conversation she had just had with Rose and Mick.

Queenie crossed herself. "Jesus give me strength. Will my family ever learn to live in peace?" She sighed. "I'm sorry they pestered you like that Kate but I'm glad you didn't discuss my condition with them. When I've had my operation, I want to be the one who's told what's causing this wretched jaundice and how long I've got. Then I'll be the one to tell them what I think they need to know. That's fair isn't it?"

"Quite fair," Kate agreed.

"Is that a promise as well then?"

Kate looked at Queenie. In the days she had been on the ward she seemed to have shrunk both in body and spirit. She had continued to lose weight. Her cheeks were hollow, the bony prominences above and below her eyes now standing out in sharp relief, her forehead lined due to anxiety or perhaps fear. Her voice was weaker and her smile less frequent. Although she still strived to put up an outward appearance of cheerful determination, Kate could see though the bravado and felt sorry for her. She drew a finger across her heart and smiled.

"Certainly it is."

"They're thinking about my money you know, Kate. It may surprise you but I've a bob or two put by for a rainy day. But money's a terrible thing; I wish we could live without it, but I suppose we can't." She thought for a moment. "You know, I think it would be for the best if I wrote something down. If I don't, they'll be fighting over my coffin. But I wouldn't be knowing how to go about it."

"Then you need to write a will, "Kate replied, "and if your family are likely to fight over it, perhaps it would be best to get a solicitor to advise you; then you can be sure it's watertight."

"Can you arrange that for me?"

This was a question Kate had not met before. "I'm not sure, but I can make some enquiries for you if you like."

But when Kate asked for advice, she found that the hospital didn't have a legal department and that an outside solicitor would need to be approached.

The whole episode left Kate much disturbed. Mick had frightened her with his aggressive attitude and threatening behaviour. She didn't like to think that Queenie had to contend with such difficult family problems as well as having a cancer of the pancreas which Paul had explained was certain to be the diagnosis and expected to be incurable. Queenie's decision to share intimate family secrets left Kate with mixed emotions. She felt honoured to have been the one to whom Queenie had opened her heart but she was also aware of the responsibilities now resting on her shoulders. Queenie had suffered a hard life. Kate admired her spirit and was coming to regard her more as a friend than a patient but she remembered her training; *'Nurses mustn't get emotionally involved with their patients,'* she had been taught. *'To be professional, they must remain detached.'*

Chapter Fifteen

Joe Johnson was 23 years old, good looking and cocky. He had just moved to the city's first division football team for a record fee. His photograph had been prominent in both local and national newspapers whilst the transfer deal was being negotiated. Although highly talented and already an international player, there had been considerable speculation about the wisdom of signing him. He had been in trouble with the police on several occasions, usually in connection with late night drinking, pretty girls or fast motor cars. It was feared that he might be a bad influence on the younger players in the club. The club's manager however had been quick to reassure supporters that he was no more than 'a bit of a lad' and that with hard work and discipline administered under his close supervision, there wouldn't be any problems.

Because a groin hernia was found at the medical assessment that was part of the transfer arrangements, Joe was admitted to the City General to have it repaired. Inevitably, his arrival on the ward, unannounced and unexpected, caused quite a stir. As he walked jauntily to the bed to which he had been allocated, accompanied by one of the nurses, there was urgent and excited whispering between the other patients.

"Hey, isn't that Joe Johnson?"

"It certainly looks like him."

"If it isn't, it's his spitting image."

The moment that Joe had changed into his pyjamas and the screens drawn back, his neighbour plucked up courage and asked the question that was on everyone's lips.

"You're Joe Johnson, aren't you, the lad who's just been signed to play for the Rovers?"

"Aye, that's me, Grandad. Recognised me did you? Here pass me that paper, the one with my photo in it. I'll let you have my autograph."

Although his neighbour was old enough to be his father rather than his grandfather, he declined to take offence. He would gain considerable kudos from being able to chat to this young star.

"Thanks, Joe," he said, genuinely pleased. "I'll give it to my boy. He's football mad and a great fan of yours. He'll be green with envy when he hears that you're in the bed next to me. He'll come to visit me every night now."

Quietly he decided to milk some information from Joe; he might hear some juicy tit bits that could earn him an easy fiver if he passed them to the local newspaper.

"So tell me what made you decide to come to the Rovers when other clubs also wanted you to play for them?" he asked innocently.

Sure enough, Joe was pleased to sit and chat and was cheerfully sharing football gossip with his neighbour when Janet Smith, Mr Potts' houseman, came to examine him and formally admit him to the ward. She was armed with Joe's notes, a sphygmomanometer and various other items of medical equipment.

The most junior doctors on the ward, fresh out of medical school, were termed 'housemen', so called because they lived in the hospital. They were known as housemen irrespective of their sex. The hospital became their home whilst they completed the compulsory twelve months apprenticeship before they were admitted to the General Medical Register and allowed to practice unsupervised.

Janet was not in the usual Leslie Potts mould. Certainly she was young and strikingly good-looking but her hair, though blond, was unfashionably short and tousled. Worn shoulder length and well groomed it would have been her crowning glory but she made no attempt to make it look attractive. With her slim figure, clear complexion and high cheekbones, she could have been a model but devoid of make-up, her face was unsmiling; indeed her expression often suggested that she had smelt something disagreeable. It was her eyes though which were her most notable feature. They were the palest of blue and had a directness that seemed to challenge those who met her gaze.

The clothes she wore were severe. She was usually to be seen dressed in a formal grey or black trouser suit with a white or cream blouse always sealed with a brooch at the neck. She was the only member of staff who was not intimidated by Mr Potts, perhaps because she was engaged to a young Australian and planned to emigrate as soon as her house job was complete. She cared not a jot what Mr Potts thought of her or what sort of reference he might write for her when she left. If the consultant bandied words with her, she gave as good as she got and strangely, Mr Potts seemed to enjoy these exchanges! He made frequent attempts to engage her in casual conversation but invariably got short shrift. Unless the topic was relevant to one of his patients, her responses were cool and abrupt. It was generally assumed that she was aware of Mr Potts' reputation as a womaniser and had decided to keep him at arm's length!

Blatantly Joe examined Janet's figure from head to toe, his gaze lingering on her chest and legs. He was impressed by what he saw. In his mind he allocated girls to one of four categories, *'slags' 'tarts' 'regular birds'* and *'high class hot totty'*. He didn't consider that any of them were beyond his reach. Janet definitely belonged in the top category and given half a chance he would chat her up. What a tale he could tell his new teammates if he managed to score with this young doctor.

All went smoothly while Janet took Joe's medical history. She learned that his groin ached when he played football and there had been occasions when he had been forced to miss training. Once he had been unable to join England's under-21 squad for an international match which had been a huge disappointment to him.

Having recorded Joe's story in the notes, Janet needed to examine his rupture. She pulled the screens round the bed and asked him to lie down and lower his pyjama pants. Whilst she conducted the examination with cool clinical efficiency, probing his groin with long elegant fingers and carefully manicured nails, Joe was acutely conscious of the closeness of her attractive figure. Desperately he tried to prevent his emotions becoming aroused but only with limited success. Janet aware of the effect her examination was having on Joe, quickly marked the rupture with an indelible pen then told him, in a voice as cold as ice, to pull up his pyjama trousers. She now needed to check that Joe was fit for an anaesthetic.

"Take your top off please, I need to examine your chest," she ordered.

"I'll let you examine my chest, if you let me examine yours," Joe responded in a flash, a cheeky grin on his face.

For a second there was silence then Janet raised her arm and slapped him hard across the face. Taken by surprise Joe fell back on to the pillows. For a second he looked angry then began laughing out loud. "You're a frisky young minx aren't you? Come here girl; give me a kiss and we'll call it quits!" He sat up and made a grab for her waist.

Immediately, Janet realised that her spontaneous reaction, justified as it may have been, was entirely inappropriate. If she had slapped a spirited boy friend who had made a suggestive remark, there wouldn't be a problem; but she was a doctor and Joe was her patient. And she had hit him. Horrified at what she had done she fled from the scene.

SisterAshbrook found her two minutes later sobbing quietly in a corner of the office.

"What on earth's the matter, Janet?"

Janet blurted out the whole story, confessing that she had struck Joe as hard as she could across the face. She was certain that she would be sacked.

"I've only been a doctor for three months," she sobbed. "No one is going to employ me after this. My career's ruined and I've spent five long years at Medical School to get where I am. What on earth can I do?"

"If I were you, I should go immediately and speak to Mr Potts," Sister Ashbrook suggested. "I'm sure he will be able to sort things out. Meanwhile," she added a grim and determined look on her face, "you can leave Joe Johnson in my hands. He's going to be with us for at least three days. I'll make sure he has good cause to remember his stay with us." She already knew exactly how Joe was to be rewarded for his insolence!

Unfortunately when Janet spoke with Mr Potts' secretary, she learned that the consultant was away receiving further training on vascular surgery and wasn't expected back in the hospital until the next morning. Miserably she returned to the ward and tried to concentrate on her duties. Later she was to spend a long sleepless night convinced that her medical career was over before it had really begun.

Back on the ward, Joe's neighbour, who had overheard the exchange, slipped quietly to the corridor where the trolley phone used by patients was stored. His opportunity to earn a little extra beer money had arisen rather sooner than he had anticipated.

****

It was a pale and anxious houseman who went to see Mr Potts the next morning. She approached his office door with the apprehension she had once felt as a school girl when sent to see the headmistress.

"Mr Potts," Janet blurted out, her voice high pitched and trembling, "I've a terrible confession to make. I've struck one of your patients."

"You've done what?" the consultant asked, incredulously.

"I'm terribly sorry, Sir. I hit one of your patients. I wanted to tell you yesterday but you weren't in the hospital."

"Who on earth did you hit?"

"Joe Johnson, Sir, the young footballer."

"And where did you hit him?"

"He was in his bed Sir, in the middle of the ward."

"No, I didn't mean where was he at the time; I meant which bit of his anatomy did you attack?"

"I slapped his face Sir."

Mr Potts motioned her to a chair. "Then I think you'd better sit down and tell me all about it."

Quietly Janet recounted the events of the previous afternoon.

As he listened, a smile crossed his face. "And did you hit him hard, my dear?"

"As hard as I possibly could, Sir," Janet admitted. "But I didn't do it deliberately. It was sort of instinctive. It just happened before I had time to think."

"So now you've come to make a clean breast of it have you?" Mr Potts said, now laughing out loud and emphasising the noun in the middle of his sentence. "Well it sounds as if he deserved it. I think we'd better go right away and sort it out, hadn't we? Is he still on the ward?"

"Yes, Sir, he's having his operation this afternoon."

"Right then, you come with me."

Mr Potts strode purposefully to the male ward, Janet following a yard behind. The consultant marched straight to Joe's bed. The young man looked up in surprise. Brusquely Mr Potts drew the screens and stood over his patient, bearing down on him, his face stern, hands on his hips.

"I believe you were extremely rude to this young doctor yesterday," he declared. "You made a highly inappropriate and sexist remark." His voice was loud and authoritative.

"Y..yes, I'm afraid I did, but only in fun. I..I didn't mean any harm," the young man stuttered, his normal self-confidence having deserted him.

"And what would happen to your reputation if such behaviour were to come to the ears of the press or your club manager?"

Joe looked horrified. "Please, you can't let that happen, Doctor. I can't afford any more bad news stories. You see, I've been a bit of a bad boy in the past; I've been in bother with the law. But my contract with the Rovers has a clause in it about my behaviour. They can turn me out if I get into any more trouble and I'm on good wages. I really am very sorry." He turned to Janet. "I do apologise Miss. I wasn't thinking. It was just a flip remark. I truly didn't mean what I said." He turned back to face Mr Potts. "Please Doctor, can we let it pass?"

Mr Potts addressed Janet. "Are you prepared to let the matter drop if he apologises to you?"

"Yes, Sir, I am, and I ought to apologise to him for striking him."

"Not at all, my dear, you were entirely justified. Such behaviour is not to be tolerated. Now, young man, let's hear what you have to say for yourself."

Joe duly obliged with a grovelling apology which Janet received with great relief.

"There you are, my dear," Mr Potts said to his young house officer as they walked back to the office, "I don't think we'll hear any more about the matter. But you really oughtn't to be so sensitive you know. A good looking girl like you is bound to get the odd suggestive remark and occasional wolf whistle from time to time. You really ought to be flattered." He patted her bottom. "Now off you go and get on with your work and we'll say no more about it."

Janet seethed with anger. Her boss was not quite as direct with his sexist behaviour as Joe but he was just as bad. It was all she could do to stop herself from slapping his face as he smiled at her before turning back towards his office.

Mr Potts had suggested that would be the end of the matter, but he was wrong. Joe's neighbour in the adjacent bed was again on his way to the telephone in the corridor.

****

Later that day a seedy looking man in a shiny suit knocked on the door of the ward office whilst Janet was writing up some notes and Sister Ashbrook was struggling with the following weeks staffing roster.

Sister looked up. "Yes, what is it?" she said, irritated at being disturbed.

"I've come to have a word with Joe Johnson," the young man said.

"Can I ask who you are and what you want to speak with him about?" Sister asked. "It's not visiting time, you know."

"I'm from the National Recorder" the young man said. "I believe he's propositioned a female member of staff and had his face slapped for his trouble. It'll make a great exclusive. I just need to verify the story."

Janet looked up in alarm. "How on earth did you hear about that?" she blurted out, without thinking.

"So it is true, that's great," the reporter commented, suddenly excited. "So who hit him and what had he done to deserve it?"

"It was......" Janet began, red faced and flustered.

Sister though interrupted her and took control of a situation which was rapidly spiralling out of control.

"It's time for you to leave," she said firmly, rising from her seat.

The reporter though was an old hand and recognised that a great story was within his grasp.

He turned to Janet, knowingly. He saw how attractive she was. "It was you, wasn't it? So what did he do to you? Did he try to lay his hands on you or kiss you?"

Janet was appalled. After her chat with Mr Potts she had believed the matter was closed. Now she could see her name being splashed all over the national newspapers; her reputation in tatters.

When Janet didn't reply, the reporter added. "He's done it before you know. You're not the first girl he's molested. You'll be doing everyone a favour if you make an example of him."

Still Janet said nothing but the reporter was not going to turn his back on an exclusive.

"I can make it worth your while, Doctor. There are big bucks to be made out of a story like this, you know. I can see the headline now; *'Soccer star's sex assault on hospital doctor'*. If you would give me an interview and perhaps we could have a photo of you, perhaps wearing something a little more....."

"Out, out," Sister Ashbrook shouted as she ushered the reporter from the room but not before he had noted the name badge on the lapel of Janet's white coat.

The reporter's next stop was the hospital canteen where, over a cup of tea and a biscuit, he had no difficulty in finding a group of student nurses with whom to chat. They unwittingly confirmed the story that had been the hottest bit of gossip on the hospital's grapevine for many months. It had indeed been the tall and attractive Dr Janet Smith who had slapped Joe Johnson's face after the young footballer had made unwelcome advances whilst wearing nothing more than his pyjama bottoms. He located the public phone in the hospital's main corridor and spoke with his editor who promptly changed the headline on the paper's front page.

Back in the office, Janet was inconsolable and again in tears. Sister Ashbrook remained furious with Joe for being the root cause of the problem and felt desperately sorry for Janet. She determined to do her utmost to support the houseman whom she respected for standing up for her sex. It would be a disaster for her if her name was splashed all over the national newspapers. Tight lipped she went in search of Mr Potts.

****

Half an hour later, Mr Potts rang the offices of the Recorder and asked to be put through to the editor.

"Oh hello Charlie," Mr Potts began, "I was at the golf club this weekend and I see you've managed to reduce your handicap again. We must have a game sometime; then I can see how good you really are."

Charlie smiled to himself, not fooled by these introductory pleasantries. He knew that Leslie Potts was a busy man and wouldn't ring in the middle of the day simply to have a chat about golf.

"Come on Leslie," he said, "I know what's on your mind. It's to do with young Joe Johnson and that lovely lady doctor you have working for you, isn't it? I'm told she's an absolute stunner. You always did have an eye for a pretty face and a shapely figure"

"I've just rung to let you know that nothing at all happened. It seems that the young man said something that was misunderstood and then the rumour mill embellished it. The story seems to have got completely out of hand."

"That's not what I heard at all, Leslie. I heard that young Joe got fresh with the young lady and had his face slapped good and hard."

"No Charlie, I assure you it's simply a rumour that's got out of hand. It wouldn't be wise to publish it. If you took the trouble to come to speak with the lad, or my doctor, or indeed the ward sister, you'd find they all flatly denied that anything significant happened."

"Come on Leslie, I can understand you wanting to keep a lid on things but we both know that Joe tried it on with that doctor."

"Just a rumour, Charlie, just like the rumour I heard that you turned up in our casualty department recently somewhat the worse for wear after Rovers cup win over United."

For a minute there was silence at the other end of the phone. "You wouldn't Leslie, not to an old friend."

"Yes Charlie, I would. Indeed I will if any word of this gets into the newspapers. Airing dirty washing in public works both ways."

Charlie took a moment or two to consider his options. "OK" he said finally, "you win but it's a shame. It would have made a great news story."

"So would *'Newspaper chief in drunken brawl with boy friend'*."

Chapter Sixteen

As on the female ward, everything had been tidied in preparation for Sir William's arrival. The male patients had been instructed to stay in their beds, preferably sitting smartly to attention. To show respect they were expected to remain silent. Most were happy to oblige but as Sir William entered the ward, Sister spotted a patient of Mr Potts sitting on the side of his bed with his legs dangling down. He had one slipper on and one slipper off; his pyjama jacket was wide open revealing an obese belly and a hairy chest. He was reading the Racing Times. As Sir William drew ever nearer this errant man, Sister despatched a nurse to plead with him to tidy himself up.

In a voice loud enough to be heard by the rest of the ward and certainly loud enough to reach Sir William's ears, he remarked, "An important person you say; is the Queen to visit us today?"

When the hospital's senior consultant arrived at his bed, the punter lowered his newspaper an inch or two, smiled sweetly, said 'Good Morning' and then calmly resumed his racing selections.

Paul rather hoped that he would add to the drama of the situation by asking Sir William for a tip for the 2.15 at Kempton Park but unfortunately he didn't. Sir William fixed him with a beady eye for a second or two as he passed, 'tutted' and then marched on without comment. Later the wayward patient was to feel the sharp edge of Sister's tongue for lowering the tone of the ward and he subsequently came to suspect that the needles used for his daily antibiotic injections were significantly larger than they been before!

Then a further incident enlivened the ward round. Sir William was in mid-sentence explaining to a builder how long he should be off work following his stomach operation when loud, angry shouting was heard from the opposite side of the ward. The voice was unmistakably female.

"Stop that. Stop that at once. Don't you dare! Take your hands off this minute!"

The voice came from behind the screens which were drawn round Joe Johnson's bed. Sister Ashbrook was the first to respond. Without a word of apology to Sir William, she dashed to investigate, fiercely protective of her young nurses. If Joe was up to his tricks again, molesting her staff, she would throw him out onto the street, no matter what the consequences. It took her no more than five seconds to reach Joe's bed.

"What on earth is going on here?" she demanded as she flung the screens open.

Joe was lying on the bed, an attractive athletic figure wearing only a pair of white football shorts. A pretty young physiotherapist sat beside him. Both looked up in surprise at Sister's sudden appearance.

"Nothing, nothing at all." the physio replied sounding puzzled. "Why Sister, what did you think was going on?"

"Is Mr Johnson being a nuisance? Has he made a pass at you? Did he put his hands on you?"

"Why no, Sister. Not at all," the therapist replied whilst thinking that perhaps she wouldn't have minded too much if he had.

"Well what was all that shouting about 'keeping your hands off you'?"

"He didn't have his hands on me, Sister. I was trying to get him to do his exercises; trying to mobilise him after his operation. He's supposed to lift his legs off the bed on his own, using only his leg muscles but he keeps using his hands to take the weight."

"Are you quite sure?" Sister demanded, still suspicious.

"Yes Sister, quite sure."

"That's just as well then. I'll leave you to get on." She shot a fierce glance at Joe. "I'm watching you, young man. You misbehave and I'll have you out of here so fast your feet won't touch the ground."

"Now I wonder what Sister thought I was doing," Joe commented, grinning at the physio the minute Sister's back was turned and the screens were again drawn. "Would you shout out if I showed you?"

The physio smiled back at him. "Yes, I would, and you might find that your exercises suddenly became ten times more painful. Now get that leg in the air and let's have less cheating!"

In due course, Sir William with his entourage of doctors, nurses and medical students reached Joe's bed. Since he was a patient of Mr Potts', it was to be expected that Sir William would walk straight passed but Sister Ashbrook had other ideas!

"Would you mind advising on a little problem with one of Mr Potts' patients Sir William?" she asked innocently. "Mr Potts is on leave at the moment."

Joe was making a good recovery after his hernia repair though the wound was proving a little more painful than he had anticipated. Nonetheless he was enjoying his stay. His celebrity status made him the centre of attention and, to Sister Ashbrook's dismay, her young nurses were making a fuss of him. After the episode with Janet and his subsequent reprimand by Mr Potts, of which Sir William had no knowledge, he remained cheeky with a ready tongue and light-hearted manner though in fairness, he had been careful not to overstep the mark.

Sir William looked to Paul to be told the nature of the 'problem' to which Sister had referred but Paul was not aware that there was a problem. He had seen Joe earlier in the day and thought that his convalescence was unremarkable. Nevertheless he told Sir William of Joe's occupation and his hernia operation all the while hoping that Sister would interrupt and disclose her concerns. True to form, Sir William then spent ten minutes telling Joe how to minimise the chance of the rupture recurring. He was only to undertake light training for the first month and not to expect to be match fit for at least two months. Having forgotten that there was said to be a 'problem' he was about to move on when Sister Ashbrook decided the moment was ripe for Joe to be taught a lesson that would forever remind him of his stay on her ward.

"I don't think Mr Johnson has moved his bowels since his operation, Sir William," Sister Ashbrook said.

Having worked as his ward Sister for many years, she knew exactly how the consultant would react. In fact, his reputation for ensuring that his patients avoided constipation after surgery was legend throughout the hospital. She knew all his favourite expressions. If she had heard him say it once, she had heard him say it a hundred times. *'If you don't put your finger in, one day you will put your foot in it!'* True to form Sir William responded exactly as she knew he would. He raised an index finger in the air like an umpire confirming a batsman's fate. It was a signal the nurses knew well. They were to pass him the rectal tray.

"Just turn onto your side" instructed Sir William.

Reluctantly Joe complied not realising what was in store for him. "Now drop your shorts," Sir William continued.

As he placed an examination glove on his hand and applied a generous portion of lubricating gel to his index finger, Joe suddenly realised what was about to happen.

"With all these people around?" he protested, suddenly alarmed.

"Don't worry, they're all doctors or nurses, they've seen it all before," Sir William reassured. "Now draw up your knees and try to relax."

But Joe was far from relaxed, he was mortified. With a dozen people crowded within the screens, his cheeks reddened with embarrassment and he covered his face with his hands to hide his humiliation.

"Everyone should be prepared to do the humblest of jobs on a surgical unit," Sir William commented as he performed a rectal examination. It was another of his favourite sayings.

"Well done, Sister, you were quite right. He's really bunged up. But I'm sure a couple of suppositories will do the trick!"

Two suppositories were peeled out of their plastic wrappers, dropped into his hand and then thrust into Joe's anus by Sir William's chunky finger.

"There you are young man.," he said as he wiped the young footballer's bottom with a dry swab. Give those suppositories half an hour to work and then slip down to the toilet. When you've moved your bowels you can go home."

Joe pulled up his shorts, muttering something unprintable under his breath, though not loud enough for the nurses to hear - which was perhaps as well! Meanwhile Sister Ashbrook returned to the office looking smug and quietly satisfied.

Chapter Seventeen

Queenie's operation, having been postponed whilst her diabetes was sorted out, then further delayed to allow for the abnormality on the chest x-ray to be resolved, was deferred yet again, this time at the insistence of the anaesthetist when she developed a chest infection. Sir William was concerned. All the while her jaundice was getting deeper which was not only sapping her strength but was also interfering with her bloods ability to clot. He felt they were trapped between the devil and the deep blue sea. The danger was that in safeguarding her from the chance of a post operative pneumonia, they were simply swopping one risk for another. He took Paul on one side.

"I'm afraid I shall be away in London for the next couple of weeks," he said, "I'm acting as an examiner for the College of Surgeons. I had hoped that we could have operated on Mrs O'Hannagan before I left but we can't possibly leave it until I get back. I've had a word with the anaesthetist and he agrees that we need to proceed. I'm quite happy to leave the operation in your hands; you've dealt with similar problems before. The blockage is bound to be caused by a tumour in the pancreas which will certainly be incurable. It will simply be a question of making a by-pass so that the obstruction is relieved allowing her a few months without the jaundice."

As the date of Queenie's operation approached, Paul arranged rigorous physiotherapy to clear her chest and extra vitamins to help her blood to clot. He wanted to give Queenie the very best chance of surviving her surgery but despite these precautions, everyone accepted that the procedure would be hazardous.

Paul was not unduly anxious as he scrubbed up in theatre on the following Monday morning. He had performed similar procedures before and whilst there was always pressure when operating on advanced malignancy in the elderly, there was a much greater responsibility when performing surgery on benign conditions in babies and children. In any case, he knew he could seek Mr Potts' advice and assistance should he run into any difficulties. To his delight and astonishment, when he opened Queenie's abdomen, he discovered that the cause of the blockage was not an advanced incurable cancer at all. Instead there was a large gall stone obstructing the bile passage. Further he was able to remove the stone without any great difficulty.

Kate and the rest of the ward staff were overjoyed when Queenie was returned safely to them a couple of hours later. During the time she had been a patient, she had become a firm favourite and the news that her condition had been curable delighted them. She still had to recover from her surgery, of course, but there was now the prospect that she could be restored to normal health and return to her old lifestyle. Sister Rutherford arranged for her to receive intensive nursing care through the first night and she allocated Kate to 'special' her the next day. 'Specialing' involved allocating a fully trained nurse to attend solely to the needs of a single patient deemed to be 'high risk'. It involved extra responsibility but Kate was happy to do it.

By the next afternoon, Queenie had recovered from her anaesthetic though she remained heavily sedated in a single bedded side room. Kate offered her a sip of water to moisten her parched lips which she gratefully accepted.

"Thanks, Nurse," she croaked, as she struggled to lift her head off the pillow. "I needed that. My mouth was as dry as old leather."

"Another sip?"

"Perhaps in a minute."

Kate heard the noise of the door being opened. She turned and looked up; Mick and Young Rose had arrived to visit.

"You have visitors," Kate whispered as the pair approached the bed but as she glanced at her patient she noticed that Queenie's head was back on the pillow and her eyes were now closed.

"You're feigning," she thought. "You sly old thing. You don't want any hassle, do you?"

"How is she?" Rose asked, concern obvious in her voice.

"I'm pleased to say, she's doing fine," Kate replied.

"It was cancer, wasn't it? How long has she got?" Mike demanded impatiently.

"I'm afraid we haven't had a chance to talk to your mother about her operation yet."

"But you can tell us, we're family."

"I'm sorry but I'm afraid I can't," Kate said, speaking quietly, aware that Mick had a short fuse. "You see, before she had her operation we chatted about who should and who shouldn't be given medical information. Your mother decided it would be best if she did the telling."

"Jesus Christ, Nurse," Mike exploded. "I'm her son, I live with her. I look after her. I've a right to know."

"I'm sorry but you don't have a right to know. Your mother was quite definite. She expressly stated we were not to give any information to you or indeed to anyone else; and that of course includes your brother. No doubt, in due course, she will tell you herself but in the meantime we must keep our promise to her."

Although Kate spoke slowly and firmly, her heart quickened when she saw Mick's reaction. His face reddened and his fists clenched. He strode towards Kate until he could have reached out and touched her. He glared at her. "Now look here Nurse, you tell me straight what that surgeon found. I've not come here today to......"

Then he stopped and looked past her as the door to the room opened again. It was Brendan. Like his older brother, he too was a big man, broad across the shoulders with the same dark features, but whereas Mick was wearing faded old jeans with a loose fitting jacket thrown over his vest, Brendan was wearing a smart grey suit, a collared shirt and tie and polished black leather shoes.

"What the fuck" Mick exclaimed. "Just look what the cat's dragged in. You can bloody well get the hell out of here."

But Brendan continued to advance towards them, walking slowly, palms raised in a gesture of reconciliation.

"Hello Mick, hello Young Rose," he said, now with his right arm extended offering a handshake. "Come on, no hard feelings. Surely with our Mother so ill, this is a time to put old differences to one side." The words were spoken quietly, the voice cultured, all trace of an Irish accent gone.

"I might have known Bren that you'd turn up when our Mam's on her death bed," Mick snarled. "Got the sniff of money did you? Well you won't be getting a penny, I'll see to that. Now fuck off, or I'll beat you with my bare fists just as I did when you decided you were too good for the likes of us. Me and Rose will look after her 'til she's gone."

"I came because Mum wrote asking me to come; she wanted to see me," Brendan replied, keeping control of his anger with difficulty. "She thinks it's time we made up and so do I. It has nothing to do with inheritance."

As the brothers faced each other, hatred burning in Mick's eyes, Rose intervened, speaking scornfully to Brendan.

"Just look at you standing there, all smug and righteous, with your pretty clothes and posh talk. You burned your boats when you took up with that fancy Proddy tart. Mammy made it quite clear that she wanted nothing to do with you, so piss off and leave our Mam alone. We'll be the ones to sort out her affairs."

Kate was certain that Queenie was not only awake but was aware of what was being said. She tried to keep her composure though her heart was beating wildly.

"This is neither the time nor the place to have such a conversation," she said. "You should all leave and if you must have an argument, have it elsewhere."

For a moment there was silence and then Brendan spoke. "You're quite right Nurse. I'll go and wait outside. I'll call back later when Mum's on her own."

Kate looked at Queenie whose eyes remained firmly closed. She turned to Mick and Rose. "Your mother needs to rest and her observations are due. I think it would be best if you left as well."

Alone once more with her patient, Kate went to check that the door was firmly closed. "They've all gone now Queenie," she said softly. "You are awake aren't you?"

Slowly, Queenie opened her eyes which were moist with tears.

"Yes Nurse, I am. You told them didn't you? You broke your promise."

Even though the words were slurred, the accusatory tone in her voice was unmistakable.

Kate was puzzled, not understanding what she had done wrong. "Told them what?" she asked.

"Told them that I had cancer and was dying."

Kate reached for her hand. "Queenie," she said. "I told them no such thing. They're jumping to conclusions and what's more they've jumped to completely the wrong conclusion. Although the doctors were expecting to find cancer, they didn't. Your jaundice was due to a great big gall stone. There was no cancer at all. There's no reason why you shouldn't make a full recovery. Everyone's delighted for you. We've saved the stone for you to have as a keepsake. It's in your locker if you want to see it."

"Well, what do you know? May the Saints be praised! And there was I, busy tying up the loose ends of my life. Now tell me; that was Brendan come to see me wasn't it? I didn't dream that?"

"Yes, it was. That's what you wanted wasn't it?"

Queenie though had closed her eyes again but the contented expression on her face told Kate all that she needed to know.

****

Before Kate went off duty at five o'clock she had a quick word with Paul on the phone. Aware that he would be anxious about Queenie after he had performed her surgery the previous day, she wanted to reassure him that his patient continued to make excellent progress. She also wished to know at what time she should prepare their evening meal. If he promised to be home at a reasonable hour, she would wait for him so they would be able to eat together for a change.

"I'm nearly through now," Paul had replied, "I should be home within the next half hour, or so."

But Paul wasn't home at five thirty or even six thirty. He was called to see a problem on the male ward and despite it being his evening off duty, he stayed with the patient until he started to show signs of improvement. It was almost seven when he left the hospital to walk along the gravel path through the hospital campus to their flat. Half way home, concern for Queenie came into his mind. He had planned to pop in to see her before leaving but had forgotten. He hesitated. Kate had 'specialed' her all day and had reassured him she was fine. She had said Queenie's diabetes was well controlled and that her observations were fine, but she had mentioned a temperature of 99 degrees. That was really only to be expected after her surgery and yet equally it might indicate a developing chest infection. Paul hesitated. Queenie had a weak chest as a result of the TB she had as a child, and she also had a tendency to bronchitis - should he go back to have a quick look at her? It would be a disaster if she died of a chest infection when, miraculously, the cause of her jaundice had been a simple gall stone. No, he would leave things to the night staff; they were experienced nurses; they would call the duty doctor if they were worried.

He walked on but the demon in his head nagged away at him like an irritating stone in your shoe. It would not be quietened. He cursed. He knew only too well that if he didn't check Queenie for himself he would spend a restless evening and a sleepless night worrying about her. So he turned on his heels, returned to Queenie's side ward only to find that she was sleeping peacefully and making a completely normal recovery from her operation. And unsurprisingly, when he finally got home, for his troubles he found Kate in an angry resentful mood.

Chapter Eighteen

With Sir William away for a few days subjecting aspiring surgeons to a grilling in the examination hall of the Royal College, Paul was deputising as tutor for the medical students. It was a task he enjoyed though the intrusion into his working day often resulted in a late finish and potentially to a cool reception from Kate when he finally made it home. Without exception, the students were intelligent; had they not been bright they would not have been admitted to medical school. Generally, they applied themselves diligently to their studies, but they differed greatly in their ability to communicate with patients. Some had a natural empathy; patients opened their hearts quickly and easily to them and as a result they found little difficulty in eliciting their patient's symptoms. Other students however, maybe because English was not their first language, possibly because of their natural reserve or occasionally because of a superior or haughty manner found talking to patients difficult. An essential task for their teachers was to observe the interaction between student and patient and to guide and advise as necessary.

On this occasion it was the turn of Sunil Solanki to demonstrate what Sir William had taught the students the previous week. Sunil had been nick named 'Sunny' because of his cheerful disposition and ready smile. Paul gathered the students round the bed of a rather deaf octogenarian who hailed from Pontefract in Yorkshire.

"Now, Sunny," he began, "Mr Howell has a problem with his bowels. I would like you to get him to describe his symptoms."

He turned to the other students. "The rest of you should listen carefully and be prepared to chip in and make comments but only if you feel it is something important."

"Right, away you go Sunny."

Sunny approached the bedside somewhat nervously. "Good morning Mr Howell," he said politely in a manner of which Sir William would certainly have approved.

"What's that you say young man," the patient shouted.

"I said, Good morning Mr Howell."

"Aye that's me, 'owell's me name."

"I am hearing that you are having trouble shitting," Sunil continued.

"Ouch", interrupted Miss Croft. "I don't think you should use the word 'shitting'. Many patients, especially ladies would be most upset."

Sunny looked puzzled. "But 'shitting' is the same as 'crapping' I am told. I have a friend who is telling me all about English as it is spoken and that is what he says."

"Yes, that's true. But 'shitting' and 'crapping' are both rude words – not words to be used in polite society or with patients," Paul explained. "Were you taught any other words for the act of moving the bowels?"

"Yes," Sunny replied as if he had suddenly remembered. He turned again to Mr Howell.

"Are you having trouble with your ha ha?"

"With what young man?" Mr Howell yelled, a cupped hand to his ear.

"With ha ha?"

The patient turned to Paul.

"I 'ope 'e's not laughing at me. I'll not stand for that."

"No certainly not," Paul said laying a hand on Mr Howell's arm.

"Sunny, I'm afraid there are lots of words in English for our various bodily functions. 'Ha ha' is a phrase sometimes used by children. 'Number twos' and 'having a poo' are other expressions; but again only by youngsters. But they're not words you would use to an adult. 'Moving your bowels' is probably as good a phrase as any, though the proper verb is 'defaecation'. Now start again."

Now both confused and embarrassed, Sunny tried again.

"You are having trouble with your defaecation?" he said raising his voice.

"Beg pardon young man?"

"Trouble with your defaecation?" Sunny repeated even louder.

"I don't know owt about 'defee whatever that is'. And there's no need to shout, young man; I may be a bit daft but I'm not deaf."

At Paul's suggestion Sunny asked if Mr Howell was having trouble with his bowels.

"My balls did you say." Mr Howell shouted back. "Let me tell you lad, I've only got one ball. I lost the other one years ago. Jerry shot it off in that little scrap we had with 'err 'itler! But I've found that one works just as well as two, if you know what I mean," Mr

Howell replied with a dirty laugh while giving Sunny a dig in the ribs which surprised and mystified him.

It took the best part of forty minutes for Sunny, prompted by Paul, to draw out the story of Mr Howell's bowel problems. Having previously had a regular bowel habit, he now had a constant desire to go to the toilet but when he went, passed little more than a small amount of stool mixed with blood. Paul hoped that as a result of the session, the students would remember the significance of a change in bowel habit and the presence of blood in the stool. Unfortunately Mr Howell had a tumour in his rectum.

Later, back in the tutorial room, Sunny again raised the subject of colloquial English.

"If number twos is the same as defaecation," he asked, "is number one pissing?"

"Yes, it is," Paul explained, "but 'pissing' is also a rude word. 'Having a pee' or 'spending a penny' are better phrases. More often you would ask a patient if he has trouble passing water. The formal medical term of course is micturition."

"If number one is peeing and number two is moving the bowels, what is number three? Is it fucking?"

Paul couldn't help but laugh. "Sunny, you need to learn which words to use in different circumstances or you're going to find yourself in some embarrassing situations. There isn't a number three and since the number system is used by young children they wouldn't know about number three, even if it was what you suggest. In any case the word 'fucking' is extremely crude. 'Humping' and 'screwing' are almost as bad but you might just get away with 'rumpy pumpy'. If you wanted to ask a patient about sexual relations you would speak of having intercourse or having sex."

"Another expression would be 'making love'" Miss Croft added quietly, catching Paul's eye and offering him a coy smile as she did so.

"Sunny," Paul continued, ignoring the interruption despite it having caused his concentration to falter for an instant, "I fear the friend who helped you with your English may have been having a laugh at your expense. I suggest you ask one of the other students to write down the terms used for bodily functions and to list those that are acceptable and those that are not.

Now if there are no more questions I think......."

Suddenly he was interrupted by the loud emergency tone emitted by his bleep. *'Cardiac Arrest... S 5 female. Cardiac Arrest.....S5 female.'* The telephonist's voice was cool and precise.

Lucky woman doesn't have to deal with the emergency, Paul thought bitterly; she only has to put out the crisis call. His heart quickened, as it always did in these circumstances. Despite the fact he was now quite experienced and had dealt with similar situations on many occasions, the call to an 'arrest' always worried him. He felt his pulse rise and was aware of beads of sweat on his brow. Would he be able to cope, or was this emergency the result of a condition that he had never encountered before? Did other doctors suffer from such insecurity? If so they never seemed to show it.

"One of you, follow me," Paul shouted, as he ran from the room leaving the group of students in a state of some alarm.

When he had been a student he hadn't witnessed a cardiac arrest and his inexperience had shown when he had been faced with his first emergency as a newly qualified doctor. It was one thing to read about resuscitation procedures in a textbook, quite a different matter to put them into practice in a high pressure situation with a patient's life at stake. He couldn't allow the whole group to attend, they would simply get in the way, but at least one of them could benefit from the crisis.

Leaving them to decide who would join him, he dashed to the female ward, wondering which of his patients had collapsed. He knew them all, of course, and was familiar with their medical conditions. At least that made things a little easier. Being called to an emergency on another ward or in casualty knowing nothing of the patient was far more difficult.

Arriving at the ward doors, his heart thumping, he looked in vain for the screened bed which normally indicated the location of the arrest and shielded the victim from curious eyes as the nurses commenced resuscitation.

"In the toilets, Doctor," one of the nurses said breathlessly as she dashed passed him on her way to get the emergency trolley.

As Paul ran down the length of the ward, he noticed that Queenie's bed was empty. His worst fears were soon confirmed. Queenie was lying face down, half in and half out of one of the toilet cubicles. Sister Rutherford was there with two of her nurses. Desperately they were trying to drag her into the open where they could start resuscitation. The cubicle door was ajar and Queenie was wedged, knickers round her ankles, one leg either side of the toilet bowl; her head and arms lodged behind the door. She had fallen forward from the toilet seat. Paul had to climb over her and drag her back into the cubicle whilst Sister freed her arms before it was possible to pull her into the more spacious washroom. He noticed that one of her legs was swollen. It was twice the size of its neighbour. All the while Queenie was ominously still, her face and hands dark blue. There was a deep cut on her forehead but it wasn't bleeding. Paul quickly established that there was no pulse, nor was she breathing. Sister Rutherford, now at Queenie's head, started mouth to mouth resuscitation. On his knees by her side, Paul commenced cardiac massage.

Within seconds the duty anaesthetist arrived, quickly followed by the nurse with the resuscitation trolley. The anaesthetist passed a tube into Queenie's windpipe. He forced oxygen into her lungs. He checked her pupils and found both to be twice their normal size. They failed to react when challenged by a bright light. He caught Paul's eye and grimaced. Paul understood his unspoken words. It was almost certainly too late for Queenie to be saved.

"Did anyone actually see Queenie collapse?" Paul asked, his voice soft, concerned.

It was a junior nurse who replied. "I don't think so. I was told that Queenie had fallen by Mrs Jenkins; she's one of the other patients. She was the one who found her and raised the alarm."

"Please go and have a word with Mrs Jenkins. Ask her if she actually saw or heard Queenie fall or whether she was she already on the floor when she arrived," Paul requested.

Within a couple of minutes the nurse was back. "Queenie was already on the floor when Mrs Jenkins arrived; she also said she was a terrible colour."

"I'm afraid that things don't look good," Paul commented, knowing that, as well as doing the right thing for Queenie, he had to manage the feelings and expectations of the nurses, some of whom were quite junior. They were very fond of Queenie; she had become quite a favourite in the weeks she had been on the ward. "Perhaps someone would fetch an ophthalmoscope so that I can look into her eyes."

The swelling of her leg had not been present when Paul had examined her the day before. The implication was that a clot had formed in her leg veins and had then broken free and floated in the blood stream up to the chest where it had blocked the circulation through her lungs. Such an event was unpredictable, unpreventable and frequently fatal. Since she had been on the floor for some time before she was found and there had also been a delay before resuscitation had commenced, it seemed likely that Queenie had been dead for some time. If so, further resuscitation was futile. Gently Paul explained the situation to the nurses.

"However we must continue with cardiac massage until we're sure," he added.

Two minutes later though, Paul's examination confirmed that the blood in the vessels of the eyes had clotted indicating that Queenie had indeed died. He turned to the anaesthetist. "Can I just ask you to confirm?" he asked, not because he was unsure of his diagnosis but for the benefit of the nurses. They needed to see that no stone had been left unturned.

"Sadly, you're right," the anaesthetist said a moment or two later. "I'm afraid there's no point in carrying on. There's nothing more we can do." Gently he withdrew the tube from Queenie's throat, then laid a hand on the arm of the nurse who was continuing the cardiac compression. Miss Croft, the medical student, who had chased after Paul when the alarm was raised, silently turned and left, tears in her eyes. It was the first death she had witnessed. Sister Rutherford, ever observant, quietly indicated to her staff nurse that she should follow and offer comfort. "I'll stay and tidy up here," she said.

Paul sadly was all too familiar with the situation since the overwhelming outcome for patients with a cardiac arrest was unfavourable. Knowing he had no further role to play at the patient's side, he also departed. He had to write an account of events in the patient's case record and also had to inform the Coroner; a legal requirement for all deaths occurring so soon after surgery. As he walked back to the office between the two lines of beds, he was conscious of the tension in the air. The patients were all painfully aware of the drama that had unfolded in the washroom only a few feet away. They had seen the frantic activity as the doctors and nurses dashed to and fro carrying emergency equipment. They knew that it was Queenie who had collapsed and whispered conversations were held as they speculated on her condition and outlook. Later when they observed the long faces of the staff as they walked back through the ward returning various items of equipment to their rightful places, they realised that their efforts had been in vain and that Queenie had passed away.

Sister Rutherford arranged that every patient should remain behind drawn screens whilst Queenie was gently returned to her bed. A few moments later, when the screens were opened, only one bed remained shielded allowing the nurses to perform their unhappy task of laying out and dressing Queenie's body in preparation for its transfer to the hospital mortuary.

Queenie's death on the ward had a profound effect on the other patients. Had her demise been anticipated she would have been moved in advance to a side ward where the death would have occurred in relative privacy. A sudden or unexpected death however, particularly if it occurred on the open ward, was intensely shocking. Inevitably a sombre mood developed. In years gone by, death was less of a stranger for it frequently occurred in the home, the body of the deceased often remaining in the house for several days before the funeral. With the passage of time, the number of people who have witnessed death at first hand has diminished. For most, the collapse of a patient in the next bed, the screams for help, the rush of nurses and doctors to the scene and the sight and sounds of frantic resuscitation was a frightening experience.

Paul wrote up the notes with great sadness. In the weeks she had been with them on the ward, she had been a breath of fresh air; a real character. She was cheerful, outgoing and always ready with an encouraging word if one of the other patients was anxious or depressed. Paul had been delighted when she had been cured simply by the removal of a gall stone, especially as everyone had assumed that her jaundice was due to an incurable tumour. He was pleased too that Kate had not been on duty and had not witnessed Queenie's death. Having been drawn into Queenie's family problems, she had become rather more emotionally involved than Paul considered wise.

For the next few hours, there was an unnatural stillness amongst the patients on the ward. Queenie was somebody with whom they had shared their anxieties during long days of bedbound inactivity. She was the one with whom they had shared a joke the previous evening, from whom they had borrowed a newspaper that very morning and with whom they had grumbled about the food at lunchtime. When the nurses had completed their morbid task the ward fell silent when two brown coated porters arrived pushing the metal coffin on wheels, disguised by being covered with a white cloth that would carry Queenie's body from the ward.

The atmosphere remained sombre long after Queenie's departure and even the next morning the mood remained gloomy. In the afternoon a new patient was allocated to the bed that Queenie had occupied and her neighbours wondered whether they should tell the newcomer what had become of the previous occupant. Fortunately nobody did!

****

The rain was falling steadily from a leaden sky when a slim young man, wearing a smart city suit parked his car in the hospital's main car park. Carefully he opened the leather brief case he had placed on the front passenger seat and checked that he had all the papers he required for the task before him. Satisfied that everything was in order, he put on his gabardine raincoat.

He had an inherent dislike of hospitals. He had been a sickly youth and lino floors, white tiled walls and the pungent smell of antiseptic brought back painful childhood memories of unpleasant examinations, needles and long periods of separation from his mother. He stopped in front of the large direction board in the hospital's lobby and learned that to reach the Surgical Five Unit he had to proceed down the main corridor, turn down the second corridor on the left and then take the stairs to the first floor. As he walked, his eyes hugged the floor as he sought to isolate himself from the hustle and bustle of the hospital. He ignored a group of chattering domestics, turned away from patients being escorted between different departments and disregarded a group of medical students, their stethoscopes slung round their necks in an attempt to impress the nurses. However he was forced to stand to one side as two porters wheeled a low, cloth covered metal trolley passed him.

Reaching the ward, he found that the office door was open. Within, working at her desk, he saw a round faced, homely looking woman wearing a dark blue uniform whose grey curls peeked from under her starched white cap. He hesitated, wondering whether he should knock on the door or cough gently to attract her attention. After a moment's hesitation, he decided to knock. Sister Rutherford looked up.

"Can I help you?" she asked.

"Is this the Surgical Five Female ward?" she was asked in a voice that was as timid as the knock on the door had been.

"Indeed it is," Sister said, a smile on her face. Her visitor was actually standing below a sign that confirmed this information!

"I've come to see Mrs O'Hannagan, Mrs Rose O'Hannagan."

Sister was surprised. Queenie's two sons had both visited on a number of occasions and were known to her. Fortunately, after the acrimonious confrontation at their first visit, they had subsequently avoided each other but whether this was by accident or design she didn't know. However this was a new face to her and it was clear that he was unaware that Queenie had died. "May I ask if you are a relative of Mrs O'Hannagan or perhaps a friend?" she asked.

"My name is Clarke, Brian Clarke. I'm a solicitor from the firm of Jones, Jones and Jackson on the High Street. I understand that Mrs O'Hannagan asked for a visit. Apparently she wanted to write her will."

"I'm afraid Mrs O'Hannagan is no longer with us," Sister said quietly.

"You mean she's been discharged?"

"No, I'm sorry. I've not made myself clear. I'm afraid Mrs O'Hannagan died earlier today. In fact we're just waiting for a member of the family to come and collect a death certificate. Because it was sudden and unexpected, her death will have to be reported to the coroner as I'm sure you appreciate."

For a moment, Mr Clarke looked nonplussed. Sister rather expected that he would utter some words of sympathy but none were forthcoming. Instead his face lightened.

"Then I'm afraid I've come on a wasted journey. I'm sorry to have troubled you," he said.

He looked relieved as he turned to leave; pleased that he was able to escape without having to go onto the ward to interview his client, glad to be able to escape from the hospital and return to the comforting and reassuring surroundings of his city office!

Chapter Nineteen

As Paul drove his battered old Morris Minor through the ornamental wrought iron gates of the Davenport Park Golf Club, in the rolling countryside ten miles outside the city, he realised he had made a terrible mistake. To have accepted an invitation to play golf with Leslie Potts at the weekend when he should be spending quality time at home was utter insanity. He had felt the full weight of Kate's fury before he left home that morning and he knew that her anger was fully justified. He ought to have refused - firmly but politely. Kate had been in tears when he left the house; he had never seen her quite so upset.

'What's the point of us being married if we never see each other?' she had shouted as he closed the door. Perhaps today he had been left with little choice, but he vowed that it would never happen again. The risk to his marriage was just too great.

The club house was approached via a drive all of a mile long. It meandered through a small copse of silver birch, then alongside a small lake in whose smooth waters the trees on the opposite bank were clearly reflected. Finally it opened into pleasant parkland where the attractively landscaped golf course had been created. Paul had never seen anything like it. The undulating fairways looked wonderful, the grass cut in neat diagonal stripes with not a pitch mark or divot to be seen. The tees were raised; each with a large board to illustrate the hole, detailing the various hazards and their distance from the tee. Most impressive of all though, were the greens. At one point, Paul got out of the car and inspected one of them. It was immaculate; beautifully manicured, not a single blade of grass out of place. The felt on a billiard table could not have been smoother. It looked so perfect it seemed it would be a sacrilege to walk on it.

Eventually Paul reached the car parks; one for club members, the second for visitors. He left the Morris Minor looking somewhat incongruous, sandwiched between a silver Bentley on one side and a red Italian sports car on the other. The imposing clubhouse was a large, mock Georgian building; marble pillars either side of an impressive oak front door. This was quite unlike the municipal courses at which he had played in the past, where the car park was a muddy patch of ground and the clubhouse a wooden shack where a bored attendant checked that you weren't wearing hobnail hiking boots before charging you two pounds and allowing you to play. Fortunately Paul was reasonably attired, having remembered that jeans and a rugby shirt were not *'de rigueur'* on private golf courses.

There was a reception desk just inside the clubhouse.

"May I help you, Sir?" Paul was asked by a bland looking man of indeterminate age wearing a uniform with sufficient gold braid that wouldn't have been out of place at The Ritz Hotel. As he spoke, his eyes roved over Paul, managing to make him feel small and insignificant.

"I'm a visitor," he explained. "I've come to play golf with Mr Leslie Potts.

"Ah yes...er Sir." Paul felt the word 'Sir' had been added with some reluctance. "Mr Potts said I was to look out for you. You will find him in the gentleman's locker room. It's the second door down the corridor on the right hand side."

There were half a dozen men in the locker room all of whom turned and gazed at Paul as he entered. Once more he gained the impression that he was being inspected and assessed for his acceptability. He was pleased to spot Mr Potts, very nattily attired in tartan plus fours, a roll neck shirt and a bright green sweater, bearing the clubs crest.

"Lambert, there you are. I'm glad you could make it. Let me introduce you to my pals. This is Brigadier Winstanley, our club captain; Tom, of course, you know from the hospital, and this is Geoffrey Clarke one of our local GPs. Rather formally, Paul shook hands with them all. Tom Lester was well known to him. He was a consultant anaesthetist at the City General and regularly worked with the surgeons in the Surgical Five theatre. He was quietly spoken, polite, and conscientious. Always down trodden by Leslie Potts, in verbal exchanges he was no match for the ebullient surgeon. Paul wondered whether the same relationship existed on the golf course.

"We're due on the tee in 15 minutes, Lambert," Mr Potts continued, looking at his watch. "Perhaps you would like to get changed."

"I've only got to change my shoes, Sir," Paul said. "I'll do that in the car park."

"I would prefer that you didn't do that," the Brigadier responded sharply. "We like to uphold certain standards at this club; jacket and tie in the clubhouse, no women at the bar, that sort of thing."

Paul hadn't thought to bring a change of clothes with him and suddenly remembered the drink at the nineteenth that was the norm after a game of golf. Perhaps though, this was a blessing in disguise; it provided him with a good excuse to slip away the minute they had finished playing. Chatting informally with Mr Potts and his friends wouldn't be easy or relaxing and in any case, he was in enough trouble with Kate already. Heaven help him if he spent an extra hour at the club and then came home smelling of beer. He would escape at the first possible opportunity.

"You go and get yourself ready, Lambert and we'll all meet on the first tee in ten minutes," Mr Potts said, leaving Paul in some doubt as to whom he would be playing with. His understanding had been that he would just be competing against his consultant.

****

Mr Potts, Dr Clarke and the Brigadier were standing with two others by the first tee when Paul joined them. Mr Potts addressed the Brigadier.

"Our tee time is actually before yours but of course, it's the captain's prerogative to go first."

"Not at all," came the reply. "You're a 'two ball'. There are four of us. We would hold you up if we went first. Besides, it will mean that you'll get back to the club house before us. You can have a stiff whisky ready for me when I come off the course. Off you go."

That clarified the situation. It was simply to be a game between Leslie Potts and Paul. Although that came as a relief, it meant that Dr Clarke, the club captain and the two other club members would be watching as he played his first shot. Paul wished he had arrived at the course earlier. That would have given him the chance to hit a few balls in the practice net. Desperately he tried to recall the basic principles of a good golf swing. He had played quite a lot at college but hadn't hit a ball for over twelve months. His flat mate though had been an excellent golfer. He'd been the captain of the university team and had played off a handicap of one. He had instilled the fundamentals of the game into Paul but that was many years ago.

Mr Potts pulled his driver out of his golf bag and marched confidently onto the tee. He took a brand new ball out of his pocket and stripped it of its wrapper.

"I'm playing a Dunlop 65, Number Three he announced," in a very professional manner. He placed the ball on a tee peg then gazed down the long, wide, fairway in front of him. He took a couple of practice swings then addressed the ball. The club moved back in a graceful arc, the sun glinting for a moment on its shaft at the top of the back swing. There was a pause, then the club came down, slowly at first, smoothly and then accelerated through the ball. It was a perfect swing and a wonderful shot. The ball flew as straight as a die, becoming a white dot against the blue sky. It landed and bounced two or three times before coming to rest 200 yards away, dividing the fairway into two.

"Good shot, Leslie," said the brigadier in a crisp voice "couldn't do better myself. I can see the lessons you've been having from the club professional are paying dividends. Now let's see what the lad can do."

Paul picked a six iron, a fairly forgiving club, out of his bag. Given the time that had elapsed since he last hit a golf ball, there seemed no point in risking the driver. With a sickening sense of impending disaster, he tried to remember what his college roommate had taught him. Get as many things as possible right before you start your swing. Shoulders and feet square to the target, correct grip, two V's pointing to the right shoulder, ball in the middle of the stance, relax and try to swing slow, take the tension out of your arms and shoulders, imagine the line along which the club should swing and above all else, watch the ball. There were so many things to remember and all to be implemented in the half second that it takes to hit a shot.

Paul was as nervous as a kitten as he placed the ball on its tee peg and took a practice swing. The club felt strange in his hand. He could feel the eyes of Mr Potts and the club captain boring into his back. As he prepared to hit the ball, his hands trembled, his legs felt weak, he became light headed and the ball became a blur on the ground in front of him. He knew with absolute certainty that this first shot would be a total disaster. Why the hell had he agreed to play!

Chapter Twenty

The fact that Paul gave Kate breakfast in bed before going off to play golf made no difference whatsoever to her mood. She was furious. For the first time in over a month her weekend 'off duty' coincided with his and she had been looking forward to spending some time relaxing together. It had been arranged that they would spend the weekend with Sally and Colin walking in the Lake District. Sally was Kate's closest friend. They had spent three years together training as nurses and Sally had been her bridesmaid when she had married Paul. Kate had reciprocated when Sally had subsequently married Colin. Accommodation at their favourite B. and B. was already booked.

Instead she was stuck in the flat whilst Paul, damn him, was playing golf. He wouldn't be home until mid afternoon at the very earliest. They would only be able to join their friends late in the evening, if at all. A whole day wasted. To make matters worse, the forecast was for a dry and sunny weekend and Paul was ruining it by playing golf with Mr Potts. It was unforgivable. Why on earth had he agreed to it? Why had he been so weak? All he had to do was to politely refuse and explain that he had already made other arrangements. But oh dear no, he had been too keen to suck up to his boss and stay in his good books.

What particularly infuriated Kate was the knowledge that other junior doctors did stand up to Mr Potts. Janet Smith for example stood no nonsense from him - and she was a lowly house officer. The nurses marvelled at the bold fashion in which she responded to Mr Potts whenever he made sexist or facetious remarks. Standing up to the consultant didn't seem to do her any harm, indeed Mr Potts appeared to enjoy the exchanges.

She dragged herself from bed and got dressed wondering what on earth she should do until Paul returned. Often, when she was on her own, she would invite Sally round for a cup of coffee and a chat, but Sally would already be half way to Windermere. Moodily, she drifted down to the kitchen and boiled an egg for her breakfast. Later she started to read the morning newspaper but found she couldn't settle. She sat brooding wondering how their marriage had gone so wrong.

Initially they had been so happy, so contented, so much in love but insidiously, almost imperceptively, Paul had changed. He had always had a serious disposition, not the sort to be the life and soul of the party but in those early days, when 'off duty' he had been relaxed, good company, able to forget his responsibilities as a doctor. And his love for her had been so obvious. In an evening, when the day's work was done, they used to sit together on the settee like two love birds, happily sharing the latest hospital gossip or telling each other the interesting or amusing things that had occurred on the ward. As often as not, Paul would have a map on his lap planning a walk or be organising an outing to the theatre or cinema.

Now, when Paul came home in the evening, he was tired and listless. To use a popular expression, his 'get up and go' had got up and gone! He looked gloomy, he rarely smiled and Kate couldn't remember the last time they had shared a good belly laugh. He sat for long periods without initiating any conversation and if she asked what was on his mind he would admit to being worried about one of his patients, as often as not someone upon whom he had operated.

Kate wondered if it was ambition that drove him so hard, that made him put in all those extra hours; a desire to be the best, to impress his consultants so that he could rise quickly through the ranks. She knew of others who were undoubtedly driven by ambition. She had seen them trying to ingratiate themselves with their bosses, laughing at their jokes, offering assistance when none was required and complimenting them at every opportunity. But that wasn't Paul's nature. He put in his extra hours early in the morning and late into the evening, long after the consultants had gone home. And in any case, he wasn't one that yearned for the trappings of success; rather the opposite, he was content to have a small car, unpretentious clothing and a modest home.

Kate's frustration and anger went round and round, fermenting in her head. To play golf with Mr Potts when they should be enjoying themselves with friends in the Lakes was the last straw. When he left the house this morning she could happily have screwed his neck! It was inexcusable. He had known all about their plans to get away for the weekend. Damn it, he wasn't even a golfer; he hadn't touched his blasted golf clubs since he left medical school.

In a cold fury, Kate washed and dried the dishes, stuck some dirty clothes in the washing machine, tidied the bedroom and living room in an attempt to work off her rage but all to no avail. With time on her hands, and seething that Paul had behaved so badly, so thoughtlessly, so selfishly, she tried to read a nursing journal but was no more successful than she had been with the newspaper!. There must be more to life than this, she thought. If Paul is going to be away so much, neglecting me, leaving me on my own like this, then I must find something to occupy my time, something meaningful to do. I'm damned if I'm going to spend the rest of my life just mooching around doing nothing.

Back in the kitchen to make herself another drink, she pulled at the cupboard door to get the coffee and sugar. It was a new cupboard that Paul had fitted above the working surface a few days earlier. This damn door's too stiff, she thought, as she gave it a fearful tug. With an ominous crack, the screws securing the top of the cupboard to the wall came loose and the cupboard hinged forward towards her. As it did so, the cupboard doors swung open, catching her a glancing blow on her forehead.

"Help!" she cried. "For God's sake someone help!" But there was no one to hear. Syrup, sugar, tea and jam spilled over her shoulders, down her dress and onto the floor. Pushing upwards with both hands, she managed to stop the cupboard coming completely off the wall but try as she might, she couldn't push it back into place. Even had she done so, it would again have fallen forward onto her the minute she let go. Again she screamed for help as desperately she hung on - but to no avail. Eventually her arms tired and she was forced to let go. The entire cupboard and contents came crashing over her on to the floor.

Bewildered, her head aching, she sat on a chair and surveyed the damage. Broken cups, plates and their best china tea set, the one her father had given her as a wedding present, lay in pieces amongst the sticky syrup and jam on the floor.

"Damn Mr Potts and damn Paul too," she shouted out loud, as the tears began to flow. "If he'd been here and fixed the bloody cupboard properly this would never have happened."

For ten minutes she sat lonely and miserable contemplating the mess around her. Again her thoughts turned to her relationship with Paul. She couldn't let things continue as they were. They were drifting apart. If this went on any longer they would have to split and go their separate ways. She loved her nursing, loved the contact with her patients but she needed more from life. She simply had to find something that would bring them back together, something that would rekindle their relationship, something that would make Paul want to spend time with her. Sadly she remembered the days when just the thought of a night alone in the flat with her was the only magnet needed to drag him away from his patients but even that didn't seem to attract him anymore.

Then an idea struck her, a thought that had been in the back of her mind for some time. It was only the germ of an idea but it excited her; and the more she thought about it, the more it appealed to her. But would she dare to carry it through? Would she be brave enough? It would mean deceiving Paul, something she'd never done before and not something that she would want to do. But if she were to share her idea with him, he would most certainly reject it, as he had rejected it when she had spoken of it previously. In which case nothing would happen and they would continue to drift apart. Yet if her plan did come to fruition, there could be no turning back. The day would arrive when he discovered that he had been deceived and when he realised what she had done, he would probably be furious. Well so be it. If it wasn't for his selfish behaviour, she wouldn't now be sitting with a sore head surrounded by the chaos resulting from his inexpert DIY efforts, their plans for a weekend spent together in tatters. In that instant, she came to her decision; she would implement her scheme and if he didn't approve of what she was going to do, that was just too bad. To hell with him!

Feeling more cheerful, she tidied the kitchen as best she could, then went upstairs to inspect the damage to her forehead in the bathroom mirror. She couldn't feel any blood but a swelling had appeared and some early bruising was developing. She would have a black eye to explain to Sister Rutherford when she reported for duty on Monday morning. As she looked at her reflection in the mirror, it reinforced her resolve to take matters into her own hands. The woman she saw was young, she was vibrant and energetic, not the type to sit and mope at home all weekend waiting for her man to come home; she would do something about it.

She opened the bathroom cabinet and found the bottle of aspirins. She swallowed a couple of tablets to ease her headache then picked up the other tablets that shared the same shelf. They were in a blister pack arranged with seven tablets in each of four rows. She studied them for a moment, then taking her courage in both hands, she burst the blisters one by one and dropped the contents into the toilet. As each one fell into the water with a satisfying 'plop', she felt fiercely elated and liberated. Quickly before her nerve failed her, she slipped into the bedroom and collected a similar pack of tablets from her handbag, this one already half empty. She disposed of these into the toilet as well. Finally she put the remains of the two packs in her pocket; she would dispose of them in the dustbin later where Paul would not find them.

For a moment, Kate stood looking at the collection of small pink pills at the bottom of the pan, pills that had been standing between her and her heart's desire, stopping her from fulfilling her dreams, preventing her from becoming a real woman. Just for a moment she hesitated then, her decision made, she pulled the toilet chain and watched as the water rose, bubbled and swirled before finally subsided. The contraceptive pills that she had never wanted to take had been washed away. She had no idea what the result of her action would be, that was now in the lap of the Gods, but as she looked down and saw the water now calm and clear, she too felt calmer and clearer in her mind than she had for a very long time.

Chapter Twenty One

Paul was certain that his first golf shot in his match against Mr Potts would be a disaster and so it proved. There were simply too many thoughts chasing round in his mind. Inevitably he swung the club too fast, was far too tense and lifted his head instead of watching the club strike the ball. The ball scuttled forward along the ground and came to rest on the lady's tee some 40 yards away. He heard a suppressed laugh.

"Oh dear," he heard the Brigadier say, great satisfaction evident in his voice, "you'll have to wear a skirt when you play your next shot, young man."

Paul looked round at the smiling faces. Only Dr Lester looked sympathetic. "Hard luck, Lambert," he said.

Paul put the six iron back in his bag and walked forward with Mr Potts. He comforted himself with the thought that the club captain wouldn't be in such close attendance when he played his second shot. Sadly though, Paul's next attempt was a carbon copy of his first, as was the one after that. *Watch the ball, for God's sake!* a voice screamed in his head but he was so anxious to see where the ball had gone, that he lifted his head every time. Fortunately the ball stayed on the fairway but it took a further four shots before he reached the green. All the while Leslie Potts looked on; the expression on his face revealing that he was distinctly unimpressed.

By the time they had both putted out, Leslie Potts had completed the hole in five shots, Paul had taken eleven!

"I think that's just my hole, Lambert," Mr Potts said sarcastically.

"Look, I 'm sorry about that, Sir" Paul said as they walked to the next tee. "Just give me a moment to have a few practice swings. It's a long time since I last played."

"Well just for a minute or so," Mr Potts replied. "Don't forget we have the club captain playing behind us. It wouldn't do to keep him waiting."

Paul stood to the side of the tee and took some practice swings making sure he was still looking down as the club swished through the grass.

"Right, that's enough," Mr Potts said a few moments later. "The next hole is a par five. There's nothing very difficult about it; it's just long and straight. There are no particular hazards; you can practice as you play it."

Paul stood back and watched as his boss again took out his driver and played his shot. He had to admire it. The swing was full and smooth, there seemed to be very little effort in it and if indeed he had only been playing for a couple of years, he had made remarkable progress. Maybe it was the result of a lot of expensive lessons from the club professional as the Brigadier had remarked, but even so Mr Potts had a natural ability. Once again the ball flew long and straight, landing in the middle of the fairway.

Paul made no attempt to match Mr Potts' drive. He simply concentrated on watching the club make contact with the ball, attempting to play gentle shots down the fairway. He duffed a couple but at least two were reasonable. He reached the green in six shots; Mr Potts was there in three!

"Sir," he said, "it's a long time since I last picked up a golf club. Truly I can't give you a game. Wouldn't it be better if I just play for practice? We could forget about the match."

"Certainly not! By all means regard it as practice if you like Lambert, but the match must go on. You see the captain said he thought you would win, so I bet him a fiver that I would beat you by at least four holes. Fortunately, that won't be a problem; I'm 'two up' already!"

If Paul hadn't already been determined to do his best before this exchange, he certainly was now! His boss was being cocky, bragging like that to the Brigadier. He hadn't particularly taken to the club captain but he would rather he won the money than Mr Potts!

For the next few holes, Paul played all his shots with his six iron. Inevitably he was out driven by Mr Potts who continued to hit beautiful tee shots with his driver but as a little of his old rhythm returned, Paul's play gradually improved. He continued to fluff the occasional shot but mostly hit the ball cleanly, managing to keep the ball on the fairway and stay out of trouble.

Unfortunately though, after nine holes, the halfway point in the round, Mr Potts was 'three up', which became 'four up' by the time they reached the thirteenth. This was a 'dog leg', just 250 yards long. It required a short shot to the corner, then a similar shot to the green. Mr Potts struck off first but hooked his ball into some grass that was so long and dense Paul reckoned it would be almost impossible for him to play his ball even if he managed to find it. It presented him with a great opportunity to reduce the deficit.

Paul plucked his trusty six iron from his bag then, concentrating hard, played his shot. Although the contact was good, the ball flew slightly to the right and settled adjacent to a tree. It wasn't an ideal result but Paul looked to be far better placed than his opponent.

Paul wasn't aware there was anything in the rules of golf that said you are required to search for your opponent's ball but it was the courteous thing to do, and certainly the wisest if you were a junior doctor playing with your boss! They had a rough idea where it was but the grass was knee deep and the ball wasn't visible. It seemed unlikely they would find it unless they chanced to tread on it. Working as a pair, they walked slowly backwards and forwards, taking small steps, systematically flattening the grass. Five minutes passed then six and seven and still the ball hadn't been found. Paul was well aware that the official time allowed to search was five minutes, after which the ball was deemed to be lost and penalty shots were incurred. Mr Potts however continued the search.

Ten minutes had elapsed before Mr Potts finally said "You go and play your ball Lambert, while I have one last look."

Paul walked across to the other side of the fairway and was pleased to see his own ball was sitting up nicely on some short springy grass. When he took his practice swing however, he found that his club just touched a twig that was dangling from an overhanging tree. Not wanting it to interfere with his shot, he changed to a shorter club, struck the ball and was delighted when it settled on the heart of the green, no more than a couple of yards from the pin. With Mr Potts in trouble, this was a hole he must inevitably win.

Well satisfied, he turned just in time to see Mr Potts play his ball from the fairway adjacent to the flattened grass where they had been searching. Paul hadn't seen him play his second shot but had to believe that not only had the consultant managed to find his ball, he had successfully got it back into play. Had he been very lucky, or had there been some sleight of hand?

"Lambert," Mr Potts said as they approached the green. "When you took your practice swing for that last shot, you dislodged some leaves from the tree you were under. I'm afraid that breaches rule 13.2 and costs you the hole."

"But Sir, it didn't affect the stroke I played at all," Paul protested as boldly as he dared.

"I agree it's a shame but with money at stake, we must play to the strict rules of golf." There was finality in Mr Potts' voice that indicated that the matter was not for further discussion.

Paul was furious. He had come to play what he had presumed would be a friendly game of golf. He hadn't imagined it would become a highly competitive match played strictly to the rules of the Royal and Ancient Club. His determination increased tenfold; he was obviously going to lose but he would do his damnedest to see the game would cost Mr Potts his fiver!

The next few holes were halved, but Paul managed to win the seventeenth thanks to an extremely lucky shot which, to Mr Potts' dismay, landed short of the green then ran all of twenty five yards before dropping into the hole! Paul was now just four down with one hole to play.

The eighteenth was a long par four. The lake that Paul had noticed as he motored up the drive ran the length of the fairway on its left hand side. Had he not been so intent on the game, Paul would have stopped to admire the scene. The grass on the banks was neatly mown, water lilies floated on the surface and a decorative fountain sent concentric ripples across the water where ducks and moorhens swam peacefully. The eighteenth green was situated at the far end of the lake, beyond which stood the splendid clubhouse. Paul could see club members enjoying drinks in the sunshine on the patio overlooking the green.

Paul looked down the fairway. It was quite narrow and the water on the left was an obvious danger. Did he need to risk using his driver? Probably not. He took his five iron out of his bag. Nice and easy, he told himself, and for God's sake watch the ball. Fortunately the contact was sweet; the ball flew straight and finished in the middle of the fairway. Paul heaved a huge sigh of relief.

"Not a bad shot," Lambert, Mr Potts commented, "but surgeons need to be bolder than that. Remember the old maxim. *'Surgeons need the heart of a lion, the eyes of a hawk and the hands of a lady'*. They should have no fear. Here let me show you."

Without the slightest hesitation he pulled out his driver. Paul had to admire his confidence. His ego knew no bounds. He watched as

Mr Potts placed his ball on a tee peg. Please let him hit it into the water, Paul's malevolent brain said silently. But he didn't. He hit another perfect shot and the ball flew over two hundred yards straight down the middle of the fairway, at least fifty yards beyond Paul's.

"There you are, my boy," the consultant said. "That's the way to do it!"

Paul knew as he walked down the fairway that the odds were now stacked against him. Reaching his ball, he decided his best strategy was to avoid the water by playing down the right hand side even though that made the distance to the green slightly longer. Choosing another iron, he played a perfectly acceptable shot which left him nicely placed eighty yards from the green.

Meanwhile, Mr Potts had marched down the fairway and was standing by his ball. He was some 170 yards from the green, but with the lake abutting on the putting surface, he would have to fly his ball all the way to the target. Anything short would end up in the water. Paul joined him as he pondered what shot to play. He picked a four iron out of his bag. Great, Paul thought, he's going to take a risk that he doesn't need to. All he needs to win his bet is to halve this hole. If this shot ends in the water, his ego will be the cause of his downfall.

Concentrating hard, Mr Potts made two practice swings before settling over his ball. Then he had second thoughts. He put the four iron back in his bag and selected a six iron instead. Paul swore to himself. Mr Potts was opting to play to the right of the water. It was the sensible safety shot.

"Has the lion lost his heart?" Paul asked, applying a bit of gamesmanship.

Mr Potts looked at him and smiled. "No, he hasn't," he replied, "but that old adage ought to have an extra line in it, you know. Surgeons also need to be as wise as an owl and this is a moment for a bit of wisdom."

With that he played his shot. Possibly the pressure of playing when fellow members were watching affected him, perhaps he was still debating whether to attempt the high risk shot or maybe Paul's remark had piqued him; but the ball flew a long way to the right of his intended landing area. It finished on a concrete path that separated the fairway from some rough ground adjacent to the car park.

"Damn," Mr Potts muttered. "My worst shot of the round."

The consultant continued to mutter as they strolled together to where Paul's ball lay. With no hazards to contend with, Paul played a simple shot onto the green, the ball coming to rest some eight yards from the pin.

Meanwhile Mr Potts had walked to the path and picked up his ball.

"I obviously can't play off concrete; I'll take a free drop," he said as he tossed the ball back onto the fairway.

"I don't think that's allowed, Sir. That will put you nearer the hole."

"But it will be quite unplayable over there," Mr Potts protested pointing to the brambles on the far side of the path. "Surely common sense says I can take a drop where I have some chance of getting the ball back into play?"

Paul knew he had a decision to make. Was it worth antagonising Mr Potts while playing a game to which he should never have agreed? Would the consultant hold it against him when he needed a reference? Probably not but in any case, the way Paul felt at that moment, he really didn't care whether or not he upset his boss. In picking up his ball, Mr Potts had just assumed that Paul would be too timid to raise an objection. And Paul hadn't forgotten the episode with the leaves that he was said to have dislodged on the overhanging tree. Well Paul certainly did object. He objected strongly and he wanted to puncture the man's over inflated ego.

"I'm sorry, Sir but you said we were playing the strict rules of golf and the rules say you can't move your ball nearer to the hole."

It was the first time he'd ever stood up to his boss and he could feel his heart beating ten to the dozen. Surely Kate would have been proud of him.

Reluctantly, a scowling Mr Potts picked up his ball and tossed it into the brambles. Paul decided there was no need to chide him for not dropping the ball from his shoulder in the accepted Ancient and Royal fashion. He knew it would be well nigh impossible for the consultant to play the ball onto the green.

So it proved. Twice he hacked at it and on neither occasion did he shift it more than a couple of inches. In disgust he picked up his ball and put it in his pocket.

"Your hole, Lambert," he said sourly, "But I think you'll agree that I beat you soundly."

"Yes indeed you did Sir; you were three up at the end. Well done. Now if you'll excuse me, I think I'll slip away. My wife and I have plans for this evening."

****

As Paul drove home, he felt reasonably pleased with the way the afternoon had gone. After a dreadful start, he had played some reasonable golf. True he had lost the match but that was only to be expected given the time that had elapsed since his last game. More importantly, he had caused Mr Potts to lose his bet. That would teach him not to be so cocky.

Paul though had two worries. The first was that his boss was clearly irritated that he hadn't been able to bully him into allowing him a free drop on the last hole. He hoped there wouldn't be a price to pay at some stage in the future! His second and far greater concern was that Kate would still be furious that he had deserted her for the day but as it happened he needn't have worried. He found Kate in a surprisingly good mood. She greeted him with a hug and a kiss, didn't mention his absence or their earlier row, made light of the chaos in the kitchen and chatted cheerfully as they drove to join Sally and Colin. And when they turned in for the night, he found that she was wearing the same flimsy negligee she had worn on their honeymoon.

Chapter Twenty Two

Victoria Kent had already worked alongside Mr Potts on the Surgical Five wards for a couple of years before Paul arrived on the unit. She was battling against a well-established prejudice within medicine, that of sex discrimination. 50 years previously, the consultants at the City General Hospital had all been male, as the portraits on the walls of the main corridor bore testament. Even at this time, women comprised only a tiny proportion of consultants in the NHS. Some had made the grade in less competitive specialties but there wasn't a female surgeon in any hospital within fifty miles. Yet academically, women were just as capable as men. They were equally dexterous and just as able to undertake technical surgical procedures. In general, they were better communicators than their male counterparts; they couldn't possibly have been worse in that respect than Leslie Potts!

Paul would have been loath to admit that he harboured any sexual prejudice, but in truth, before meeting Victoria, he had wondered if she might be a tough hirsute 'hockey type', with a flat chest and a booming voice. Such irreverent thoughts were quickly dispelled when he first met her. Of average height, she had a natural fresh complexion which made her look younger than her 32 years. With her hair worn short in a practical fashion and wearing clothes that were comfortable and discrete, she was accepted without question by the nursing staff. She had warm brown eyes and an engaging smile that quickly put patients at their ease. The more Paul saw of her, the more he liked and admired her. Unassuming, without any airs or graces, she was thoughtful and quietly spoken, yet her words were chosen with care. What a shame, he thought, that Victoria had opted off the surgical training ladder and settled for a staff grade post; she would have made an excellent consultant.

Victoria had worked for Mr Potts long enough to have become aware of the flaws in his character. When Paul first arrived on the unit, she had offered him some words of advice.

"There's something I need to warn you about Paul, as one junior doctor to another." Paul had smiled. The term *'junior'* when applied to hospital doctors meant anyone who was not a consultant. Some *'juniors'*, such as a newly qualified doctor undertaking their first weeks work on the wards were indeed very inexperienced. Others, such as Victoria were quite senior. She had been qualified for nine years and was able to carry significant responsibility and perform complex surgical operations.

"In recent months, certainly since you worked here last," Victoria explained, "Mr Potts has taken exception to the presence of orthopaedic patients on our ward. It happened a lot last winter when there was snow on the ground. People were slipping on the ice and breaking wrists and ankles. The orthopaedic beds were all full, so some of their patients overflowed and 'lodged' on our ward."

"That's what happens in every hospital I've ever worked in," Paul commented, "don't tell me the boss objects."

"Unfortunately he does. He gets extremely angry and we all suffer. So please, for the sake of a quiet life, try to keep orthopaedic patients out of his beds if at all possible."

"What's his objection to them?"

"I honestly don't know," Victoria replied. "Perhaps he's had a disagreement with one of the orthopaedic consultants at some stage; maybe one of his patients couldn't be admitted because there was an orthopaedic patient blocking a bed on our ward. Frankly though, if there's a major road accident with multiple victims, they have no option but to place their patients wherever a bed is available. What makes Mr Potts' attitude even more unreasonable is that from time to time we lodge patients on the orthopaedic wards!"

"It's also unreasonable to involve us in disputes between seniors," Paul commented. "Life's stressful enough, without the worry of preventing arguments between consultants."

****

It became apparent that Sister Ashbrook was also aware of Mr Potts' intolerance of orthopaedic lodgers when she rang Paul at 7.45 one morning. He was fresh out of bed and his face was covered in shaving foam. From the tone of her voice it was obvious that she was worried.

"Paul, I've just come on duty and found that an orthopaedic patient has been admitted during the night. What's worse, he's in one of Mr Potts' beds. You'd better get rid of him fast or there's going to be a dreadful scene when he arrives to take his ward round later this morning."

Paul recalled Victoria's warning about orthopaedic lodgers. Now Sister Ashbrook was in a flap. It seemed that Mr Potts' rages at orthopaedic lodgers must indeed be fearful to behold.

"Not to worry, Sister," he reassured her. "I'll have a word with their houseman and get him shifted."

Paul chanced to meet Jane Holme, the orthopaedic house officer, at the breakfast table. She looked weary having been up for a couple of hours in the night. He spoke to her about the orthopaedic lodger.

"Oh, he's an old boy of about 85," Jane replied, spreading marmalade thickly onto her toast. She believed that a good helping of sugar would help sustain her through the day. "He fell yesterday whilst he was out shopping. He's broken his wrist and sprained an ankle. His wrist was straightened under an anaesthetic last night."

"So I presume he'll be discharged this morning," Paul said, relieved that the problem had been so easily resolved.

"Normally he would but he lives alone, he's got no close family and no carers. We're going to have to fix him up with some support before he goes home. But don't worry; he'll only be with you for a day or two."

"Have you no beds on the orthopaedic ward?"

"Sorry but we haven't. Yesterday was a busy day for us. We've overflowed onto Surgical Two as well."

It was obvious that the lodger would have to stay where he was on Surgical Five and Mr Potts would just have to accept the situation. Paul wasn't particularly concerned, after all, only the week before, when all their beds were full, a patient of Mr Potts had been placed on the orthopaedic ward.

As usual, at 8.30 Paul met Victoria on the male ward to undertake a quick review of the patients before Mr Potts arrived. By this time however, Sister Ashbrook had become quite agitated.

"You simply must get rid of the orthopaedic patient. All hell will be let loose if you don't."

Paul explained that the patient couldn't be discharged home for social reasons, nor was there any prospect of moving him back to the orthopaedic ward.

"Don't worry, Sister," he added. "I'm sure Mr Potts will understand."

"No he damn well won't," Sister replied. She looked pleadingly at Victoria who turned to Paul.

"Paul," she said, "you do a quick ward round and make sure everything is shipshape before Mr Potts arrives. I'll see what I can do about this orthopaedic patient."

As Paul worked his way, patient by patient, down the ward, it was impossible for him not to notice the orthopaedic lodger. He was in a bed half way down on the left hand side; his freshly applied 'Plaster of Paris' cast and brilliant white triangular sling stood out like a beacon of light in the midst of the general surgical patients. A pair of crutches and a walking frame stood at his bedside. It simply will not be possible, Paul thought, for Victoria to hide his presence from the eagle eyed consultant surgeon.

Chapter Twenty Three

A couple of hours later, the team congregated in the office on the male ward for Mr Potts' formal round; it was one of the highlights of the week. There was always a tense atmosphere in the room on these occasions. Whereas Sir William could be relied upon to be the perfect gentleman, generous with his praise and constructive with any criticism, Mr Potts was unpredictable. If in good humour, he could be charming and affable. However some minor incident could upset him and then his mood would rapidly change; his brow would darken and he would become irritable and short tempered. Woe betide any junior who crossed him at such a time. He was quite capable of reducing a junior nurse or medical student to tears and at times seemed to take delight in doing so!

Victoria, having worked for a dozen or more surgeons during her training, was in no way discomforted by Mr Potts' behaviour. Easy going and confident, she was well informed of the patients and there were no gaps in her knowledge which could be criticised. Besides she knew from experience that the boss always chose easier targets when he needed to let off steam. Paul, conscientious as always, had prepared himself well for the ward round. It was unlikely the consultant would find any reason to give him a roasting but that didn't stop him from being mildly apprehension.

Janet Smith, the house officer, didn't give a damn for the consultant's personality or his temper tantrums. She was grateful for the support he had given her over the McGovern affair and would allow him a little bit of rope but she despised his attitude to women and if he made any personal or sexists remarks, she would give as good as she got. She had already lined up her next job in Sydney, Australia and she didn't give a fig for Mr Potts' opinion of her.

It was the medical students however who were trembling in their shoes. This was to be their first encounter with Mr Potts and all knew of his fearsome reputation. Students who had already passed this way had forewarned them of the fate that befell anyone who upset him. Each of them had been allocated a patient by Sir William and they were expected to be fully informed about that patient's diagnosis and treatment. During the round at least one of them would be picked on to present the case to the consultant. But which one of them would it be?

Sir William could be relied upon to walk through the doors on the dot of ten but, as with his moods, Mr Potts was capricious. Victoria, Paul and Janet had many other tasks awaiting their attention and found the waiting an irritation. Minutes wasted during the day meant extra time to be worked in the evening before going off duty. For the students though, each of them reading and rereading the case histories they had prepared, waiting for the consultant to arrive simply increased their anxiety.

Finally, half an hour late, Mr Potts burst through the door a beaming smile on his face. "Sorry to be a few minutes late," he boomed, "I had a bit of a problem in the private patient's wing; one of my patients had a spot of bother with constipation. I should have got old Sir William to pop in a couple of suppositories shouldn't I? Happily it's all resolved now." He laughed then noticed the medical students who had sprung to attention the moment he appeared.

"Now what have we here? Another bunch of students for us to whip into shape, eh?" He turned to Victoria. "Well let's hope they're a bit brighter than the last lot. They wouldn't have made the grade as vets never mind as doctors!"

Mr Potts looked along the row of the eight students, assessing them in turn. There was the slightest sniff as he noted the two overseas students, his eye lingered for a moment on the tall blond Eleanor Croft then fixed on Steven Morris who was the last of the line.

"Unless that fungus growing on your face is a religious necessity, shave the damn thing off," he instructed. "I don't allow beards in theatre, they're stuffed full of germs."

Morris, embarrassed and not wishing to discuss the assault that had caused his facial scarring, was stunned at so sudden and unprovoked an attack. Gamely he tried to explain.

"Mr Potts, Sir, I er have... that is to say.,,, I er..." he started but Victoria came quickly to his rescue.

"Sir, perhaps I can explain the reason for the beard to you later," she said quietly, "and in private," she added giving the consultant a meaningful look.

For a moment Mr Potts looked puzzled.

"Alright then, if there's a reason for the beard, you can keep it but shorten it by at least 50% and whenever you come into theatre you will cover it with two masks instead of one. Is that understood? Now, we've wasted enough time already; let's go and see the patients."

Mr Potts left the office and to Paul's surprise turned right towards the side wards instead of turning left and passing through the double doors onto the main ward.

"All your patients are on the main ward, Sir," Paul commented.

"Not today, they're not Lambert." The consultant raised an eyebrow to Sister Ashbrook. "Which side ward Sister?" he asked.

"Room three, Mr Potts."

Paul's heart gave a lurch; surely there couldn't be a patient of whom he was completely unaware. What the hell could he say if the boss asked about him?

Paul looked at the occupant of the side room in some surprise. He was a man in his fifties who, unlike every other patient on the ward, was wearing his outdoor clothes, a man whom he had never seen before. Paul prided himself on always being well informed of all the patients, particularly those of Mr Potts. Where was the patient of Sir William's that Paul had seen in this very side ward not two hours before? How on earth had this man gained access to the ward without his knowledge? No new patients were scheduled for admission that day, nor had it been their day to accept emergencies. Presumably the patient had been slipped in from the consultant's private rooms, like the local MP Harry Grimshaw and if so, it must have been arranged by the house officer. He would have a word with Janet later to stress that he needed to be kept informed of new patients.

"Hello, Mr Walton," Mr Potts began, "I'm grateful to you for agreeing to come in like this at short notice. It will help me to judge just how bright these 'would-be doctors' are."

He turned to the students who were crowding around the bed, each hoping that they would not be the one he picked on. Unsurprisingly, his eye fell on Miss Croft!

"Miss Croft, you look to be a bright attractive young thing. Come and examine Mr Walton's legs." The prejudice in the words was lost, or possibly ignored, by the student but not by Janet who bridled at the sexual implication. She was bursting to express her indignation but managed to hold her tongue at the last minute.

Mr Walton took off his trousers and lay on the bed. The sight that met Paul's eyes was quite extraordinary. Not only did the patient have the worst varicose veins he had ever seen, but both legs were discoloured by severe varicose eczema that extended from his ankles to his knees. A small ulcer was developing on the inner aspect of one ankle.

"Now Miss Croft, describe carefully what you can see" Mr Potts instructed.

Belying the old adage that all blonds are dumb, Miss Croft accurately and succinctly described the appearance and correctly made a diagnosis of varicose veins with associated complications.

"Well done, well done indeed. Not only good looking but smart as well," Mr Potts remarked beaming.

This second remark was too much for Janet.

"What on earth is the relevance of Miss Croft's appearance? Surely what matters is the accuracy of her diagnosis."

Mr Potts face creased into a huge smile. He enjoyed these exchanges with his prickly house officer. They amused him immensely; adding a little spice to his day.

"Well, my dear, diagnostic accuracy is important of course, but coming from pretty lips makes it easier on the ear, don't you think?"

"So would you have made a comment on the appearance of one of the male students?"

"I doubt it, Janet, my dear, I doubt it very much."

"My name is Miss Smith, or Doctor Smith if you prefer, as you well know; and I am not *your dear*." Janet's voice was clear, cold and precise.

Paul was astonished at Janet's bravery in challenging Mr Potts in such a bold direct manner and amazed that she always got away with it.

Mr Potts stifled his laughter. "Touché," he remarked, holding up a hand to show that the exchange was at an end. He then turned to the rest of the group.

"Now I want you all to watch very closely whilst Mr Walton performs his party trick. Afterwards I shall ask you to explain what you see. Miss Croft, will you help Mr Walton off the bed please."

As he spoke, he nodded to Jimmy the ward orderly who had slipped into the room unnoticed. With a great smile on his face Mr Walton sat up, Miss Croft supporting him by one arm as he did so. As the patient swung his legs over the side of the bed, Jimmy positioned himself to support the other arm. For a few seconds Mr Walton stood facing the students who were wondering what they were supposed to observe. Then quite suddenly, the colour drained from his face, he swayed slightly then with glazed eyes, his knees buckled and he collapsed. Fortunately Jimmy, who clearly knew what to expect, caught Mr Walton before he hit the floor and shovelled the unconscious patient back onto the bed. Miss Croft, taken completely unawares, gave a high pitched yelp partly in surprise and partly because one of the Mr Walton's flailing arms had struck her a forcible blow across the chest as he fell.

Jimmy made the now comatose patient comfortable and with a quick thumbs up to Mr Potts, left the room as silently as he had entered.

"Now," Mr Potts asked, "Who knows what the patient's pulse will be right now?"

The students were too stunned to respond.

"Well who can tell me how we should treat the patient?" Again there was silence.

But Paul knew and so did Victoria. Appalled that Mr Potts was prepared to leave the patient to recover spontaneously they both dashed to the foot of the bed, grabbed one leg each and elevated them as high as they could. 30 seconds later Mr Walton slowly came round. He still looked a ghastly colour and his brow glistened with sweat. Suddenly he retched. Sister Ashbrook grabbed a vomit bowl from the bedside locker just in time to prevent Mr Wilson's partly digested breakfast spraying over the bedclothes.

Mr Potts ignored the patient as he quizzed the students on the events they had witnessed. Why had Mr Walton lost consciousness, had they noticed what had happened to his veins when he adopted an upright posture, what had happened to his pulse before and after his collapse, why had his face been so pale? Despite being prompted by the consultant, it took the students several minutes to regain their composure and explain what they had seen. Eventually though, Mr Potts helped them to understand that the minute that Mr Walton stood up, such a vast quantity of blood had dropped into his huge varicose veins that there simply hadn't been enough blood available to be pumped to his head. His blood pressure had dropped dramatically and his brain had been starved of oxygen causing him to faint. Paul was appalled. How many brain cells had suffered as a result? And the way in which the patient had performed this 'party trick', suggested that this wasn't the first time Mr Potts had arranged this demonstration for the benefit of students.

"Thanks Mr Walton, that was very helpful," Mr Potts said. "We'll get you a cup of tea and some toast and give you a couple of minutes to recover before you go. If you pop in to see my secretary on your way out, she'll see you alright for your trouble."

He turned for the door. "Now let's get on with this ward round."

As was his custom, Mr Potts strode to the far end of the ward and saw his patients one by one as he worked his way back to the door. This allowed him to exit directly into the office. He disliked finishing at the end furthest from the door since that gave patients an opportunity to high jack him with additional questions as he returned to the office. To the student's great relief, he ignored them while he worked, seeing his patients in a brisk, one might say brusque, but business-like fashion.

Paul was anxious to see whether Mr Potts' reaction to the orthopaedic lodger would be as fearsome as Victoria and Sister Ashbrook had intimated but to his great astonishment, the patient had vanished. The bed was empty; indeed it had been remade with fresh linen. The bedside locker was bare. The patient, together with his plaster cast, triangular bandage, crutches and walking frame had disappeared into thin air. The empty bed awaited its next occupant. Paul looked at Victoria in amazement as they walked past the spot where the lodger had been. She caught his eye but said nothing, she just winked and her face eased into a slightly smug smile. In due course the round was completed without undue incident, without any temper tantrums and to the students' great relief, without any of them being required to present their patients to the consultant - but the minute Mr Potts departed, Paul demanded to know how Victoria had managed to weave such magic.

"Easy," she said. "The patient had his wrist fracture reduced last night. That means that he needs a check x-ray today to see that the bones have been set in a satisfactory position. The patient is now in the radiology department having his x-ray. The rest of the transformation is down to Sister. She goes along with the subterfuge for the sake of peace and quiet. We've both seen Mr Potts' reaction to orthopaedic lodgers and believe me, when you've witnessed it once; you don't want to see it again."

"Well done, well done indeed," Paul commented, admiration evident in his voice. "Now what are we going to do about Mr Walton. Every time he performs that 'party trick' of his, he's knocking off dozens of brain cells; I don't suppose the boss has explained that to him."

Victoria, whose views on the matter coincided with Paul's, suggested that they ought to express their concerns so together they went back to the side room. Mr Walton was just gathering his things together before going home.

"Did you come here today purely to help to teach the students?" Victoria asked.

Mr Walton grinned hugely. "Yes it's something Mr Potts asks me to do a couple of times a year. It allows me to have a day off work and he gives me a bob or two for my trouble."

"Has he ever suggested operating on your veins?" Paul asked, fearful that Mr Potts might be deliberately deferring Mr Wilson's treatment to enable this demonstration to be repeated for the benefit of each new batch of students.

"Yes he has. I'm on the waiting list, though first I have to get rid of this nasty ulcer and angry skin rash. That's why I wear these compression stockings."

"That's fair enough," Victoria commented, "but if I were you I should call it a day. You see, every time you faint, your brain gets starved of oxygen. It won't be doing you any good in the long term."

"But I quite enjoy it and if it helps the students to become good doctors."

"Well the decision must be yours, but if it were me, I should definitely put my own health first!"

"And so would I," Paul added emphatically.

Chapter Twenty Four

"Hello, is that the surgeon on call at the City General Hospital that I am speaking to?"

The accent was unmistakably Indian and Paul assumed it was one of the local GP's referring a patient to be seen in casualty with a view to admission. Being continuously on call from Friday morning until Monday tea time made for a long and exhausting weekend. He had hoped that this Sunday evening would be quiet; he desperately needed to catch up on his sleep. Unusually, he hadn't been disturbed at all during the Friday night but had been called to casualty twice after midnight on Saturday. One of the patients had a perforated ulcer and he had worked for a couple of hours resuscitating him and getting him fit for his operation. Having patched him up in theatre on the Sunday morning, he had then spent the afternoon doing the ward round that he would normally have finished before Sunday lunch.

"Yes, Paul Lambert here. I'm on duty for the surgical side," Paul replied wearily.

"I am sending you man with very bad aneurysm. Blood pressure in boots. He is one very shocked patient."

"You're sending me what?" Paul exclaimed, now very much alert.

"Man with aneurysm of aorta. Wanted to let you know so you can get prepared. I send blood by taxi when ready but will not be full cross match."

"Who is that speaking?" Paul demanded much alarmed. Mr Potts was on a week's leave and no-one else was trained to undertake vascular surgery.

"I am Doctor Samit Ahmed, casualty officer at Middleton Hospital."

"But you can't send him here. We haven't got a surgeon able to treat him."

"He die if he stay here, so he already in ambulance on the way to you. He leave us five minutes ago. He is called Mister Baxendale. I send his wife with him."

'Christ Almighty', Paul thought. 'What the hell am I to do?' The Middleton was about twenty minutes away but an ambulance with a blue light and siren on a Sunday evening when the traffic was light would make it in half that time. The patient would arrive at the City General within the next few minutes. All he could do was pray that Dr Ahmed had got the diagnosis wrong. He rang casualty and warned them to expect a shocked patient, possibly with a ruptured aneurysm and then ran down to the department. He arrived at the same time as the patient and within seconds he knew that the diagnosis was correct. The patient was a man in his sixties. He was indeed profoundly shocked; he was pale, was sweating with a racing pulse and low blood pressure. And there was a large pulsating mass in his abdomen. Without surgery the man would die within the next couple of hours but there was no one available to perform the surgery that he so desperately needed. The nearest specialist centre was in London and there was no way that the patient would survive the journey.

In his panic, he had forgotten to ask Dr Ahmed how much blood he had requested or how long it would be before it was available. He grabbed the casualty officer.

"Get eight pints on emergency cross match. Tell the lab to ring the Middleton, they will already know the blood group – that may save a little time."

He needed help but from whom? He rang Sir William. The phone rang... and rang.....and rang. Please, please, please don't be out, Paul pleaded to himself. Finally the phone was answered.

"Oh, it's you Lambert. Sorry to be a bit slow coming to the phone. I was just tidying up the vegetable patch in the garden and had to take my boots off. Now what can I do for you?" It was reassuring for Paul to hear the consultant's calm voice. Quickly he explained the situation.

"And you don't think he would survive another transfer?" Sir William queried.
"Not a chance, Sir. He really is *'in extremis'*."

There was a long pause as the senior consultant considered the situation. Finally he spoke.

"Well Lambert, if he won't survive another ambulance journey and he'll die if he doesn't have an operation - then we have no choice. We'll have to perform the surgery here. I'll join you in theatre in a few minutes."

He rang off, leaving Paul to organise the theatre, the anaesthetist and to ring the Middleton Hospital to find out how much blood they had arranged and how soon it would be available.

As Paul waited for the patient and Sir William to join him in the theatre, he wondered how his boss would cope operating on an aneurysm, never having performed this type of surgery before. He was well read of course, but he was in his sixties and about to retire. In theatre, he was slow and methodical; Paul doubted he was equipped for such a dramatic emergency.

"Lambert," Sir William said, as they changed into theatre gear, "before we start, there are a couple of things we need to recognise." Although there was a thoughtful, almost stern look on his face, his voice was unruffled as always.

"I think you've seen Mr Potts perform this operation haven't you?"

"Yes Sir, twice, but they were planned procedures; I haven't seen an aneurysm that has ruptured."

"Well that's two more than I've seen but the bottom line is this. If we don't operate the patient must inevitably die. Even in the best hands the procedure is extremely hazardous. I believe the death rate for operations when an aneurysm has ruptured is about fifty percent. So together we'll try to save this patient but if we fail, as we probably will, then at least we shall have given him a chance. Since you've seen this type of surgery already and I haven't, I want you to do the operation. I will assist. Do your best but if we fail there must be no recriminations. Now tell me, what's the patient's name and has anyone spoken to his wife?"

"The patient is called Bernard Baxendale. I presume someone at the Middleton has spoken with his wife, but I don't know for sure. There hasn't been any time to speak with her here. I think she's probably in the anaesthetic room now if you want me to have a word."

"No, I'll go." Sir William replied. "You crack on here. It's important that she realises exactly what the situation is; I don't want her to be under any illusions about the outcome."

With blood being pumped into both his arms, it wasn't cross matched but at least it was the same blood group as the patient, the operation commenced. Paul made the same huge incision that he had seen Mr Potts make and then shifted the patient's intestines to one side. He was totally unprepared for the sight that met his eyes.

Arising from the back of the abdomen was a haemorrhagic swelling the size of a grapefruit, looking like a large blood soaked bathroom sponge. This was quite unlike the two operations he had seen when the aorta had been clearly visible. When he had assisted Mr Potts the aneurysms hadn't burst; you could see the normal aorta above and below the blow-out. How was he supposed to put a clamp across the biggest artery in the body to control the bleeding when he couldn't even see it? And how was he to avoid damaging the enormous vein that ran immediately adjacent to it, which was similarly invisible?

"Sir," he said, his voice quaking. "I really have no idea how to begin to control the situation. The minute I open this mass, the haemorrhage is going to be catastrophic. Would you care to take over?"

"Normally I would, Lambert," Sir William replied quietly, "but I'm afraid that I have even less experience of these cases than you. Just do the best you can. No one is going to blame you if you fail. Whatever happens you will have my support."

Tentatively Paul began to dissect through the upper part of the mass trying to locate the normal artery above the aneurysm but as soon as he did so he was greeted by fresh bright red bleeding. He could feel the vessel he was aiming to locate because it was still pulsing weakly, but he couldn't see it. He abandoned the scalpel he was using and tried to find a way through with his finger hoping that this would cause less bleeding but it didn't; the nearer he got to the aorta the worse the bleeding got.

There was an anguished cry from the anaesthetist. "I can't keep up with the blood loss. If you can't get that clamp on in the next minute or two we're going to lose him."

Desperately Paul pushed on, finally getting a glimpse of the aorta. Sister passed him the specialist clamp that had to be placed across the artery that was an inch across. He had seen Mr Potts carefully separate the aorta from the adjacent structures before applying the clamp but he simply couldn't see clearly enough to do that and in any case there was no time. He opened the clamp, passed one jaw behind the aorta, the other in front and snapped it closed. The result was a disaster. Immediately the bright red bleeding was replaced by a flood of ominously dark blood. He knew at once what had happened. One of the jaws of the clamp had punctures the huge vein that lay alongside the artery.

Within seconds the heart monitor screeched its warning that the heart had stopped beating.

"Do you want me to start cardiac massage, Sir?" The anaesthetist's question was directed at Sir William, not at Paul.

"No, I don't think that would be appropriate," Sir William replied. "We've done all we can but regrettably to no avail." He turned to Paul. "I'll leave you to tidy up here Lambert. I'll go and have a word with his wife."

A death in the operating theatre was a rare event and one that had a profound effect on the staff. Normally, when a procedure is in progress the atmosphere is one of calm efficiency. Then, when an operation is concluded, a lighter mood of easy camaraderie prevails as the patient wakes from the anaesthetic and the ward nurses come to collect them and return them to their bed. Inevitably a death leads to gloom and despondency. Little is said as the patient's wound is closed, the anaesthetic machine is turned off and all the drips, tubes and monitor leads are disconnected. The deceased is covered with a sheet and the staff proceed with their various tasks in silence; clearing away instruments, emptying laundry baskets and cleaning the floor and any other surfaces that have become soiled, whilst waiting for the mortuary attendants to remove the body.

When Sir William returned to the surgeon's room ten minutes later, he found Paul slumped in a chair, the cup of tea that the theatre sister had provided with a sympathetic word, going cold on an adjacent table. To stop Paul brooding, Sir William walked with Paul back to the doctor's mess and then stayed with him awhile for a coffee and a chat.

"You mustn't blame yourself, Paul." Sir William said before he departed, "We were placed in an impossible situation. There was nothing more we could have done to save him. I'm sure you understand that had we not operated, he would be just as dead as he is now."

Paul found consolation in Sir William's words. He knew in his heart that they were true. He also realised it was the first time that the senior consultant had referred to him by his Christian name.

In bed that night, unable to sleep, he mulled over the events of the day, asking himself repeatedly if he could have done anything differently to save the patient's life. Eventually, he concluded that he couldn't, nor could he be held responsible for his lack of experience; after all, Mr Potts had only just started to perform this procedure and he had yet to tackle an aneurysm that had ruptured. Then, as he tossed and turned, unable to find sleep, he became angry. He should never have been put in this situation. When Mr Potts set up this new service, he should have arranged that appropriate staffing be available, particularly if they were going to accept emergency cases.

It dawned on him that the staff at the Middleton hospital must have been told, presumably by Mr Potts, that the City General was now able to take such emergencies. Had other hospitals in the region also been told? Did it mean that they could now expect to receive a string of such cases? He needed to clarify the situation as a matter of urgency. He decided to raise the subject with Sir William. Surely after the fiasco in which they had both been involved, he would understand the need to appoint a second surgeon with experience in vascular surgery. When he spoke with Sir William the next day, he learned that was exactly what was planned - but only when Sir Willam retired. This alarmed Paul greatly; what, he wondered would happen in the three months until that happened?

Chapter Twenty Five

A few weeks later, as Paul entered the female ward to undertake his routine early morning visit, he was met by Sister Rutherford. In her mid-fifties, motherly and plump, she was warm, friendly and caring. A superb ward sister, she was loved by her patients, appreciated by her nurses and respected by the consultants. The junior doctors thought she was perfect. She was always helpful, particularly to the newly qualified house officers; someone to whom they could turn for advice. She guided them in a firm but friendly fashion; nursing them through their early difficult months and always ready to revive them when they were weary with mugs of hot tea and words of encouragement. She had been the ward sister on the Surgical Five unit for many years and loved her job. She harboured no ambitions to be promoted to a teaching or administrative post. Her third grandchild had just arrived and Paul was sure she made a wonderful granny. How they wished that Sister Ashbrook on the male ward was as pleasant and easy to work with!

Sister Rutherford greeted him with a smile. "Good morning Paul, bright and early as usual, I see."

"Yes, though it's hard to get out of bed on these winter mornings. Kate is lucky. She's enjoying a lie-in today. She's not on duty until the afternoon."

"It will do her good Paul. She works ever so hard, in fact you both do. I do hope you're managing to spend enough time together. You must look after her you know. She's a lovely girl; one of the best nurses that I've ever had working with me but remember; she'll want to see plenty of her husband as well as caring for the patients on the ward."

Paul smiled. He was proud of his young wife and delighted to know that others appreciated her but he recognised that Sister was also offering advice. Since the episode when he had wasted a Saturday playing golf with Mr Potts, he had tried, albeit without too much success, to spend less time in the hospital and more time at home. Certainly Kate seemed more content than before; presumably she appreciated that he was trying to mend his ways. Recently she had complained less about the hours that he worked and the atmosphere in the flat had certainly improved.

He was about to say he knew how lucky he was, when his pager went off. It was Sister Ashbrook on the male ward.

"Paul, I've just come on duty and found another orthopaedic lodger on the ward. He must have been admitted during the night. Mr Potts will be starting his round in a couple of hours. You've got to get rid of him." As before, the anxiety in her voice was obvious.

It was time to speak with the orthopaedic houseman once more. She answered her pager almost at once.

"Hi Jane," he began, trying to sound cheerful, knowing that he had a favour to ask. "I believe you've placed a lodger on our ward. We need the bed for today's admission," he lied. "I'd be grateful if you could take him back to your ward as soon as possible."

"Don't tell fibs," Jane chided him. "He's on your ward because you *haven't* any admissions today! I know because I checked. You've got a Leslie Potts ward round this morning, haven't you; and you're afraid he'll cause a scene? I've heard all about his allergy to our orthopaedic patients. What happens if he comes into contact with one, does he swell up and come out in blotches?"

"So far I haven't actually seen what happens, but I'm told he loses all sense of proportion and breathes fire and brimstone like a dragon. Apparently he roasts any junior doctor who happens to be around, folk like Janet, Victoria and me. But OK, you're quite right, I confess we haven't got an admission today – but it still means that you've got to take him back pronto!"

"I'm sorry Paul but that won't be possible. There was a major road accident on the by-pass last night. We've got lodgers all over the place. I'm afraid one of you will have to act as St George!"

"Is there no chance of moving him at all?" Paul pleaded. Much as he would like to slay Mr Potts, he didn't think he was up to it.

"No; and frankly I really don't see why your team are always pushing for special treatment. None of the other units harass us the way you do. You lodge patients on our ward from time to time. You should be prepared to give and take."

"I know that Jane and I don't mean to hassle you, but unfortunately Mr Potts isn't as reasonable as some of the other consultants."

"Well as I say, I'm sorry," Jane said emphatically, "but the fact remains. We've no slack on our ward and if we had a spare bed, we would bring a lodger down from Surgical Four. We've three patients up there, you've only got one. Anyway it would be difficult to move him. He's trussed up on a 'Balkan beam'."

Paul groaned. This was a real problem. A 'Balkan beam' was a bed adapted by the addition of four vertical posts; one at each corner. It looked like a four-poster bed with cross beams at the top. The frame was used to support a fractured femur in a sling and in all likelihood there would be a giant weight swinging at the foot of the bed, applying traction to the leg. Although the bed could be wheeled gently on the flat, to move the patient down to the orthopaedic ward in the lift would mean taking it apart, causing the patient pain, risking disturbing the alignment of the broken thigh bone, then reassembling it. The whole process would take at least an hour. Paul sighed. It seemed he was destined to witness Mr Potts' reaction to a lodger, though he doubted it would be quite as dramatic as Sister and Victoria suggested.

Then he had a brainwave, a moment of true inspiration. He rang the male ward and had another word with Sister Ashbrook. He needed her assistance if his plan was to work but, recalling how she had been complicit in hiding the elderly man with the broken wrist, he felt sure that she would agree to help. He had seen Victoria pull the wool over Mr Potts' eyes when she had made a lodger melt into thin air. Would he be as successful, or would his deceit land him in trouble? Would the slightly devious use of language that he would have to employ, save them all from an unpleasant scene? It would be risky though. What would Mr Potts' reaction be if the plan didn't work? Presumably Paul would become the focus of Mr Potts' fury and since the consultant's attitude to Paul had been distinctly cool since their game of golf, Heaven help him!

An hour later, when Mr Potts arrived to do his round, he led Victoria, Janet and Paul together with Sister Ashbrook and one of the staff nurses to the far end of the ward as was his custom.

It was noticeable that his approach to patients was very different to that of Sir William. Gone were the open questions that invited a frank and honest reply. Mr Potts was much more abrupt.

"You're feeling better," he might say.

Although the slight inflection in his voice suggested that this was a question, the words were actually spoken as a statement. Should the patient not be feeling better, they had to contradict the consultant to make this known, something few had the confidence to do. Sir

William's technique was quite different. "How have you been feeling since I saw you last?" he would have inquired.

There was, in fact, very little communication between Mr Potts and his patients. The consultant stood at the foot of the bed with his entourage and the conversations that took place almost exclusively involved the doctors and nurses, the poor patient scarcely being involved at all. Further, the discussions were held in hushed voices almost suggesting that it was inappropriate for the patients to hear what was being said about them, their illness and their treatment.

It was also noticeable that Mr Potts encouraged brevity. He conducted the round in a brisk, many would say brusque manner. He also showed great trust in the competence of his staff, particularly in Victoria.

Victoria might say, "Yesterday's hernia Sir, no problems at all, probably home on Wednesday."

Mr Potts would wave at the patient from the foot of the bed and say "good, good" and then move onto the next patient. Inevitably, patients felt excluded from such consultations and it became the house officer's responsibility to return later in the day to tell them of decisions taken about their treatment. It seemed Mr Potts was happiest when his patients were anaesthetised in theatre when he didn't need to talk to them at all!

The team moved down the ward, Janet pushing the trolley containing the patients' notes from bed to bed.

"Good practice for your future pram pushing days," Mr Potts remarked with a grin on his face. He enjoyed teasing his house officer, always pleased if he could get her to react. Paul hoped that on this occasion she wouldn't. There would be fireworks if he realised there was a lodger on the ward and it would be ten times worse if he was already riled. Janet glared at the consultant, met him eye to eye, but kept her lip buttoned; she had already decided that on this occasion her response would not be verbal. As the group moved to the next patient, she deliberately left the trolley behind. They were three beds further down the ward before Mr Potts asked for some information that required looking in a patient's clinical records.

"Where are the patient's notes?" the consultant wanted to know, his eye searching in vain for the missing trolley. As one, the group turned and saw the trolley isolated and abandoned like some wartime casualty after the cavalry had raced on.

"I parked the *'pram'* five minutes ago," Janet replied coldly, standing tall, glaring at the consultant and making no movement to go and retrieve it. She added the word, "Sir," somewhat belatedly.

A shocked silence enveloped the group in anticipation of an imminent storm. A flash of anger crossed Mr Potts' face. Then his features softened, then broke into a smile and finally he laughed out loud.

"So you have, my dear, so you have. I do so like a pretty girl with a bit of spirit. Well done." Then he stopped and with a twinkle in his eye added, "I suppose you wouldn't care to carry the notes in your arms rather than push the pram would you? Carrying notes is a bit like carrying a baby, you know – good practise for later life." Seeing the expression of disgust on Janet's face he added, "No, I don't suppose you would."

He turned to face Paul. "Let me give you a bit of advice, Lambert," he said, with mock seriousness. "In a few years' time, when you're a consultant, be very careful when appointing female staff. By all means employ a woman to be your house officer. They won't be with you long enough to get pregnant and in any case you'll work them so hard that they won't have the energy to take the preliminary steps. But never appoint a woman to a long term post. Invariably they get pregnant and it plays havoc with the duty roster.

Now Sister Ashbrook, do you think one of your lovely nurses would be kind enough to act as mother for me and fetch the trolley. It's time we got on with our work?"

Thereafter as the round continued, Mr Potts was in an effervescent mood, enjoying himself immensely as he continued to tease Janet.

"Now tell me about this next patient, my dea..... Oh I'm so sorry Miss Smith, or is it Doctor Smith? For the life of me I can't remember which you prefer and I'm not allowed to say 'my dear', am I?" he quipped. "I can't get used to all this political correctness; you really must forgive me."

Janet simply ignored him. She had decided not to rise to the bait and never to push the notes trolley for Mr Potts ever again!

During these exchanges, Paul had become increasingly apprehensive. They were coming to the last few patients and so far nothing had raised any suspicion in Mr Potts' mind that there might be an orthopaedic lodger on the ward. But the most critical, most dangerous part of the deception was yet to come. All that remained was to see the patients in the side wards which were shared by the two consultants. As Mr Potts saw the patient in the first room, Paul lingering at the back of the group so that he would be the first to exit when the consultation was over.

The door to the second room was closed; the blind covering the window pulled down. Paul made sure he reached the door first. Mr Potts normally barged straight in without knocking, but found Paul barring his way.

"I'm afraid we had a death on the ward earlier today, Sir" he said. Strictly speaking it wasn't a lie, though it was very misleading!

For a moment Mr Potts looked concerned.

"Not one of mine I hope," he said.

"No, Sir. He wasn't a patient of yours," Paul replied honestly.

The consultant's cheery disposition seemed to be enhanced by this information.

"So! Old Sir William has been killing them off, has he?" he joked. "What was it; a simple toe nail operation that went wrong?"

Remarks like this were commonplace between medical staff at all levels in the hospital; it wasn't unusual for one consultant to have a laugh at the expense of another, or for surgeons to rib the physicians. Victoria and Paul smiled dutifully at the remark but Sister Ashbrook took exception.

"Sir William may be nearing retirement," she protested, "but he remains a very safe surgeon and a very fine gentleman."

"I'm only joking, Sister dear. There's no need to spring to his defence. But you must admit, he is getting a bit beyond his prime."

Paul knew he was only teasing, but wasn't sure that his ward sister did. Sister Ashbrook looked furious but without Janet's self-assurance didn't have the confidence to bandy words with the consultant.

Thankfully, the rest of the round passed off without further incident and when Mr Potts had departed and the tea and biscuits had appeared Paul turned to Victoria.

"Did you happen to notice the orthopaedic lodger on the ward today?" he said, helping himself to a chocolate biscuit, a satisfied expression on his face.

Victoria looked surprised. "No, I didn't."

"Actually he has a broken leg and is strung up on a Balkan beam. I'm amazed you didn't spot him."

Victoria thought for a moment. "Ah," she said, "that must be the 'deceased' patient in the side room! I can see you're learning Paul; obviously a candidate for promotion as Mr Potts remarked a few moments ago. But when you make consultant grade I do hope that you'll ignore his intolerable sexist advice about appointing female members of staff."

Chapter Twenty Six

"Mr Lambert, I have an outside call for you."

It was Dave on the hospital switchboard. Paul groaned, irritated to be interrupted in the middle of a busy clinic. Friends and family knew not to call during the day unless it was urgent; staff members who needed to speak with him always came through on the internal phone.

"Hello, Paul Lambert speaking," he said brusquely.

"Good afternoon Dr Lambert. This is the Coroner's Office here. I have Mr Frobisher, the Coroner, for you. I'll put you through."

Paul's heart skipped a beat. Why did the Coroner wish to speak with him? It must be about the death of Mr Baxendale on the table. He'd have to explain in court how the poor man had bled to death because of his lack of skill. No, damn it – it wasn't his lack of skill; it was his lack of experience. It would become public knowledge that he had been left exposed as a result of Mr Potts' decision to tell other hospitals that the City General now offered a vascular service. The press would make a meal of it – but surely the coroner should be approaching Sir William. He had been the senior surgeon present even though he'd been acting as the surgical assistant.

"Ah Dr Lambert, I hope I haven't called you at an inopportune moment but I need to speak with you about one of your patients, a Mrs Rose O'Hannagan." When Paul heard Queenie's name he breathed a sigh of relief. Certainly she had died after he had operated upon her, but her death had simply been unfortunate, nothing for which he could be blamed.

"You will recall you reported her death to me a week or so ago." Mr Frobisher continued, his voice was cultured, clear and precise. Paul guessed that he was probably a lawyer rather than a doctor. What was the correct way to address a Coroner, he wondered?

"Yes, Sir," he said opting for safety and respect, "I remember her very well. She was with us for some time. I presume you received the report I wrote for you?"

"Yes, I did thank you, and I also have reports written by your consultant, Sir William and by Dr Higgs who performed the autopsy. He confirmed that the cause of death was a pulmonary embolus as you suspected. It seems that a blood clot formed in one of her legs then floated free to block the circulation through her lungs."

"Yes, I did know that. I was shocked when she died so I went to watch the post mortem myself to confirm my suspicions. It also gave me the opportunity to review the surgery that I had performed."

"In the beginning, it all seemed to be very straightforward," Mr Frobisher said, "but now a complication has arisen which obliges me to hold a formal inquest into the lady's death. You see, I've received a letter from a member of the family. He is alleging malpractice and specifically it is aspects of your involvement that concern him."

Paul was stunned. What on earth had he done with which the family could possibly take issue? The operation had gone smoothly, there had been no complications attributable to it and her death, whilst regrettable, was essentially an act of God. A blood clot floating to the lungs was something which happened from time to time. It was an event that was unpreventable, unforeseeable and if major, as Queenie's undoubtedly had been, untreatable and fatal. He tried to think what aspect of her treatment the family might be concerned about but his mind was numb.

"Hello, Mr Lambert, are you still there?"

"Yes Sir, I am. May I ask which member of the family has complained?"

"It's the son. He has the letters LL.B after his name and the letter head is from a legal office in London, so I presume he's a solicitor."

Oh my God, thought Paul. So Brendan wasn't simply a junior in a bank or a small office somewhere. He had clearly risen in the world.

"That would be Brendan, the younger son. I didn't know he was legally qualified," he said, now ten times more worried. "Does he say what he's concerned about?"

"No," the Coroner replied. "That's the reason I wanted to speak with you. The letter is very vague about the nature of his disquiet, though very specific that it relates to your involvement. In due course I shall contact him to clarify the situation but I wondered whether you could shed any light on the matter. If you can, perhaps you may wish to consider writing a supplementary report."

Quickly Paul cast his mind back over his involvement in Queenie's care, from the time of her admission to the moment of her untimely collapse and death. He knew himself to be very self-critical, frequently chastising himself for some minor error or omission but in this case he could think of nothing that he could or should have done in any way differently.

"Sir, it was very unfortunate that Mrs O'Hannagan should collapse and die as she did but I can think of nothing that could be the cause of any complaint. The only contentious issue that arose was that she insisted she be the one to give news of her condition to her family. She made us promise not to speak with them about her illness."

"Fair enough. Anyway we'll leave it there but should you think of anything that might be relevant do please let me know. Obviously I shall have to call you as a witness in court when the inquest is held and I'll have to give the son an opportunity to ask you some questions. My staff will be in touch to let you know when the inquest is to be held."

As Paul put the phone down he was visibly shaken.

"Are you all right?" the clinic nurse asked, as she came to see what had delayed him.

"Yes thanks," he muttered as he returned to the patient whom he had abandoned mid-consultation.

For the rest of the morning, Paul couldn't settle. What had he done that he shouldn't have done? Or had he perhaps omitted to do something that might have prevented Queenie's death? He wracked his brains trying to think of any possible justification for complaint but could think of nothing. Then he realised he'd never actually spoken to Brendan, so why was Brendan specifically criticising him? He remembered his meetings with Mick of course. He recalled how, in Queenie's caravan, he had felt threatened by his remark that *'he would make damn sure his mother was well cared for'*. He also knew how frightened Kate had been by Mick's outburst when he was denied information about his mother's operation. It didn't seem likely but perhaps the two brothers had settled their differences and Brendan, since he was a solicitor, was acting as spokesman for Mick and it was in fact Mick who had his knife out for him.

By the time the clinic ended his mood had changed from one of anxiety to one of anger. Damn it, he worked long hours, he did a responsible job to the very best of his ability. His troubles at home, Kate's irritation and frustration at being left on her own night after night, came because he was so conscientious. He always put the patients first and now he was being hauled up in court for no reason.

He knew he would suffer sleepless nights before the court appearance worrying about it. It simply wasn't fair.

To save time, Paul normally took lunch in the hospital canteen but, on a whim, decided to make an exception, and slipped back to the flat. Kate had been heavily involved in Queenie's care and might be able to throw some light on the situation. She was surprised and delighted to see him but soon realised there was a problem.

"Come on, Paul, spit it out. A problem shared is a problem halved," she said. "Something's worrying you."

"Queenie's son has contacted the Coroner. Apparently he's not happy with the way I looked after his mother."

"That will be Mick, her eldest. He's a nasty piece of work. He was aggressive with me and with some of the other nurses. On one occasion I'm sure he would have hit me had Young Rose not been there."

"No, that's the strange thing. It isn't Mick who's complained. It's Brendan, the younger brother, though he's probably only acting as the family spokesman. Apparently he's a solicitor which makes it worse."

"That can't be right," Kate responded, "the two brothers hate each other's guts. They almost came to blows when I was there. We had to keep them apart and make sure they didn't both visit at once."

"Well it's definitely Brendan that's written to the Coroner. I had it from the horse's mouth."

Kate was silent for a moment, thinking hard and then the penny dropped. "There's more to this than meets the eye," she concluded. "It will be to do with money, with their inheritance. Queenie said as much to me. *'Money's a terrible thing,'* she said, *'I wish we could do without it.'*"

"Yes, I remember you telling me that at the time."

"Brendan was estranged from Queenie and the rest of the family. He'd abandoned the gypsy way of life and Mick wanted to keep it that way. Mick was the eldest son and with Brendan out of the way, he would expect to inherit. But when Queenie thought she was dying, she wanted to make her peace with Brendan. Do you remember she asked me to post a letter to him?"

"That's right; she'd decided to write a will and didn't you arrange for a solicitor to come to see her? Presumably she wanted to do the right thing by Brendan."

"I did," Kate continued, "but the solicitor arrived after Queenie had died. She never did make a will. So Mick as her eldest, as her next of kin, will inherit. Brendan's missed out. I bet that's why he's upset."

Paul considered Kate's theory. "You could be right Kate. When Sir William took me to the gypsy camp he did comment that theirs was a rich family. The caravan was enormous and had all mod cons. It wasn't the old wooden van that you see in picture postcards and there was a very expensive car outside. But how does having a go at me improve his chances of inheriting?

"I'm not sure Paul but I bet that's at the bottom of it."

PART TWO

Chapter Twenty Seven: November 1970

At four in the morning, distraught after his futile battle fighting for the life of William Wilson and feeling utterly wretched, Paul trudged from the theatre changing room to the ward where Mrs Wilson was waiting for news of her husband. Informing someone that their spouse had died was a duty with which he was familiar, but that didn't make the task any easier. No matter how gently or sympathetically the words were chosen or spoken; the news delivered was brutal and final. If the death was expected, perhaps after a prolonged battle with cancer or some other progressive debilitating disease, comfort could be offered that their loved one was now free of pain, their suffering at an end. But when death was sudden and unexpected, perhaps when a husband had gone to work fit and well in the morning but had failed to return at night, nothing could be done to soothe or console the bereaved.

Never before though, had Paul needed to impart such dreadful news after a death for which he held himself responsible. He accepted that someone could bleed to death at the road side after a nasty accident or in the pub after a fight with knives or guns but it shouldn't be possible to exsanguinate on an operating theatre table with a trained surgeon at their side. What on earth was he to say? Turning into the ward, he passed the side room where he knew Mrs Wilson would be waiting. He had hoped to slip into the office and ask the night nurse to join him; a sympathetic female presence was always helpful when imparting bad news, but he didn't get the chance. The door was ajar and Mrs Wilson saw him passing. In a flash she was on her feet, her face anxious and drawn, hoping for the best but fearing the worst. One look at Paul's ashen face confirmed her fears. "I've lost him haven't I?" she said.

"I'm afraid so." Paul's voice was flat and lifeless. The night's events had taken their toll and he was overcome with physical and emotional exhaustion.

He waved Mrs Wilson to a chair then drew one up beside her.

"The main blood vessel to his legs had burst and I wasn't able to stop the bleeding," he confessed. "I'm so sorry."

"It wouldn't have helped that he's a bad heart would it? He had a heart attack last year, you know; and he's had angina for years. Did he suffer a lot?" Mrs Wilson asked.

"No, not at all. Within five minutes of you seeing him last, he was asleep; anaesthetised. He would know nothing of the operation at all."

"When I saw him in the casualty department, I was afraid I would lose him. I've never seen anyone quite so ill or in so much pain. He was bowling with his friends when he collapsed you know; he would have had a pint of beer to hand too, I've no doubt." Mrs Wilson commented, a wan smile on her face. "He would have been enjoying that. You know, Doctor, my Bill was a good man; I suppose I've been lucky. We've been together for almost forty five years and we've had some good times. We've been blessed with three fine children. We have six grandchildren too; and they're all doing well. The eldest is off to college soon; she wants to be a teacher, though Bill's not sure she has the patience to deal with a classroom of little ones."

For some time she spoke, largely talking to herself while Paul just sat and listened. Finally she stopped and looked Paul full in the face.

"Thank you Doctor, for trying to save him. I know you did your best. That's all I could have asked of you. And will you thank the nurses for me as well. We're so lucky to have people like you, working through the night to help those in need."

"I just wish we could have been more successful," Paul replied.

"So do I, but unfortunately it wasn't to be. Now Doctor, may I see my husband please?" Mrs Wilson asked, tears in her eyes.

Paul was thrown by the question. In hospital, deaths normally occurred on the ward where the nurses dressed the deceased and make them look respectable. But Mr Wilson had never been in a hospital bed. He had been rushed straight from casualty to theatre. Paul wasn't sure how things were arranged when a death occurred in theatre.

"If you'll excuse me, I'll see what can be arranged," he said.

"I'll wait here then," Mrs Wilson replied. She took Paul's hand in both of hers, "and thank you again Doctor for trying to save Bill."

With Mrs Wilson's gratitude grating on his conscience, Paul rang the night Sister.

"Leave it with me," Mr Lambert," she said, when Paul had explained the situation, "I'll arrange for him to be popped into a side room somewhere. It wouldn't be right for his wife to see him in the theatre. "Now, you get to bed. It's been a long night, you must be worn out."

Finally as the clock approached five, Paul fell into his bed still in his theatre greens. Though mentally and physically drained, sleep evaded him. His mind dwelt on the events of the night; his attempt to save Mr Wilson's life, his battle to staunch the bleeding and his utter and complete failure. Yet Mrs Wilson had been grateful to him; that made him feel more wretched than ever. He felt worse than he had after Bernard Baxendale's death. On this occasion he hadn't even had the comforting presence of Sir William at his side to console him.

Still tossing and turning at seven in the morning, he abandoned all hope of sleep, rose and stared moodily out of the window. The first hint of dawn heralded another grey day. Pleasant summer days had come and gone, autumn leaves had enjoyed their brief moment of glory, been felled by November rains and now lay sodden and trampled on the city's pavements. Paul watched with unseeing eyes as men and women hurried to work wrapped in coats and scarves to keep out the chill wind. Some hastened through the light drizzle towards the city centre, collars turned up and hats pulled down, but many entered the hospital to clock on for their morning shift. All too soon as the nights drew in, there would inevitably be weeks of fog when cars would drive at a snail's pace and wise folk would stay indoors. Then finally winter would hold the city in its icy grip.

Dramatic though the seasons were in the outside world, they largely went unnoticed by those who lived and worked in the City General. There would be a slight change in the pattern of disease they would treat, more wrist and shoulder injuries as people slipped and fell on icy pavements, more patients with chest and heart problems if a cold winter smog enveloped the city but otherwise the usual hurly burly of routine work would continue. The blinds were pulled down and the curtains drawn earlier as the days shortened but it was always warm and dry in the wards, clinics and theatres.

Paul continued to brood on the nights events. What a catastrophe it had been. Mr Wilson's corpse would now be in the large freezer cabinet in the hospital morgue, wrapped in a white sheet awaiting the post mortem that the coroner was legally bound to arrange. Paul always tried to find time to watch the autopsies of patients he had treated. Watching the pathologist reveal the cause of death helped doctors understand illnesses that had defied diagnosis during life and it was especially valuable to surgeons, enabling them to review procedures they had undertaken. He would hate witnessing this particular post mortem though; it would bring him face to face once again with his own inadequacies, but watch it he must. He would ask to be allowed to dissect the aneurysm himself to see exactly where he should have applied the clamps that would have controlled the bleeding and would have saved Mr Wilson's life if only he had been sufficiently competent and skilful.

By the nature of their job, surgeons leave their mark on their patients but patients also leave their mark on surgeons. These scars may not be physical but they are real enough. Paul would never forget this night; it would be indelibly etched in his memory. From time to time, perhaps waking him from sleep in a cold sweat, or during some idle moment during the day, Bill Wilson would return to haunt him. But there was a more immediate concern. Sir William's replacement had still not been appointed. If a similar emergency arose next week or next month when Mr Potts was unavailable, Paul would have to face this entire nightmare again. That would be more than he could bear.

Chapter Twenty Eight

Mr Wilson's death on the operating table had a profound effect on Paul. Previously, although by nature a quiet self-contained individual, he had generally been at ease with himself and reasonably cheerful and optimistic. He enjoyed his work, happy to put in long hours for the benefit of his patients, finding surgery stimulating and rewarding. Now he withdrew into himself and with his confidence in tatters, he worried excessively over the decisions he had to make on his patients. He recalled that during his student days, he had attended a lecture given by a psychiatrist in which different types of personality had been explained. Paul had decided that he must have an anankastic tendency. Certainly from time to time he would leave the house but stop when half way down the path, needing to feel in his pocket to check that he had his wallet or retrace his steps to ensure he had locked the front door. Now though, he became pathologically cautious and as a result took even longer to complete his duties. He wished he could adopt a more relaxed attitude to his duties but realised this was unlikely to happen. In life, wherever you went, you took your personality with you. It wasn't like moving house and leaving your old self behind.

It might have been expected that Kate would become ever more annoyed by the excessive hours he worked but in fact her reaction when he came home late became somewhat unpredictable. Occasionally she would let rip and berate him quite viciously but generally she seemed calmer and more accepting of the situation. When Paul returned to the flat in an evening, inevitably later than he had promised, he would often find her curled up contentedly on the sofa reading a book or watching television having already eaten her supper. His would be on one side in the kitchen ready for him to warm up. Paul found it unsettling not knowing what to expect when he walked through the door.

Others noticed a change in Kate as well. One day in the accident department Paul was chatting with Sally, Kate's best friend from her student days. Her husband Colin was an accountant and Kate and Paul found it refreshing to be in Colin's company. Sir William often said that when they were off duty they should leave their white coats and stethoscopes behind. It was good advice and being with Colin stopped them talking 'shop' and reminded them that there was life beyond the walls of the hospital.

"I've never seen Kate looking so well," Sally had said a smile on her face and a twinkle in her eye. "She really is blooming. She seems to have a new lease of life these days. Marriage must be doing her good."

Paul had laughed. "It's certainly suits me and it doesn't seem to be doing you any harm either."

"No, it suits me well enough too. But you will look after Kate won't you? It wouldn't do to tire her out; she's running a home as well as working full time you know."

"Kate's a strong and healthy young woman. You don't need to worry about her." Paul had replied and promptly dismissed the conversation from his mind but it wasn't long before Sister Rutherford also had words to say on the matter.

"Hey Paul, What are you doing here at this time of the day?" she had demanded to know as he walked onto the ward at eight one evening to check that all was well before he went off duty.

"Just taking a drop of blood from Mrs Illingworth, Sister," Paul replied as he armed himself with a syringe and needle to take blood from one of the sicker patients. "I want to check her haemoglobin after her operation this morning."

"But you're not on duty tonight? It's Surgical Three's night on call."

"Yes, I know it is, but her blood pressure has been a bit on the low side all day and I thought it wise just to run a test, purely as a precaution."

"I see," Sister replied. "That's fine but perhaps you would pop into the office when you've finished. There's something I want to chat to you about."

Two minutes later, the blood sample taken, placed in a bottle and neatly labelled ready to go to the laboratory, Paul went to see what was on Sister's mind. She rose when he entered the office, closed the door behind him then sat down next to him.

"Paul, if you're not on duty, why are you still here at this time of night?"

"Mrs Illingworth had a major operation this morning. I just wanted to keep an eye on her."

"But you're not on duty tonight. The nurses here will be monitoring all our patients overnight and Surgical Three's registrar, Bob Turnbull, is perfectly able to check on anyone they're worried about. And in any case, why are you taking blood? Surely the housemen should be doing that." Sister's voice was firm, though the words were kindly meant.

"I guess I'm not very good at delegation, Sister. I like to do these things for myself, then there's no doubt in my mind that the job has been done."

"In some ways that does you credit, but you can't run the hospital single handed, can you? You must remember that you're a member of a team. The nurses and housemen we have at the moment are all excellent. Monitoring patients and taking blood is their job, not yours. Do you want them to think that you don't trust them?"

"Of course I trust them. They're all first class. We're very lucky to have them."

"Well then, you should have given one of them a ring and asked them to take the blood samples. I know it's none of my business and perhaps I oughtn't to mention it but I don't like to see you working so hard."

Paul had the greatest regard for Sister Rutherford. For twenty years she had run the female ward with calm efficiency. Thanks to her wisdom and experience, many young house officers had been helped to become better doctors. Much less frequently she had felt the need to guide registrars which was the task she had now set herself. She was afraid that Paul would crack under the pressure to which he subjected himself if he failed to mend his ways.

Paul couldn't deny that Sister's words were not only well meant but were true. He already knew that he had to learn the art of delegation. The trouble was that whenever he passed a job to Janet, he felt the need to check that it had been satisfactorily completed and yes, he had seen the look of irritation on her face when he had done so.

"Thanks Sister. I hear what you say and I know you're right. I'll just take this sample to the lab and then I'll get off home."

"Oh no you won't," Sister responded, "you'll ring for a porter to deal with the specimen. And before you go Paul, there's another thing I want to mention, and again you must forgive me if you think I'm speaking out of turn. Remember you're a married man. When you were single, you only had yourself to think about but it's different now. While you're working here, Kate is on her own. I thought she looked a little tired when she left the ward today; in fact I let her go home a few minutes early."

"You don't think she's sickening for something do you?" Paul replied anxiously, remembering the long illness Kate had suffered when she had been training. She had been hospitalised for six weeks with rheumatic fever, an illness that was prone to recur.

"No, I don't think that at all; but she's young, she's newly married, I've no doubt she wants to see something of her husband. She won't be happy sitting night after night in an empty flat watching the clock! She's a pretty young thing. She's not short of admirers. Make sure you don't take her for granted."

"Are you suggesting that .....?"

"No, I'm certainly not suggesting that her head has been turned. Far from it; I'm just asking if you're certain you've got your priorities right. As a married man Paul, you have other responsibilities as well as those as a doctor."

Paul went back to the flat reflecting on Sister Rutherford's motherly words. Was she right? Was there a danger that he was neglecting his young wife? Certainly it was true that before they were married, they often went out in the evenings and found time to go walking at weekends. When they were courting, they regularly visited Kate's father in the Lake District and then, exhausted from a long day in the fresh air, would end up with some wholesome food in a country pub. Their life was certainly quieter these days, in fact he couldn't remember when they last went out for a casual drink together; and they hadn't been to a good party for a year or more.

He found Kate with her feet up reading in front of the fire. "I've had my meal, Paul," she called as she heard the front door open. "I hope you don't mind. I've left yours in the fridge. It won't take you more than a minute or two to warm it up," she added, as she turned the page and started to read the next chapter of a romantic novel.

Paul ate his meal on a tray at her side. Sister had given him much to think about. He respected her views and knew her advice wouldn't have been offered unless she had been concerned. Certainly, in recent weeks it had been his own problems that had dominated his thoughts. He glanced at Kate. There were slight shadows round her eyes and a certain heaviness to her face that he hadn't noticed before. Yes, she does look tired he thought and then felt guilty that Sister had noticed before him.

"Can I get you a drink, Kate?" he asked.

Kate looked up surprised. "That would be lovely, Paul, thank you. I felt a bit queasy earlier but a cup of tea would go down a treat now."

Chapter Twenty Nine

"Kate has just collapsed!" Paul recognised the voice on the other end of the telephone. It was Sister Kenyon, one of the theatre sisters.

"What," Paul exclaimed, much alarmed.

"I think it was probably just a faint though," Sister continued reassuringly. "She's come round now, so there's no need for you to be alarmed."

"Did she fall? Has she hurt herself? Are you sure she's OK?" Paul rattled off the questions, anxiety evident in his voice.

"She doesn't seem to have hurt herself but if you're free, perhaps you could slip along to theatre," Sister replied. "As I say, she appears to be fine now but it would probably be wise for her to go home and rest up for an hour or two."

With a quick apology, Paul left the patient he was examining and went to see what had happened. He needed to reassure himself that Kate was alright.

It was by no means unusual for staff to faint in theatre. Usually it was student nurses who were there for the first time, apprehensive of what they were about to witness. It requires a strong stomach to watch as a scalpel blade cuts into human flesh and draws fresh red blood. But it was not something that had happened to Kate before; and what, he wondered, had she been doing in theatre? She was a ward nurse. Presumably Sister Rutherford had released her to broaden her experience because the ward was quiet.

Since the theatre floor is tiled, fainting is potentially dangerous. There had been a nasty incident a few months previously when a nurse had suffered a sizable head wound as the result of a faint. Fortunately she was in the right place to be rapidly assessed and expertly stitched! As he hastened to theatre, Paul's suspicions fell on Mr Potts; the longer he worked alongside the consultant, the greater his loathing of him. Despite acknowledging that the man was a superb surgical technician, he was finding it increasingly difficult to mask his feelings towards him. For Paul surgery was a vocation; it allowed him to relieve suffering, to make a real difference to people's lives. Mr Potts though seemed to regard it merely as a vehicle for his over inflated ego, enabling him to flaunt his skills to the nurses whilst embarrassing and belittling his subordinates. He didn't see his patients as real people suffering with debilitating problems; he saw them as the canvas on which he performed his art. He was also happy to make a fortune from his private patients whilst those on the NHS got short shrift.

Ever the showman, Mr Potts loved to have an audience when he was operating and if he could make one of the nurses feel queasy, or better still see them carried prostrate from the theatre, the happier he was. His best opportunity came during operations on toe nails. The patient would usually be a young man with a painful and infected nail that needed to be removed. Mr Potts' party trick was to infuse the area with local anaesthetic in an anteroom out of the nurses' sight. This meant that the patient could walk into theatre and clamber onto the operating table unassisted. Then gathering the nurses round so they all had a good view, he raised the tension with a vivid description of what was to follow. 'This toe nail is exceptionally painful and needs to be removed', he would say. 'Watch closely. You will see me insert a pair of forceps under the nail. That used to be a way of torturing prisoners in days of old, you know. Then I will slowly force the instrument up to the very root and tear the nail off in one swift movement. Don't be alarmed if you see quite a lot of blood.'

Unaware that, with his toe already frozen, the patient would feel no pain, many in his audience, already alarmed by these words, promptly felt sick when Mr Potts proceeded to do exactly what he had described. The theatre sister and theatre orderly, well aware of the consultant's tricks, always kept a close eye on the junior nurses and at the first sign that any of them looked pale or queasy, whisked them away much to Mr Potts' annoyance! Mr Potts was known to have muttered '*Spoil sport*' to Sister under his breath on more than one occasion.

****

Arriving in theatre, Paul was relieved to find that Kate, though looking a little pale, was sitting in the office whilst Sister Kenyon fussed over her with a mug of hot sweet tea. Fortunately she had been caught before she hit the floor and had not injured herself in any way. She was embarrassed that Paul had been called from his ward duties.

"I'm sorry Paul. I don't know what came over me. One minute I was fine, the next I found myself flat on my back here in the office."

"Perhaps you would stay with Kate for a few minutes?" Sister requested, "I need to see that things are running smoothly in theatre."

"Of course Sister," Paul replied, "I'll wait 'til Kate has finished her tea then take her back to the flat."

Ten minutes later, when Sister Kenyon returned, Kate had finished her drink and was pink cheeked and fully alert.

"I think Kate has recovered sufficiently for you to take her home Paul," She said. "When you get there, let her lie down and rest for an hour or two. I've spoken to Sister Rutherford who completely understands the situation; she says that she can manage this afternoon without her."

Paul heard the emphasis on the word 'completely' and frowned. Was he missing something? He saw Kate and Sister Kenyon exchange a glance before Sister spoke again, a smile on her face.

"It was rather strange that you should faint today Kate, wasn't it?"

"It was Sister but let's not go into that now," Kate replied quickly, curtailing the conversation before Sister had time to elaborate. "Are you free to walk me back to the flat, Paul?"

Paul escorted Kate home and made her another cup of tea. Since she refused to go to bed, he sat her on the settee, insisting that she rest up for the remainder of the day. He was puzzled though by Sister's remark. Did she have some idea why Kate had fainted? Paul was at a loss to explain it. Kate was young, fit and strong. When out walking she could match him stride for stride, indeed a couple of weeks before, when they had managed to spend some time together, they had covered ten or twelve miles over rough terrain. Perhaps on reflection, Paul recalled, she had struggled a little up some of the steeper sections which was unusual. He hoped that she wasn't sickening for something.

"Are you sure you're alright Kate?" he asked, frowning. "You're not keeping anything from me are you?"

Kate had known for at least a month that this moment must inevitably arrive. She had been waiting for a suitable opportunity to break the news to him but whenever the moment seemed right, afraid of Paul's reaction, she had chickened out. Now there was no escape; he had to be told. She had deceived him, she had gone against his wishes, but in the circumstances surely he wouldn't be angry with her.... or would he?

Kate looked Paul in the eye, put a hand on his, smiled softly then with her heart in her mouth replied. "Well actually I confess that I have rather held something back." There was a long pause before she added, "I'm pregnant."

Paul looked startled; he was completely lost for words. It was the one cause of fainting that he hadn't considered.

"You're what?" he echoed.

"I'm pregnant Paul. We're going to have a baby. You are pleased aren't you? It is what we both wanted," Kate asked anxiously.

In that instant and quite instinctively Paul recognised that the wrong answer would ruin their marriage. It would be a disaster if Kate came to believe she was carrying a baby that he didn't want.

"Well.... yes...I'm... Of course, I'm delighted," Paul stuttered. "It's just that I'm surprised. No, I'm more than surprised, you've rather startled me."

"Startled happy or startled alarmed?" Kate demanded to know.

"Oh happy; a bit shocked maybe but certainly happy. I just had no idea. How far on are you?"

"About three months." She would let him find out that she was nearly four months gone when they went to the antenatal clinic!

"So you've missed a couple of periods."

"Yes I have."

"I'm sorry Kate. I didn't know."

"Don't worry Paul. There's no reason why you should have known. I've always been lucky and fairly light with my periods and the one's I've missed have fallen on weekends when you've been living in the hospital. I've feel a bit guilty that I haven't said anything sooner, but I wanted to be sure before I told you."

"Well those contraceptive pills weren't much good were they, or has my super stud status overcome them?"

This was the real moment of truth, when her deceit was to be exposed. Dare she be honest?

"Well, I may have missed taking one or two," she replied looking at the floor, afraid to face Paul.

Suddenly Paul realised where the truth might lie. With a finger under her chin, he tilted her head up so that he could look her in the face. "One or two tablets or one or two months?"

Although Paul's voice was quiet and serious, Kate somehow knew he wasn't going to be angry.

"Well, four or five months actually."

"You wicked, wicked woman; I really ought to put you across my knee and spank you," Paul replied laughing as he took her into his arms. "That's amazing news. I'm thrilled. So I'm going to be a 'daddy'. I might have known you wouldn't faint without there being a good reason. Is that what Sister was referring to in theatre just now? Does she know you're pregnant?"

Kate paused before replying. "Yes, she does know, and," she added quietly, "and she's not the only one; I'm afraid most of the staff on the ward also know. It's been an open secret for a week or more. In fact, I believe there's a sweepstake going on to guess how long it will be before you cotton on."

Paul was dismayed, then angry. "That's unfair Kate. You should have told me before blurting it out to all and sundry. I suppose they've all been laughing at me behind my back."

"No, Paul, truly I didn't tell anyone. They worked it out for themselves, at least Sister Rutherford did. She was the first to notice. She saw me running for a bus. Apparently I slowed down then walked to the bus stop letting the bus go without me. She knew that I would normally have caught it without difficulty. And I was late for work on a couple of mornings because I felt a bit queasy. Sister Rutherford is a mother and grandmother. She's been in charge of a ward run by young nurses for twenty years or more; she notices these things."

"And I suppose I don't," Paul responded bitterly.

"Let's just say you work too hard," Kate replied softly, putting her arms round him and planting a kiss on his cheek. "You leave the house at the crack of dawn, you work hard all day and you come home exhausted."

"Not too exhausted to put you in the family way though," he replied realising there was no point in being angry. Suddenly he remembered the huddle of nurses he had seen when he had walked onto the ward earlier that day and their giggling, guilty expressions when they had seen him. Damn it, they all know, he thought, I'm a laughing stock.

"I know I really ought to have told you," Kate confessed, "but everyone thought it such a joke and I didn't want to spoil their fun."

"I'm going to get a lot of ribbing now aren't I?"

"Yes, that's true. But you are pleased? Tell me you're happy with the news."

"Of course I'm happy. I'm absolutely delighted. I just wish you'd told me first."

"That's good then. Now tell me, what were you doing before you were called to rescue me in the theatre?"

"I was examining a patient on the male ward."

"Was he undressed?"

"Yes, he was!"

"Well hadn't you better get back to complete the job before he dies of cold?"

Paul turned to leave then stopped as a germ of an idea formed in his head. "Kate, I suggest you don't let on that I know about the baby," he said, "then maybe I'll be able to turn the tables on them."

Chapter Thirty

Paul was genuinely delighted with Kate's news but aggrieved that the staff on the unit knew of his wife's pregnancy before he did. He felt that Kate ought to have told him first but equally had to admit that he should have been the first to notice. Looking back, he did recall she had complained of heartburn on a couple of occasions, indeed he had even raided the drug cupboard for some antacid tablets for her, and once or twice she had spent an extra hour in bed when she was not on the early morning shift. Sadly, he just hadn't noticed and come to the obvious conclusion. Kate was right; he was too wrapped up in his work. Still it was great news and now that he knew, he determined to be more attentive to his young wife.

Embarrassed to think that the staff had been laughing at him behind his back, Paul decided to play them at their own game. He recollected a similar event a number of years previously. Sir William's ward rounds lasted so long, not least because of his obsession with his patient's bowels, that to help pass the time, a sweepstake was organised to estimate the number of suppositories Sir William would insert in the course of the morning. Initially Sister Rutherford had declined to participate, unhappy that her favourite consultant was being made the unwitting central character in the charade. When the sweepstake had continued despite her protestations, she had informed Sir William and between them, they had turned the tables on the surgical team. Joining in for the first time, and with the consultant's connivance, Sister Rutherford had won the jackpot and donated the proceeds to ward funds. Paul decided he would attempt something similar. He would pretend he remained unaware of Kate's condition even after her recent fainting episode.

Inevitably, when Paul next visited the operating theatre, the questions came thick and fast.

"Well Paul, how is Kate today? No ill effects I hope."

"Wasn't it strange that a strong and healthy person like Kate should faint?"

The questions were posed with a smile on the face and a knowing look in the eye.

Paul feigned to look puzzled.

"Yes" he replied, "very strange indeed. I really don't understand it. She says she's never fainted before, but I'm pleased to say she's now fully recovered. Let's just hope it doesn't happen again."

He had his chance to take the deception further when Sister Rutherford similarly enquired after Kate.

"She's absolutely fine," he said, "and I was delighted to hear the news she had for me."

Sister laughed. "So you know about that now do you. Well can I say that I'm thrilled. Many congratulations. She's a lovely girl; but you do need to look after her. No-one should ever take their wife for granted. There is life outside the hospital you know, Paul."

"Thanks Sister. I hear what you say. I should have spotted what was going on much sooner. But now that I do know, I promise I'll take care of her. By the way, officially I don't know about the pregnancy, so if you want to make another contribution to the ward's amenity fund, you should join the sweepstake; perhaps place a bet on next Tuesday."

"So you know about that as well do you?"

"Yes I do, Sister. I wasn't best pleased at first but I suppose there's no harm in it."

"None at all; it's a sign of a happy unit and it's good for morale."

Paul would have enjoyed teasing the staff and pretending he still hadn't realised that his wife was pregnant but it wasn't to be. When Kate came to work the next morning, she was immediately asked why she hadn't told Paul she was expecting and she confessed she had told him and that he finally knew. Inevitably Paul came in for some teasing after that. 'Hadn't he noticed that she'd stopped drinking coffee?' he was asked, 'or that she left the room if anyone started to smoke?' He took it all in good heart but felt incredibly guilty that he hadn't noticed these things for himself. It was a 'wake up' call; in future he needed to do more to help his wife, to care for her. He had to stop being so obsessed with his own problems, particularly the fear that he might again be left to operate on another ruptured aneurysm.

Kate's excitement and happiness knew no bounds. Her pregnancy dominated her thoughts both at home and at work. She chatted to anyone and everyone about her condition including the patients that she nursed on the ward. If they had children of their own, she wanted to know whether they had delivered at home or in hospital, their views on breastfeeding, how much maternity leave they had taken and how they had coped with the heartburn and constipation that had started to trouble her. Then she would share what she had learned with the other nurses during coffee and lunch breaks. Her pregnancy so dictated her thoughts that one day Sister Rutherford took her to one side and had a quiet word with her.

"Kate, it's lovely to see you looking so happy and progressing smoothly with your pregnancy. We all wish you well but......."

"Yes, Sister," Kate interrupted, "It's marvellous isn't it. I can't believe how lucky I am and...."

It was Sister's turn to interrupt. "Kate, listen for a moment. We're all pleased for you. I remember my first pregnancy. I recall how excited I was and how I wanted to tell the whole world my good news but there's something you may be forgetting. Not everyone is as lucky as you. There's one member of staff here who's trying desperately to get pregnant, others who would loved to have had a baby but for whatever reason found that impossible. They may find it difficult if you are talking about it all the time. Be happy for yourself but please bear in mind that not everyone has been so fortunate."

"Yes, Sister, I'm sorry. It's just that I feel so excited; I want everyone to share my happiness. I'm afraid I didn't think. I will be more considerate in future."

Thereafter, Kate tried to keep herself in check but found it exceedingly difficult to do so.

At home though, her true feelings shone through and in the weeks that followed, Kate was happier than Paul had ever seen her. She blossomed both physically and mentally. As her breasts and abdomen swelled, she radiated health and contentment. In the evenings she sat and rested for hours on the sofa with her hands on her belly and a smile on her face. She had known Paul wanted to have children but she had agreed, albeit reluctantly, to his suggestion that they wait until he no longer had to work overnight in the hospital. She had been afraid that he would be furious when he realised she had deceived him. To see his obvious pride and pleasure in her condition delighted her.

"Pregnancy suits you," Paul remarked as he observed his young wife. "You seem to be glowing with good health."

"I feel wonderful. My only sadness is that Mum isn't here to share my happiness with me. She would have loved to have a grandchild. She had a wonderful way with children and I'm sure she would have given me useful advice and helped me along the way."

"But I'm here to do that," Paul replied.

Kate rewarded him with a sideways glance.

"So says the last person on Surgical Five to realise I was pregnant!" she observed.

Paul had never met Kate's mother but he knew a very close bond had existed between mother and daughter and recognised the loss that Kate felt after her mother's death.

"However," Kate continued, "I do have someone to talk to about the heartburn, varicose veins and piles that I'm told I can expect; Sally's pregnant too. I think she must have conceived about three weeks after I did."

"That's great," Paul replied, aware that he still had to sleep in the hospital every fourth night and fourth weekend. It would be helpful for Kate to have a close friend with whom to chat and compare notes.

As Kate's pregnancy progressed, Sally frequently kept Kate company on evenings when Paul was on duty. Together they knitted baby cardigans and bootees, discussed different types of cots and prams and considered the merits of home or hospital delivery. Sometimes Paul would come home to be told what had been decided and after this had happened a couple of times, he began to feel a little excluded.

"Hey, Kate, this is my baby as well you know," he remarked one evening.

"I know, darling, but you're away so often and there's such a lot to plan and decide."

"That's true enough but it's still early days you know. You're only four and a bit months' pregnant. There's still a long way to go; plenty of time to get organised."

"But we do need to talk about these things Paul. There's the question of my work, after the baby is born. Do you think it would be all right for me to continue to work full time?"

"Surely that's something to decide when the time comes. When you hold the baby in your arms, you may want to spend more time at home. What about going part time or even stopping altogether and becoming a full time Mum? Money would be tight of course but my salary would just about cover it, if that was what you wanted."

"Sally says we should go back to work when we've taken our maternity leave. She says we can put the babies into nursery and if one of us has to work a late shift, the other can take care of them both."

"Never mind what Sally says! Don't you think I might have a view on the matter?"

"Don't be angry Paul. I just think it's lucky that my best friend and I are pregnant at the same time. When the babies are born we'll be able to help each other."

"No, I'm not angry," Paul said in a resigned voice, "I'd just like to be consulted that's all."

"And so you shall be," Kate replied, giving him a big hug. "Now let's get out that list of baby's names. Which names do you like?"

"It would be lovely to have a daughter. I was one of three boys. We were a very male household, all football, fighting and tom foolery. It would be wonderful if our first was a baby girl. And if it is a girl, I should like her to be called *Joan*," Paul said. "It's simple, uncomplicated and it goes nicely with our surname."

"I think *Sally* Lambert sounds better," Kate replied, "It has the same letters in both the Christian name and the surname, it has a lovely ring to it."

Paul bit his tongue as Sally's name cropped up again. There was a pause, "and if it's a boy?" he asked.

"Definitely *Thomas,*" Kate replied, "and I feel certain the baby's going to be a boy. In fact, I'm so sure that I've started knitting in blue." She held up the front panel of a blue and white cardigan she was working on.

"How can you be so sure? It's simply a fifty-fifty chance you know and if it's a girl, she will look a bit silly dressed in blue."

"I just feel it in my bones and Sally says that a mother always knows."

"And I'm telling you it's no more likely to be a boy than a girl," Paul responded unable to mask his irritation.

He recognised that his work prevented him from being as involved as he would have wished but he resented Sally's constant involvement. Before the two girls became pregnant, he and Kate had been great friends of Sally and her husband Colin. They had socialised regularly as a foursome and had even been on holiday together but Kate now seemed to take more notice of Sally than she did of him - and it annoyed him.

He thought it best to change the subject. "Look, let's discuss babies' names after we've had something to eat; I've had a long day."

The truth was that he was tired and worried. A patient he had operated on that morning was unwell. He planned to slip back to the ward later in the evening to check things for himself. He was afraid that a further operation might be necessary; babies' names were not top of his list of priorities at that particular moment.

Chapter Thirty One

Paul became increasingly apprehensive as the day of the Coroner's Inquest into Queenie's death approached. In his more rational moments, he was convinced that his involvement in her care had been beyond reproach. He had reviewed the medical notes and rerun events in his mind but could think of nothing that could possibly justify any complaint. He also felt confident that had he mismanaged the case in some way, Sir William, in his usual gentle and constructive manner, would have mentioned it to him. However that did not prevent the demon in his head demanding to know why Queenie's son, a solicitor no less, was planning to interrogate him in court. In his introspective way, Paul tried to analyse the nature of his demon. Was it his conscience, or some misplaced sense of guilt or simply his basic insecurity? He couldn't be sure, but whatever it was, it was a curse. It lay in hiding just below the surface of his brain, a snake in the grass, lurking ready to strike at any time. It would not be silenced; at night it woke him in a cold sweat; by day it flashed unannounced into his thoughts at inopportune moments making his heart skip a beat.

Paul knew he had to become more like Sir William; he had to keep things in perspective; he had to control his negative feelings and his self-reproach. Yet even as he analysed his anxiety about Queenie's inquest, his demon was at work reminding him of a second concern; it was surely only a matter of time before the coroner invited him to write a report on the death of Mr Wilson. Would he dare to explain that Mr Potts had left him unsupported to perform surgery that was beyond his experience and capabilities or should he keep quiet and take the blame himself?

Something the Coroner had said on the phone when he spoke to Paul about Queenie also troubled him. He had suggested Paul might care to write a supplementary report. Was he aware that a chance to prevent Queenie's death had been missed; was he offering Paul a lifeline to justify himself? He discussed his worries with Kate over breakfast one morning.

"Kate, you got to know Queenie well, indeed I think you were a favourite of hers. You also met Brendan and the other members of her family. Did any of them express concern about her care whilst she was on the ward?"

"No, not at all; they were too busy squabbling amongst themselves. They were upset we wouldn't discuss Queenie's medical condition with them but that, of course, was Queenie's express wish. There were never any complaints about the nurses or doctors."

"So why is Brendan having a go at me?"

"I can only assume he knows his mother intended to write a will, presumably one that would have benefitted him, and he's angry that she died before she could put pen to paper. Honestly Paul, you must stop worrying all the time. You really do worry about the slightest little thing. I'm sure the inquest will go off smoothly"

However, despite Kate's support and reassurance, Paul did worry and continued to have restless nights.

Since Sir William had also been called as a witness at the inquest, he suggested they travel to the Coroner's Court together. On this occasion Rufus was not physically present in the car though an unmistakable doggy odour lingered.

It was a cold bright December morning and the consultant, sensing Paul's unease, sought to put him at his ease.

"I understand that this is the first time you've given evidence at an inquest," he commented. "There's no need for you to be concerned. I've appeared before several coroners in my time, but old Mr Frobisher is by far the best. He may be a bit old fashioned but he does things strictly by the book and he's always scrupulously fair. He accepts that medicine is not an exact science and that outcomes aren't always predictable. He also believes that, in general, doctors and nurses are caring people who do a difficult job and he supports them whenever he can."

As they entered the court room, which was only remarkable in how plain it was, Paul was surprised to see how few people were present. Dr Higgs, the pathologist from the hospital who had conducted the autopsy was there. He also recognised Mick and Young Rose sitting on the public benches. Apart from them, only two other people were present. One, wearing a crumpled suit and a bored expression, was a slightly built man barely out of his teens, still sporting his adolescent acne. He held a pen and notepad in his hand and Paul presumed he was the reporter for the local newspaper. His discontent stemmed from his editor's insistence that he sit each week in the Coroner's Court where nothing of sufficient interest ever happened to allow him to demonstrate the extent of his literary ability. His honours degree in English literature was being completely wasted. How he longed to report on an inquiry into a major rail disaster with multiple fatalities, the death of a local celebrity in embarrassing circumstances or a juicy murder.

The only other person in the public area was smartly dressed in a city suit, shirt and tie. He was tall, broad across the shoulder and good looking with a mop of dark hair atop his swarthy face. Bearing a striking resemblance to his brother, Paul realised that this must be Brendan O'Hannagan, the London solicitor, his adversary. For a second their eyes locked. Paul quickly turned away but continued to feel Brendan's gaze burning on the side of his face.

If Paul expected the Coroner to be wearing a horse hair wig and black gown, he was to be disappointed. Mr Frobisher was casually dressed; corduroy trousers, a hand knitted pullover beneath a sports jacket with leather elbow patches which gave him the appearance of a country gentleman. Although Sir William had referred to him as '*old*' Mr Frobisher, Paul gauged him to be in his late fifties, probably five or so years younger than the consultant! He had a round and rather ruddy face suggesting an interest in gardening or hiking, bushy eyebrows and a good head of unruly white hair. The manner in which he conducted proceedings was informal. In his introductory remarks he stated that the purpose of the inquiry was to investigate the circumstances surrounding the sad demise of Mrs Rose O'Hannagan. He emphasised it was not a criminal court, that the proceedings were not adversarial and accordingly there was no requirement for lawyers to represent any of the witnesses. Dr Higgs was then sworn in and invited to read his report to the court. Since Paul had been present at the post mortem, Dr Higgs' evidence yielded no surprises.

When he had finished, Mr Frobisher explained for the benefit of the lay persons present, that a pulmonary embolus was a blood clot that formed in the legs then travelled to the chest, blocking the flow of blood through the lungs. Since blood normally passes through the lungs on its way to every other organ in the body, including the brain, a complete blockage inevitably leads to sudden death. He asked Dr Higgs whether such an event was accepted to be a random and unpredictable event.

"Yes it is," the pathologist replied.

"And can anything be done to prevent it happening?" the Coroner wanted to know.

"Sadly no," came the reply. "It's a problem that can happen to the patients of the very best surgeons in the finest hospitals in the land."

"When you were performing your post-mortem, I take it you examined the area from which the gall stone had been removed. Were you able to make any assessment of the adequacy of the surgery that had been performed?"

"The operation site was free of infection, the tissues were healing satisfactorily and the surgery seemed to have been performed in a skilful and competent fashion."

The words were like manna from heaven to Paul. Surely Dr Higgs' testimony put him beyond reproach.

"Thank you. Now before you stand down, do any members of the family wish to ask Dr Higgs any questions?"

He paused for a moment looking towards the public benches.

"No. Then may I invite Sir William Warrender to take the stand."

The report that Sir William read to the court was detailed and delivered, as Paul would have expected, in a clear and confident fashion. Again his evidence held no surprises for Paul who, in preparation for this moment, had relived every minute of his involvement with Queenie.

"Sir William," Mr Frobisher asked, "I understand you were on leave when Mrs O'Hannagan's operation was undertaken. Did you ask Mr Lambert to perform it in your absence?"

"I did."

"And, in doing so, did you feel the procedure was within his competence."

Sir William frowned a little. "Of course I did Sir, otherwise I would not have asked him to undertake it."

Again, the Coroner invited questions from the family but again none were forthcoming.

Paul knew that it was now his turn to take the stand and give his evidence. Within the next few minutes he would find out exactly what aspect of his care Brendan O'Hannagan considered to be negligent. It was inevitable that when Mr Frobisher next invited members of the public if they had any questions, Paul would be interrogated. The solicitor had not come all the way from London without a reason.

Paul was sworn in and expected to be asked to read the report that he prepared.

"Mr Lambert," the Coroner began. "We have heard Sir William's account of the care Mrs O'Hannagan received prior to her operation and we have Dr Higgs' report that the surgery you performed was more than satisfactory. Rather than ask you to read the whole of your report, may I ask you simply to tell us about her care from the day of her surgery until the day of her death?"

"Essentially, she was making a completely unremarkable recovery," Paul said. "We were very pleased with her progress."

"Was there anything, anything at all, to suggest that she might be at risk of having a blood clot in her leg which could float to her lungs and cause such a catastrophe?"

"Nothing at all, Sir. The notes record that her legs were examined on the morning of her death and there was no sign of swelling or thrombosis at that time."

"Thank you, Mr Lambert. Now I understand there are members of the family who wish to clarify some aspects of their mother's care and this is their opportunity to do so."

Brendan raised his hand.

"Perhaps I could ask you to stand and identify yourself before you put your question." Mr Frobisher said.

"Of course, Sir. I am Brendan O'Hannagan, son of the deceased. I should like to ask Mr Lambert if he is aware that it's not just operations that result in blood clots forming in the legs but that prolonged hospitalisation is also a major and significant factor?"

Stay cool and calm Paul said to himself, though his heart was racing. You know far more about medical matters than he does.

"Yes, I do know that," he replied. "It's something that can affect anyone who is confined to bed for a long time. For example, it occurs on the medical wards when patients lie in bed for long periods for conditions such as strokes or heart attacks."

"Why then," Brendan demanded, in an accusatory tone, "was my mother kept in bed for three and a half weeks before the operation was performed?"

Paul felt a surge of relief. If this was what had been worrying Brendan, he would quickly deflect his criticism with medical fact and logic.

"Well," he replied, "it is true that your mother was in hospital for many days before her operation but during that period she was not confined to bed; she was ambulant on the ward. She was a restless soul; indeed on many occasions she helped the nurses by serving meals to bed bound patients and clearing away the dishes afterwards."

"But why was the surgery so delayed? All the while you were dithering and wasting time, my mother's jaundice was getting deeper and her general condition was deteriorating. She was getting weaker by the day. The operation was deferred even after Sir William went on leave."

"I agree that in ideal circumstances the operation would have been performed sooner, but we discovered that your mother was diabetic and there was a delay whilst that was sorted out. Then unfortunately she developed a chest infection which needed to be treated with antibiotics and physiotherapy. In consultation with the anaesthetist we were trying to pick the safest possible moment for the surgery."

"Does that answer your question?" the Coroner intervened.

Somewhat reluctantly Brendan agreed that it did. "But there is another matter I wish to raise with Mr Lambert," he added.

Inwardly Paul groaned and he felt sweat on his forehead. What was he to be accused of now?

"And that is?" the Coroner prompted, sounding a little impatient.

"Why did Mr Lambert give my mother injections of Vitamin K before her operation? My mother died of a blood clot and my inquiries inform me that this vitamin actually causes blood to clot. Surely this was the very last thing my poor mother should have been given." Brendan's voice had a triumphant ring to it, so certain was he that he could prove negligence. The junior reporter sat up and licked the end of his pencil in anticipation of a good story.

But Paul felt so relieved he could have laughed out loud. His accuser was dabbling in things of which he was wholly ignorant. It was on the tip of his tongue to tell Brendan in sarcastic fashion that he didn't know what the hell he was talking about, but he thought better of it. Since he was in a public court he had better deliver the 'coup de grace' with dignity.

"You're quite correct," he explained patiently. "Vitamin K does indeed help to make blood clot. The trouble is that when a patient becomes jaundiced the level of this vitamin falls. This means that the blood's ability to clot is reduced; it's as if they have developed haemophilia. Had we performed your mother's operation whilst her

Vitamin level was low, she would have bled excessively. All we were doing was replacing something that was missing."

Brendan looked deflated but was not finished yet. "But how do you know that you didn't give too much making the blood clot too readily."

"Because we monitored the situation with a regular blood test and I can assure you that your mother's blood test was satisfactory on the day of her operation."

Mr Frobisher raised an eyebrow in Sir William's direction and the consultant responded with a confirmatory nod.

"Do you have any more questions, Mr O'Hannagan?" Mr Frobisher asked of Brendan.

"No, thank you."

Disappointed, the junior reporter returned his pencil and note pad to his pocket. He would have enjoyed writing a good *'negligent local doctor causes gypsy woman's death'* story. He had endured another frustrating morning.

"In that case you may stand down Mr Lambert, and thank you for addressing the court."

"Now it's time for me to sum up the evidence that we have heard," Mr Frobisher said, "but before I do, I feel I should read the final paragraph of the statement Mr Lambert provided for me." He paused, and then cleared his throat in a theatrical fashion.

"In the weeks that Mrs O'Hannagan was with us on the ward," he read, *"or Queenie as she insisted everyone should call her, she greatly impressed the staff with her good humour, cheerful personality and positive attitude. She was quite a character and a real tonic for the other patients. The medical, nursing and ancillary staff who became acquainted with her were deeply saddened at her passing and asked for their condolences to be passed to her family."*

The Coroner then paused and for a few moments there was silence in the court. Then he placed Paul's statement on his desk, looked up and addressed the court.

"Having read the reports that have been submitted to me and having heard from the various witnesses present today, it is clear that Mrs O'Hannagan's death, albeit sudden and unexpected, was due to an unfortunate complication that could neither be anticipated nor prevented. No fault can be attributed to the medical or nursing staff who clearly did everything in their power to minimise the risks associated with her operation. The verdict is one of death due to natural causes."

Mick's reaction was immediate. He raised himself to his feet and with a broad grin on his face embraced Young Rose. Then he turned towards his younger brother. "There I told you so, you stupid bastard," he shouted. "Now piss off back to London and stay out of our lives."

The Coroner was about to issue a stern rebuke but Mick had already turned his back and was making for the exit. Startled, the young reporter reached for his pencil and ran after him, hoping that perhaps he could interest his editor with a *'gypsy brothers in slanging match in court'* story.

As Paul gathered together the papers he brought with him and prepared to leave, he saw the Coroner have a quiet word with his assistant and nod in his direction. He was so relieved his worries were at an end that he didn't know, or frankly care what the implication might be. He turned to Sir William who had come to join him.

"I'm glad that's over," he said a big smile on his face. "I really didn't see what the son could possibly be holding against me but it didn't stop me worrying."

Sir William placed a hand on Paul's shoulder. "In that case, go home and take your wife out to celebrate," he said kindly.

As they were leaving, the court assistant stopped him. "Before you go," he said, "Mr Frobisher would like a word with you."

Oh no, what now, thought Paul, as a pang of anxiety hit him in the guts, please don't let it be about Mr Wilson bleeding to death on the theatre table. But he quickly found that he had no cause for concern, the Coroner was kindness itself.

"I'm sorry I had to ask you to appear in court and allow Mrs O'Hannagan's son to harangue you in that fashion," he said, "but I thought it was the best way to clear the air. From the letters he wrote to me, it was obvious he was intent on pursuing a formal claim of negligence against you. That undoubtedly would have been far more stressful for you than today's hearing. It would also have been much more expensive and could have dragged on for many months when clearly there was no justification for complaint. As it is I shall make it clear in my formal verdict that the medical care was beyond reproach and that will be the end of the matter."

Paul smiled his thanks, the interview was at an end and he went home with a spring in his step, feeling more cheerful than he had for several weeks.

Chapter Thirty Two

"If you're training to be a doctor, you should look like a doctor, not like some scruffy labourer from the local building site. Jeans and an open neck shirt are not suitable apparel. Leave at once and don't come back 'til you're properly dressed."

Leslie Potts was in the outpatient clinic with the medical students and Steven Morris was learning the hard way that the consultant expected certain standards to be maintained. The unfortunate young man left red-faced and angry. The remaining students looked apprehensive, fearful that they would be Mr Potts' next victim.

Poor Steven often seemed to bear the brunt of Mr Potts' ill humour, possibly because the consultant had been forced to back down on the issue of his beard. However, having previously been advised by Sir William of the standard of dress expected, he ought to have known better, particularly in the light of an incident that had occurred a few days earlier. Paul had been teaching the students how to examine the chest. He was using Steven as a model but unfortunately Steven hadn't had a bath or a shower since he'd played football a couple of days before and the body odour when he took off his shirt was overpowering. One of the girls had rather pointedly opened all the windows in the room. The December draught created quickly cleared the odour but poor Steven, who was naked form the waist up, was left shivering from the cold.

Mr Potts regarded the students as a mixed blessing. He could get through his morning's work much faster when seeing patients on his own, but being an extrovert with a big ego, he also enjoyed demonstrating his knowledge and experience to an audience. For their part, the students approached these sessions with considerable trepidation. Although they benefitted from seeing some interesting medical problems, the male students were fearful of being castigated in front of their peers if their answers to the consultant's questions were incorrect; the criticism often heavily laden with sarcasm. By contrast, Mr Potts was quite charming to the female students irrespective of their surgical knowledge; his remarks to them invariably being complimentary, though frequently rich in innuendo.

"Now let's get back to work," Mr Potts said to the remaining students. "I've got a letter here from one of our local GPs. I'll read it to you and then we'll see the patient."

Dear Mr Potts
Re   Anne Nichols

This lady is the wife of a local farmer. She has noticed a lump in her left breast. The lump is not painful and does not vary with her periods. Two years ago she had a lump in the opposite breast which proved to be benign.
    I should be grateful if you would kindly see and advise on further management.
With thanks
David Evans

"No attempt to offer a diagnosis, you'll notice," commented Mr Potts drily as he beckoned Sister to show the patient in. "What else is missing from this letter?"

He addressed the question to Brian Booth, a quiet diligent student who, although highly intelligent and well read, lacked self-confidence. Had Brian been in an examination hall with paper and pen to hand, he would have had no difficulty in suggesting that the GP might have given the patient's age, stated how long the lump had been present, whether it was increasing in size and half a dozen other pieces of information. But in the presence of the patient, a couple of nurses, surrounded by his fellow students, and with Mr Potts glaring at him he became flustered.

"I, er,   um, well, I'm not sure Sir," the poor man stuttered. "Perhaps whether she's married or has a family."

Mr Potts sighed sadly. "I told you that she's the wife of a farmer; that means she's married doesn't it, Booth? That was one of the few things the GP did say in his letter. My God, when I saw you standing there in your white coat, I thought you were training to be a doctor, but if you're part of the maintenance staff come to do a bit of decorating you should have waited 'til the clinic was over."

He turned to one of the girls. "Miss Johnstone, you look as though you're a bright young thing, for heaven's sake, help him out."

Mr Potts believed that such criticism stimulated the student to work harder but in practice it had the opposite effect. It crushed the confidence of the unfortunate victim, filled his fellow students with apprehension and embarrassed the patient.

Mrs Nichols proved to be a pleasant woman, 36 years of age, who had kept her figure despite having two young children. Wearing a plain thick woollen skirt and a chunky roll necked sweater and with her rosy cheeks and broad calloused hands, her appearance spoke of a healthy life of hard work spent in the open air.

In response to Mr Potts' interrogation, she described how she had noticed the lump a few weeks earlier. It had gradually increased in size but had not been painful. She stated that although she did a lot of physical work, she had no recollection of having bumped or knocked her breast. Apart from the contraceptive pill, she wasn't taking any medication.

"Nothing there to suggest what the problem might be," Mr Potts remarked to the students before asking Sister to take Mrs Nichols into one of the examination cubicles.

In the privacy of the cubicle, Mrs Nichols enquired whether she would be seen by Mr Potts alone or whether all the other young men with him would also be present.

"If you like I can ask him to see you on his own," Sister replied, though the inflection in her voice indicated she was not optimistic that she would be successful. In fact her request fell on deaf ears.

"I've brought a number of young doctors with me today," Mr Potts began when he entered the cubicle. "They do have to learn you know, so they'll be able to look after patients with breast problems in the future. Now if you would care to remove that dressing gown."

Hesitatingly Mrs Nichols did as she was told.

For a moment, Mr Potts stood back and regarded his patient. "Now sit up straight and show me where this lump is."

"Frugis ruris vero largae sunt," Mr Potts remarked, a smile on his face and with a sideways glance at his students. Some of the medical students had studied Latin at school; one sniggered; the rest looked surprised and embarrassed. The non Latin scholars looked puzzled. Mrs Nichols, realising that a personal remark about her appearance had been made looked hurt; her eyes turned to Sister appealingly. Sister also conscious that an inappropriate remark had been made, though not understanding what had been said, looked daggers at Mr Potts but said nothing.

"Right, let's see what this lump is all about."

He examined Mrs Nichols quickly though thoroughly. He was about to instruct one of the students to examine Mrs Nichols as well but Sister beat him to it. In a flash she had the dressing gown back in place and a protective arm round Mrs Nichols' shoulders.

Mr Potts stood back, a grave look on his face. "I'm afraid that you have a bit of a problem there," he said. "Dress up and I'll come and have a chat with you in a minute." Without waiting for a response, he led the students out of the cubicle.

"What did that Latin phrase mean?" one of the students whispered to his colleague.

"The land produces bountiful fruits," he was told.

Whilst Mrs Nichols was dressing herself in the examination cubicle, Mr Potts spoke to the students. "I'm afraid that's rather a large tumour," he said, before going on to explain that it was unusual to find a cancer in such a young patient. Unfortunately it meant that the prognosis was poor.

"Sister obviously didn't want you all to examine her today but when she comes in for her surgery, I want every one of you to take the opportunity to examine her so you'll learn what a breast cancer looks and feels like. Now," he said, looking at his watch, "we're running behind schedule. You go and read up about the conditions you've seen this morning, whilst I have a word with Mrs Nichols. I've several more patients to see before I'm able to get my lunch."

Chapter Thirty Three

Whilst he was working in the outpatient clinic the following afternoon, Paul was surprised to be summoned to the phone by the duty administrator.

"Mr Lambert, I'm sorry to trouble you but we have a problem with the 'on call' rota. Unfortunately Mr Turnbull went off sick this morning with tonsillitis; he was due to be 'on call' tonight as the surgical registrar. I've rung the agency to try to get a locum but I'm afraid they don't have anyone available to cover. Mr Smith is unavailable; Mr Ahmed is on holiday out of the country so I'm afraid that just leaves you."

"Normally I wouldn't mind helping out," Paul replied, "but I've already lived in the hospital one night this week and I shall be on duty next weekend as well. I really don't fancy another night on duty."

"I appreciate that it may be awkward but I'm afraid I must ask you to change your arrangements."

"And I'm afraid that I'm not prepared to do that. I already have plans for this evening. My wife and I are going to the theatre."

"In that case I must remind you that your contract requires you to cover in case of emergency. Of course, we will be able to pay you the going rate for working overtime," the administrator added as an afterthought."

Paul cursed, not least because he knew Kate would be livid. Desperately he asked himself if there was any way he could get out of it.

"Are you still there Dr Lambert?" the administrator queried.

"Yes I am. Look, I'll speak with Mike Smith to see why he's not free tonight but I guess one of us will have to do it."

"That's great. Then I'll leave you to sort it out." He sounded relieved to have off loaded his problem.

Paul immediately contacted his surgical colleague

"Mike, I've just been told that Bob Turnbull has gone off sick. Kate and I have already arranged to go out this evening so I wondered------"

He was interrupted "Don't think that I'm going to do it Paul, because I'm not. It's too damned easy for the bloody admin department to get us to deputise. I don't believe for a minute they've tried to get locum cover. They know it's cheaper to get us to do it."

"Are you really unable to cover tonight? Kate and I have a genuine arrangement. We've got theatre tickets so it------."

"Listen Paul, I did an extra night a couple of weeks ago and didn't get a word of thanks for it. I'm not prepared to do any more extra work. There are more important things in life than working for this bloody hospital. I'm not available tonight and that's final."

Paul heard a click as the phone went down.

For a moment or two Paul sat with his head in his hands. The previous evening Kate had announced that there was a play on at the Odeon in the city centre. The theatre manager had rung the Nurses Home and offered a number of complimentary tickets. Apparently they were happy to give away seats for the opening couple of nights of a new production if ticket sales hadn't been good, preferring the theatre to have some atmosphere rather than to be half empty. Kate had been allocated tickets and had made Paul promise to be home in time for them to have their evening meal and be at the theatre for seven thirty.

Paul looked at his watch; it was three thirty. It was Kate's half day so the chances were that she would be in the flat. With a sinking heart he phoned her.

Kate immediately sensed that something was amiss.

"What is it Paul? You're usually too busy to phone in the middle of the day."

"I'm afraid there's a problem, Kate. We won't be able to go out tonight. Bob has gone off sick and I've had my arm twisted to cover."

As anticipated, Kate was furious. Paul explained and apologised but Kate was not to be placated.

"It's just not good enough Paul. You're letting me down yet again. You always put the wretched hospital first. We haven't been out together for weeks and you promised faithfully you'd be free tonight."

Stung by this criticism, Paul pointed out that he hadn't been given any choice in the matter. The department had a service to run and it wasn't his fault that Bob had gone down with tonsillitis.

"Look, let's go to the theatre later in the week," he said. "We'll have a meal out before the show like we did in the old days."

"But we've got tickets for tonight – free ones; and I've been looking forward to going out. If you won't take me, I'll damn well go on my own."

"Look Kate, I truly am sorry. Don't you think that I'd rather have a night out than work another night in here? But it's no good blaming me. There's nothing I can do about it. Anyway I've got to get back to work now. I'm in the middle of a clinic."

"Of course, you can do something about it," Kate snapped "Simply say that you're not free tonight; then they'll have to get a locum. You've got to learn to stick up for yourself Paul and not let them walk all over you."

"It's not as easy as that, Kate and you damn well know it. Now, I shall have to go, I've got patients waiting."

"That's right. Always put your patients before me," Kate said. "Well you go and see your precious patients and see if I care!" She put the phone down with a bang without waiting for a reply.

It was their worst row for several months and Paul was deeply concerned. If he was stuck in the hospital overnight, it would be five or six the following evening before he saw Kate again. She would be alone for the duration, fuming that yet again he had put his patients before his marriage.

He went back to his clinic room but didn't immediately call for his next patient. He hated having any sort of disagreement with Kate, usually being prepared to back down rather than push his point of view. Of course, this wasn't the first time they had clashed over his inability to control his work and in his heart he knew that Kate was justified in being annoyed.

He recalled the very first lecture he had attended when he joined the medical school as an undergraduate almost a decade before. The Dean had entered the hall and without saying a word to the students had written the words 'TIMES THREE' in large letters on the blackboard. He then explained that doctors had three times the suicide rate, three times the incidence of alcoholism and three times the divorce rate when compared with the general population. His message was clear; although a doctor's first duty was to his patients, he also had a responsibility to look after himself.

Although Paul felt wretched, there was no way he would consider ending his life, and he drank very little, far less than other doctors that he knew; but the possibility of losing Kate was unthinkable. Was his marriage at risk? The thought horrified him. He couldn't imagine living without Kate. Looking back, he realised they had married without seriously considering the nuts and bolts of a life spent together. They hadn't discussed his work load, the salaries they might earn, where they might live or the challenges they might face. They had been blinded by their love for each other and had naively imagined that marriage would be a dream world of log fires and country walks, with a couple of healthy children and a dog thrown in for good measure. In fact, marriage was a step into the dark, a journey into uncharted territory, a blind leap of faith.

He wondered if Kate also had concerns about the state of their marriage. Was it possible that she wanted to start afresh? With hindsight he realised how selfish he had been. He had put his own career before everything else, simply expecting Kate to play second fiddle. She had been desperately keen to start a family; he had been the one who was happy with the 'status quo'. How inconsiderate that had been.

The more he thought about it, the more he realised that he just couldn't go on. He had to act to change his life; the risk of losing Kate was too great. He couldn't let that happen. He wouldn't let it happen. He had to find a way to escape the pressure and he needed to find it quickly. Then, quite suddenly, the answer to his problem struck him. It was so obvious and so simple he was surprised he hadn't thought of it sooner. It was staring him in the face. He had to quit surgery.

There was a knock on the door and an angry outpatient Sister entered.

"I've come to see what's causing this frightful delay. Can't you see we're running half an hour behind schedule? My nurses need to go off duty at five. It's not fair to delay them. I'm going to call your next patient."

"Get out and leave me alone," Paul snapped angrily.

Sister was startled. She was about to issue a brisk reprimand but she had worked alongside Paul for many months. She knew him to be a quiet and courteous young man. This was totally out of character, something was wrong.

Paul also realised how inappropriate his reaction had been. Perhaps he was cracking up. This wasn't him at all. Nor were the tears that he felt welling up in his eyes.

"Look, I'm sorry Sister," he said quietly, "I didn't mean that. Just give me a few moments on my own, to sort myself out. I'll call the next patient myself when I'm ready."

After Sister had left and closed the door, Paul reflected on the decision he had just made. Surely it was the right thing to do. Life would be so much pleasanter if he had a 'nine to five' job with less responsibility. It wouldn't mean quitting medicine altogether, he could do research at the university or maybe get a teaching job. The relief from not having to do out-of-hours 'on call' duties would be enormous. He could still earn enough for them to be comfortable and he could spend every evening and weekend with Kate and with their baby. Yes, that was the way forward, it was an attractive proposition. Would he miss surgery? Surely not; surgery was making him miserable, it was threatening their marriage. He would tell Kate of his decision as soon as he saw her. She would be delighted of course, and then he would inform Sir William and Mr Potts.

Feeling more cheerful than he had for many weeks, he went to the door and called for the next patient.

Chapter Thirty Four

Kate's anger burned inside her after her row with Paul on the phone. He had promised to take her out, insisting that for once he would come home on time. She had been looking forward to it; it would certainly have made a pleasant change from sitting on her own in the flat looking at the four walls as she did so often these days. Maybe it wasn't Paul's fault that Bob was sick but it was time he learned to stand up for himself. Damn it, he was 28 years old, he should simply have said *'no. I'm not doing extra work tonight'*. Why was he always the one who said *'yes'* when there were problems to be solved? Did it never occur to him that he was letting others down? No it didn't; as long as he was looking after his precious patients, he didn't give a damn about anyone else. He was selfish; it really was too bad.

She had already chosen the loose fitting outfit she was planning to wear that evening. She was getting bigger by the day; it wouldn't be long before she would need a maternity frock. With a sigh, she drifted upstairs to put the dress away then, on a whim, picked up the phone and spoke with her friend Sally, as she often did when something was bothering her and she needed someone to talk to.

Bitterly she explained how Paul had let her down yet again and how angry and frustrated she felt.

"I'm totally pissed off," she said. "It happens over and over again. Afterwards he always apologies and says he will mend his ways – but he never does. We haven't been out together for ages. In truth, I don't think he's capable of changing."

"Well, Clare and I also have tickets for the show tonight," Sally said. Clare was a mutual friend who had also been in the same nurse training year as Kate and Sally.

"Why don't we go as a threesome? Let's forget the men and have a jolly good girl's night out. It will do you good, and besides you could take us in Paul's car; that will save us traipsing into town on the bus."

On the phone, Kate had threatened Paul that she would go to the theatre on her own. She hadn't meant it, of course; her words had been spoken in anger. Had she not spoken with Sally, she would simply have stayed at home nursing her resentment, but a night out with her girlfriends would be fun. It would cheer her up and be a real tonic. She decided she would go and if Paul didn't like it, then that was just too bad!

"Come to the flat at six fifteen," she said, "I'll be waiting for you."

****

Having driven into the city centre and parked the car, they had time for a coffee before the show in a cafe on the High St. It felt good to be away from the hospital and the three girls chatted and giggled happily before going on to the theatre. The seats they had been allocated were up in 'the Gods' but that didn't matter. They hadn't expected to be gifted the best seats in the house. Kate particularly enjoyed the production. It was a pleasant diversion, helping her to forget her domestic troubles for a while. The play was *'She stoops to conquer'* by Oliver Goldsmith, which she had studied for her 'O' level English exam many years before and it brought back happy memories of her school days.

It had started to rain by the time they came out of the theatre and all three got soaked as they ran back to the car. Claire tried to persuade Kate to call at one of the city centre pubs for a drink before they went home but with Sally and Kate pregnant and both having to be on the ward before eight the next morning, she was overruled.

On the return journey, Sally commented that the plot in the play was so complicated, there being so many twists and turns that she hadn't quite followed it all. She was amused however that the heroine, who also chanced to be called Kate, had acted as a common serving wench to seduce Charles Marlow, the man of her dreams. Had Kate engaged in any such subterfuge to snare Paul, she wanted to know.

"Not at all," Kate replied laughing, as they cleared the city centre and joined the main road that led back to the hospital, "though I admit Paul was just as shy as Charles Marlow. I did have to make it pretty clear to him that I would say yes if he asked me for a date."

"And is it true that he asked both you and Carol Jenkins on that first date?"

Kate chuckled as she slowed to overtake a cyclist, "Yes. He had two tickets for a party. Carol and I happened to be standing together when he asked if we would like to go. It wasn't clear whether he was inviting both of us or just one – and if so, which one.

As the memory of those early days of their relationship returned to her mind, Kate felt a sudden wave of affection for Paul. How she wished he would be waiting for her when she got home, just as Sally's husband, Colin would be waiting for her. The flat would seem cold and empty when she turned the key in the lock. Why couldn't they spend more time together? Why did he have to be so conscientious about his work? Yet she knew that she truly loved him despite it. In her heart she accepted she would always have to share him with his patients. She couldn't imagine life without him.

"So what happened?" Claire asked.

"We both said yes at exactly the same time. So being the perfect gentleman, Paul took us both - though I was the one he kissed at the end of the evening!" "That's hilarious, Paul must have been so embarrassed," Sally responded, "I hope that when you got to the party you......"

A huge dark shadow suddenly flew towards the side of the car. "Look out!" Sally screamed. But there was no time to take avoiding action. A lorry hit the driver's door with tremendous force. There was an enormous crash and the sound of breaking glass. The car was thrown across the road and was hit by a van coming in the opposite direction. Thrown onto its side, it ground to a halt. Within a few seconds, the lorry driver and two pedestrians were checking the wreckage, anxious to see what had happened to the occupants. Gently they helped Sally and Claire to clamber out into the road. Both were shaken and badly bruised. Kate though, had been thrown bodily from her seat, her head had smashed into something metallic and she lay motionless, slumped across the steering wheel.

****

"Have you ever taken out an appendix, Malcolm?"

"No, I haven't though I've assisted plenty of times of course."

"Then perhaps you would like to do this case and I'll assist you for a change?"

Malcolm was a research worker on 'Surgical Three'. He had enjoyed his house job on Sir William's unit the previous year and had decided to make surgery his career. Had he known how disillusioned Paul had become and the decision he had taken to quit surgery earlier that afternoon, he might have reconsidered! His academic post did not involve any 'out of hours' work, thereby allowing him plenty of time to study for his postgraduate exams. For a moment, he looked surprised at Paul's suggestion. He had been itching to be given the chance to perform a proper operation; to date he had only been allowed to stitch up minor cuts in the casualty department. He jumped at this unexpected opportunity.

"Yes, I'd love to; but you'll have to be patient with me and watch me like a hawk."

It was eleven in the evening. A couple of hours earlier, Janet had examined Roger Wilkins in the casualty department and suggested a diagnosis of appendicitis. In accordance with protocol, Paul had reviewed the case and agreed that the appendix was indeed the root of the problem. Roger was a slim healthy young man, a labourer from a local building firm. His symptoms had only been present for 15 hours making it unlikely that the inflammation would be too severe. Malcolm had already shown himself to have a neat pair of hands when suturing wounds so Paul was in no doubt that this was a suitable operation for him to perform. He would be there to supervise, ready to take over should the need arise. Understandably the anaesthetist was not best pleased with the arrangement. He would have preferred Paul to operate, knowing that his chances of getting to bed before one in the morning would have been improved had the operation been performed by the more experienced surgeon!

Normally Paul would have preferred to undertake the operation himself. Until the last month, he had enjoyed a warm sense of satisfaction from feeling in control when undertaking a straightforward procedure, particularly one that cured a potentially life threatening condition like appendicitis. This case might have gone a little way to restoring that confidence. However he remembered how grateful he had been when others had taken the time to supervise his early surgical endeavours. Unfortunately many consultants were unwilling to act as the assistant, preferring to perform the surgery themselves. Partly this was understandable as it saved time but common sense dictated that trainees ought not to perform operations without supervision. Yet it continued to happen, as Paul knew to his cost after his botched attempts to deal with a burst aneurysm. It was not an arrangement that was in the best interest of patients!

Learning to operate is like learning to drive a car. Malcolm could learn a lot by sitting as a passenger in the front seat; watching theatre routine, learning aseptic technique and understanding the importance of counting instruments and swabs at the beginning and end of every procedure. But to make progress he had to take the wheel. He had to learn how to tie surgical knots left handed without letting go of the suture at any time. He had to learn how much pressure to apply when cutting different tissues, to appreciate that skin is reasonably tough, offering resistance to the scalpel blade, like cutting through thin cardboard, whereas incising the subcutaneous tissues is akin to slicing through soft butter with a hot knife. As he gained experience he would also learn that the scalpel is not simply used to cut tissues but also allows the surgeon to get feedback through his hand about the tissues being incised; if it is rubbery it is probably benign; if gritty almost certainly malignant.

Understandably Malcolm was nervous as he commenced the procedure, incising the skin and dissecting his way tentatively through the various layers of the abdominal wall, all the while keeping the bleeding under control. Then, under Paul's guidance he opened the peritoneum, the thin membrane lining the abdominal cavity. Some cloudy fluid welled out of the wound indicating that the diagnosis of appendicitis was correct. Without being prompted, the scrub nurse handed Malcolm a syringe so that a sample could be taken for bacteriological examination. The results would influence the choice of antibiotic that would be given. Malcolm now had to locate the appendix. He struggled for a couple of minutes, but was unable to find it.

"Have you noticed what the consultants do if they're having difficulty seeing the target organ? Paul asked.

"Make a bigger incision?"

"Yes, that's right. It's always safer to enlarge the incision than to risk damage to some vital structure because of inadequate access. If you remember, the patient's pain was a little lower down the abdomen than usual, so I should extend the incision at the bottom end."

"Please may I have the skin knife again, Staff Nurse?"

Paul laughed. "Sir William would have loved to hear you say that. He's a stickler for courtesy. He regularly reminds us that a *'please'* and a *'thank you'* are good for staff morale; and quite right too."

The nurse, at his side whispered ,"Shhh Paul."

Paul wondered what had caused the warning but a second later was startled to hear a movement behind him. He turned to find Sir William gloved and gowned and obviously ready to join the surgical team. He also became aware that an ominous silence had descended on the theatre. No one was talking, no one was moving and all eyes were fixed on him.

In the moment before Sir William spoke, Paul felt a dreadful sense of foreboding, an ominous feeling that something terrible had happened, like a policeman arriving unannounced and knocking on your front door, something that affected him.

"Lambert, I need a quiet word," he said, holding his hands to his chest to avoid desterilising his gloves. He took a couple of steps back so they would not be overhead.

"I'm afraid that your wife has been involved in a road accident; she's been taken to the casualty department as an emergency. I'm afraid I have no other details. I suggest that you go and see how she is. I'll take over here."

Stunned, Paul muttered his thanks, threw off his gown and gloves, pulled his white coat over his green theatre suit and ran to casualty.

Chapter Thirty Five

Kate became dimly aware that she was cold. She felt her whole body shivering uncontrollably. As consciousness slowly returned, the discomfort began; at first a dull ache which rapidly became an unbearably sharp, agonising pain. Her whole body felt as if it had been dragged through a mangle but it was her head and chest that hurt most. Curiously she wasn't afraid, rather she felt puzzled. She struggled through a grey haze to understand why she was lying on something hard and why water was splashing onto her face. She came to the conclusion that she must have been involved in some sort of accident though she couldn't imagine what. She decided to wiggle her toes to see that they were still there and was reassured to find that they were! Then she tried her fingers with the same pleasing result. Tentatively she opened her eyes.

"Ah, so you've finally decided to wake up," a gruff voice said in a kindly tone. "That's good news."

She tried to focus but could only make out a bright light shining down at her against a dark backcloth. She blinked as a rain drop fell in her eye and everything became more blurred than before.

The voice spoke again. "Just lie still. We're going to lift you onto a stretcher. We'll have you at the hospital in a jiffy." Slowly, painfully she turned her head in the direction of the voice and tried again to see who was there. Vaguely she made out someone wearing a dark uniform.

She felt two pairs of arms link under her body and as she was lifted, the pain became excruciating; it stabbed like a dagger into her chest. She winced and tried to tell them they were hurting but her words were inaudible. Then her eyes closed as she lapsed back into coma.

When she next woke she found herself on a couch in a cubicle with nurses fussing round her. "I'm cold," she managed to mutter, "terribly cold."

"I know, my love. You're shivering all over. But don't worry. Nurse Atkins has gone to the linen cupboard to get a couple of blankets. We'll have you warm in no time at all. You just try to lie still while we get you sorted out."

Through the haze Kate recognised Sister James and realised that she must be in the casualty department of her own hospital.

"What's happened to me?" she asked.

"You've been involved in a road accident," Sister replied as she wrapped Kate in two warm blankets then slipped a blood pressure cuff round her arm. "I don't know the details but Nurse Taylor and Nurse Flynn were also involved. They arrived a few minutes before you did."

"Are they alright?"

"They are being examined but I think they've got away with just a few bumps and bruises."

She recorded Kate's pulse, temperature and blood pressure on a chart which she placed on the locker. "The doctor will be along in a minute to check you over but I'm sure with that bump on your head, he'll want to admit you for observation. Oh, and I think we'd better tell your husband that you're here, don't you?"

As Sister left the cubicle Kate tried desperately to remember what had happened. She recalled working on the ward in the morning. 'I think we were planning to go to the theatre', she said to herself, 'but what happened after that?' But try as she might, she could remember nothing of the trip into town, or the show, or the accident on the return journey.

Dr Jim Dovey, one of the casualty officers, entered the cubicle. He knew Kate well, both as a colleague in the hospital and as Paul's wife.

"Sorry, Kate but I'll have to give you the once over," he said, knowing how awkward it felt to be examining someone, or indeed being examined, by someone with whom you were acquainted.

Twenty minutes later, having completed a comprehensive assessment, he slipped back into the office to arrange for some intravenous fluids, some precautionary x-rays and to write up his case notes. He had been especially thorough and left nothing to chance.

****

Arriving in casualty, Paul was prevented from entering Kate's cubicle.

"We're busy sorting your wife out at present, Mr Lambert," the staff nurse said. "We won't keep you a moment."

For fully five minutes, he fidgeted and fretted outside the door fearing the worst. When finally he was allowed in, he felt a surge of relief. Kate was conscious and had a reasonable colour in her cheeks. Despite an eye that was rapidly closing with a developing bruise, she managed a wan smile when she saw him.

"I'm sorry Paul; it seems I've been in an accident. The trouble is I don't remember anything about it." She winced as she spoke, holding a hand to her side.

"You must have been to see that play in town. Sally and Claire must have been with you. The ambulance men say there were three of you in the car and that you were driving. Don't you remember that?"

"No, I don't. I remember working on the ward but after that everything's a blank. I don't understand. I thought you and I were going to go out, but you say Sally and Claire were with me. Oh Paul, I do hope that I haven't caused a crash or that the car isn't too badly damaged."

"Damn the car," Paul replied, "How are you?"

"Not too bad. I've bumped my head and it aches like hell, but it's my ribs that hurt most. I feel as if I've been crushed in a vice. I'm to have an x-ray to see if they're broken."

"Nowhere else damaged?"

"Jim says not. But Paul, what about Sally and Claire? Sister says they aren't too badly hurt but please check for me and let me know."

"Sure."

The door opened and Sister returned, a porter at her side. "We're taking you to x-ray now and then to Ward One. I'm pleased to say that they have an empty side ward for you. Whether or not you've broken some ribs, you'll have to be monitored overnight because of that nasty head injury."

Paul accompanied Kate to the x-ray department and thirty minutes later was relieved to learn that the x-ray had not shown any broken ribs. Then having seen Kate settled on the ward, he went to bed. With reasonable luck her observations would be satisfactory and she would escape without any serious or permanent injury. She might even be allowed home the next day.

The night's events were a real jolt to Paul. Seeing Kate dazed and bruised brought home to him just how much he loved his wife and how foolish it was to let anything threaten their relationship. He would be pleased to mother her for as long as it took for her to recover. He would tell her that he had decided to give up surgery and move into something less demanding, a 'nine to five' job that would allow them to spend more time together. It would give him a chance to show her that he cared; an opportunity to make up for the way he had neglected her in the past. He wondered whether the car was still at the roadside and how badly damaged it was but decided that could wait until the morning. Even if the car was a write off, it wouldn't matter so long as Kate was alright. However he did worry what had caused the accident. He knew Kate would never forgive herself if she had been to blame.

****

Although sedated, Kate found it impossible to settle. Her head throbbed and whenever she moved, a severe spasm of pain struck her in the ribs making her wince. Worried about the accident, she wracked her brains but could remember nothing about it. They said she had been to see a show at a theatre in the city but her mind remained a complete blank. She couldn't recall the name of the show or anything about it. Her head was full of questions. How badly was the car damaged? Had she been the cause of the accident? Had she hit another car, or worse, a cyclist or pedestrian? Had anyone else been hurt or even killed? Please God no.

She felt terribly alone and afraid, desperate for someone to comfort her. She needed a shoulder to cry on, someone to wrap their arms around her, to hug and protect her. Her first thought was not for her husband but for her mother – why did you have to leave us Mum, when I still need you so much?

She had no idea what time it was though she could see it was dark outside. There was no clock in the room so she looked for her watch but couldn't find it. She found that she was wearing nothing but a hospital nightgown. Who had undressed her? Where were her clothes, her watch, her handbag? The more the questions went round in her head, the more anxious she became. Eventually she acknowledged that she had no way of answering them so she closed her eyes and tried to get some sleep. However sleep wouldn't come. She developed a pain in her back and grew concerned. They hadn't x-rayed her back. Had they missed something? Had she fractured her spine? Aware of the devastating complications of back injuries, she wiggled her toes and reassured herself that her spinal cord was intact. Then a severe cramping pain started in her belly and she panicked.

"My baby," she cried out loud. "I must have hurt my baby." She pressed the nurse call button and when no one responded within a few seconds, she pressed it again urgently and persistently.

A middle aged woman whom Kate didn't recognise opened the door. She was wearing a staff nurse's uniform; she looked tired and irritable. She cancelled the nurse call alarm, then hung it on the wall, out of Kate's reach.

"Now what is it? I've a ward full of sick patients to look after. I can't be doing with any unnecessary interruptions."

"I've got a terrible pain in my belly," Kate wailed. "It must be the baby. I'm sure I've hurt my baby. You've got to call the doctor."

The nurse gave an audible sigh. "Look Mrs Lambert, there's no need for you to get excited. I'm sure everything will be okay. Babies are tough little fellows. I've had three so I ought to know."

She busied herself taking Kate's pulse and blood pressure, then checked that the drip was running satisfactorily.

"Everything's fine," she declared. "There really is no need for you to be so alarmed. The doctor did write you up for something a little stronger that could be given if you needed it; I'll get that organised. Then you get off to sleep."

Two minutes later she gave Kate an injection of morphine. "There, I'm sure that will help. Now try to get some rest."

"Are you sure everything's alright?"

"Absolutely. It's four in the morning; there's certainly no need to go waking the doctor. You just relax and go to sleep. We're short staffed you know; you must let me get on with my jobs."

Kate lay awake, unconvinced. Although she closed her eyes and tried to sleep, the cramping pain in her belly increased in intensity despite the morphine she had been given. The spasms were incredibly severe for a couple of minutes then just when she thought they might have passed, they returned even more fiercely than before. The pain and her anxiety about her pregnancy meant that sleep was impossible. Then her worst fears were realised. She felt wetness between her thighs. In horror she lifted the bedclothes and saw blood. A pool of dark red sticky blood was spreading over the sheets. Her nursing training told her exactly what was happening. She let the bed covers fall back into place, curled into a ball and wept uncontrollably.

Chapter Thirty Six

At a quarter to eight the day staff congregated in the office for the daily 'hand over'; the ritual that took place when they came on duty each morning and was repeated every evening when they departed. The agency nurse who had been in charge overnight was detailing the care that each of the patients had received during her shift. Sitting round her in a wide semicircle were the Ward Sister and her nurses, all listening intently. Thanks to the staff shortage, it had been a long and tiring night. She was looking forward to getting home for a soak in the bath to ease her aching feet followed by a long restful sleep. She reported on each patient in turn, most of whom had spent an uneventful night. If relatives rang to enquire after their progress they would probably be informed that they were 'comfortable', an odd expression to use given that they all had distressing symptoms of one sort or another! Finally she spoke of the only patient who had been admitted while she was in charge.

"In the side ward we have Mrs Lambert. You probably know her better as Staff Nurse Meredith. She works on the Surgical Five Unit. She's the wife of Dr Lambert who's the registrar there. She was involved in an RTA last night, bumped her head and was concussed. She was admitted for observation, but her 'obs' have been fine. No bones were broken but she's a bit shaken up and bruised; she's got a lovely big black eye. She had some abdominal pain at one stage but it settled with morphine. I looked in later but she was asleep, so I didn't disturb her. The doctors are to review her today with a view to discharge this afternoon."

"Okay Staff Nurse, I'll look in on her later," Sister said.

It was over an hour later when Sister opened the door of the side room. She found Kate curled up in the foetal position sobbing quietly.

"Hey, what's the matter? I'm sure there's no need to cry."

Kate turned away and buried her head in the pillow.

"Now, now, Mrs Lambert, I'm sure there's no need for tears. Just tell me what's upsetting you."

"I've lost my baby," Kate sobbed. "I've lost my precious little baby."

"Straighten up and lie on your back," Sister instructed, angry that no-one had mentioned that Kate was pregnant.

Suddenly noticing that Kate was clammy and ominously pale, she realised that she had an emergency on her hands. She pressed the 'nurse call' button.

"Have you been bleeding?" she asked.

Kate nodded weakly. Sister turned down the sheets to find the bed full of blood, some fresh and fluid, some old and clotted.

"Oh, you poor dear," she said, quickly replacing the bedclothes before Kate had a chance to observe that amongst the blood clots was her perfectly formed but still born baby boy.

A student nurse appeared.

"Nurse, bring me a BP machine and prepare another intravenous drip," she ordered. "Then call for the registrar to come immediately to see Mrs Lambert. And ask Dr Lambert to give me a ring," she added as an afterthought.

"I've lost my baby, haven't I Sister?"

Sister put a comforting arm around Kate. "I'm rather afraid that you have," she said softly.

The morning passed in a whirl of activity of which subsequently Kate had little memory. She was seen by the registrar who arranged for an urgent blood transfusion. As he left, Paul arrived. Kate clung to him, eyes red with tears.

"Paul, I'm so sorry. I've lost our baby." Paul hugged her offering words of sympathy but Kate was not to be consoled.

Then Dr Walker a gynaecologist from the neighbouring St Margaret's Hospital for Women called. He asked Paul to leave while he examined Kate. As he left he had a quick word with Paul in the corridor. He spoke quickly in the matter of fact manner that was normal between medical colleagues.

"I'm afraid your wife has suffered a miscarriage. As I'm sure you know such events are really quite common but in this case, it's probably the result of last night's accident. Normally, given the ongoing bleeding, we would arrange to perform a D and C to evacuate the uterus straightaway but given her head injury and concussion, I doubt the anaesthetist will allow us to do that today. I suggest that your wife be transferred to St Margaret's and all being well we'll do it tomorrow."

"Have you explained this to her?" Paul asked.

"Yes, I have but I doubt that she took it all in. Perhaps you could go over it again for her. As I say, I'm sorry, but do tell her that these things happen and not to be too upset."

Dr Walker glanced at his watch. "Look, I'm afraid I must dash. I was supposed to be in my clinic twenty minutes ago."

For Kate, the next 48 hours were a nightmare. Gradually her memory of much of the previous night's events returned such that she remembered leaving the theatre and driving home. She relived the terrifying moment when the lorry had suddenly appeared and the sickening crash as it hit the side of the car. Curiously though, try as she might, she still had no recollection of lying in the rain on the pavement or of the ambulance journey to the hospital.

When she was transferred to the gynaecological hospital she found herself in a four bedded room with three other women. All had been admitted to have a D and C on Dr Walker's next operating list.

A girl of about 19 approached her. "Hello there, welcome to the clearing house. I suppose you're in the same boat as the rest of us; in for a quick scrape to get rid of our little mistakes?"

She was a dyed blond, and might have been quite attractive with her blue eyes, curly hair and cheerful smile had it not been for the purple lipstick she wore, the tattoos on her arms and the obvious love bite on her neck. She spoke cheerfully, as if she hadn't a care in the world, in no way intimidated by the medical environment.

Kate was unable to reply. She simply burst into tears.

"You might well cry love, if your fella' gave you that shiner as well as a bun in the oven. For God's sake get rid of him as well as the bloody baby. But hey, don't cry about it, darling. All things considered, this is the best way for us girls to get out of a difficult spot."

"What do you mean?"

"Well, look at me. This is the third time I've been put in the family way. How can I hang on to my job with a baby to look after? And how many men will look my way if I've a snivelling child in tow?"

"So...so you...," Kate began.

"So I'll have to be a bit more careful in future. Doc Walker was a bit shirty with me this time; says he won't be so keen to help me if it happens again." She laughed, "Mind you, I can always go to the hospital down the road, can't I?"

"You mean you don't want your baby?" Kate asked, bewildered that anyone could be so callous about an unborn child.

"Of course I don't. I've just been a bit careless that's all. But don't you worry love; under the anaesthetic you won't feel a thing. By tomorrow you'll be back at home and free to live your life again."

Horrified, Kate turned away and found herself facing a woman of about 35 in the next bed.

"Are you getting rid of your baby as well?" she asked.

The woman paused, realising that Kate's situation was very different from her own.

"Yes, I am," she said quietly. "I'm not sure it's really what I want but I've three children already and there's no man in the house. I simply can't afford to have another one."

She came across and put out her hand to take Kate's. "You want your baby don't you?" she said gently. "I'm sorry."

"Don't touch me," Kate cried. "Don't you dare touch me?" She turned away, closed her eyes and her tears returned. She said not a single word to any of them until she was discharged 48 hours later.

****

When Paul visited Kate that evening, he found her curled up in her bed, her back turned on the other patients in the room. The three other women who had been in the ward when Kate was admitted had been treated and discharged and had been replaced by three more, all wanted their pregnancies to be terminated. They were of various ages and backgrounds but all eager to be rid of their unwanted babies. Kate ignored them, her face a mask of despair. She was inconsolable.

"Paul, I'm so sorry," she sobbed over and over again. "It's my fault. I shouldn't have gone out. I should never have gone to the theatre. When I knew you had to work, I should have stayed at home."

"Don't be silly, Kate," Paul said, sitting on the bed beside her, holding her hand and trying to put a brave face on the situation. "It was just an unfortunate accident, just one of those things."

"But if I'd stayed at home this wouldn't have happened, would it?"

"We don't know that, do we? That's the nature of accidents. One minute you're fine; then something completely unforeseen happens. It was just bad luck. Something might just as easily gone wrong had you stayed at home; just like it did when that cupboard fell on you."

Desperately, Paul tried to cheer her up. He reassured her that Sally and Claire had escaped with just a few bumps and bruises. He told her that the police had been in contact and confirmed that the accident was not Kate's fault. The lorry driver was to be prosecuted for dangerous driving, for exiting a side road without stopping. He didn't tell her that the car was a 'write off'.

Kate though was not interested. Her mind was focussed solely on the baby they had lost.

Paul got up and pulled the screens round the bed to shield Kate from prying eyes. Then he sat beside her whilst she wept silently in his arms. For fully fifteen minutes, neither spoke as they offered comfort to each other. They were disturbed when the Ward Sister put her head round the curtains.

"Kate, I've finally managed to find a side ward for you. If you gather your things together, I'll show you the way. You deserve a little privacy; I'm sure you'll be happier having a room to yourself."

Kate didn't reply; she simply nodded and moved to collect her belongings.

"Thank you, Sister. That's very kind," Paul said on her behalf.

"Perhaps you could wait outside for a moment Dr Lambert, whilst I move your wife and get her settled in," Sister added. "I'll take the opportunity to repeat her observations, change her pads and generally freshen her up."

As Paul exited the screens, he noticed one of the women in the bed opposite, a woman whose face seemed familiar. He was certain he had seen her before but couldn't place her. She was tall and slim and despite being in a hospital bed, had obviously taken some pride in her appearance. For a second, she caught Paul's eye, then immediately turned away and buried her head in a book. Paul went across to her.

"Hello there," he said. "I'm sure that I should know you." The woman looked up briefly. "No, I don't think so. You must be mistaken," she said curtly.

It was the voice, with its somewhat 'plummy' tone, that reminded Paul exactly who the lady was. It was Anne Cullen and immediately, as if a key had suddenly unlocked a compartment in his mind, all the memories of his previous dealings with her came flooding back. He recalled every detail of the consultations in the outpatient department both when he had seen her on his own, then later when accompanied by Sir William. She had tried to persuade them to repeat her husband's vasectomy operation. He remembered her supreme acting ability and her absolute denial that there had been any extramarital activity. He recalled her husband's desperate desire to believe in her fidelity and his willingness to undergo further surgery rather than face an unpalatable truth. He even remembered the wink she had given him when an alternative, if unbelievable, explanation of her miscarriage had been suggested. It also brought to Paul's mind Sir William's wisdom in not forcing on Mr Cullen the evidence of his wife's adultery. Yet since all the women in the room had been admitted for termination of pregnancy, it was clear that Anne Cullen was continuing to deceive her husband.

"I do remember you now," Paul said. "It's Mrs Cullen, isn't it? You've got yourself pregnant again haven't you?" There was a cold hard accusatory tone to his voice.

"Perhaps I have; but it's no business of yours."

"Does your husband know?"

"Again that's none of your business."

Paul's normal self-restraint cracked. He attacked her angrily.

"He doesn't know, does he? You've been cheating on him again, haven't you? What a cheap tart you are for all your airs and graces."

"As it happens, he doesn't know, he thinks I'm visiting my sister in Bristol but if you so much as breathe a word to him, I'll have you in court for breach of confidentiality."

Paul recalled that she worked in a solicitor's office. During their previous encounters he had actually wondered whether one of the young solicitors might have been responsible for her previous pregnancy.

"I'm not likely to meet him, am I?" Paul responded bitterly, "and just so that you know, the last time we met, we knew exactly where the truth lay, but we gave you a second chance for the sake of your children. You clearly didn't deserve it."

Paul turned his back on the woman who now disgusted him.

Chapter Thirty Seven

After the accident, Paul was shocked to discover the depth of Kate's grief at losing her baby though truly he ought not to have been surprised. He knew how badly she wanted a child; she had mentioned it often enough before she abandoned the pill! He had seen how thrilled she was when she finally told Paul that she was pregnant; Sister Rutherford had needed to curb her excitement when talking to the patients and staff on the ward and her happiness had been very obvious each evening as she sat watching the television with both hands massaging her swollen belly or when knitting baby clothes with a contented smile on her face.

Now witnessing her sorrow, dismayed at the level of her anguish and despair, Paul knew he should have anticipated her distress. Kate had watched her body change, felt the baby growing and moving inside her. Whilst pregnant, she had read the manuals on labour, breast feeding and child care far more assiduously than she had as a nursing student! And she had done everything possible to protect this new life from harm. She had eaten sensibly, had avoided smoky rooms, stopped drinking alcohol, exercised in moderation and insisted to Paul that their love life should be infrequent and restrained. She had established a bond with her unborn child of which Paul, busy at work and obsessed with his own problems, had been blissfully unaware. He was left feeling guilty about his thoughtlessness.

Paul's reaction to his wife's pregnancy had been restrained. His initial surprise and delight when Kate had finally plucked up the courage to tell him her news had been replaced with a small quiet satisfaction that he was going to be a 'daddy'. Certainly, he had enjoyed the congratulations and good wishes received from friends and family but working long hours and worrying about his patients, he hadn't subsequently given the matter a great deal of thought. His early irritation that Kate and Sally had taken control of matters had evolved into an acceptance that they, together with the midwives in the maternity department would take the appropriate decisions and make the necessary arrangements. Perhaps selfishly, his concerns throughout had been for Kate's well-being, not for their unborn child. He had imagined that any feelings he would have for the baby would begin when it was born. He now recognised that he too should have developed a greater attachment for the baby as it developed in Kate's womb. It left him unprepared for Kate's pain and misery.

It would have been nice had Kate and Paul been allowed some time to come to terms with their loss but the fact that there had been such an emotional event in their personal lives did not stop the work in the hospital from continuing as usual. The wards and theatre were just as busy as before and whilst Kate was in St Margaret's, Paul was expected to work as normal which meant the usual nights on call, early starts and late finishes. Whilst this distracted Paul from his domestic problems, it did not leave him much time to support Kate in her sorrow.

So it was that the next morning, with Kate still in hospital and due go to theatre herself later in the day, Paul found himself working alongside Sir William in the outpatient clinic. Sir William, sympathetic to his assistant's problems, suggested that Paul leave the clinic early so he could visit Kate at St Margaret's. However, just as he was about to slip away he was contacted by Sister Rutherford. She was worried. Anne Nichols, the lady with the ominous lump in her breast whom Mr Potts had seen in the clinic a week or so before, had been admitted to have a mastectomy. Janet had 'clerked her in' but Mrs Nichols had a number of questions that Janet had been unable to answer.

"I need you to come to the ward and calm her down?" she said before going on to explain that Mrs Nichols was distraught because she'd heard that many patients died of breast cancer despite disfiguring surgery. The operation was planned for the next day and Sister wanted Paul to offer some words of encouragement and reassurance.

Paul found Anne Nichols to be a likeable and uncomplicated lady who asked little more of life, than to be able to care for her husband and her two young children. A couple of years before, she had developed a lump in the opposite breast that had proved to be a simple cyst.

"That only required a tiny operation," she explained. "I was home within 24 hours and back at work within a couple of days."

She had been horrified to learn that on this occasion she had not been so lucky. Mr Potts had told her in the clinic that removal of her breast was essential.

Paul was painfully aware that the outlook for patients who developed breast cancer at such a young age was particularly bad; regrettably the majority of patients would succumb to their cancer despite surgery and x-ray therapy. Mrs Nichols poured out her worst fears to Paul.

"I'm terribly frightened," she said. "Obviously I don't want to lose my breast, but I suppose I'll get used to that eventually."

"I'm sure that you will," Paul replied. "It's an operation we have to perform quite commonly. We're seeing more and more patients with this problem these days. If it will help, we can arrange for you to meet one of our patients who has already had a mastectomy. You could have a chat with her and she could show you how to disguise the operation. When you're dressed with a pad in your bra, no-one will be any the wiser."

"I'm sorry, Doctor, I'm not making myself clear. It's not me that I'm worried about."

"You're married aren't you," Paul replied still misunderstanding Mrs Nichols' principle concerns. "Well obviously you won't be able to disguise it from your husband but if he truly cares for you, he will understand."

"Of course my husband would prefer that I didn't have to have my breast removed but that's not what worries me. My real concern is the children; they're so young, they're still at primary school. John is nine and Becky's only six. At that age they need a mother. They'll need me for many years to come. On his own, my husband won't be able to care for them or give them the support they need. You see, my mother died of breast cancer when I was a teenager and I know how much I missed her.

And there's something else as well, Doctor, something that truly terrifies me. I watched my mother as she died; it was awful seeing her distress as she lost weight and faded away. She had a great deal of pain. I used to hear her tossing and turning in the night, moaning. Sometimes I would go and try to comfort her but she always sent me back to my room. I used to cover my head with my pillow because I couldn't bear to hear her suffer.

But that's not all doctor. Towards the end, she was confined to bed and she developed awful bed sores. I remember them to this day. Even now when I think about her, the smell of those terrible ulcers haunts me. I don't want my children to go through that. I want to be around to see them grow up safely. I've got to stay healthy until they're able to look after themselves, old enough to be independent."

Belatedly Paul realised that any concerns that Mrs Nichols had about her body image were overshadowed by her fears of dying of cancer and leaving her children without a mother.

Sitting at the bedside, screens drawn, despite knowing that the odds were stacked against this young patient, Paul explained that many patients with breast cancer did survive, indeed they lived into old age but Mrs Nichols, in her own mind, equated a diagnosis of breast cancer with death from breast cancer. She begged Paul to promise that when she was dying, he would arrange for her to be admitted to hospital, so that her children wouldn't witness the terminal stages of her illness.

Again Paul tried to reassure. "Believe me Mrs Nichols, the majority of patients with breast cancer are cured by the operation." Although, taken literally, this statement was true; Paul knew that it was misleading in this particular case. "Admittedly the operation is somewhat radical," he continued, "but that is the price to be paid for being rid of the problem."

"But what happens when the cancer returns?"

"You mustn't assume that it will return."

"But it usually does come back, doesn't it, Doctor?"

"In most cases it doesn't," Paul replied, again guilty of verbal deceit, "but even if it did, we should still be here to help you."

But Mrs Nichols was not to be reassured. Regrettably the consultation ended with the patient in tears. Paul prescribed a large dose of a sedative and arranged for sleeping tablets to be available should they be needed to help her sleep through the night. He left her with one of the nurses attempting to comfort with her with kind words and the inevitable cup of tea.

****

Paul glanced at his watch. Twelve thirty. If he hurried he would be able to slip to St Margaret's, see Kate and still be back in time for Mr Potts' afternoon ward round. The women's hospital was only a couple of hundred yards from the City General and he ran most of the way there. Arriving somewhat short of breath he made straight for Kate's side room. It was empty. Damn, had Kate already gone to theatre? He wandered onto the main ward looking for the nurse in charge hoping for some news. As he walked between the lines of beds, he attracted a low wolf whistle and some sexist comment from the younger women. An all-female group could match the chauvinism of men given an appropriate environment and a gynaecology ward was undoubtedly such a place. Normally he might have responded with a smile or a wave but he was in no mood for such levity.

Sister spotted him as she came out of the sluice, a bedpan in her hand. She smiled a welcome.

"Dr Lambert, I'm pleased that you've come. There's something I want to chat to you about. Could I ask you to wait in my office please?" She smiled, and then added, "you're exciting my ladies too much standing there. I'll join you in a minute."

Paul waited for at least five minutes before Sister was free to join him. Praying that Kate's operation was going well, he wondered what Sister wished to talk to him about. The office was similar to those at the City General. A large desk stood in the middle of the room, with chairs scattered around where the nurses sat for the twice daily hand over. The notes trolley was parked against the end wall and there were numerous cupboards used for storing instruments and the many forms used by doctors and nurses to record patient's observations, to write reports and to request investigations from other departments. The walls were largely obscured by numerous notice boards and Paul glanced idly at them. The off duty rota was prominently displayed, as were several notices from management relating to the rules and regulations that governed the lives of the nurses and doctors. There were unofficial notices too; nurses offering their services as babysitters to supplement their meagre pay and advertisements of item for sale such as a second hand prams and push chairs. One particular notice caught Paul's eye; it was the list of operations to be performed in the gynaecological theatre that day. Neatly recorded were the names of the patients, their dates of birth, their hospital numbers and the procedures to be performed. It had been neatly typed, presumably by the secretarial staff but Kate's name had been scrawled at the bottom in ink in a rough hand.

'Mrs Kathryn Lambert 23yo 51284 ERPC'

Paul had seen the initials 'ERPC' hundreds of times on operation lists during his time as a hospital doctor and had never given them any real thought. In his mind he had equated them to '*D and C*' the Dilatation of the cervix that allowed the surgeon access to Curette (scrap) the lining of the womb. It was the commonest of all gynaecological procedures. But in fact ERPC stood for the Evacuation of the Retained Products of Conception. For a moment he stood looking at the letters, then froze as the cold reality hit him; the Products of Conception that the surgeon was evacuating, possibly at that very second, were all that remained of their baby; the baby they would never know, the child they would never hold, never nurture and love and for the first time he had a glimpse of the grief that Kate was suffering. In that moment he felt her pain and began to understand the depth of her despair.

Then other thoughts came crowding into his mind. What had happened on the night of her accident? Had the baby been born intact? Were the surgeons now just removing the placenta that had been left behind or had Kate only lost part of the foetus and its remains were now being evacuated? And if the baby had been born intact where it was now? What had happened to it? He realised he hadn't even asked Kate if she had seen the tissue that she had lost? How crass and unfeeling he had been. His concern for Kate's physical well-being had blinded him to her emotional state and he had given no thought, no thought at all, to the fate of the baby.

Paul was still staring blankly at the operating list when Sister entered the room. She noticed what had attracted his attention.

"Yes, it's very very sad, isn't it," she said softly. "I'm so terribly sorry for you both."

She waved Paul to a chair and took her place behind the desk.

"As well as offering you my sympathy I must also offer you an apology. It was very unfortunate that your wife had to share a room with the women who had been admitted for abortions. We try desperately hard to separate such patients from those having miscarriages but given the pressure on our beds it isn't always possible.

However, that's not the main reason that I wished to speak with you. Am I right in thinking this was your wife's first pregnancy?"

"Yes, that's right."

"I'm afraid she's likely to suffer quite an emotional reaction to her loss. Miscarriages are really quite common and patients react to them in different ways but already it's obvious that Kate is more traumatised than most."

"She was involved in a road accident as well of course."

"Yes, so I believe. I understand your wife was about twenty four weeks pregnant which is much later than is usual for a miscarriage. She will have felt the baby move inside her and will know that the midwives have heard a heartbeat. She will already have formed a bond with her child and that inevitably makes the loss all the more upsetting. I fear it will take Kate a long time to recover and she's likely to need a lot of support, particularly in the early days."

"Is there anything special that I need to do?" Paul asked.

"No, just be there, be sympathetic and supportive."

"Anything else Sister?"

"Well, most of all, you will need to be patient, very patient and remember that professional help is available if you should need it."

Now," she added in a more businesslike tone, "I think it would be best if we kept your wife in hospital overnight. Perhaps you could come to take her home at about ten in the morning."

"Certainly Sister," Paul replied but already he was wondering how he could manage that. He was due in the clinic in the morning and twenty patients had been booked for him to see!

Chapter Thirty Eight

Returning to the City General, Paul found Victoria and Janet together with Sister Ashbrook and the eight medical students waiting in silence for Mr Potts to review his patients. There was a general feeling of anxiety, a sense of foreboding in the air, felt by different members of the group for different reasons.

Victoria was worried because she knew Mr Potts of old and was anticipating trouble! With a degree of subterfuge, the cooperation of the nursing sisters and thanks to a run of good luck, she and Paul had managed to conceal the presence of the occasional orthopaedic patient from the consultant's eagle eye. Good fortune however, does not last forever and the day had arrived when Leslie Potts was destined to find an orthopaedic lodger in one of his beds. To make matters worse, there were actually two lodgers, both highly conspicuous, in beds adjacent to those of Mr Potts' patients, right in the middle of the ward! It was inevitable that the consultant would spot them! One lodger had a surgical collar around his neck and an arm encased in plaster of Paris as brilliantly white as virgin snow. The other was imprisoned in a Balkan beam, his leg in a heavy metal splint exposed above the bedclothes, with numerous weights and pulleys hanging over the foot of the bed. Desperately, Victoria and Sister Ashbrook had tried to conceal them but without success. Neither needed to leave the ward for further x-rays and there wasn't a side ward available into which they could be hidden. Consideration had even been given to placing them on the veranda for the duration of the ward round but since it was December, the temperature outside barely above freezing and snow was falling, this wasn't a practical proposition. It seemed that for the first time Paul would witness the consultant's displeasure and discover exactly what it was that made Victoria and Sister Ashbrook so apprehensive. The two junior doctors were both painfully aware that when Mr Potts was in a bad mood, they were the ones most likely to suffer.

The students were also apprehensive. They too were familiar with Mr Potts' moods. They recalled vividly the manner in which he had objected to Steven Morris' beard when they had met the consultant for the first time and also the way Steven was despatched from the outpatient clinic for his untidy appearance only a few days before. They were expected to be fully informed about the patients that had been allocated to them and feared that if their knowledge was found to lacking they would be harangued and humiliated by the consultant, in front of both patients and nurses.

The nerves of the patients awaiting the consultant's visit were also jangling. Most had heard that Mr Potts was a bit of a tyrant, not a man who suffered fools gladly. Their concerns had been heightened by witnessing the preparations made for the round; the nurses anxiously tidying lockers, straightening blankets and fluffing pillows. They had seen the porters, orderlies and cleaners being shooed from the ward. They had been given strict instructions to stay in their beds and avoid unnecessary noise. However as they waited for the consultant to arrive, their main concern was for themselves and the health problems that had caused them to be in hospital. There were major questions in their minds. *'What did my investigations show? Am I to have an operation and if so, when is it to be?'* Or perhaps; *'What did you find at my operation? Was it anything serious?'* And the all-important question; *'Can my problem be cured?'* Different questions in the minds of different patients, each vital to their health and happiness, perhaps even pivotal to the life of the individual concerned, all to be resolved in the next few moments.

Unfortunately though, not all the questions had definite answers. *'We're still waiting for the results of your tests. Sometimes patients with your problem never have any more trouble, but unfortunately a few do.'* Then the phrase that is meant to reassure but often doesn't; *'Don't worry. Whatever happens, we shall continue to keep a close eye on you so we can deal with any problems that may arise.'*

****

On this occasion, Mr Potts was a mere ten minutes late and as he breezed into the room he appeared to be in a good mood. He had a smile on his face as he ran his eye along the line of students.

"I'm pleased to see that you're all turned out smartly this afternoon, especially you Miss Seddon, if I am allowed to say so. Even Mr Morris seems to have made a special effort today."

Then he put a hand loosely on Janet's shoulder, still addressing the students. "And our lovely House Lady also looks well this morning doesn't she, although I'm not supposed to say that either, am I my dear?"

With time Janet had come to regard her boss with contempt. She had learned that reacting to his provocation simply encouraged him so she simply ignored the remark and waited for the hand to be removed. If the consultant was aware of her feelings he didn't show it.

"Right let's go and see our patients," Mr Potts said as he strode purposefully through the double doors and onto the ward. Sister was at his side, Victoria and Paul followed behind. Next in line was Janet. Holding to her resolution, she strolled alongside the notes trolley which was being pushed by a student nurse. The eight medical students brought up the rear. They walked fearfully in silence. Mr Potts stopped abruptly the moment his eye fell on the two orthopaedic patients. The entourage behind also came to a sudden halt, each bumping into the one in front, like railway trucks in a shunting yard. The consultant jabbed a finger at the two lodgers then glared at Sister Ashbrook, eyebrows raised, brow furrowed and face flushed, his blood pressure rising.

"What are those patients doing on my ward, Sister?" he demanded. "They are orthopaedic patients. They should be on the orthopaedic ward." His voice was loud, the tone angry.

Sister hesitated, flustered. Victoria interceded on her behalf.

"I'm sorry, Mr Potts but there was a nasty accident at the steel works late last night. All the beds on the orthopaedic unit were taken, so unfortunately these two patients had to be placed on our ward."

"Well get rid of them at once!" he bellowed.

"We've already tried to do that, Sir. We've spoken to the staff downstairs to see if they have any spare capacity, but regrettably they haven't. They admitted some patients this morning from their waiting list for surgery tomorrow. All their beds are full."

"They've no damn right to admit more patients to their ward when we have their blasted lodgers here. Go downstairs immediately, Miss Kent and send their new admissions home. I will not tolerate orthopaedic patients on my ward. They're a bloody nuisance; they upset the staff and interfere with the smooth running of the ward."

"I'm afraid I have no authority to do that Sir, any more than the orthopaedic registrar has the right to come here and discharge our patients." Victoria spoke quietly and respectfully. What she said was completely true, but her words cut no ice with her angry boss.

"Then go downstairs and tell their registrar to discharge their new admissions. It's quite intolerable that they should carry on admitting when their patients are clogging up my beds."

Had Paul been wise, perhaps had he not had other more important worries on his mind, he would have kept quiet, but unfortunately he didn't. Set against his own problems, a couple of patients on the wrong ward seemed no more than a minor inconvenience particularly as the beds on their ward would otherwise have been empty.

"I know it's awkward Sir," he volunteered, "but they did have some of our patients on their ward only last week. Surely it's simply a matter of give and take."

For a moment, there was silence, and then Mr Potts roared, "When I want your advice Lambert, I'll ask for it. Until then shut up."

In the silence that followed all eyes turned on Paul, no-one daring to say a word for fear of aggravating the situation. Then Mr Potts started giving orders.

"Miss Smith, you stay here. Sister, you prepare those two orthopaedic patients for transfer. You students go and find something else to do 'til I get back. Miss Kent and Lambert, come with me. We'll go to the bloody orthopaedic unit and we'll find some empty beds, even if we have to discharge their patients ourselves. I'll show them they can't scatter patients around the hospital like confetti whenever and wherever they please."

As Victoria and Paul followed Mr Potts off the ward, there was alarm on the faces of the patients in the vicinity. Stunned by the behaviour of their consultant, they wondered whether he threw temper tantrums like this when operating and if so, were they wise to entrust themselves to his care?

Leslie Potts flew down the stairs two at a time and flung open the doors of the orthopaedic ward. A ward round was in progress. The orthopaedic junior doctors were present, together with the ward sister and a couple of her nurses. At their head was Mr Keenan, the orthopaedic consultant, a man built like an ox, who would not have been out of place in the front row of a rugby scrum. With his thick neck, broad shoulders and with pectoral muscles scarcely contained within his tight fitting shirt, he towered over his fellow consultant.

Mr Potts, blinded by rage, was not intimidated and marched straight up to him, David face to face with Goliath! Victoria and Paul following apprehensively, a dozen paces behind.

"Sam, I need words with you!"

Sam Keenan looked up and saw Mr Potts, his face flushed and bristling with anger. Knowing his colleague of old, he summed up the situation in an instant.

"Ah Leslie," he said, in a quiet appeasing voice. "I've no doubt you've come to have a little chat about the two patients we've had to lodge with you. I'm genuinely sorry about that. Come into the office with me and we'll see what can be done about it."

Before Mr Potts had time to respond, Mr Keenan draped his arm round his consultant colleague's shoulder and gently guided him to the privacy of the office. Victoria and Paul stood a little way apart from the orthopaedic team and awaited events.

"Well," Paul said, "you did warn me, but I've never seen anything like it. Why on earth does he get so angry? It's obvious that when one ward is full, urgent admissions have to be placed on another ward. It's give and take. Sometimes we lodge on their ward; sometimes they lodge patients on ours. It all balances out in the end."

"Yes, obviously it does, but Mr Potts doesn't see it like that. He believes that the beds on his ward are sacrosanct. And to be fair, the orthopods ought to have taken their lodgers back this morning before they arranged further admissions to their own ward."

"But why does he get upset?"

"I honestly don't know. There's obviously some bad blood between them, though I can't see Mr Keenan ever upsetting anyone. He really is a gentle giant and the most obliging man you could hope to meet. Maybe Mr Potts fell out with the orthopaedic consultant who retired recently. Perhaps he had a bad experience with a broken limb as a child. I really don't know, but I could do without it. There are more than enough problems for us to worry about without having to deal with explosions of rage by the consultants."

The door of the ward office remained firmly closed for the next five minutes. Then the two consultants emerged and rather formally shook hands. Mr Keenan, a twinkle in his eye and the hint of a smile on his face looked perfectly calm. Leslie Potts still looked tense, though he now appeared to have control of his emotions, his rage having abated somewhat.

"Right," he said to his registrars, "now that's sorted, let's get back to our own patients."

Victoria and Paul would love to have overheard the exchange between the two consultants and to learn what agreement had been reached but that remained a secret between them. However they were fascinated to observe that both the orthopaedic patients had disappeared by the time they visited the ward the next day and it was to be many months before any more orthopaedic lodgers found their way into Mr Potts' beds!

Chapter Thirty Nine

Back on their own ward Mr Potts began his round. His expression was severe, his manner towards his patients curt in the extreme, his speech monosyllabic. Conducting his round at great speed he left two women visibly distressed before arriving at Anne Nichols' bed. Despite the attempts by Paul and Sister Rutherford to offer her reassurance, anxiety was etched into her face. The screens were drawn around the bed and Mr Potts instructed that Mrs Nichols' nightdress be removed. As she sat vulnerable and exposed, it was obvious that Mr Potts was completely unaware this might be in any way awkward or embarrassing for the patient; and as the consultation continued, it became clear he was equally unaware, or possibly unconcerned, of any feelings she might have. No wonder that Anne should burst into tears.

"No need to cry, my dear," Mr Potts remarked impatiently. "No-one's going to hurt you. We just want to sort out this little problem for you."

The abnormality of her breast was very obvious, even to the dullest of the students and most junior of the nurses who were squeezed around the bed. The lump was so large that it caused the nipple to be distorted and pushed to one side. The overlying skin was stretched and pale. Mr Potts examined his patient in a cursory fashion and then invited Victoria to examine as well. Whilst she did so he retreated to the foot of the bed, turned away from the patient and addressed the medical students.

"A fairly large mass, typical carcinoma, about two inches across. Pretty big really," he said in a 'matter of fact' tone. "It's a good job she's big busted. It's always easier to do a complete operation if the patient has large breasts. The best plan will be to whip off the breast and remove the glands in the arm pit while we're at it."

His voice was loud enough, not only to be heard by Mrs Nichols but also by those in the neighbouring beds, the screens insulating from sight but not from sound.

Paul and Victoria glanced at each other, the same thought passing through each of their minds. Sir William would never have behaved like this. He would have put the patient at ease, restricted the number of people round the bed to the minimum, undertaken his examination gently and then discussed the position quietly and sensitively with the patient. He would certainly not have bellowed like a fog horn for half the ward to hear. How could Mr Potts be so insensitive? Surely had his wife been treated with such lack of feeling, he would have been absolutely furious, the first to complain? Suddenly Paul caught Janet's eye, the feminist house officer whom Mr Potts loved to provoke. Her face was a picture of furious indignation, her anger about to explode in an outburst of criticism and rebuke. Hurriedly he frowned and put a finger to his lips as a warning. Mr Potts was in no mood to have his conduct questioned.

Mr Potts lacked all insight, seemingly unaware that Mrs Nichols was distressed. He appeared to have no more regard for her or for her feelings than a carpenter might have for a block of wood. Victoria, Janet and Sister Rutherford had all witnessed the exchange and were appalled. They shared Mrs Nichols' embarrassment and humiliation and they empathised with her. How had such an insensitive man risen to become a consultant? Had he perhaps hidden his true feelings towards patients when he was being supervised as a trainee? Or had he subsequently become immune to their feelings because he had treated so many cancer victims that he had simply forgotten they were human beings? Did he now regard them merely as academic exercises to be resolved by his knowledge and experience? Paul wondered if there was any higher authority to whom he could express his concerns but of course there wasn't. The consultants were the highest authority; that was what enabled some of them to act as Gods!

When Victoria had completed her examination, she stood back and Sister Rutherford immediately helped Mrs Nichols to replace her nightdress. Like the Sister in the clinic two weeks earlier, she was not going to give Mr Potts the chance to invite any of the students to undertake a further examination. She then sat on the bed, her arm around her patient's shoulders, offering words of comfort.

Victoria looked worried. She turned to Mr Potts, and then spoke quietly and hesitantly. "Do you think Sir, that it would be wise to take a sample biopsy of the lump as a first step? That would enable us to confirm it was indeed a tumour before the whole breast was removed."

Mr Potts however, was adamant and dismissive. "There's no need to do that Miss Kent. There's really no doubt about it. It's a cancer and a big one at that."

Then he turned back to face Mrs Nichols, "Don't you worry about a thing, my dear. We'll remove the breast tomorrow. You'll be fast asleep. You won't know a thing about it. The appliance lady will sort you out afterwards. The 'falsies' are pretty good these days. We'll have you home in a week or so and nobody will know that you're a bit lopsided."

A voice inside Paul wanted to scream, 'her husband will know and in any case, that's not what she's worried about. She's worried she's going to die a painful death from her cancer and leave her children alone in the world without a mother.' But fearful of a public verbal lashing, he didn't.

As Mr Potts moved to the next patient, Mrs Nichols again began to cry. Sister indicated that the screens should be left around the bed. For a brief moment, before following the consultant down the ward, Victoria took hold of her hand and whispered, "I'll be back as soon as I can to explain it all to you."

However, Victoria was not the only one aware of the distress that had been caused. Sister asked one of her staff nurses to ring for her husband and one of Sir William's patients from the opposite side of the ward was already moving across to offer comfort.

****

20 minutes later, back in the office, the ward round over, Victoria again expressed her concern about Mrs Nichols' proposed operation.

"Do you think Sir, there's a possibility that the breast lump might be benign?" she asked tentatively, by which she actually meant, *wouldn't it be wise to take a sample of the lump first, before being committed to a full mastectomy?*

Paul wondered if the consultant would explode at having his decision questioned a second time. He didn't, but he was unyielding, his view unchanged.

"That would simply mean two operations and two anaesthetics; one to take the biopsy, then a second to remove the breast. It would also give the patient false hopes that would inevitably be dashed. It'll come to the same thing in the end, so we might as well get on with it."

Paul was not sufficiently qualified or experienced to question the consultant's diagnosis, but he could see that Victoria remained unconvinced. Furthermore, bravely, she was prepared to stand her ground.

"She's had a breast cyst in the past Sir, although I admit that was on the other side. Don't you think we should stick a needle in the lump first just to be sure?"

Paul recalled the history he had taken from the patient and knew that a minor operation had cured Mrs Nichols' previous breast cyst.

"Look Miss Kent, do that if you must, if it will put your mind at rest but don't go spreading any cancer cells around. With big tumours like this, the prognosis is bad enough as it is," Mr Potts replied. He was suggesting that if a needle was inserted into the tumour, cancer cells might be displaced from the lump and seeded into the surrounding tissues. Paul though was sufficiently experienced to know that this argument was false. If the patient subsequently had a mastectomy, all the surrounding tissue would be removed anyway.

Mr Potts looked at his watch and turned to leave. "Now I must be off. I'm committed to removing a gall bladder in the private wing in a couple of minutes. Miss Kent you can come and assist me."

As Victoria departed with the consultant, she whispered urgently to Paul, "Put a needle into that lump Paul. If it's solid, then I accept that it's probably a tumour but I still think there's a chance it's just another cyst."

****

The minute they left, Sister Rutherford shooed the medical students out of the office, despatched her nurses to their routine tasks, closed the door then turned to Paul. "I'll swing for that man one day! How can he be so insensitive?"

With the consultant gone, Janet also glared angrily at Paul. "It's no good you '*shushing*' me like that. Only a man could behave in such a deplorable fashion," she said scornfully. "Someone needs to tell him that his conduct is simply not acceptable."

"That's as may be," Paul replied irritably, "but don't let that someone be you, unless you want your medical career to end before it's begun. I was only trying to help you."

Then Sister Rutherford and Paul walked back down the ward. The screen remained drawn around the bed and within, Mrs Nichols was still being comforted by one of the nurses; yet another cup of tea on the bedside locker, this one being ignored and going cold.

She was distraught; her face streaked with tears.

"It's not the operation that worries me," she wailed. "I don't care about that. My husband's a good man. He'll get used to it. You can take them both off for all I care. It's the children; they're both so young. They need me. My husband works long days on the farm. I've lost my mum and dad; there's no-one else to help. I must be there for them."

Once more Paul attempted reassurance. "You're still assuming that all patients with cancer die. They don't. The whole purpose of the operation is to remove the tumour, to get rid of it, so that you can be healthy afterwards."

"But many patients do die, don't they?"

Paul couldn't deny this but didn't want to get involved in a discussion on the success rate of surgery until he had done the needle test.

"Yes, that's true," he admitted, "not everyone is cured of cancer but many people are. But first, Mr Potts has agreed that we do a little needle test on this lump for you. Let's get that over first. We can talk about other things afterwards."

Once again Sister helped Mrs Nichols to remove her nightie and then asked her to lie on the bed with one arm above her head. In this position the lump was so prominent, distorting the overlying skin, that it amazed Paul that she had only noticed it so recently. Mrs Nichols must have read his thoughts.

"I always examine myself at period time. Five weeks ago the lump was tiny. At first I wasn't even sure there was a lump there at all. Now it feels enormous. I'm scared. The cancer must be growing ever so quickly."

"This will only take a couple of minutes," Paul said as he attached a needle to a large empty syringe. "You'll feel a sharp pin prick in the skin, like the one when we take blood samples from your arm. I suggest you look away while we do it."

Fixing the lump firmly with his left hand so that it would not run away from the needle, Paul swabbed the skin with an antiseptic solution and then plunged the needle into the heart of the mass. Immediately the barrel of the syringe began to fill with pale yellow fluid. As he aspirated more and more fluid, he could feel the lump getting smaller, collapsing beneath his fingers. He felt exhilarated. A feeling of pure joy swept through him. Victoria had been right. This wasn't a cancer at all. It was an enormous cyst. It would have been an absolute disaster to remove Mrs Nichols' breast. He glanced at Sister Rutherford and saw all the anger and frustration that Mr Potts had caused, melt from her face.

Soon the syringe was full and Paul had to replace it with a fresh one as the cyst continued to empty. When all the fluid had been removed the breast looked and felt entirely normal. Two minutes earlier, there had been a large hard mass in the heart of the breast. Now the lump simply didn't exist and there were 60-70 millilitres of clear pale yellow fluid in the kidney dish on the bedside locker.

Nursing sisters are trained not to show emotion but Paul was sure he saw moisture in Sister Rutherford's eyes. Ever so gently Sister took Mrs Nichols free hand, placed it over her breast and asked her to feel for the lump. It was an absolute delight to watch her face as her fingers probed in vain for the lump that was no longer there.

At first her expression was one of bewilderment, then incredulity and then one of enormous relief. The last time that Paul had seen such joy on a patient's face had been during his student days at the maternity hospital when he had placed a newly born baby into its mother's arms. This memory instantly brought to mind his own problems and a wave of sadness hit him so hard that it made him feel sick. With pain in his heart, he found himself unable to speak as he thought of Kate, childless, her womb now empty, evacuated of its contents, recovering from her anaesthetic in the neighbouring hospital. Distraught, unable to face Sister or Mrs Nichols, he turned to one side, his head bowed.

"It's gone!" Mrs Nichols exclaimed, astonished.

Noticing Paul's distress, Sister answered on his behalf. "Yes, it was a cyst, just like the last one. It wasn't a cancer at all," she said and showed her the fluid on the bedside locker. Without warning and still naked from the waist up, Mrs Nichols threw both her arms round Paul's neck and dragging him to her, giving him the most tremendous bear hug. Relief and gratitude triumphing over modesty.

"Hey," Sister cried, "be careful; your husband's due at any minute." But it was too late. At that very moment Mr Nichols appeared through a gap in the screens escorted by one of the nurses.

"What the bloody hell is going on here?" he exclaimed, his face showing surprise and anger.

With difficulty, Paul tried to extricate himself from her embrace, but Mrs Nichols was not for letting go. She kissed him on both cheeks before releasing him.

Paul stood back, red-faced, moist eyed and flustered. "I think you'd better explain to your husband what's happened," he muttered.

He had been hoping to make a quick getaway but Mrs Nichols clung on to his hands. She looked at him through tear streaked eyes, "Thank you Doctor, thank you so much, and you too Sister."

A junior hospital doctor's job was hard work. There were long hours on duty, disturbed nights and there were times when they were so exhausted that they could scarcely think straight but events like this made it all worthwhile.

"It's Miss Kent that you need to thank," he said quietly, "not me. She's the one who insisted the needle test should be done."

With his emotions in turmoil, he walked to the office, picked up the phone and spoke to the staff in the operating theatre.

"Tomorrows mastectomy operation is cancelled," he said, "the lump in the breast has disappeared."

Then he rang St Margaret's to enquire after Kate.

Chapter Forty

When Kate was discharged from hospital, she was advised to take four weeks off work to allow her time to regain her strength and recover from her grief. Unfortunately though, the young woman who emerged from St Margaret's bore little resemblance to the one who had gone to the theatre to enjoy an evening out with friends just three days before. Previously Kate had been energetic and cheerful. When working on the ward she had been a confident, hard-working and conscientious nurse who greeted her patients with a smile and dispensed care and encouragement in equal measure. Off duty, she was easy going and sociable; able to tease others or take a tease, and she could enliven any group with interesting comments, anecdotes and with her infectious laugh.

Regrettably, she had lost the spark that had made her such good company. She drifted round listlessly. It became an effort for her to perform the easiest of tasks and she hadn't the energy or the initiative to take any exercise. She lost her appetite and started to lose weight. She only spoke when spoken to and then with just a few words in a voice that was barely audible. For long periods she sat in silence, brooding. If the television was on she stared at it with unseeing eyes, the pages of her book remained unturned.

Her mood was low, her thoughts negative and she showed little interest in the day to day activities such as cooking, shopping and cleaning that previously she had enjoyed. She neglected her friends and withdrew into herself. An invisible barrier developed between her and those who tried to support her and of course it didn't help that Paul worked long hours such that she was left on her own for lengthy periods.

As well as his concern for Kate, Paul had another worry. He was acutely aware that he hadn't told Kate about his decision to quit surgery. With Kate ill, discussing the matter with her would surely upset her further. It wasn't that he had changed his mind, rather the opposite for he felt sure it was the right thing for him to do; it was simply that he realised that such a move would cause a massive disruption in their lives. He would inevitably suffer a period of unemployment resulting in a financial loss. That would have stretched them to the limit at the best of times but with Kate now on half pay because she was 'on the sick', for him to resign his job would be inconceivable. Then there was the problem of the hospital flat. They were entitled to live there on a peppercorn rent by virtue of his contract as a hospital doctor; if he quit his job they would have to find a new home. Reluctantly Paul was forced to the conclusion that his plans to change his career would have to be shelved for the time being.

The four weeks passed and then another four but still Kate showed no sign of improvement. She went back to work for a couple of days but found the effort too much and once again signed off sick. Paul did his best to keep the atmosphere in the house bright and cheerful. He tried to persuade her to socialise and to take some exercise but with little success. He encouraged Kate to express her feelings, to bear her soul about their misfortune, believing that bringing her emotions into the open and airing her sorrow might help her to accept what had happened and allow her to move on. But his various attempts to help all failed and gradually he became frustrated that his efforts reaped no reward. Mentioning their loss seemed to make matters worse, causing her to cry and retire even more into herself. Consequently their still born baby became a taboo subject; it ceased to be mentioned despite the enormity of its presence in their home.

Frequently, when he returned home, he found Kate sitting on the sofa, listless and with tear stained eyes. It was clear to him that she was depressed and believing her mood would be lightened with medication, he offered to make an appointment for her to see the doctor but this suggestion like many others was refused. In desperation he went himself to see her GP. She was sympathetic but explained that she couldn't help unless Kate was prepared to come and see her in person. Subsequently, when he admitted to Kate that he had spoken to her doctor he was rebuked for going behind her back.

One day, in desperation, he decided he would risk a further attempt to persuade her that their loss was not the end of the world; that there could be happier times in the future.

"To lose a baby like that is a horrible thing to happen Kate. It's bound to be upsetting," he said, "but there's no reason why we can't have another one. We're both young and healthy. You got pregnant easily enough last time. When you're stronger we can try again."

"But exactly the same thing will happen next time. I just know it. For some reason I'm being punished. I must have done something terribly wrong."

"That's nonsense, Kate and you know it. It was simply a case of bad luck."

"But last week, when I saw Dr Walker in the clinic, he said that miscarriages are very common. He said some women have multiple miscarriages. I've read all about it in my nursing books. Some women never manage to carry a baby through to term. There's obviously something wrong with me, some problem with my womb."

Such talk frustrated Paul and his irritation showed in his voice. "I'm sorry Kate but that's just plain silly; you're talking nonsense, you're making no sense at all. There's no reason to think that you have a problem. It's perfectly obvious that the miscarriage was caused by the accident. Had it not been for that stupid lorry driver, you would be as right as rain. You wouldn't have lost it."

"I'm not being silly and it isn't '_it_'," Kate responded, her words bursting out in an angry torrent. "You simply don't understand do you Paul? '_It_' as you call him, was my baby – our baby. For weeks he's been growing inside me. I've felt him move. I've talked to him, sung to him, I've dreamt about what might have been, what should have been; giving birth, seeing him for the first time, holding him in my arms, loving him, feeding him, watching him grow up. I was looking forward to showing him to my father. Living alone, having lost Mum, it would have made him so happy to have a grandson. He would have played with him and introduced him the countryside. I was going to show him the animals in the fields, let him listen to the birds and when he was older take him up into the hills behind Dad's house. Now everything I wanted, everything I dreamed about has gone. What have I got to look forward to now?"

Kate's mother had died when Kate was still in her teens and Paul knew how Kate still grieved for her. He also knew how close she was to her father.

"Would it help if you were to spend a week or two with your Dad?" he queried. "It might help you to get over things, to get things in perspective."

"No it wouldn't," Kate replied angrily. "I just want to be left alone. You don't understand. Nobody understands. All I feel is emptiness and you just go off to work acting as if nothing has happened." She stormed out of the room and Paul heard the bedroom door slam.

Paul was aware that whenever Kate referred to the baby she always said 'he' or 'him'; never 'she' or 'her' and this concerned him greatly. When Kate had been pregnant, although Paul had insisted that she was being illogical, she had been certain she was carrying a baby boy. Was that why she now spoke of 'him' or was there another reason? The thoughts that had flashed through Paul's mind when he had seen the letters ERPC on the gynaecological operating list all those weeks ago came flooding back to him. Had Kate seen their baby? Had she held their still born child in her arms? Did she actually know that he was a boy? He didn't know the answer to these questions; he had never asked her about it. Then there were other questions. Did Kate know what had happened to their baby's body? How did they dispose of still born babies? Surely they didn't just ......!

He forced himself to stop thinking about it – it was simply too painful. But was this why Kate was grieving so terribly?

Paul was at a loss, not knowing what to do for the best. He felt he ought to raise the issue, go upstairs, talk to Kate and bring it into the open but his courage failed him. If these really were the questions worrying Kate, discussing them might help to improve her depression. But if these thoughts had never entered her head, raising them now would surely make the situation ten times worse. He went into the kitchen, made himself a sandwich and then, feeling exhausted, he collapsed in front of the television. He wondered if he should try to talk some sense into her later but realised it would be a waste of time. He would just be rebuffed again.

As the weeks became months, there was precious little improvement in Kate's state of mind. She showed no interest in Paul's accounts of events on the ward and little inclination to go out; nor did she encourage visitors. She neglected the flat and spent her days drifting, feeling empty and longing to hold a baby in her arms.

One afternoon, her old friend Sally called hoping to cheer her up. She was wearing a maternity smock and the bloom of late pregnancy. Kate boiled a kettle intending to make a cup of tea, then, consumed with envy, abruptly asked her to leave. She then took herself off to bed. *'Why me'?* she asked herself. *'It simply isn't fair.'*

Once or twice Paul did manage to persuade her to open her heart and let her feelings out.

"People don't understand," she explained. "You don't understand. You don't take it seriously. Nobody does. They say it was just bad luck, that I'll have another one. It's as if they think that losing this one isn't important; but it is. I had a baby growing inside me, our baby. I know in my heart it was a baby boy and he died. I lost him and I grieve for him. I grieve for what might have been, for what should have been. I want him back but he's gone and I can't have him. My Mum would have understood and she's not here for me to talk to."

Paul felt desperately sympathetic but also felt completely impotent; he didn't know how to respond. Should he comfort and console and wait for her depression to pass or should he tell her to 'snap out of it' and forget what might have been? He was used to dealing with physical disease, problems that could be excised with a scalpel in the operating theatre, not these intangible mental problems. Whatever he said and no matter how hard he tried, he simply couldn't get through to her; and he found his constant attempts to lighten the atmosphere exhausting. He had no idea how to help Kate cope with a broken heart and, although he tried not to show it, he was annoyed that she still refused to seek advice from her doctor. Surely she would be helped if she took some antidepressants tablets.

As Kate spent more and more time silently brooding, the atmosphere in the flat chilled. Gone was the laughter and gaiety that had characterised the early days of their marriage, gone the easy familiarity, the teasing and the light hearted banter; gone also the comfort, warmth and satisfaction of the leisurely love making they had previously enjoyed. Paul found he had to steel himself when he returned home at the end of each day. Anticipating a cool reception he forced himself to be positive, to be bright and cheerful. Standing on the front step, before he opened the door, he thought of any news and gossip he had heard on the hospital grape vine that might interest Kate only to find she paid little attention; he was rarely able to arouse her curiosity. The friendly camaraderie in the hospital contrasted with the cheerless mood at home and gradually Paul found himself making excuses to stay at work longer in the evening.

Kate's father came down from his cottage in the Lake District and suggested that Kate should spend a week or so with him. Kate tried to turn down the offer but her father insisted.

"When her mother died," he told Paul, "Kate took solace in the hills. I'll take her on some long walks; give her some good country air to see if that will help."

Paul was grateful for her father's offer and pleased to accept but it left him feeling that he was a failure; that he ought to have been able to help his wife through this crisis without his father-in-law's help; but he accepted that he couldn't.

Chapter Forty One

Kate returned a fortnight later. Her sick leave had come to an end and she was expected to return to work. Paul thought there was a slight improvement in her mood but he remained concerned. No longer did she burst into tears for no apparent reason but she still retreated into her own dark world for prolonged periods. When she reported for duty on the ward, Sister Rutherford allocated her some light duties then quietly observed how she performed. With dismay she watched as Kate drifted through the morning showing little enthusiasm for the job. She shouted at one of the student nurses, ignored an elderly lady's request for a bed pan and was irritable with a number of the patients. She was quite unlike the pleasant patient cheerful nurse that Sister knew her to be. By lunchtime, she had seen enough and told Kate to take the afternoon off. Then she rang Paul and asked him to drop by for a chat.

"I'm truly sorry to see Kate in her present state," Sister began," she's not herself at all. What can we do to help?"

"I honestly don't know, Sister. I'm at my wit's end. I try to be sympathetic but everything I say seems to make matters worse. I end up afraid to say anything at all for fear of being shot down."

Sister Rutherford smiled. "They say that you always hurt the one you love, don't they? Do you think it would help if I went round and had a chat with her? I had a similar experience myself early in my married life so I know how she must be feeling. I also know it can be difficult for a man to fully understand her sense of loss."

"I would extremely grateful if you would. The alternative would be to persuade her to change her mind about taking antidepressants but we had a terrible row the last time I suggested that!"

"I suspect some medication would be helpful but there may be other ways. I'll see what I can do."

"Thanks, that's most kind. Incidentally Sister, I am heeding that advice you gave me a little while ago. I've been trying to stop myself from running the hospital single handed, particularly whilst Kate has been so low. And this afternoon I've only got to tidy up a few loose ends so you can tell Kate I'll be home by five."

"That's good. I'm sure she'll be pleased to hear it."

However Paul didn't get home at five. As luck would have it, half way through the afternoon, he was called to see a patient who had arrived in the Casualty Department. Cliff Fielding, a 45 year old electrician, had collapsed at work and been rushed to the hospital by ambulance. Clutching his belly he was shocked, in pain and when the duty doctor examined him, he found a large pulsating mass in the centre of his abdomen. He rang Paul.

"Sorry Paul, but I've a man here with a ruptured aneurysm. We're busy resuscitating him but he'll have to go to theatre. Get down here as soon as you can. He's fading fast."

Immediately, a pang of fear hit Paul hard in the stomach. It made him feel physically sick. Not another blasted aneurysm. This would be the third in as many months and the previous two had died on the operating table. For the first, he had at least been supported by Sir William, although it had been moral support only; the hospital's senior consultant had less experience of vascular surgery than he did. The second was Frank Wilson whom Paul had operated on without senior support. He too had bled to death despite Paul's frantic attempts to save him and the experience had devastated him.

Please God, not again. He was still haunted by the memory of the man's lifeless corpse lying on the theatre table, waiting for the porters to take it to the morgue. He could still see the red sticky puddle on the changing room floor where blood had dripped from the gowns in the laundry skip. He recalled also the painful conversation he had endured with Mrs Wilson after the event; the pathetic gratitude she had expressed to Paul for doing everything in his power to save her husband whilst he silently cursed himself for his inexperience and incompetence. Paul couldn't bear to face another experience like the last, it would destroy him.

He needed to find Mr Potts and get him to perform the surgery. However it wasn't Surgical Five's duty day so the consultant wasn't 'on call'. He might be available or he might not. Nevertheless Paul had to find him and find him fast. He picked up the phone and told the switchboard operator to locate the consultant.

"Ring his home, ring his private consulting rooms, ring anywhere that you think he might be, but find him," Paul instructed desperately.

Then he hastened to see the patient dreading what he might find. Guiltily he knew he would actually feel relieved if he found the patient had already succumbed by the time he got there. He was almost tempted to delay his arrival in casualty to increase the chance of that happening.

Any hopes that the casualty officer had made the wrong diagnosis were quickly dispelled. The patient undoubtedly had a leaking aneurysm and had lost so much blood that he was barely conscious. Paul went to meet his wife. He told her that the chance of a successful operation was virtually nil. He had learned from Sir William that it was always wise to give a bad prognosis. *'Don't raise expectations too high'*, the consultant often said, *'or you set yourself a standard that you may not be able to fulfil'*.

"Then why will you operate?" she asked.

"Because without surgery the chance of death is 100%," Paul stated bluntly. He was about to explain that he wasn't certain Mr Potts was available but thought better of it. There seemed little point in distressing the woman further.

A nurse popped her head round the door.

"Switchboard for you, Mr Lambert."

Paul hurried to the phone. "Sorry, Mr Lambert, but I can't find Mr Potts anywhere."

"Then send the police round to his house. Get them to see if he's in the garden. If he's not, get them to ask the neighbours if they know where he might be or leave a note on his door; but get him to the hospital as soon as possible."

"I'm not sure we're allowed to do that Mr Lambert. I'll need to check with my supervisor."

"There's no time for that," Paul shouted. "Just do it."

In less than an hour from the moment Mr Fielding arrived in the hospital, he was in theatre, the anaesthetist endeavouring to pump blood into his arm, at the same time giving him gas and air to put him to sleep. Paul was scrubbing his hands and arms, gowning and gloving, all the while desperately hoping and praying that the theatre door would swing open and Mr Potts would breeze in. But he didn't. He glanced at the clock. It was four thirty; it was over forty minutes since he had told the switchboard to get the police to find his boss; perhaps there still was a chance the consultant might appear. Then he suddenly remembered he had sent a message to Kate via Sister Rutherford that he would be home by five. He spoke to the nearest nurse.

"Ring my wife for me and explain what's happening. God knows what time I'll be home. And ask the switchboard if they've managed to find Mr Potts."

As he applied sterile drapes to the skin, he took a last desperate look at the door, only to be disappointed.

The nurse returned.

"Switch say they've tried everything but have no idea where Mr Potts might be."

Paul cursed that he had been placed in this impossible situation yet again. Damn Mr Potts and damn the hospital's management! They had no right to advertise a vascular service until they were fully staffed with experienced surgeons. Bitterly he reflected just how wrong it was and so desperately unfair on him. When Mr Fielding died, as surely he would, and he was called to give evidence at the inquest, he would tell the whole truth and nothing but the truth. Why the hell should he protect the reputation of the hospital or his consultant when they treated him as they did? He had met the coroner, he knew him to be a reasonable and fair man. He wouldn't hold back. He would explain with great clarity that he had been left unsupported to attempt emergency surgery on a critically ill patient when Mr Potts knew the situation was beyond his training and experience. To swear to that under oath in court in front of the consultant would most certainly end his surgical career, even if he hadn't already resigned of his own volition, but the way he felt he didn't give a damn. But even as these wild thoughts ran through his head, he knew he couldn't tell the whole truth. To do so would leave Mrs Fielding carrying the additional burden of knowing her husband had died unnecessarily.

However, now clear in his mind that whatever happened he was not culpable, a cold determination came over him. He would stay calm, he would do his best but if the patient died, so be it.

He held out his hand. "Knife please, Sister."

Chapter Forty Three

Mrs Fielding, the patient's wife, found herself sitting frightened and alone in the anaesthetic room. She had accompanied her husband as he had been rushed through the hospital corridors to the theatre suite, she sat on a stool and held his hand whilst the anaesthetic was administered but had been left behind apparently forgotten when the action moved into the operating theatre itself. She had his jacket and trousers over her arm, his wallet and keys in one hand and a tear stained handkerchief in the other. There was a small porthole window in the door between the anaesthetic room and the theatre but she dared not go and see what was happening. A religious woman, she recognised how ill her husband was, had seen the urgency with which he had been treated and had heeded Paul's words when he had been so pessimistic about the chances of a successful outcome. Now she put her faith in God and her trust in the doctors and nurses. She had been surprised how young Paul looked, yet impressed how efficiently he had arranged for the operation to be performed. How wonderful, she thought, that someone of such tender years should have the experience and expertise to perform surgery for such serious conditions.

She was still there five minutes later when the theatre technician slipped into the room to fetch another bottle of plasma. He was surprised to see her.

"I'm afraid you can't stay here," he said, wondering where he should advise her to go. "Do you want to go home, or would you prefer to wait in the hospital?"

"I couldn't possibly go home. I'll wait in the hospital."

"There hasn't been time for your husband to be allocated a bed so I suggest you wait in the hospital canteen. You can get a drink there and we can contact you if necessary."

"How long will it be, do you think?"

"I'm afraid that's impossible to say," the technician replied gently. It might be ten minutes if the bleeding couldn't be stopped, anything up to four or five hours if the patient survived.

Before she went to the canteen, Mrs Fielding rang her daughter. Thanks to an earlier call, she already knew that her dad had been rushed to hospital. She had collected her little girl from school and was giving her tea but promised to come as soon as she was able to arrange child care and get a taxi. Mrs Fielding then went to the canteen , ordered a drink and a biscuit then, fearing the worst, settled down to wait in a quiet corner.

One hour passed, then a second. Her daughter arrived and still she waited, desperate for news. Was the fact that the operation was taking so long a good sign or a bad one? Or had her husband already died and they were afraid to come and tell her?

Another thirty minutes passed and still no one had contacted her. Whenever anyone entered the canteen or the telephone rang, her heart jumped thinking there might be a message for her.

"I can't bear this any longer," her daughter finally said. "Surely there should be some news by now."

"You don't think they've forgotten about us do you; they were so busy with your dad it's quite possible."

"But who can we ask; none of the people in here will know anything about it?"

"I'm going to ask one of the nurses over there. I'm sure they will know what we should do."

Hesitantly she approached a group of nurses who were sitting chatting at a nearby table. One of them went to the canteen phone and rang the theatre on her behalf.

She returned a couple of minutes later.

"Your husband's still in theatre," she was told gently. "I'm afraid you'll just have to wait. But they do know you're here and they've promised to send someone down to speak with you when they've finished."

****

Paul looked apprehensively at the ring of stitches he had placed at the top and bottom ends of the graft. Amazingly he had managed to remove the section of diseased artery which had ruptured. He had then bridged the gap by replacing it with a length of artificial tubing. Whilst he had been working, clamps placed across the artery had kept the area free of blood. When he removed these clamps, blood would once again flow to the patient's pelvis and legs. The suturing had not been easy. The teflon graft was strong and held the sutures well but the artery to which it had been joined was far from healthy. Some parts were distinctly soft, like cheese and he had experienced difficulty getting the sutures to hold. Other areas contained hard plaques like tiny buttons, too rigid for the needle to penetrate, making it impossible for Paul to place the sutures evenly. The question was, would the two junctions hold when the clamps were released and blood under pressure flowed through them. If either of them was not strong enough, the patient was doomed. There was only one way to find out!

"Sister," he said," it's time to test this anastomosis. Let's have some large swabs handy."

He turned to the anaesthetist. "Bill, I'm going to release the clamps one by one. We may well get some significant bleeding. If we do, I'll clamp them off again. Is that OK with you?"

"It will have to be won't it," Bill replied with a wry smile, "otherwise we'll never get him off the table."

"OK, here we go then." Paul placed large swabs over the two suture lines and asked Janet to apply some gentle pressure. This was the last of several critical moments in the operation. If the sutures held, the procedure would almost certainly be a success; if they didn't, Mr Fielding would follow Mr Baxendale and Mr Wilson to the hospital mortuary. Paul's heart was in his mouth. He simply couldn't bear the pain of another surgical disaster, another failure, another death on the table. Mr Wilson's death had devastated him; completely destroying the confidence he had in his own ability. It had left him close to despair, to the point of deciding to resign his post and move to a less taxing, less demanding, less traumatic branch of medicine.

In truth, in recent weeks, a trace of his former self belief had returned. His friends and colleagues had argued that he was being placed in a wholly unacceptable position by Mr Potts. The consultant had undergone training to prepare him to perform surgery on aneurysms. He was operating on elective cases, when the artery was diseased but hadn't yet burst, where the patient was in good shape and blood had been cross matched and made available in advance. But when an aneurysm ruptured and the patient had collapsed and was rushed to hospital at death's door, his blood pressure in his boots, Paul was left unsupported and expected to perform miracles. Paul accepted the truth of these assertions but that afforded him no protection from the misery and anguish he felt with each death.

He decided to open the bottom clamp first. This would simply allow some blood to flow gently back into the graft. The real test would come when he opened the top clamp allowing blood from the heart to be pumped under pressure into the graft. Ever so gingerly, he started to release the lower clamp. There was no obvious leak of blood so he opened the clamp completely. He took the precaution though of leaving the jaws of the clamp around the artery so that if it leaked he would be able to close it again before too much blood had been lost. Silently he prayed that maybe this time he would be lucky.

"So far so good," he muttered to himself.

"The patient still looks OK to me," Bill said cheerfully. "Well done."

"I've only opened the lower clamp so far," Paul replied.

"Ah, I thought it was a bit too good to be true!"

"Right, here goes."

Paul unfastened the ratchet on the upper clamp then, scarcely daring to breathe, he opened the jaws millimetre by millimetre. At first he saw the graft fill with blood and then watched as it developed a weak pulse. The pulse got stronger and stronger as he continued to open the jaws of the clamp. Finally, when the clamp was fully open, he saw the artery spring back to life and pulse in rhythm with the patient's heart beat as blood flowed through it once again. Thankfully there was no immediate flood of blood into the swabs that Janet was holding, which were protecting the sutures and hiding them from view. Dare he hope that this time he would be successful?

"Now Janet, take those swabs away but do it slowly and ever so gently," he instructed, holding his breath, almost afraid to watch.

With infinite care Janet withdrew the swabs revealing the entire length of the graft, which was now pulsing merrily. Not a single drop of blood was leaking from the junctions at either end.

"Bloody hell," Paul remarked, relief surging through every fibre of his body, "I think we've done it."

For fully a minute, he just gazed at the graft, scarcely believing what he saw, half expecting that the sutures would suddenly fall apart in a welter of catastrophic bleeding – but they didn't.

He turned to the anaesthetist. "Bill, have a look at his feet will you, tell me whether you can feel pulses down there."

Bill lifted the drapes over the patient's feet and examined them carefully. Paul waited anxiously. Had they avoided the danger of blood clotting in the legs while the circulation had been switched off?

"Bingo," Bill declared, "All pulses present and correct. Well done."

A sense of pure joy flooded through Paul. He couldn't believe what he had achieved.

"Hell's teeth," he said to himself, "I've actually done it."

Paul was ecstatic, he felt like singing, shouting or doing a jig around the theatre but forced himself to concentrate as he checked the swabs and instruments, sutured the wound and applied a dressing. He looked at the theatre clock. It was eight thirty; the procedure had taken nearly four hours but such had been his concentration that he'd been oblivious of the time. He couldn't have said whether the operation had taken ten minutes or ten hours.

Deliriously happy and enormously relieved, he dragged off his cap and mask and tossed them into the skip. Despite his labours, he didn't feel in the least bit tired. He had the most enormous smile on his face and had to restrain himself from hugging and kissing every nurse in the theatre.

After the patient had been found a bed, lodging on the orthopaedic ward as it happened since all Mr Potts' beds were full, the theatre staff sat down for a celebratory tea and biscuits. A sense of euphoria filled the room. Working together they had achieved something very special. It was an historic first for the hospital, indeed a first for the city. Inevitably Paul received the greatest praise but readily acknowledged it had been a team effort and following Sir William's example, he thanked each and every member of the staff for their efforts. He was overjoyed. The near panic and grave anxiety he had felt when he heard that another patient with a burst aneurysm had arrived in casualty was now replaced by a sense of exhilaration the like of which he had never experienced before. For weeks he had been despondent, painfully aware of his lack of experience and expertise, pitifully conscious of his mental frailty, living in constant fear that another aneurysm would be admitted before Sir William's replacement arrived; but this was a moment to cherish, an achievement of which he could be justly proud.

He was just about to set off for home when the telephone rang. It was the canteen supervisor ringing on behalf of Mrs Fielding, the patient's wife.

"Oh, my God," Paul said. "I forgot all about her. She'll have been worrying herself to death whilst we've been sitting here relaxing. Tell her I'll pop down and see her."

Janet was quick to intercede. "No Paul, it's late. You go; I'll have a chat with her."

Paul thanked the theatre staff yet again then headed for home. Flushed with success, singing quietly to himself, he almost knocked over a couple of nurses in the corridor as he turned a corner too quickly. In the half light of the evening, he jogged along the path that led from the hospital to the doctor's flats. It was only when he saw their front door that he hesitated. Drunk on his own success, he had forgotten Kate's anxieties and depression. He had said he would be home at five and it was now after nine. Once again, he had let her down; inevitably she would be furious. He was bursting to tell her about the operation, to share his happiness, his moment of triumph but it would be a grave mistake to barge in full of the joys of spring when she had spent a lonely evening in the flat. He slowed his step and considered the best approach. Yes, he would tell her of his success but first he would apologise profusely for being late and enquire after her first day back at work. He fervently hoped that it had gone well.

As he opened the door, quietly apprehensive of the reception he would receive, he was pleasantly surprised to be met with the appetising smell of fresh baking. He threw his jacket onto its usual hook and walked through to the kitchen. The room was empty but cleaner and tidier than it had been for some time.

"Hello, I'm home," he called. "I'm sorry to be so late."

"Just coming," Kate shouted from the bedroom.

Paul watched anxiously as she came slowly down the stairs. She looked strained and had obviously been crying but she greeted him with a watery smile. Paul offered the brief peck on the cheek which had become the norm in recent weeks. To his surprise she clung onto him, hugging him with all her might. Then great sobs wracked her body and her tears flow free. Paul had no idea what had caused such emotion but held her tight delighted to feel her body close to him once more. He felt her tears wet on his cheek, was conscious that her nails were cutting into him as her hand gripped his shoulder; but still she clung to him. Gradually she leased her hold and her tears subsided. Paul held her from him and gazed at her blood shot eyes, her tear stained face and bedraggled hair. He thought she had never looked more beautiful.

"Sister Rutherford popped in for a cup of tea this afternoon," she whispered. "She really is a lovely person."

"She said she might and I see the two of you have been cooking. There's a lovely smell in the flat."

"Yes, she helped me to make some scones." There was a long pause. "I've something to show you Paul." Her voice was barely audible.

Paul noticed a small white envelope in her hand.

"Is that what you want me to see?"

"Yes, it is."

Paul took the envelope. It was quite small and square, the sort that might contain an invitation to a wedding or special event. It wasn't sealed. Paul lifted the flap and took out a small card. It was clearly of good quality with silver crenated edges.

Paul recognised Kate's hand. The message was beautifully presented, the words clear, the lines equally spaced. It had clearly been written with great care as one might for a handwriting competition. Paul began to read.

Dear Thomas

It has now been over three months since you left our lives. I will always love you and reflect on what could have been but the time has come when I must say goodbye.

I think about you and the happiness we should have shared all the time. You will always be in my heart. Please don't think I am not grieving for you, but I need to be strong again. My patients need me and so does Paul. They can see the sadness in my eyes and I know that I am not helping them as I should.

I love you with all my heart, you were my hopes, my dreams, my precious baby, but love alone could not keep you here. If it could, you would never have had to leave us.

I will never, ever forget you and what we should have had, but some things are not meant to be and we have to accept that. I pray for the angels to keep you safe and tuck you up at night.

So I say goodbye and let you go.

With love to take and keep until we meet again.

My precious little baby, I love you.

Mummy xx

Paul read the letter, then read it a second time. He looked at Kate. Again tears were streaming from her eyes but there was a small sad smile on her face. Paul put his arms round her and held her close.

"What are you planning to do with it?" he asked softly.

"I'm going to put it with the letters and photos I have of Mum," she said, "in the box under the bed. And then I'm going to ask Sally and Colin to come round for a drink."

"Are you sure you can cope with that?" Paul asked anxiously.

"Yes, I am. She's my best friend and I owe her an apology."

Once more, Paul took Kate into his arms and hugged her. She clung to him as if she never wanted to let him go. He was so delighted to feel her close, to see the change in her mood and sense her determination to move on that he completely forgot to tell her that earlier in the day, he had successfully dealt with a ruptured aneurysm and saved the life of a forty year old man.

Message from the author

Writing this novel has allowed me the pleasure of reminiscing about days gone by, occasionally with a glass of wine at my elbow! I hope that you've enjoyed reading it. Should you have any questions or comments about it, or about life on a surgical unit in the 1960s and 70s, I should be pleased to hear from you. I can be reached via the 'contact' tab on the website www.petersykes.org

Sir William's Ten Commandments
(For Clinical Records)

Thou shalt write legibly

Thou shalt sign thine entry

Thou shalt also record thine name in CAPITALS

Thou shalt, in addition, record thine status in the organisation

Thou shalt date thine entry……

And time it as well

Thine entry shall be concise and relevant

Thou shalt NOT write flippant comments about thine patients, his   friends or family

Thou shalt NOT criticise thine colleagues

Thou shalt remember that thine words might one day be read back to thee in judgement by thine elders